W9-ADD-234

Jane Grimes Thomas

n. C. setting

WITHDRAWN

Gramley Library
Salem College
Winston-Salem, NC 27108

The Scarlet Thread

BY THE SAME AUTHOR

Tall Houses in Winter

Gentle Insurrection and Other Stories

90 - 1683

PS
3552
.E84
S2
1964

The Scarlet Thread

by Doris Betts

Harper & Row
PUBLISHERS
NEW YORK, EVANSTON,
AND LONDON

Gramley Library
Salem College
Winston-Salem, NC 27108

Chapter 5 in this volume was originally published in *The Student*, publication of Wake Forest College.

THE SCARLET THREAD. Copyright © 1964 by Doris Betts. Printed in the United States of America. All rights reserved. No part of this book may be used or reproduced in any manner whatsoever without written permission except in the case of brief quotations embodied in critical articles and reviews. For information address Harper & Row, Publishers, Incorporated, 49 East 33rd Street, New York 16, N. Y.

FIRST EDITION

LIBRARY OF CONGRESS CATALOG CARD NUMBER: 62:14552

M-O

To Lowry

To Lowry

NOTE

The piedmont of North Carolina is a real area, but the town of Greenway in Stone County is mythical. So are all these people and the things which happen to them.

". . . and afterward came out his brother, that had the scarlet thread upon his hand."

—GENESIS 38:30

". . . and she [Rahab] bound the scarlet line in the window."

—JOSHUA 2:21

PART I

Esther

❦

JUNE, 1897—NOVEMBER, 1898

Chapter

◄§ 1 §►

THE HILLS OF PIEDMONT North Carolina are laid in a series of ripples. They rise and dip like the crooked stiles for all the crooked men going their uncertain miles; and the earth in the middle part of that state gets ready in stages to become the Blue Ridge and Great Smoky Mountains farther west.

In such a land, unwilling to lie flat and stretch seaward, soil and clay practice at being hillsides. The April rains flow, by turns, in rapids or silty streams, pouring down and then stopping to rest in a hollow like some temporary lake. Small ravines cut themselves into dirt the color of old orange rinds, and the summer sun shatters its surface with cracks, and these become rivulets, and they work at becoming new ravines. Then the sides lean inward and slice off in hard slabs and fall in to clog up the work of the previous season. So it is that August undoes April, and September repairs the summer and March makes it seem that autumn has never been.

The land paced the journeys of men who came to settle. Here they rushed upriver, flung out a fence and hurried their seeds into the ground; and here they paused and a long gap stretched between them, and honeysuckle made something new out of a deserted chimney. Those who stopped in the east had a long, flat land; bought and sold it in long pieces, set tall houses upon it; and lived there, looking inward and out to sea. And in the west they tacked their houses on the hills and walked on a slant; and lived there looking inward and up to sky. But in the middle of that state, men looked forth into Virginia and South Carolina; they built the state's business and commerce and manufacture. It was a land where all the red rivers were coming-from and going-to. Now was the time to stop them long enough to grind one sack of corn in the space between came and went.

When time itself paused between coming and going after 1865, and prosperity was carried off by circumstance the way whole piedmont fields can wash down on the rain and bleed orange into creeks and streams, the systems of nature failed. The balance of chaos there had been very delicate—rains to deposit and erode, sun to bake and nourish, clay that fell off and filled in; but now that so much had been destroyed, creation could not catch up. And the people, lacking coastal pride or mountainous isolation, could see a reflection of their hungers stretching from Richmond to Charleston.

Some of those people lived in a town called Greenway, built on the Katsewa River, which traced the western boundary of Stone County, and sometimes traced it in flood, and sometimes traced it as a sluggish stream.

It was no typical piedmont town and nobody typical lived there. Sam Allen, his wife, Mildred, and their three children did live in Greenway in the dimpled middle of that state. It was summer, 1897, and Thomas Allen was the middle child.

She stood at the kitchen door, calling.

"Thomas? Esther? David!" The names descended in order of most to least responsible, and each one grew louder. Thomas would surely answer. David was a last resort.

She shaded her eyes and studied the slope of tan grass where, like balled caterpillars, they might be rolling downhill with eyes glued tight against the dizziness. "Thomas? You children hear me?"

None of them answered.

All three were underneath the house with a small mirror, trying to put their fingers through it to grope in the world on the other side. It was Esther's idea. When they had learned to do it very well with fingers, she said, they might go all the way to Hobbs Dry Goods in town, where the big one was, and walk right through like Father, Son, and Holy Ghost, without looking back.

An hour before, this had seemed a wonderful plan. David could still picture himself growing misty as he marched dead ahead through that looking glass, but Thomas had already bent back the nail on one finger and his hand was stiff from trying to find exactly the right position.

Esther turned the mirror until again it caught a sliver of light through the boards above their heads. "Right there," she whispered. "And curve as you come in."

Thomas poked at it halfheartedly.

"No, no—come flying in! You must know you'll be passing through."

"You do it then," he said crossly.

Esther explained for the fifth time that the first two through the mirror must be boys, since she had reserved for herself the role of Holy Ghost.

Mildred Allen stepped onto the back porch and called them again. The door slammed. Both boys looked at Esther.

"Don't answer," she whispered. They squatted motionless in the shadows and Thomas looked up to where his mother's feet must be. Esther began moving the glass again to catch the light. "Not a word," she hissed.

They said nothing, but David stretched up to lay his hand against the underside of the cool boards, an inch from his mother's shoe soles. She was tapping her foot. He felt her temper coming gently onto his fingertips and, once more, believed it was true that one could slide somehow through all the solid things of earth.

"Let me try!" he said.

"You've used up all your turns."

Thomas was listening to his mother's vibrating foot. "She's very angry," he said.

Esther reached over and pinched him. "She'll go away."

The drumming of the foot loosed a shred of dry clay and it fell from the cracks in the porch to the ground. "Thomas! Answer me!" Sharp steps passed over their heads, came back, made a subfloor trail of dust puffs as they crossed to the back door again and went inside.

At this Esther smiled and in the dirt she drew a small circle within a larger circle, a secret mark of hers. Sometimes Thomas felt all of Stone County must be drawn over with Esther's mark. "I'm tired of this game," he said.

"We'll rest a minute," said Esther, "and go on."

Under the Allen house it was cool and mysterious. The family's dozen hens drowsed here on summer days, and had feathered the dirt as soft and gray as coffin dust. Six of them lay now against the far brick underpillars, where they had drifted when the children came; sometimes they stirred and muttered, or stood to stretch and resettle. Round hollows were left where they had slept, and their feet had spattered the surface with a thousand crucifixes. On the boards above, dirt daubers' nests clustered like small orange fruit, and long strings of dust hung through the cracks in filaments, and swung, and sometimes broke.

"I'm hungry," David said.

Thomas rolled some of the dirt, powdery as ash, in his hand. "It's so soft here," he said, thinking of the surrounding clay fields.

"No rain, no sun," said Esther, who knew everything. "No loud noises." One of the hens made a sleepy murmur to prove it. Thomas put the dirt down and ground it in.

Esther had arranged the mirror, shifted her mouth and eyes in just the right way, and now drove her hand suddenly toward the light. The way she dived down like a bird was so effective the others stared, half expecting to see her plunge in up to the wrist.

But nothing happened. She was disgusted. "I told you it had to be a boy the first time." She wiped the glass on her skirt and examined her dim face. She smiled at herself, snarled, thrust forth her tongue so far it seemed her whole mouth would turn wrong side out. Then she shrugged and slipped the mirror into a beaded bag she had stolen from her mother's trunk. "David," she said, "go see what Mother wants."

David, the smallest, crawled carefully without bumping his head and came out under the back steps, where he threw a small stone over his shoulder before he went all the way outside. All three carried stones each time they went under the house—another of Esther's ideas—to keep them from being drowned in light when they came out suddenly into the sun. Wintertimes even a clod would do, for the light was thinner then and did not fall so heavily into the face.

Esther lay back and her hair became dusted with gray dirt.

"You'll get no supper when Mother sees how you look."

"I don't need supper," she said lazily. Her eyes were closed.

He thought: She'll always be beautiful. Even when Esther lies dead and ancient, strangers will tell each other over her casket, "She must have been a beauty." With great care Thomas took up a handful of dirt and let it fall into her face. She came up angry, coughing, struck her head against a low beam and went for him with both hands. Two of the nearest hens clacked and flew up.

But Thomas had rolled aside and scuttled like a lizard for the opening, trying to aim at her as he whizzed his own protective stone behind him; and he stumbled into the back yard already running in a crouch. He pounded down the hill, letting his cramped back and legs straighten as he ran. At the foot of the slope he laughed aloud and scooped up some pine cones to throw at Esther when she appeared. He waited but Esther did not come.

Shaking out her hair, he thought, and spitting on her petticoat tail to wipe her face! He dropped the pine cones and threw back his head with laughter.

But why did I bother to throw the stone when I came from under the house?

Thomas stopped with his mouth still spread on a fading mirth. He searched the hot sky. Why did I throw her silly rock? Why does Esther make me do these things?

He lowered his head and began to walk angrily along the path toward the spring, looking for anthills he might crush. He was glad to get under the sycamores and sweet gums and beyond them into deeper shade. The light upon his face in the open had been very thick and very heavy, and he felt it had struck him like a rain of lemons.

"Where in the world have you been?" his mother snapped. "I called and called."

He felt trapped, not knowing what answer Esther had already made. "I was under the house."

"Thomas Allen, don't lie to me! I saw you myself walking up from the spring."

"Before that. I mean before that." From one corner of his eye he could see Esther smiling as she passed up and down the long kitchen table, setting out plates and forks.

"Under the house and didn't hear me call?" Mildred Allen put out both arms in the way Esther called "sugar-bowl angry," fingers to hips like a pair of china handles.

"I'm sorry, Mother," was all he could say.

She was shaking her head as she returned to the bread board in the pantry. "You children help your grandfather till supper's done. And what about David? Where did he get to?"

"Isn't he out in the woods with his string?"

"I wouldn't doubt it." Mildred Allen sighed. "Go help your grandfather now."

It was the summer David—seven years old—spent measuring the woods with his long piece of string knotted at two-inch intervals. He had been struck in April, just before the swollen buds exploded, by the symmetry of growing things, the precise space between leaflets on a twig, the wheeling and circling at the edge of leaves, inside a bloom, and laid secretly in the trunks of trees. Lately he had grown more ambitious and had taken to climbing oaks to see if all their major limbs thrust from the main trunk the same distance apart. He had already suffered two bad, unadmitted falls.

"David ought to help," Thomas grumbled. Nobody spoke. He followed Esther into the other room.

"That's not what's ailing you," Esther said over one shoulder. Behind them, their mother raised her voice to announce they were being sent in to help.

Grandfather shouted back that he didn't want their help.

Esther dragged a chair across the room and sat by him. "You'll have us anyway," she said.

"Well," said Grandfather. "Well. So. God. Damn." He always swore very deliberately, pausing to savor each word, as if he had time to watch his blasphemy mount to Heaven and run down rows of angel wings in a ripple and a stir. He grinned at Esther with teeth which were very brown.

"What are you doing?" said Thomas politely.

"Any fool can plainly see."

Any fool could. He was shelling dried bean pods, a task he hated, and dropping the small white beans into a pan. Esther put a handful in her lap.

"Want some help?" said Thomas.

Grandfather snorted. "If you know what's good for you."

The bean pods were yellow and wrinkled and tough. Esther had trouble shelling them since she bit her fingernails, and when no one was watching she would nip off the end of the pod with her teeth.

Bean shelling was work for women—mothers-in-law and poor relations—and Grandfather was bitter when he was put to it. His daughter Mildred thought he would be miserable and feel unwanted without something to keep his hands busy, and every year she planted extra rows of beans and dried them for weeks on the porch roof. Everyone else knew how he hated the beans, and Grandfather was hoarse from the effort of trying to tell it to her. She only smiled at him wisely and pressed more beans into his hands out of pure kindness.

Mildred was a very Christian woman, like her mother. Grandfather sometimes said that only after his wife died did he get out of the weekly trip to church and thus (here he inserted, distinctly, a God. And a Damn) escape from the Presence of Grace into the Presence of Good Works. Of the two, he said, Grace was the easiest to take.

"Don't speak ill of the dead," Mildred always warned him.

Mildred Allen came in now from the pantry, wiping flour from between her fingers onto her apron, and smiled at the picture of her father and two of her children busy over the bean pan. "A fine job," she said. "Don't know what I'd do without you to help."

"Don't put them in your mouth," said Thomas to Esther. "You're dirty." He wanted his mother to see the cobwebs hanging in Esther's hair.

But she went back into the kitchen without noticing and began to sing one of the psalms—"Marvelous kindness . . . marvelous kindness . . . he hath shewed me marvelous kindness . . ." They stopped to listen. Esther took up a bean pod and began absently to poke it into her ear.

"Hear that," said Esther, and for a minute Thomas thought she meant the bean. "Mama can sing."

The tone was thin, but high and sweet. "How great the goodness Thou hast stored . . . In secret for Thy Saints, O Lord . . ."

"Must be very secret," Grandfather grumbled, for he took the viewpoint that earth was a vale of troubles, and when he and his daughter discussed religion it came out the Book of Job versus the Book of Revelation every time.

"Is David out playing inchworm again?" said Grandfather.

Esther nodded. "He's got a pencil tied on his string today. He's working on the curves inside leaves."

Grandfather said he was glad nobody ever asked David to make the world in any seven days. "He'd still be making the darkness and the deep, down to the last teaspoonful." He set his beans onto the floor between his feet. "Ya'll keep shelling," he ordered, and took a long, lazy stretch. He slipped a hard bean kernel into his mouth and munched on it, for he was proud of having kept his teeth and often irritated Mildred by crunching bones at the table like a hound dog. Leaning forward, he pulled a string of dust out of Esther's hair. "Been under the house?"

"It's cool there," she said. "If you'll just open the pods, I don't mind the shelling."

"I mind opening the pods," he said firmly. "I mind all of it." She nipped another with her teeth. "You sure are dirty," he went on. "Worse than David when he's been up all the trees for miles around. You never going to grow up, Esther?"

"Never," she said.

"Smart girl. It don't get better with the years." A look of gloom and self-pity settled on his face. "Better to die young. Better to be a butterfly. Grow up, start the next generation and then die off." He thought of David, measuring off the created earth in precise inches. "God should have stopped with butterflies. He didn't know when the Garden of Eden was well off."

Neither of the children paid any attention. They both knew Grandfather was terrified of dying. The whole household was in league with him against his own end, yet he talked forever of the importance of dying young. He seemed to take the view that since Death had missed him forty years before, with a falling tree or a long fever, it had no right to come at him now when he'd had time to think on things.

Grandfather raised his voice to make them listen. "That way you wouldn't count on anything, see? Butterflies don't have time. You'd know that's all you were here for. This extra time is what's confusing." He looked from one to the other to see what they thought. When he saw neither was listening, he was overcome with fury and kicked out at the bean pan and scattered pods all the way to the kitchen doorway. "It's all a lie!" he bellowed. "Especially the part about children heedin' the words of wise old men!"

"Look what you've done!" clucked Esther, and when her mother came to see what the racket was, Esther said the wise old man had done it, which made Grandfather speechless with rage. Thomas was set to picking up all the beans. Grandfather pulled out his tobacco plug, wrenched off a huge mouthful and announced his intention of spitting on Mildred's clean floor.

At this Mildred Allen leaned to one side in the kitchen doorway and closed her eyes against the sight of him. She reminded herself of all the Israelites in the wilderness, their own hopes fading and the Promised Land moving farther and farther away.

Then she opened her eyes and fixed all three with an angry glare. "We are going," she said grimly, "to have a peaceful evening. We are going to be a happy family." Her temper got the best of her. "You are going to love each other if it kills me!" she said in a loud and rising voice.

David ran in just then, carrying a pine cone and calling for them to look! Look how it was built from base to top, each fragment lapping over the other, spun out in rising spirals off the branch of the mother tree!

"And squirrels bury the seeds to save for winter, and some get lost, and the new trees grow. Isn't that something? The way it's all worked out?" He stood there, joyous, as if he held in his hand not a pine cone but the massive, interlocked universe.

"It's God's plan," said Mildred, smiling, and remembering all the certain patterns.

"Think of the waste," Grandfather snapped.

Now Mildred faced him with defiance. "Not a sparrow falls but that He knows!"

"They go on falling, don't they?" he crowed. "Ain't creation just one dead bird after another?"

She stamped away and into the pantry, reminding herself that by honoring one's father and mother, one's days might be long upon the land which the Lord had given.

Sometimes it was a trial, honoring Angus Mackey. The children forgave him a great deal because he had once seen Stonewall Jackson. And she was able to bear with him because he was old; he was her father; he would somehow be redeemed in the end if she had to drag him into Glory by the hair. But Sam . . .

Mildred shook her head and made a noise against her teeth as she put her bread board and flour sifter back into the bin. Sometimes she thought she might split the length of her body, on a line from the crown of her head right through the navel, and that would satisfy both her father and her husband.

Gramley Library
Salem College
Winston-Salem, NC 27108

"Here!" she'd announce, somehow having been transmuted into a floating tongue of fire above the two segments. "Here, the childhood and the womanhood, neatly divided. Take your share and go." Solomon had once offered to chop up a baby like that and love had stayed his hand; but love as she knew it would only say, "About time too," and offer to whet the blade.

That's the lot of womankind, she thought now, slamming the heavy wooden lid of her flour bin; and how shall I tell these things to Esther?

The ordinary quarrels of an ordinary day had so depressed her that she needed both hands to lift the skillet to pour ham drippings out. I could sleep a year, she thought.

Angus Mackey came into the kitchen as she tipped the thick stream, golden and brown-flecked, into a little bowl.

"Dreaming again," he said, but more gently. "You always was a dreaming girl."

There it was, his half. What would he say if she turned to him now, and announced in an absolute fury, "I cannot go on being what I always was!" It tickled her to think about it, and she smiled down at her own hand.

Aloud she said, "I was thinking that's one thing they don't have in Heaven. They don't have any meat grease. Sometimes I think if I pour any more meat grease in or pour any meat grease out, I'm going to sit right down and cry."

"They got meat grease," he muttered. "They been frying sinners for a million years."

Grandfather Angus Mackey often said he was very lucky; he had one friend and one enemy, and these were the fruits of a long and useful life.

His friend was an ancient Negro named Cabiliah Henderson, whom he had known for half a century. The enemy was his daughter's husband.

Cabiliah came to visit only three times a year (Esther said it took him four months to make the trip across Stone County, walking), so Grandfather had more time invested in his enmity, on which he looked every morning and every night. Thinking up ways to annoy his son-in-law was a comfort to his old age; and bean shelling a mere detail which interfered with his full career of getting on Sam Allen's nerves. The joy of it lay in the indirection, since the two men almost never spoke to each other. Grandfather, in fact, behaved as if he were head of that household, observing Mildred's children and eating Mildred's meals. She seemed to him a widow—well out of it too—and any other male presence was no more than a stubborn ghost or a disagreeable memory. At the table, Sam Allen had to stop the serving bowls by force or else every vegetable would pass him by.

The two enemies rarely spoke out of rudeness, but it was different with the two friends. Cabiliah Henderson was a deafmute, and when he appeared like a vanguard of the changing seasons to sit away an afternoon on the front porch, Grandfather would not so much as clear his throat, out of respect for his friend's silence.

It was all done, then, without a word. Sam Allen and Angus Mackey looked aside to walls and furniture, and these bounced back their mutual dislike the way a bullet will ricochet inside a cave. And Cabiliah Henderson and Angus Mackey, after an hour's rocking, might follow with their eyes a small cyclone of leaves and then exchange one look of perfect satisfaction.

Still, there was a stretch of daylight in which Grandfather, if he were not careful, would have nothing but dried beans to occupy his time. Sam Allen left while it was still dark to ride his mare three miles down the Stoneville road and into Greenway, where he ran Hobbs Dry Goods Store. The lamps would be lit again before he came riding home. So, needing an enemy the worst way during those hours of sunshine and blue sky, Grandfather gave over the daytimes to worrying about his own death, which—he said—had held off just long enough to make him nervous.

He was vigilant against Death, which today might be curled and waiting under a broken stair tread, and tomorrow hide shrunken in a plate of spoiled food. So much did he talk of the many ways he might be ambushed that once Esther stamped her foot and cried, "Death! Death! Death! It makes me sick!" This got him so tickled that he wheezed off into a long coughing fit and had to be pounded on the back, which proved—he panted—how various are the weapons of destruction.

Now that the beans were shelled and the children sent out back to wash, Angus Mackey pulled his rocker to the edge of the front porch and waited for Sam Allen to come riding home. The sound of thunder grumbled in from a long way off, but he thought the mare would probably outrun the rain, which meant his son-in-law would come home flushed with triumph. Grandfather tried to think of something to destroy that mood in the space between gatepost and front door.

It was a singing twilight; a crowd of insects droned and whirred and clicked among the grasses. Esther said sometimes the sound was so thick you could probably walk upon it, a foot above the ground where all the seed pods hung on their long stems.

Angus Mackey smiled, for Esther was his favorite. Mildred had been like that, before she married. And Virginia had been like that, before she took her Bible so seriously. . . .

He shot upright and squinted sharply down the road. No sign yet of the mare. He relaxed and pictured Esther walking at a slow, up-lifted pace, her weight upon the voice of crickets.

Two summers before, Esther had convinced her brothers it would be possible to fly. Practice, that's all; nothing but practice, she said.

All that June Grandfather watched them working on it. They were to begin on small things, an inch or so high, and jump down lightly, moving arms to tread the air as if it had been water. Later, said Esther, a stair, two stairs, the edge of the porch and finally the roof of the barn itself; and as they flew down they would gather in armloads of leaves.

"I feel it," David whispered once in awe. The lightness seemed to creep inside them and their bones had no more substance than an odor while Angus Mackey watched. Esther, he heard, now swore she could rise an inch from her bed at night by holding her breath and stroking her fingers over the edge.

That had been quite a summer. The children planned how they would ring the Greenway church bells at night, put chairs on roofs and hang washtubs onto spires, and start all across Stone County the rumors of angels.

He'd been sitting just this way the day Esther leaped grandly off the roof of the front porch and came down screeching in front of him into Mildred's rosebush. The terror had nearly stopped his heart. He took her arms and pulled her, crying, over the banister in a heap.

"Had more sense! Shoulda had gumption!" he was spluttering. "Craziest thing! Know where foolishness leaves off and truth begins! Old enough. No more brain than a blue jay. Scare the fool out of an old man. . . ."

Esther sucked a brier out of her wrist and spat it on the porch and went on crying. She was deeply scratched on the neck and shoulder; her leg had twisted, and scarlet rosebuds were scattered and hung on her dress with thorns.

Grandfather patted her back and pricked his own finger. "Oughta know better, big girl like you; Never saw such a fool thing!" He looked down at the rising blood on the end of his finger, being pumped out that leak by his aged, struggling heart. He yelled, "Are you *trying to kill me?*"

Esther hushed. Just like that she stopped the tears, wails and shuddering; and he almost thought her will was so great she had dried her own blood in the scratches and snapped shut every wound.

"Let go of me," she said through her teeth.

David's head appeared, hung upside down at the edge of the porch roof. "Are you hurt? Esther, you hurt?"

She continued to stare at her grandfather. David edged down farther and now hung his shoulders over the edge. "Esther?"

"Don't fall," she snapped. "Grandfather couldn't stand it."

This was so unjust that Angus Mackey began to lecture—how she would understand someday; it would all come home to her; she too would be mistreated when she got old. . . .

"I won't get old! I won't!" she yelled, shaking off twigs and leaves and roses.

"You'll see what I mean then, when your time comes! When you get old!"

"I won't," she whispered, shaking her head; and he said, "Won't do no flying either."

She ran from him.

Now when Angus Mackey remembered it, the rosebush and the argument, the cries of the insects began to grate on his ear and he worked himself into an irritable mood to greet Sam Allen.

The mare was coming. He could see the growing speck of her down the road.

He leaned forward and with a great noise blew his spent wad of tobacco at the roots of Mildred's rosebush. He felt suddenly tired and his arm and shoulder ached.

Ain't worth it, he thought.

He got up to go to his own room and lie on the bed till suppertime.

In the hallway it came to him that maybe his retreat was a sign; his death, approaching, was already active inside him to mellow his speech and sweeten his action, so the last things about him to remember might all be good . . . so that, waiting through the night by his coffin, even Sam Allen would be able to say the old man had changed at the last, been nicer, easier to handle.

"Hell I will," said Angus Mackey aloud. He went back to the porch and moved his chair and a flowerpot where, in the growing dimness, Sam Allen might stumble as he came home.

He almost fell himself when thunder broke suddenly out of the sky like an accusation. He staggered and hung swaying onto the front door. The wind blew raindrops into his face. The downpour began and through it he could no longer see the road, much less the mare.

Angus Mackey went inside and told Mildred he would skip supper; he wanted to sleep. No need now, he thought, to waste good energy sitting at that table. Between the waiting rocker and the driving rain, this day's duty by Sam Allen had been done.

Upstairs, he put his dirty shoes on the coverlet of his bed and fell asleep, smiling, with a clear conscience.

Usually moonlight fell in a pale square through his upstairs window, but tonight the room was dark. The rain was almost gone and Thomas could hear the individual drips and splatters and the noise of wet boards swelling. Down the hall somebody coughed. He heard Grandfather turn, whuffing and puffing, in his bed beyond the wall, and when something thumped he decided the old man had worn his shoes to bed again.

Thomas slept on a thin feather mattress laid over a straw tick and the feathers forever puffed away on both sides and left him in a valley of prickles. He rolled over now to the edge.

Something rustled at his door. Thomas sat up in bed.

"Who's that?" he whispered, not very loud. For all he knew, something terrible might answer.

It was only Esther. She came in, barefoot, gliding in a white gown. "It's me," she said.

He told her to go away.

She stretched one arm out before her like a sleepwalker and came stiffly to his bed. "Remember the story of the Sleeping Lady?"

Grandfather liked to tell that one—how Pearlie Winters, seventeen, sleepwalked one night onto the rail of a bridge over the Katsewa River; and when her family and sweetheart found her there, the sweetheart yelled a warning, which woke her so abruptly she fell from the bridge and drowned. Esther loved that story.

Thomas leaned forward and clasped his knees. "What about it?"

"Nothing. I got you in trouble about not coming when Mama called."

"You always get me in trouble."

"I brought you something."

He saw then why she had not balanced both hands forward like Pearlie Winters; her left was holding two green branches.

"What are they for?"

"To put under your pillow. They're wet from the rain."

Thomas said he didn't want any wet leaves under his pillow.

"They die all night long," Esther whispered, "and you get to smell it."

She held out the sweet-gum leaves, five-pointed like small green hands, and a smaller branch of cedar. Thomas shook raindrops onto the floor. "You sure are funny," he said and put them under his pillow.

That seemed to bother Esther. "You think so? Why do you think I'm funny?"

"Girls just are."

"I hope that's it," she said to herself. She jumped at a sudden noise from the next room. "Did he fall out of bed?"

"He's got his shoes on again, that's all."

"I wish I was a boy," she mused. "Couldn't I be you? Couldn't we change?"

Thomas was half afraid she might know some way to do it. "No!" he said in a loud voice, and the wall beside him banged again.

"You'll be the death of Grandfather, breaking his sleep that way," Esther said calmly. "Give me back one of my leaves."

He broke off a spray and she crushed it to her nose, then sucked air through one leaf till it popped. She slipped her tongue into the hole and said thickly, "Why'd you throw dirt on me today? Under the house?"

Thomas didn't answer. She rolled the leaf into a cylinder and stuck it up one of her nostrils.

"Don't do that."

"My nose. My leaf. I started to bring in mud to throw on you after you went to sleep tonight."

"Mama wouldn't like mud in her clean bed."

"That's why I didn't."

"I wish you'd go to bed yourself. David's been asleep for hours."

"He's little. But wasn't that something about the pine cone? After supper he started breaking off the little scales, one by one. He wanted to see how many it took."

"How many?"

She chortled, *"More than this!"* and shot her hand forward into his bed and scattered a thousand pieces of pine cone. Thomas caught his foot in the sheet and fell getting out of bed after her, and by that time she had made it, giggling, to her own room and propped a chair against the door. It took him twenty minutes in the dark to get the worst of the pine bits fished out of his bed. The next time Grandfather rolled over and his shoe sole struck the wall, Thomas sat up angrily and thumped back with his fist.

It was a long time before he fell asleep. Finally he buried his head under the pillow until the odor of wilting leaves made him dizzy and then whirled him off in the black. He did not hear the other sounds beyond the wall, the cry and the strangling late in the night, nor his mother's running feet, nor that terrible racket when the doctor hurried in and fell on the front porch over a rocking chair and a flowerpot.

Chapter

❧ 2 ❧

"How is he?"

"Don't bother me now. We don't know yet." Mildred brushed by her daughter and ran up the stairs. There was no longer any need to run and yet it eased her guilt. Just before dawn she had found herself shaking her father's shoulder, screaming, "Papa! Wake up and pray!" Now the doctor said Angus Mackey would live through this one after all, but she did not give this news to Esther. She had the feeling it was wiser to spread out the fear and worry to include the children just now rising from their beds. Their concern added to hers would somehow buoy her father up, present him before the throne as a man who had been loved.

"There's mush in the pot," she called back to Esther. "Tend to the boys."

Dr. Newton was closing the sick man's door. He shook his head at her. "Slow down, Mildred, he's gone to sleep. And that's what I'd better do." He pulled out his watch and made an ugly noise at it. "No, guess I'll just eat and go on."

"I'll fix you something. Dr. Newton, will he be all right?"

"Angus Mackey's an old man. He'll live till the next one. He may even live till the one after that. He's got a stubborn heart." Dr. Newton was fat and bald and gave the impression of being freshly peeled. "Where's my horse?"

19

"Sam put him in the barn. He's fed and watered."

"If you can feed me then, Mildred, I'll get on my way. I can stop back tomorrow or next day." He steadied her on the stairs. "And don't take on so over him. You've given him a home for years. You know these days are coming. He's what—seventy-five?"

"Seventy-seven." Mildred knew he had spoken out of kindness, to prepare her, but it was so much what Angus Mackey himself bellowed in her ear seven days a week that tears rose in her eyes. She allowed herself to lean a little on the doctor's arm.

David and Thomas searched their faces as they came into the kitchen. Thomas had merely poked his cornmeal mush.

"How is he?" Esther said.

"Not well, but he'll live," answered Dr. Newton. Mildred fixed ham and three eggs while Esther finished her mush and began washing out the dish. Sam had long since ridden in to Greenway, with nothing in his stomach but pear preserves and a cold biscuit, after being up half the night to bring the doctor.

"Don't play with your food, Thomas."

He put a spoonful into his mouth and swallowed it in one lump. "He kicked the wall all night. I heard him."

"I was asleep," said David.

Thomas seemed to be struggling to get the mush down his throat. "I didn't know he was sick. Mama, I'd have called you if I'd thought he was sick."

"Grandfather kicks the wall anyway," said Esther sensibly.

Mildred passed the food and Dr. Newton patted Thomas on the shoulder as he sat on the bench. "Your grandfather isn't going to die this time, Thomas, so don't worry about a few kicks on the wall. You got molasses?" He took the jug, poured a puddle on his plate and blended butter in before sopping with half his biscuit.

"It won't be long though," said Mildred to herself. She crossed to the window. Beyond the back porch and through the framework of the well she could see two Negroes coming through the pasture. Without turning, she sent David to get the doctor's buggy hitched. "And send Ellie Faye to pick tomatoes," she called. "I don't want them laying on the wet ground."

"Fine breakfast, Mildred," said Dr. Newton.

She only nodded. She watched David racing into the pasture to tell the news to Ellie Faye and her brother Rutledge—how death had come for Grandfather and been driven off awhile. Now he had reached them and begun to talk. His arms were waving; he pointed to the house. They could have given him the name of Angus, she supposed. It was such an ugly name.

Over one shoulder she asked if her father could have anything to eat.

"Soup, coffee. Bread and gravy if he's hungry. He'll not want much today."

"I ought to go sit with him."

"Not unless it makes you feel better. He won't sleep any deeper for having you there." The doctor swallowed the last of the coffee and asked Thomas to carry his bag outside.

Mildred turned to where Esther was washing the bowls. "I never even thanked him for coming."

"He doesn't expect it. Tell me about last night."

Mildred closed her eyes. "I heard Papa choking. I ran in and he was beating the air. One of his hands hit me." She rested her fingers lightly above one eye. "I tried to talk to him. He just went on thrashing around—it was like drowning." She walked back and forth. "It looked like he was drowning."

"I didn't hear a thing," said Esther, disappointed to have missed it.

Mildred moved her hand out in front of her and looked into it, much as if she had plucked her father's blow right off her forehead for further study. "I think I will go up. Let Ellie Faye clean the kitchen."

When she tiptoed in, Mildred saw that Angus Mackey's eyes were open, fixed upward like those of a corpse. "Papa?" she whispered. He moved the eyes but not his head. She bent over him. "You feeling better, Papa?"

Still he said nothing.

"You've been sick but Dr. Newton says you'll be fine now. Can I get you anything to eat?"

"Sick," he said. His breath smelled like a swamp.

"Rosa will be over to see you later in the day. You're to rest and get your strength back."

Something—a cough or laughter—rattled inside his flimsy chest. "What was that, Papa?"

He might have been smiling. "I told you so," he said, and went back to sleep.

Sam Allen was considered a city man, although he lived three miles out of Greenway on the Stoneville road. He had run the dry-goods store on Main Street for Old Man Hobbs nearly thirty years, and now that Hobbs, at eighty-three, had suffered a stroke and could barely tell dark from sunlight, Sam expected to be left the store in the old man's will.

"Glad to hear it," Sam said now to the doctor, holding the bell with one hand while he opened the door to the street.

"I knew you'd be waiting for some news," said Dr. Newton. "He's one tough old man, Angus Mackey."

As soon as the door had closed, Sam Allen let go the bell and even slapped it a few times. Angus Mackey and Winkler Hobbs were two tough old men, and sometimes he thought they would live forever.

He peered out to make certain the doctor was out of sight, then went outdoors to stand on Main Street under the sign which read:

HOBBS DRY GOODS
We Sell Everything Except Whiskey

Shading his eyes, Sam took a quick east–west look along Main Street. The rutted road was bordered by uneven rows of trees—walnut, wild cherry, mulberry, elm; and two of the tallest ones had some kind of blight, so that even in the green summertime their leaves were halfway dead and the topmost branches scorched and nearly empty. Sam had first noticed the diseased trees in early June, and now he watched them regularly for signs of decline.

Today he took only a brief look, remembered they must have roots halfway to China, and slammed back into the store.

He could not rid himself of last night's conviction that a daytime heart attack would have killed Angus Mackey on the spot. "That old man," he said aloud to the sugar bin as he walked by, "just couldn't stand to die in front of me."

Well, he might have had the decency to pass on while Sam and the mare were racing to Greenway and Dr. Newton! Not that he'd run her full gallop all that distance. Once he had even jerked her still to watch a deer bolt for the dark woods. A soul ought to slip away like that, with some grace, he'd thought.

He should have given up long ago any hope of grace from Angus Mackey. The snake and cicada might slip from their old skins with movements like some easy dance, but Angus Mackey would have to be dragged screaming out of his.

The bell rang.

"Sam? You in there, Sam?" Peering into the dimness of the store, a skinny man stepped halfway through the doorway. "Hey, Sam."

"Stop letting in flies, Silas."

He closed the door and came across the oiled floor. "What was that, Sam?"

"Nothing." Sam blew out all the breath from his chest and sucked in deeply. Whiskey, sure enough. Some from last night and some fresh from this morning. He slid a few steps away from the smell. "I was going to send somebody out to your place this morning. The old man took bad last night. Rosa ought to know it."

"Pint jar will do," said Silas. "How is he now?"

"Dr. Newton says he'll live. You been home since yesterday?"

"I'll tell her about it. Just one pint, Sam."

"You've not even been home!"

"I was busy," said Silas. A small man, he had a rabbit's face and long ears which were laid back at an angle on his skull as if from fear. "I'll go straight and tell her. Just wrap it in brown paper."

"You got the price? I bet Rosa's worried sick."

Silas patted him on the shoulder, looked into his face, stopped patting. He put his hand in first one pocket and then another. "I ought to get on my way, her daddy sick and all." He took out a little money from here and there, spread it in one hand and moved the coins around with a finger. There was a silence. "Half a pint might be easier to carry."

Sam Allen shrugged and led the way through the curtains into the back storeroom. Then he wheeled. "You ain't sold your horse!"

The curtain flew behind him and covered the man's face. "Course not," said Silas in a muffled voice. He pushed it aside. "Was it his heart?"

"That was it. Middle of the night and I had to ride all the way to town. Scared Mildred pretty bad." He got the jar of whiskey, rolled the paper around it and twisted both ends. It seemed a waste. He doubted the paper would stay on the jar till Silas was out of sight. Sam was very thrifty about things like paper. "How's Rosa feeling?"

"She's up and down," said Silas, watching his hands. "That's fine." He reached for it.

Sam took a step back and turned the jar in his fingers. When Angus Mackey had first moved into his house, he'd argued to Mildred the old man ought to be living with Rosa, be company for her with Silas off drinking half the time. Besides, Rosa had spells; she got dizzy on stair steps and cried into the milk churn for no good reason. And there had been at least six months when all Rosa did was sing the church songs backward, everywhere from her own cellar and wood-shed to the church vestibule—the tune regular and the words reversed. It was enough to make anybody dizzy to hear the way she went at it: "Binds That Tie the Be Blest," or "Cross Rugged Old an Stood Away Far Hill a On." Rosa was just peculiar. She ought not to be left alone in that farmhouse, far away from anybody.

"I'll just carry it along," Silas was saying nervously for the second time, putting his hand out again for the jar.

But Angus Mackey had wound up with the Allens after all, Mildred answering back that with Papa's problems it would be the blind leading the blind to send him to her little sister and, besides, most of Rosa's spells were just grief for all her babies that couldn't somehow be born, but threw themselves out of her womb as off a sinking ship.

"You ought to stay with Rosa more," Sam said now, sternly.

"I'll do that, Sam. I surely will." Silas had maneuvered his hand into the air until he was able to plunge forward suddenly and grab the jar. Smiling, he laid it between his left forearm and his chest, and almost seemed to rock it once or twice, soothingly. "I'll bring Rosa over right away. Maybe tonight." Something about his face, which was full of bones and splinters, seemed suddenly to unmold. He looked over Sam's shoulder at nothing. "Maybe tonight," he repeated vaguely, making it sound a long way off.

"You go straight home now, Silas Bennett."

The little man handed over his money and drew the curtain slowly, not willing to shake the contents of his jar or send one bubble down to trouble the liquid. He said over one shoulder, "That sign don't bother you none?"

"What sign? Oh, out front. The whiskey. No, that's just business. Besides, Hobbs Dry Goods don't sell whiskey. Sam Allen sells it."

"Good whiskey too."

"Mildred likes it."

The man's eyes pushed out. "Mildred likes whiskey?"

"The sign, you fool. She likes the sign."

Silas began to walk very rapidly down the narrow aisle toward the door and Sam nearly had to run to catch up with him. "You're going straight home now, and tell Rosa about her daddy?"

The bell rang sharply as Silas stepped out onto the street. Sam, hurrying, caught the door before it could close and called, "Straight home, Silas?"

The little man was backing away down the street, his small rabbit face turned up to study the dry-goods sign, which was swaying in a hot breeze. "I don't care much for it myself," he called back in a friendly way.

"You go tell Rosa!" Sam hollered again.

Silas turned the corner.

If I listened hard, thought Sam, I could probably hear that paper coming off.

At the first noise in the darkened yard Mildred stiffened in her rocking chair and cried, "I knew they'd come!" She jerked her head forward at her husband. "You hear them?" When he said nothing, she folded her embroidery neatly over the hoop and put it on the mantel. "I knew Rosa would come when she heard about Papa."

Sam had been half asleep in his chair. "Wanting supper, I bet," he mumbled.

"I don't begrudge my sister supper!"

Mildred met them at the door, opening it wide as it would go for Rosa, who was very fat. The ins and outs of Rosa's swollen face made her look old and wicked, although at thirty-three she was eight years younger than Mildred and had always been a gentle, quiet girl. She turned herself sideways now, and edged in on small steps. "Is he all right? I'd have come sooner . . ."

"He's sleeping." She made an effort to be soft. The very sight of Rosa made Mildred raise her voice, as if by yelling she could pierce through these bloated walls and reach her little sister.

Mildred saw she was still holding the door open to the empty night. "Isn't Silas with you?"

"He took a walk down to the pines. You know how he is, Mildred."

She knew exactly how he was.

Rosa gave a high laugh. "Silas never could stand sickness. He likes people to be—" She stopped abruptly and spread her right hand over her belly as if to hide it. "It was too hot to stay inside, he said.

Maybe Sam would like to walk out with him?" She gave Mildred a worried look. "You think Sam would like a walk?"

He'd like the rest of his nap, thought Mildred, but Sam was already coming into the hall to join them. The corners of his mouth were pulled down and into his cheeks.

"I'll walk out back with Silas," he said politely, making it sound like a threat.

By old habit the two women walked down the hall to the kitchen. Mildred said, "I bet you never stopped to eat."

"Just a mouthful." Rosa's eyes were already darting here and there, to the cabinet where there might be half a lukewarm berry pie or baked sweet potatoes shriveling in their skins.

Mildred set out biscuits, cold bacon, the last of the milk in a jar which still held the coolness of the cellar. She took a tomato off the windowsill and cut it into quarters in a saucer. The molasses and a jar of pickles were still on the table from supper.

Rosa began to eat. She gave no appearance of enjoyment, but cut and spread and chewed with a rhythmic efficiency as if this were a skill she had acquired from years of training. She ate like an eating expert, without interruption or wasted motion, every bite the same size, every morsel chewed the same solemn length of time; until the table was as bare as the fields of Egypt after the locusts passed.

Mildred watched her for a while and then she didn't watch her. She found an apple and began nervously to peel it. When she was done, Rosa shook the salt above it and took a large bite and wiped her mouth delicately with the handkerchief she carried in her sleeve.

"I'm eating for two again," Rosa said.

"When did you miss?"

Mildred tried not to sound skeptical but in these matters Rosa was always lying. The blood did not dry in her before she swore she was with child, and that meant twelve extra disappointments every year besides the real ones. There had been three of those, and the things never as big as a child's fist before they came hurtling out for Silas to bury in the orchard. He wouldn't even tell Rosa where he had dug those not quite graves for the babes which had never quickened in her womb; and sometimes she went out in the dark and lay in the grass among the rotting apples and called her children by name.

"I've not missed yet but I just know it, Mildred. I can tell."

Mildred made two cups of tea and sat at the table and blew into hers.

"Papa taking sick like that, it's like a sign. If it's a boy, I'm going to name him Angus. Angus Mackey Bennett."

"He'll be teased and called Agnes, like a girl."

"We can call him Mackey. Mack when he's older. I'm going to tell Papa tonight."

"Don't tell him yet. Wait till you're sure. Another month, Rosa."

"I'm already sure," said Rosa, but her eyes brimmed with sudden tears. "This tea is too hot. I hope Sam found Silas. Men don't like to be around when women are talking about death or birth—you noticed that?"

"I've noticed it," said Mildred shortly. She waited a minute before going ahead to speak her mind. "I wonder, Rosa, if it wouldn't be better for Silas if you quit so much talking about babies, anyway. You give him so many promises; every week you're sure. And maybe it's like serving a man the same thing for supper every day." She saw that Rosa, to explain the increasing tears, had begun to scald her mouth by drinking the tea. "It was just a thought and I'm probably wrong. Rosa? Rosa, don't burn yourself."

In a small voice Rosa said, "Did Silas say something?"

"Of course not. I said it was just my thought. Rosa, children aren't everything." She took her sister's hand, clumsily, because there was so much of it to hold. The palm was hot from being wrapped around the cup. "If you knew how I worry about mine—they're all so different." Mildred knew she was fumbling now. "Need such different things. And they're different from me too; it doesn't seem possible they came from me at all. They just happened to me in a way, can you understand that?" She saw Rosa could not understand it and she let go her hand and sipped cautiously at the tea. "About Papa now . . . Dr. Newton thinks he'll be all right, at least for a while. Someday his heart will just stop; we all know that."

The thought rang in her head. *Someday his heart will stop. Stop, stop, stop.* She found she was doing it to the rhythm of the tall clock in the next room. When Thomas came into the kitchen and spoke politely to Aunt Rosa, she was relieved. "Thomas could go down cellar for some more milk . . ."

"That was more than enough, on top of this tea. Thomas, you get an inch taller every time the sun comes up."

"I'm big as Esther," Thomas said with a frown.

"You're both growing up. Is your grandfather still asleep?"

"Yes, ma'am. I've been sitting with him. David's up there now."

"David?" Mildred's voice was sharp. "What happened to Esther?"

"She went out back to see Uncle Silas. I told her I'd stay." Thomas waited to be praised for his high sense of duty.

But Mildred was too worried about what Esther might see and hear, out in the dark where Silas was probably sitting atop the woodpile with his whiskey.

"Maybe one jug of milk to take home," Rosa was saying. "You know our old cow's gone dry."

Mildred had just been ready to send Thomas outdoors after his sister. Now she told him in a cross voice to fetch Rosa a bucket of milk from the crock in the cellar, the crock on the left, not the buttermilk. She knew what that meant: water to draw at the well to rinse the bucket out, a candle to carry, that chain on the cellar door to wrestle with . . . "I ought to call Esther," she said uneasily.

"They'll look after her. Let's go see Papa now."

Mildred thought wearily of the effort of getting Rosa up those narrow stairs. "I'm sure he's still asleep."

But Rosa, carrying her weight with care as if it might spill, had already started on her tiny steps. "If it's a girl," she was saying, "I thought about Mildred. Mildred Rose? Or do you think Virginia Grace after Mama?"

There was nothing to do but follow.

Outside in the dark, Esther was doing just what her mother feared.

When she first crept down the steps from the front porch and placed one foot on the dew-wet grass, she had become a Cherokee princess, swift and silent in her walk, and now she carried a sharp stick (knife) between her teeth as she crept from tree trunk to tree trunk. She had gathered her skirts into a wad on her stomach to stop their rustling against grass or stones. In the shadows she went forward in a crouch, sometimes putting one palm against the earth in front of her to see whether it vibrated from the hoofbeats of an enemy.

In this way she reached the long, flat planes of wood sliced from tall pines and stacked in the shape of wigwams. After drawing a circle within a circle in the pungent layer of bark chips, she sat down upon it, protected. Beyond this wooden tower an oblong pile of cut wood, slabs sawed from these very lengths, had been braced between two small oaks and on top of this pile Silas was sitting with his head thrown back like a hound preparing to howl at the sky. Esther could hear her father's voice.

"I wish you'd come down from there," Sam was saying, "before you set all that wood rolling."

At first Esther could not understand Silas, who seemed to be singing. Then she could tell he was simply droning the same words over and over. "I figured it out I figured it out I figured it out," twanged Silas.

"Do your figuring down here on the ground."

Esther wiped her wet knife blade on her skirt and stuck it into the ground. The dang thing broke and ruined everything.

"I figured it out," came the singsong voice beyond her. "I figured out why I can buy whiskey just as good as yours from any nigger at half the price. Years I been thinking on it. I figured it out."

"Ought to be buying seed and tools and getting that cow bred. You ought to get Rosa one decent dress!" called Esther's father.

But Silas went on telling the moon. "Now here's what I figure, Sam. I figure I'm paying for that sign. All these years I thought I was buying whiskey and it's been that sign."

"I know your daddy's farm never was much," Sam Allen persisted, "but you could have made it pay. You could have worked that place. Now it's all rust and rot."

"Now here it is, Sam. You listening? You want to hear me now?"

"I'm listening."

"Some places you buy things at, you pay for the reputation, right? Some stores are known to give good measure, ain't that so? Some places you never need to count your change."

"I never cheated you."

"You're missing it, Sam. Now listen at this: when I walk in Hobbs Dry Goods Store . . ." He went off in a wheeze of laughter. "When I walk in Hobbs Wet and Dry Goods Store with my throat dry all the way down to the heels, I pay extra for your reputation. And your reputation says you don't sell whiskey. That's why it costs me so dear, Sam. I figured it out."

"Silas, let's go inside."

"Oh," cried Silas, "Oh, oh, *oh*, it costs me dearly high for you to be respectable."

"I don't aim to argue with you now."

Silas let out a trill of laughing. "How many more cents on the bottle will that be—your even temper? How high am I bid for the Allen disposition?" He stood up, balanced precariously, and pointed his finger into the plum tree. "What am I offered?"

"Sit down before you fall down," Sam barked, and came close and pulled at Silas' trouser leg until he sat down again on the woodpile. Esther had fallen forward onto her stomach and wormed around until she could see light hit on the bottle when Silas turned it up and lowered it again.

"And Sam," he cooed, "ain't it so you charge me more than other folks?"

"Liquor's not good for you," Sam said shortly. "You're in my family, besides. And I worry about Rosa."

"Oh, it do come dear, being your kinfolk. It comes high-priced." Silas waved his right hand around and around in the air, as if he were holding a lariat. There was a sudden thud. "My God, I've dropped it! Sam, did you see it hit? Is it broke?"

"Let that bottle lay still and come in the house."

Silas half fell from the woodpile, bringing the top row of cut slabs down around him. "I didn't hear nothing break," he was wailing. "Look around you, Sam. Oh, you wood chunks, wait! You see it there?"

"It's gone till morning," Sam Allen said, slipping the bottle into a crotch of limbs in the plum tree. Esther saw the starlight shine on it once. She held her breath.

But Silas was down on his hands and knees, picking up each piece of wood hopefully. Sam threw a few back onto the pile.

"Don't throw so wild; you'll break it yet!"

"Likely it rolled downhill."

Silas seemed to be sniffling. "Ah, Sam, you know I never meant it. You wouldn't fault me for what I said. Give me a hand here, Sam. Feel around there under that tree."

"There's nothing here. We better go in. Rosa wants to get home before late."

"Where could it go, such a little fall? You know I never minded your price, Sam, you always treat me fair. Have a look behind you."

"Silas, it's gone till daylight. Come on now." He bent and lifted Silas under the armpits like a child and set him upright on the path to the back door. "I'll save it for you." He pushed Silas in the shoulder blades and, walking behind him with an occasional prod, got him to the back steps.

"I never meant it, Sam. What's a few dollars over the years? It's just moonlight talking. You know that."

"There's none in the house if that's what you mean, and don't you go asking Mildred for it."

"I never have, Sam, now have I? All these years?" The back door closed on their voices.

Esther didn't move for a long time.

She thought: If the light catches on that bottle one more time, it'll be all right to go look it over. But even though she waited and held both eyes unblinking as an Indian, no light gleamed, and finally she walked to the plum tree as quietly as she could and stood on tiptoe and hauled the bottle down. She shook it at her ear. She held it up and tried to judge its level in the dark. She smelled the neck, where whiskey had trickled down, and shivered at that, and touched the very end of her tongue on a sticky place and began spitting into the air. Shooo-Weee. She dried the inside of her mouth and the surface of her tongue on one sleeve.

Then she sat on the ground and leaned back against the trunk of the plum and tried to guess what it was in that bottle that could raise up in little Silas Bennett the power to speak truth to her father.

Esther thought he had spoken truth because this very summer she had been working out a series of sentences which would explain all the Allens, once and for all. It was another of her efforts to find a single key to unlock everything. There had been other tries. No longer ago than April, when David first set forth with his string to learn the size of the world, she had tried one such code: David must measure. Thomas must win. Esther must discover.

That had been the key in April, and it had not lasted to the end of May.

Now, shaking the bottle again to hear the power inside it move, she tried her latest one: Father wants to *have* everything. Esther wants to *feel* everything.

No, that was still not it. Yet Esther was sure, somehow, there was something very simple to which all of them could be reduced. A set of colors, or a series of sounds or words. She had tried the code on objects: David gets the circumference of the egg; Thomas throws it; Father cooks it; Mother waits for biddies; Grandfather spoils it; and Esther plants it in the ground to see what tree will grow. . . .

She sighed in the dark. Another failure, placing her too like her mother in design. It was the differences she wanted, not the likes.

She put the bottle up against her nose, closed her eyes and tried to suck the power in. David sees connections. Esther sees differences. Mother sees patterns. Father . . .

It was a silly game. Esther opened the bottle.

She pinched her nostrils together, tilted the bottle back and took one long swallow.

The heat and cough were so violent that she blew some whiskey out through the nostrils in her spasms and that set her whole skull afire. She tried to smother the choking sounds in the folds of her skirt, bending over and rocking from side to side. When she was able to sit up again she decided Silas was braver than she thought, if he could bring himself to drink this every day. She put her head back against the tree and opened her mouth to the night air. Tears ran down her cheeks and her nose was dripping. She felt as if she had swallowed some flaming sword which, even now, filled up the hard tube of her throat straight down through her chest. Lordy. Esther blew her nose on her petticoat. She cleared her throat and spit. That Silas, Lordy me.

Carefully then, she tilted the bottle and let a small amount slip into her mouth between clenched teeth. It slid down so gently that she hardly gagged at all. The taste was terrible. The roots of her teeth were smoking in her gums. She closed her eyes and blew the heat from her mouth. I bet I could brown a leaf just breathing on it, Esther thought.

Maybe it would burn less if the mouth grew accustomed first. She took a swallow, held it, forced it hotly into first one cheek and then the other. Both, she found with horror, were growing numb. Hastily she swallowed the whiskey down and it fell into her stomach like a glowing coal. Even her legs, cool through her damp skirt, began to warm and—for all she knew—to give off light. Esther paused and laid the cool glass against her face. It was like, she thought gravely, learning to read at Greenway Academy. If you could only last long enough to get beyond alphabet drill, something was out there. Dim, but out there.

She took another cautious swallow and concentrated on following it with her mind all the way down to where it splashed in a sunburst underneath her ribs. Well, sly old Silas Bennett! She drank some more, still with great care. Undoubtedly the trick lay in thinking, thinking of the throat and stomach. She tried to pretend she had been wrung off at the neck like a Sunday chicken, and was pouring directly into the cavity of her throat, beyond any taste and any odor. It was easier, now, to focus on the throat, since the entire surface of her head and face had begun to prickle, the way a cramped foot tingles when it begins to go to sleep. Esther pinched her cheek, probed her nose with a finger, ran her tongue in bulges against her lips. Her tongue felt like the puffy head of a dry dandelion. A wind would scatter her teeth like seeds.

Esther giggled and took a big mouthful and let it go. Somewhere she felt it splatter and lie in warm bubbles at the tips of her feet. Well, Silas, Silas, no wonder!

The sight of Thomas closing the cellar door made her contract and blend into the plum tree. She had not seen him coming out. He carried a bucket up the back steps and went into the kitchen. Esther began to foresee the sudden search which would be made for her, the fear, the frenzy, the strap and the prayers. She stood up with the feeling it would be wise to run in several directions at one time.

And I could too. I could get into the looking glass. I could fly over the church!

She knew too, without a sliver of doubt, that she was going to get away with it all; she would not be caught; no one would ever know about this moment but Esther herself. That might even be her magic sentence. Nobody knows but Esther herself.

She tried that aloud to the woodpile: "Nobody knows but Esther."

Then she ran, clumsily, to the front of the house, shinnied up a porch post the way she had learned years ago, and pulled herself, holding Silas' precious bottle, over onto the roof. She lay there, panting. Her lungs were full of laughter but she bit down and kept it low. She pulled the waist ribbon out of her underdrawers and dragged down a branch of the chinaberry tree and bound the bottle tight to it, pinged it once with a finger and let go. The limb dipped a little with the weight but she thought it would not be seen from the ground and Nobody Would Know But Esther.

Lazily she stood on the roof and stretched. I've got to remember to get that down before the leaves fall in October, she thought. The moon was wavering in the sky.

Esther climbed into the window of Thomas' room, whirled herself dancing down the hall to her own, flung off her clothes and fell into bed. She threw the tail of her nightgown over her head and found she could see through it quite well; she could see through the ceiling; she could see through the roof and the night; it was all out there. She lay there, shaking with strength and laughter. The tips of her fingers throbbed.

When she heard voices, Esther put a pillow over her head to muffle her own whiskey smell, and to absorb the waves of heat which must be rippling the air above her bed.

Her mother, lamp in hand, was peering in. "Why, here she is, Rosa, asleep all this time!"

"I knew she'd be all right." The bulk of Aunt Rosa came into the doorway, blocking the light. "It's wonderful how children sleep."

The door began to close and the light to shrink. Rosa was saying, "You think Papa was happy?"

"You shouldn't have told him, Rosa. Not till you're sure."

"I am sure. Some things you just know."

The door clicked shut. Esther threw the pillow onto the floor and flung out her arms wide and spread her legs and lay staring through the darkness and knew and knew and knew it all. And nobody knew but Esther.

Chapter

⚜ 3 ⚜

THAT MORNING Sam seemed to linger at the table.

"Rosa take all the milk?"

Mildred held herself very still. Then, ever so slowly, she slapped her spoon once in the bowl of egg whites she had been beating. "There's plenty down cellar," she said with control. "You want some more?"

"No, no. Coffee, I guess." He had slept poorly. Two nights lost, for Mildred's relatives. He was a stingy man? People paid dear for his kinship? Sam shot a look at his wife. "Sit and have some yourself."

Shaking her head, Mildred began to fold the meringue into her cake batter. "It's wonderful to have these extra eggs. I must send word to Mr. Hobbs and thank him."

"No, don't do that!" he said sharply. He poured his own coffee and set the pot back in its saucer on the table. "He's . . . ah . . . sick. Forgetful. By now he probably doesn't remember sending you eggs."

"I didn't know his stroke had left him that way."

Somberly he told her the old man's mind was bad, very bad, and came and went from one day to the next. "It might be any day. And the store would be ours. Any day." He began to smile.

"I hope his mind don't forget about that!" laughed Mildred.

35

This filled him with terror. "Don't even say it!" he barked at her. Hobbs was clear as a bell, even two bells or three; and what if Sam's lie had tempted God?

Mildred gathered the eggshells, crushed them carefully and put the brittle chips into a bowl. Later these would be mixed with cracked corn and fed to her own small flock of hens.

"Usually Rosa has plenty of eggs," she said. "About all that's left of the old Bennett place—that fine flock of hens—and they'd have been nothing but soup and feathers if Silas had been in charge of them. Rosa was always good at raising chickens." She began pouring batter into a pan; Sam had stopped listening. "I know some weeks that's nearly all they've had to eat—plain eggs—and how much can you do after you've tried frying and boiling? Rosa won't cook one of them hens till it gets too old and tough to eat." She slid the pan back and forth on the table, settling the batter evenly. "Lately even Rosa's eggs have got scarce; she's worried the hens might be sick."

Mildred licked off her spoon and set the bowl aside to wash. "I told her if those chickens had any disease, its name was Silas Bennett. I bet he's swapping her eggs for whiskey."

Sam heard the last part well enough. Hastily he stood up and pulled out his pocket watch and set it for the second time that morning, shaking his head.

"Late. I'm going now. You having Dr. Newton look at Esther?"

"I think I will. He's coming at noon anyway to see Papa. I never saw anybody so sick as Esther was this morning. She still can't keep water down, though she claims to be dying of thirst. Her face is cool."

Hurrying out the back door, Sam agreed it was unusual for Esther to take sick. "Nothing serious, I'm sure," he called. "See you tonight."

Rutledge and Ellie Faye waved at him from the pasture. Usually it was seven before they came along the path to the Allen house, and Sam jerked out the watch again to see if he might be really late. No. He called, "You mighty early today."

The two Negroes waved again; they were too far away to hear. The mare Sam had fed and saddled before breakfast was waiting, and he swung on and lifted the reins before he remembered. He turned her downhill to meet the two servants, who stopped in the path and waited. Rutledge let his mouth come halfway open in case it should be necessary to say "yes, sir" in a hurry. Sam could not understand why they were always so nervous with him and he frowned as he reined in, frightening Rutledge all the more.

"Rutledge, there's half a jug of whiskey stuck up in that plum tree by the woodpile—"

"No, sir, I never did," the Negro broke in, putting up his pale palms.

"Not me, Mr. Sam!" his sister cried. "Jesus be witness, I wasn't even there!"

"No, no, it's mine. I just wanted to tell you to take the thing home, Rutledge. Might need it for a winter cough one of these days."

Rutledge had begun to grin.

"No need to let Mrs. Allen see you with it. Just take it along home tonight."

"I might even work up a bad chest before suppertime," said Rutledge. "I thank you."

Sam turned the mare toward Greenway and began to organize his mind for the day. He felt any grown man ought to keep his mind sorted out at least as neat as a general store, with categories shelved in order of usage and an arrangement of aisles for easy access.

He could find no place for the accusation Silas had made to him —no box or bin or counter or shelf was the size of it. This was obviously the fault of Silas himself, who never could do anything right. Another man's insult you'd know about—it would be worth an equal insult, contempt, perhaps a fight. But Silas!

He spat into the road and gave the mare her head.

Sam Allen was a native of Kentucky. He grew up in a family which had sent men to fight under both Union and Confederate flags. After 1865, the Allens had no one to fight but each other and no weapons left but words. There was never a Sunday dinner that did not sour in their bellies before the cake could be cut, nor a Christmas that failed to end in a brawl.

In 1868, when he was twenty, Sam married Ernestine Foxx to escape from the quarreling in his house. In a new home of his own, he thought, all loyalties would be definite. Chairs would stand where they were first put and a man would be able to walk through his own rooms in pitch dark and never bump a shoe. Every week the same clothes would be boiled in lye soap and hung on the same line; he would raise pigs in an orderly progression from birth to prime size, and slaughter them for the smokehouse and hang them up in rows. Seeds would sprout evenly in his careful hills and once a year the harvest would fill his bins. Sam saw his future laid out for him the way Jacob saw the ladder at Bethel—neat, day-sized blocks building one upon the other until at last, when he had grown old and good and prosperous, Sam Allen would follow the angels into Heaven.

He never asked Ernestine Foxx what she saw in her future.

Ernestine had lived three miles down that Kentucky road all his life, along with her father and nine brothers and sisters whose faces of ascending size blurred into each other. For years Ernestine had been combined mother and sister to the Foxx family, and it was said she could boil string and stones in a pot and get a passable soup out of them. Sam Allen had seen Ernestine so many times over the years (usually working) that he married her with relief and confidence.

"Lucas," he warned his oldest brother, "when you come to my house, come smiling. And first one to mention the war gets throwed in the berry briers!"

The chairs in Sam Allen's farm cabin were fixed in their places, sure enough—and never a broom came nigh them. Left open to the rains, the washpot rusted, and nothing but brown birds were ever seen on the clothesline at Sam Allen's house. Nothing rattled in Ernestine's button box. Nobody ever whitewashed the hearth. When worms came out of the earth and sawed off his young shoots of corn, Sam had the feeling that was the fault of her general bad housekeeping too.

Once she had married, Ernestine Foxx Allen became so lazy she never ate an apple that did not drop off the tree into her apron. She would put blackberries into a bowl with a spoon, but never bake a pie; and her fires were always going out because she couldn't even remember to move a stick of wood two yards and lay it on the coals. All those years she had worked in poverty to tend her brothers and sisters seemed to have used up the work in her. Already she had worn out two lifetimes, she said to her new husband, over jelly and sausage and cow's tits and now—at eighteen—she was in her old age and planned to sit down.

The first few months she said, "I'm tired." After that, "I'm *still* tired," and at the end of their first year she'd begun to say, "You keep pestering me with complaints and I never will get rested."

Sam didn't know what to do. Fresh from a house where old war cries were ringing in all the halls, he could not bring himself to raise his voice to Ernestine, not even when the beans boiled down to cinders while she rested in her chair.

Ernestine had never been really pretty. "I wore that layer off the first year Mama took sick," she said once; and came all the way across the room and thumped him in the chest, as if it were his fault.

Her hair was thin, and looked like winter grass. One front tooth was gone and she had the habit of sucking air through the space. Her skin was like an old quilt—worn dry and thready in some places and faded or stained in others. Sam had not noticed it before they married, but Ernestine did not like to wash herself. Sometimes he felt as if he were sleeping in a barn.

All she could talk about was money. Money would pay for a colored woman—and that woman would render the lard and make the soap and heat the flatirons and sew up pine needles into cushions for the straight chairs. It wouldn't even cost much to hire a woman to come in every day. Then maybe Ernestine could get rested. Energy would flow back into her just from watching somebody else tending her tasks.

"That would be beautiful," Ernestine sighed. "Somebody else doing your work, and you watching. Beautiful."

Late in 1869—Sam Allen was then twenty-one—Ernestine took suddenly to combing out her hair and pinning it neatly in the mornings, and sometimes she ironed a fresh dress and washed the chicken manure from the bottoms of her shoes. She took long walks—"visiting my family," she said. Once Sam noticed she'd gained enough strength to hum to herself if she sat on the porch steps late at night.

That November she ran away with a man from Alabama who'd been traveling the county selling beaded breast pins and silk thread, and sharpening knives and scissors on the side. A note was left for Sam in the kitchen. The peddler must have done that; Ernestine didn't know how to write.

"I've gone with Wallace Coats and before I left I cleaned the morning dishes," read the note. It made Sam feel he'd been insulted twice.

He sold the farm, took up saw milling and cotton ginning, and rented a room at a widow woman's in town. Every cent he could get from his land or his labors he put in the bank, and every month he felt—with some pleasure—it was almost like locking Ernestine's hard-working colored woman into that savings vault.

The widow woman who ran the boardinghouse was a former school-teacher. She so admired Sam's thrift that she worked with him on addition and subtraction until he could follow what the bank said about his total. Sam didn't care much for subtraction.

In the fall of 1870, his brother Lucas came to the boardinghouse to tell him Ernestine was dead. Sam was in bed with the widow woman at the time and wouldn't open the door to his room, so Lucas had to shout it—that in Virginia, Ernestine and her peddler friend had holed up in somebody's tobacco barn during a summer storm; the lightning struck and they burned to death. They'd been near the town a week, trying unsuccessfully to join a traveling medicine show. People knew from the melted brooches who the corpses were, and buried Mr. and Mrs. Wallace Coats in the indigent graveyard behind the jail.

All this Lucas shouted through the closed door while Sam, naked, stood with his ear pressed to the crack. Goose bumps spread on him in chilly waves. He thanked Lucas for coming.

The widow woman simpered on the pillow. "You're well out of it, seems to me. God rest her soul," she said, stretching. "Nice thrifty boy like you deserves better. Not to speak ill of the dead. You need somebody settled in her ways. Come here, honey."

He looked her over.

"You're going to get sick in the cold," she said, and made a little laugh.

Without another word, he put on his clothes and rode out to the home place to say good-bye to his brothers.

He spent the night there and next morning, when the bank opened its doors, Sam was inside before they'd even unlocked the money, asking for his funds. There was a nickel's difference between the bank's figure and his own, and he raised such a racket the bank president came out and paid it from his own pocket.

By Christmas of that year Sam Allen, now twenty-two, was living in Greenway, North Carolina. There was no plan to it. He simply set out from Kentucky on horseback, looking. He wanted a small town, a job and something else. A glimpse, maybe. A hope. A vista of success, even if he could see it no more than keyhole size. But Sam

Allen didn't call it success. He called it Money. This was the only thing he saved from his marriage. Ernestine had been right about that one thing, after all. Everything else he could imagine was only a second step. First the money—then there was time to develop a fine character, or learn to worship, or even indulge in a little sin; but there was no beginning on any of these things without money. Money was the root of evil, good, pleasure, power, posterity. First the money, then. Later a wife he could tire out in his own way.

Greenway wasn't the town Sam was seeking at all. Already he had seen fifty just like it in his travels—four clay streets coming together at the square, a general store and post office, livery stable, dressmaking shop, two lawyers, a school academy and one so-called hotel.

It was just before noon on December 21, 1870. Sam decided not even to eat in this place but ride ahead to the county seat of Stoneville. Christmas he would spend in Greensboro, where he could listen to the talk of travelers and drummers about places they had seen. Then he would head east and pass through Raleigh and, if the weather held, right straight on to the sea. He had never seen the sea. The sight of it, he thought, would settle things and from there he could turn inland to choose, infallibly, the town which was waiting for him to come and live in it.

A plug of tobacco would ease the miles. Sam swung from his saddle in front of a dry-goods store. He was hitching his horse when a keg of nails rolled off the overhanging roof and struck him on the shoulder and right side of his head. The blow came without warning. He knew only that he had been hit hard, maybe by some of Ernestine's lightning. He lurched into the horse, which reared away. The muddy street floated slowly up to his face. He put his cheek gratefully into its softness. Around his head some burning barn fell in.

All that day and the next he lay unconscious on a pallet in the back room of Hobbs Dry Goods Store. No one had wanted to move him far. A doctor from Stoneville said he would likely live long enough to cuss out Winkler Hobbs, who had let two fool boys replace shingles instead of hiring it done proper, and go out on that slanting roof with a whole keg of nails instead of a pocketful.

That scared Hobbs. When he was on his feet again, this stranger might want to get even. Worse than that, he might want money.

When he heard the doctor's words, Hobbs ran to a table of shoes and grabbed a pair and hit one of his young workmen in the neck.

"You go to Angus Mackey's house and get me that oldest girl, the one that's good with the sick. Ask her to come tend this man you've nearly murdered for me!" He raised the shoes a second time. "Willie, you get out front and pick up all them nails."

So Mildred Mackey, who would not be fifteen for another month, sat for two days in the back room and watched Sam Allen and laid wet cloths on his bruises. She did not mind the long hours with an unconscious man, since it was all in Jesus' name. Most of the time she drowsed in the dim room and made up long and dreamy prayers. Some were every bit as beautiful as the Psalms of David, she thought, and she shivered with pleasure as God's finger wrote and rewrote His praises in her head.

The morning of December 23, Sam Allen began to stir and talk and holler up his horse and call out sums of money.

Mildred Mackey went into the front part of the store and pulled at the owner's sleeve. "He's coming round," she said, "and I'll be getting home."

Winkler Hobbs paid her a sack of flour. "What's he saying?"

"He talks about money."

After she had gone, toting her own flour, Hobbs knelt by the pallet and put his ear close to the hurt man's face. All he could hear was dollars and cents.

Hobbs jerked away. He went to the cash drawer and got his gun and put it into his trousers, out of sight. He paced the length of the store several times.

When he went to the storeroom again, Sam Allen was sitting up and feeling around on the floor with his hands.

"Nobody took your money," Hobbs called out.

"Nobody better."

They eyed each other. Sam saw a man in his late fifties—bifocal glasses, brown hair in tufts, a good suit of clothes with a silver watch chain showing. Hobbs saw a big man with a mouth unused to smiling, half his head reddened and bruised from the accident, dressed like a farmer. His hair and a thick mustache were black.

Hobbs said, "How you feelin', boy?"

"Head hurts." Sam touched his right temple, then the bone behind the ear. His skin felt pulpy. "What happened?"

"Barrel rolled off a roof and hit you," said Hobbs, deciding to get the worst of it over as quickly as possible. "I've been looking after you. I had a doctor in. Says you'll be all right."

"Much obliged." Sam squinted, which lit up half his head with pain. "Your roof?"

"Hired a girl to sit with you. Two days," Hobbs pressed on. "Had to keep a fire back here too, day and night. I don't keep a fire here most of the time. Them quilts is off my own bed." Hobbs shook his head, though Sam had not spoken a word. "No, no, don't thank me. It's nearly Christmas."

"Lucky I wasn't killed," was all Sam Allen said. "Who's got my belt?"

Hobbs rolled two brown crocks to one side and reached down into the far one for Sam's money belt. "Just as safe as if it was in church." He gave a halfhearted laugh.

"You count it out?"

"Not a cent missing; I can vouch for that."

So this man had put his fingers on Sam Allen's money after half killing him with a barrel of nails. Sam frowned. "I was coming in here for tobacco," he said.

It sounded threatening. "Tobacco . . . yes. Have some." Hobbs held out his own plug along with a pocket knife. When his coat flapped, Sam could see the gun.

"No, thanks. Chewing will make my head hurt worse." He began counting his money.

"I tell you none of it's gone!" Hobbs's voice was getting shrill.

"Who witnessed your count?"

Hobbs whacked off a large chunk of tobacco and put it into his mouth, sucked once, took it out. He began to cut it off in slivers, adding them one at a time to his rapid jaws. Nobody had watched him count. This man could claim anything.

"You looking for work?"

"Not much," said Sam. He nodded toward the gun showing in Hobbs's belt. "You looking for thieves?"

The storekeeper buttoned his coat. "You won't feel much like horseback riding, not this cold weather. You could work here a couple weeks before you move on. Sleep in the store. Save yourself a lot of weakness."

"Must be plenty people around here needing work," said Sam. He replaced the paper money and began on the coins.

"Steal me blind, most of 'em," snapped Hobbs. "Need work too bad. Too many hungry kids at home. A handful of beans and a pocket of cornmeal going out every day. You write figures? Measure and weigh?"

"Yes."

"All right then." He watched Sam total the last pile and nod. "Didn't I tell you all the money was still in that belt? Let me put it back in the crock for you. Good safe place."

"No." He wound the belt around his bruised neck and lay down.

"My name is Winkler Hobbs." Seeing that Sam must be at least partly honest, he thought about asking him to pay the doctor's fee.

"Sam Allen."

"You're sure that thing won't choke you in the night?"

"If I'd worn it this way before, it might of saved me getting hurt."

Hobbs squatted beside him. He decided not to mention the doctor's bill. "Set a great store by money, don't you?"

"Can't do much without it."

"I like that. Most people here in Greenway, now, they set store by things and possessions. They swap money over the counter for anything they can feel in their hands, and they always look satisfied, thinking they've swapped even." He had begun to smile. "Now that ain't never so. Always the thing is worth somewhat less than the money. Why else would people be in business? You'd think everybody could see that."

Sam closed his eyes. His head was hurting.

"You see it. I see it." Hobbs got to his feet and looked down at him. "Most people is dumb, I guess. Outright dumb."

Sam said in a sleepy, noncommittal voice, "Sometimes they learn."

The next day he became a clerk at Hobbs Dry Goods Store in Greenway, North Carolina, at a wage of two dollars a week. He didn't mind that, since he expected to stay no longer than early January and the fading of his bruises.

While he had been going back twenty-seven years remembering, Sam Allen was surprised to see that the mare from old habit had carried him forward from his home all the way to the livery stable at the end of Main Street. He was on the way to work at the store as usual, only it was 1897 and he was not twenty-two, but forty-nine.

Maybe, after all, people learned nothing—at least nothing they could use.

Yet, thought Sam Allen, he was now ready at long last to become a rich man. The vital information and methods were neatly shelved. Whiskey and egg trading and a hundred little side deals and self-denials over the years had fattened that original money belt until now he had "breeding money"—cash he could put at stud to mate with other money and reproduce in its likeness. He was ready at last, eager enough, denied long enough, taught enough, mean enough.

The only real obstacle was the same one Sam Allen had seen twenty-seven years before when first he rode down this same Main Street. He had known then, before those nails rained down about his shoulders, that Greenway was not the right place. After all these years it was still the wrong place, but he was here marooned.

Dismissing these thoughts, Sam turned the mare over to a livery boy, stopped a man in the street who owed him money and argued about it, and tipped his hat to Miss Amelia Bancroft. By some different series of accidents, he might eventually have married Amelia, whose prim face had now wrinkled up like a dry chinaberry. Better some accidents than others! Thank God for small blessings and so forth and so on, he thought, entering the store.

The interior of Hobbs (someday to be Allen) Dry Goods Store was neat and well organized, with a place for everything and everything in its place. There was no item Sam could not locate promptly. It stretched before him, orderly, thoroughly prepared, waiting for customers—like my life, he thought.

The bell rang above the front door but Sam Allen strode briskly down the aisle without glancing back. No one had come in but himself.

Chapter

❧ 4 ❧

TO HIS ASTONISHMENT, Grandfather failed to die.

He woke each morning and stared at his own bedroom walls, first in surprise, then resignation. Here I am again, he thought.

By October it had become an awed: Still here, by God! He was afraid to indulge himself in feelings of relief. He told Mildred it looked like a man could depend on nothing beyond being scared half to death. All he could ever count on was neither fair nor poor, but middlin'. Now he felt middlin', which was how he'd felt most of his life. He stated, but without any optimism, that it was high time he moved to a chair downstairs.

"We could try it," said Mildred agreeably. "And now I think about it, you could shell beans for me down there, the children off at school and all."

Angus Mackey decided right then to settle for a rocker at his bedroom window.

From this spot he watched Thomas and Esther wave to him weekday mornings before they climbed into the small wagon Sam hitched to the mare. Sometimes, just as the wagon turned left on the road that would take them to Greenway and their studies at the Academy, Esther would wave to him a second time. That pleased him so much he was afraid he would get dependent on it.

One morning he rapped on his window glass till Esther walked back toward the house and cupped a hand at her ear. He struggled to get the window up, propped it with a stick, and yelled down at her.

"What's that thing in the tree?"

"Hey? Tree?"

"I see something hung up there." Angus Mackey pointed. "See yonder? Looks like a glass jar!"

"Your eyes are failing!" Esther was laughing fit to kill. "Old birds' nest!"

Birds' nest! It sure did look like some glass jar or bottle hanging by a ribbon on that chinaberry limb. He yelled out that his eyes were better than ever and jerked the stick out so quickly the falling window almost mashed his finger. He flapped his hand at Esther. Could swear there was glass hung in that tree. Maybe he didn't even feel middlin'.

Esther laughed to herself half the way to town. It made her brother tuck his mouth in at one corner and wrinkle his brow.

"I hope this is not one of your laughing days," Thomas said to her sternly. "You make Miss Eliza nervous."

"She was born nervous."

Greenway Academy, where Miss Eliza Tilley had been teaching since Valley Forge, at least, met for two terms each year in a white frame house with a green roof. The path to its door made a half circle between two rows of small cedars, and Esther said that was the pitifullest Grand Plantation Avenue she ever saw. Even the darkies knew cedars were bad luck and smelled of death.

Although tuition was charged at Greenway Academy, which meant most families could not afford it, the studies were under the guiding hand of the Presbyterian church which stood next door. The Reverend Holt taught mathematics, history and the classics. Miss Eliza, who had the pursed, sniffing look of a squirrel, taught poetry, music, grammar, spelling and geography.

As usual, Esther was the first one called to recite. She thought Miss Eliza liked to get this done while she still had her early-morning strength.

Esther's voice was bored but dutiful as she finished the poem: "Under the sod and under the dew, waiting the judgment day."

"Very good, Esther," said Miss Eliza. She did not look up from her book. "Now tell us what these words mean to you."

Esther hated saying what words meant. She liked them to shower.

She liked them to tumble down about her head like raindrops. She looked down the bench to her brother. Thomas was very good at word meanings, but he never tasted anything.

"It means," said Esther, the note of duty heavy now in her voice, "that Yankees and Confederates both died in the war."

"And that the souls of both are equal before God," prodded Miss Eliza.

This gave Esther a disagreeable vision of souls, cool and white and specific, lined up in Glory like so many eggs. She was silent so long that Miss Eliza lifted her face and fixed her in a long, unspoken warning. "Yes, ma'am."

Esther and Miss Eliza Tilley were a trial to each other. Each felt the other did not take education seriously.

Miss Eliza had a fondness for quotations and maxims. In her off hours she did samplers in a neat cross-stitch, accumulating their fabric wisdom all year long toward Christmas giving. At the Academy she choose similar sentiments for exercises in parsing or penmanship and as punishment for the girls. Boys who misbehaved received a ruler on the palm from the preacher, but girls took their blows abstractly. Esther's copybook was full of moral lessons, each duplicated in blocks of twenty-five, and she had wiped enough righteousness off her slate to save all the Chinese heathen. The one she had written most often was:

> Thus plain, plodding people, we often shall find,
> Will leave hasty, confident people behind.

"Remember," Miss Eliza would add when she gave Esther this assignment another time, "remember the hare and the tortoise." She saw from the girl's face that this was pointless. Esther, obviously, did not even believe *that* story.

Esther hated maxims. The only one she ever gave an instant's respect was "Circumstances alter cases," and she relished that one so much Miss Eliza was sorry she had ever brought it up.

"Yes," Miss Eliza was saying now, ending their discussion of a poem called "The Blue and the Gray." "Yes, we must remember that the War was tragic for all, and that in God's sight, every dead soldier was equally sad."

"Circumstances alter cases," Esther wrote firmly in her copybook.

And by the brief, weary blink of Miss Eliza's eyes, it was easy to see she knew from the very curve of Esther's fingers exactly what had been written down in silent, stubborn debate.

"Lunch," said Miss Eliza crossly, although it was at least ten minutes early.

The students, a dozen under ten years of age and six others who were older, lined up in the hallway and marched to the back porch to wash in a basin of spring water. Then they sat around the steps, preferring cold winds to the smell of school. They swapped off baked sweet potatoes, biscuits of pork shoulder and fatback, hunks of cornbread, fried apple pies.

Nellie Grimes sat next to Esther. Her father, a lawyer from one of Stone County's oldest and most respected families, was Sam Allen's friend. Nellie was so pretty the mere sight of her made Thomas turn red as a geranium. Mildred Allen said Nellie was a born lady, and why couldn't more girls be like her? She was Miss Eliza's best pupil.

And Esther didn't like her. She drew into herself slightly as Nellie sat beside her, and thought: I have a black heart.

Nellie wore shining red shoes. Her hair hung in curled loops. "It's warm for November," said Nellie lightly. "But I hear we'll have a hard winter. So many nuts and berries in the woods."

She sounded very grown up. Esther bit into her cornbread and the grains lay on her tongue like sand.

"You always say the poems so well."

"Thank you," said Esther.

"If you'd only be nice to Miss Eliza."

"I'm nice."

"You're supposed to learn whatever she teaches you."

"I learn it," Esther snapped. Nellie moved her head in a gesture which made each curl expand and lengthen and then shrink back again to neatness. It made Esther know her own hair was full of knots, snarls, lost slingshots.

Nellie said, "If you do learn, you won't admit it."

Esther lifted the tail of her linsey dress and wiped her mouth on the underside. She might have blown her nose against her fingers for good measure had Nellie not caught her arm.

"Esther, where *is* your handkerchief!"

Esther said she forgot it again.

"Take mine then. But you'd get better marks if you'd be nicer with Miss Eliza. If you'd just smile and nod your head in class, she'd raise your mark."

Esther didn't want to smile and nod her head. She ran the handkerchief back and forth between her fingers. "They used to stand you in the barn on your birthday and cut a notch in the wall to see how tall you'd grown," she said dreamily. "Miss Eliza thinks her marks do that." She sent a sidelong glance at Oliver Martin, who was carrying in the firewood. "Ollie is the ugliest boy I ever saw."

"Hello, Ollie!" called Nellie with one of her brightest smiles. And more softly, "He can't help how he looks."

"I know that, I know that," said Esther, leaning forward slightly to cup her shoulders around her black heart.

"Father says Thomas is going to work in the dry-goods store after Thanksgiving."

"I didn't know that," said Esther, sitting up straight. "I was going to ask to do that. I can add better than Thomas!"

"You're a girl. Father says Mr. Allen has already asked if you can ride home in our buggy in the afternoons."

"I wish people would tell me things." Esther now blew her nose into the handkerchief. Delicate and edged in lace, it was the color of a creamy tea rose and had been laundered to such a point of thinness that she was afraid of exploding through it in rents and tatters.

Nellie lowered her voice even further. "What do you think about the factory?"

"What factory?"

Nellie put a finger to her lips. "My father's going to talk to your father about it."

Esther forced herself to whisper. "What kind of factory?"

Nellie jounced a shoulder in such a way that her hair loops did that little dance again. "Oh, I don't know. I'm not interested in such things. But my father says—he says a factory will change everything."

"Do you think so?" said Esther. She felt suddenly hungry, although she had just finished the cornbread. "Do you really think so?"

From the inside hallway, Miss Eliza's bell began to clang and there were movements, tying of strings around boxes, brushings at crumbs.

"Time for geography," said Nellie cheerfully. "I do hope you can bound the states today."

"Bounds, bounds, bounds!" fumed Esther. "Why can't they all just run on forever!"

Nellie said sensibly that would make an awful mess.

"I bet God didn't think it was a mess in Genesis, when he threw it all together in a week."

"*Threw* it together!" Nellie said that certainly wasn't a nice way to describe a holy thing. "Besides, even God bounded things," she added. "Divided the waters from the dry land. The heavens and the firmament . . ."

"So *that's* who started it," Esther grumbled.

In the afternoons, Thomas and Esther had several hours to themselves before their father would be ready to lock the store and pull the wagon home through the twilight.

It isn't time to myself, Thomas was thinking, It's time to *herself.* He gave his sister a resentful look.

All the games were hers. She could think up the strangest things to do, tell them with such excitement, praise him when he took part.

"We never do what I want!" he blurted now as they came out the front door of the Academy.

Esther asked calmly, "What do you want?"

He could not think of a thing. It was her fault for turning to him so promptly with her whole face open. He tried wildly to come up with a suggestion.

Esther, two steps ahead as usual, had begun to twirl her skirt of purple linsey until its yellow stripes swirled like a turning candy stick. She curtsied to a few of the cedars, calling them by human names. Then, after one grand dip and a twinkling of copper-toed shoes, she said, "You say something, Thomas?"

"I thought of a game and now you made me forget."

"I'm sorry."

He felt outraged. "I'll never be able to think of it again. It was a fine game! It would have been the best of all!"

She looked really contrite. "I'm so sorry, Thomas. I was busy thinking how nice it would be if Presbyterians still danced in praise to God. Can you imagine it? Miss Eliza and the preacher going around and around with hosannas? What does that mean—hosanna?"

"How do I know?"

"I wonder what a timbrel is."

"You don't really care about my game."

"I do, I do!" But she ran ahead between the green cedars, among all the harps and timbrels.

On the sandy walk bordering Main Street she waited for him, pulling a twig from the last cedar and making a bristly mustache on her upper lip. "Well, son," she boomed in their father's voice, "I hear you're coming to work at the dry-goods store."

"Who says so?"

"Nellie says Papa is going to let you work afternoons and Saturdays, at least till Christmas. You're to stay in town late every day, and I'm to ride on with Mr. Grimes."

Thomas could not control his excitement. "You're not teasing? It's really true?"

"Yes, really. And I am sorry I made you forget the game."

He held himself tall. "Who cares about games? I'm going to be working. Like a man! That's something you'll never be able to do, Miss Smarty Esther!"

"I guess not," she said agreeably. She tossed the cedar twig away.

"Will I be paid? Am I to get money of my own?"

"You are your father's son!" said Esther flatly. "Money, money! If father ever gets rich and Grandfather ever dies, the sky is going to split." She pointed to a patch of blue above Main Street. "Right there, all the way from sunrise to sunset."

"I'll be learning all about business," said Thomas in a dreamy voice. "Important things. Talking to men."

"The angels will fall out," Esther went on firmly, flicking her wrist to show just where the sky's incision would be made. "All over Stone County, it'll be raining angels."

"Hurry up—I want to ask Papa all about it!" cried Thomas. He ran past her and down the street to the dry-goods store.

Sam Allen and Nathan Grimes, the lawyer, were going over accounts when they came into the store. Cotton was picked and sweet potatoes dug; those who had not paid their bills by now would not. It was foreclosure time. The two men waved. Mr. Grimes was puffing on his pipe and a shaft of sunlight made a curtain of smoke and dust motes.

"Get some gumdrops and stay quiet," Sam Allen called. "We're busy talking."

Thomas and Esther went to the counter where glass jars held gumdrops and cinnamon red-hots. Esther chewed a whole handful of candy because she liked her mouth to be "sweet all at once." Thomas ate his one by one, sucking his gums carefully before he took another piece. They squatted on the oiled floor.

The voices of the two men carried to them down the aisle.

Mr. Grimes was saying, "Sam, it's different for you. What you are and believe has already been marked to go on."

"Marked by who?" Sam broke in, but was swept along.

"You can pass your ideas along to your children with a clear conscience. But I'm left over. There's no place for me except an old place—"

Here Sam tried again to interrupt, but Mr. Grimes rode over him from long practice against other lawyers in the courtroom.

"No place but an old place already small and left behind. It gives me," he persisted, "the strangest feeling that I'm really ninety-five years old and they've counted my birthdays wrong to make me feel better."

"You're forty-seven," said Sam, who liked to stick to facts.

"This foreclosing." Nathan Grimes waved his hand at the ledgers on the table before him. "I know these people. This land has come down for generations. Poor land, I'll grant you. Poor generations, sometimes. I wish I didn't know all these people."

"Can't see what difference that makes. You've never done so well as now," said Sam. "Lawyers don't suffer when times are hard. They—"

"Not just hard," said Mr. Grimes. He was good at picking up a word out of somebody else's mouth and building an argument upon it. "Not hard; entirely different. And I'm not talking about being a lawyer. I'm talking about who you are. I'm talking about values."

Sam pressed stubbornly to his point. "Lawyers have always led this state. They'll keep on leading it."

"Leading it where?" said Nathan Grimes, pulling the word trick again. "Leading everything these people own into other pockets? Northern pockets sometimes! Winkler Hobbs and his hundred pockets!"

"Lead some to my pocket then." Sam Allen grinned, trying to lighten the talk.

But Mr. Grimes was not just talking. He was *speaking*. "Besides, Sam, I wanted to be a lawyer not just for the work but because of a certain standard of excellence. Who cares whether being a lawyer is out of date or very current? It's the standard of excellence that's lost."

Sam was insulted. "When you said my ideas were still in fashion, did you mean I have no personal standard of excellence?" He thought about Silas Bennett sitting on that woodpile like an Accuser.

"No, no, Sam, of course not," said Nathan, but it didn't seem to Sam to have much conviction in it. "I was speaking generally, you understand. Just generally. This is an age to seek profit, that's all."

"High time," muttered Sam. Irritably he called, "What you young'uns doing?"

"Having candy like you said," called Thomas.

"Why don't you go play?"

"I want to talk to you, Papa." Thomas came out into the aisle where he could be seen, as if his presence would make his words that much more important.

"In a while, in a while."

Esther got up and said she was going to walk over the cemetery and did Thomas want to go since he couldn't remember *his* game?

Thomas shook his head. "Business is business," he said to her from a superior distance. "We've got to get used to it. I've got to learn how these things are done. Mortgages and . . . and business."

"I'm going to the cemetery then."

"I don't see what you get out of that."

Esther ran all the way—down the street, around the corner, along a wet path through an empty lot. The town cemetery had once been a single family plot, then a community burying ground on the edge of Greenway. Now it was inside the town, with houses on all sides and gravestones pressed up against each other.

It was damp, dank, mossy, dim; but it was not frightening. Esther followed it through the seasons and the hottest August sun never baked the earth here, so she thought the dead might give off memory like a moisture. Inside the rusted metal fence she began automatically to take deep breaths so that other lives, like a mingling of vapors, might seep into her. Sometimes when she saw a place for the first time and almost, nearly remembered, she knew the deep breathing had brought her something. Or when a certain sound or odor made her stop short and think: The last time this happened I was . . . it was because a wisp of someone else's life was lodged beneath her ribs.

When she was younger, Esther had gone through the cemetery and knelt and laid her hand flat on the graves and waited for knowledge to enter her palm. At the fourth grave she screamed out in pain, thinking for an instant a skull had reared up and bitten her with one of its rotten teeth, but it was only a honeybee under a ball of clover. She hardly knew whether to laugh or to cry.

Now that she was nearly thirteen, she went only to the far corner where in a grove of sickly dogwoods a crypt had been bricked atop the ground and covered with a marble slab. She had long since tried to move the slab and look inside but, thankfully, had not been able to make it budge.

Into the slab was cut a poem of tribute to Nora Lafferty, 1801–1847, which meant Nora had died the year before Sam Allen was born, way out in Kentucky.

Often Esther would lie flat on this slab, duplicating the crossed hands of those imagined bones beneath, and she would try (she told Thomas, who was horrified), to teach her back, her shoulders, legs, to read those words which she could feel engraved on the stone beneath her. If she could once read them, not with her mind but with her skin alone, time would open up and she—superimposed on the dead woman—would see into her life as if she had lived it in her own flesh.

"That's sinful," Thomas always said.

"How do you know?" Esther would stretch out and stare straight up at tree branches and one patch of sky and begin to murmur whatever words came into her head.

"It must be sinful!"

Today she climbed up onto the cold slab and lowered herself into the precise spot and did not miss Thomas at all. She lay very still. Her shoulder, without the slightest aid from her mind, began to sense the letters: *1847 . . . beloved consort . . . hand of God.* She tensed and then, shivering, laid her other shoulder tighter on the stone and pushed the curve of her backbone down and pressed her legs right into the carving.

It can't be true, because I've memorized what's written here, she thought.

But her hip began to pick up the left margin of the poem and the Bible verses: *She was . . . forever faithful . . . price above rubies.*

Her body seemed to be vibrating. *Wipe away all tears from their eyes.*

She closed her own eyes against a sudden dizziness and, like smoke, seemed to pass through the stone. She lay now on something dusty and soft, like the powdery earth underneath the Allen house. It seemed to her that in the darkness behind closed lids, her eyes had melted. The voice was like a little buzz:

". . . And so I married James Lafferty and began to keep his house, and the baby died, the first one. Died before he even made a sound to show he knew this world had started. That's what I hated most— all those months of growing from next to nothing and getting ready for something that was already over before he even knew it. I was a long time getting well from that and the other children—sometimes I thought they were standing in his place. Like walking a path and you can't step anywhere but on the shadow of the one ahead of you. But when I got older and tireder I had the feeling he'd been given a second try. I knew I was not with child and yet I felt a fullness of some kind of life. I put my hand to it all the time, asking it to move. I pushed at it with a finger. Push back, I said.

"But whatever it was could only grow and not birth, and I was too small for it; and oh, in the end there was nothing but pain when it all outgrew me like some great flower. And I didn't really die so much as I went down under the weight and size of it and when I fell into this place I was already running in search of the little one who should be here. How can you call a baby that did not live long enough to earn a name? Sometimes I still cry out for him in the dark; I holler, 'Baby, Baby,' but there are a thousand babies here. . . ."

"*Baby, baby!*" screamed Esther, sitting bolt upright on the cold marble slab. She slapped her own hand into her own mouth and it shook there as if her breath were a windstorm.

Her eyes, turning wildly, stopped at the little stone next to the crypt. STILLBORN SON OF NORA AND JAMES LAFFERTY. 1820.

"I knew it was there," she whispered. "I must have seen it before. I knew it already."

She leaped off the crypt and ran, stepping on graves and sliding on slick patches of moss, out the cemetery and through the brown field, and she did not slow to a walk until she was around the corner on Main Street and the dry-goods store was safely in her sight. A heart was pulsing in her throat. I hope it's mine, she thought.

Sam Allen saw his daughter come into the store a second time. Children were like that, he thought; a parent's eye registered their comings and goings no matter where the attention was. Right now his attention was still fixed on Nathan Grimes, who, for half an hour, had been explaining (a) The Plight of the South, and (b) His Own Plight locked in that larger one.

Nathan talks too much, makes it too easy to listen without hearing, he thought. Might have gone to the legislature if he didn't repeat himself so much. Folks thought if you gave him two locations, Greenway and Raleigh, you wouldn't just double his words. Quadruple, maybe. Maybe more.

"My family," Nathan was saying, "has always lived from the land and done well at it. That's part of my problem. Part of all our problems. Any fool knows that can't happen now, may never happen again. And we've behaved as if whatever the heart held onto was truth, a notion that got thousands of us killed. Most of us have no talent for selling, as you do. Or even for changing."

"It's not a talent," said Sam. "You just do it. You just work at it." He shot a glance at the other man's hands and the pale fingertips. It was so like Nathan to assume, in conversation, that his experiences were universal. Everybody, like him, came from long-weathered backgrounds and comfortable money. Sometimes Nathan would even stop a nigger on the street and say, "Ah, it's not like it used to be," and think they had shared something. "No, sir, praise God" was what the man would want to answer. "No, sir, and for me it never was."

"Every day I hear the word 'realistic,'" Nathan went on. "Be realistic about cotton, about politics, about life. It's an ugly word for me. I think of being realistic as being diminished. Cut down to commonplaces. I've had no training for it."

Sam had just been about to advise Nathan to be more realistic. Instead he said, "You've had a lot of training since eighteen sixty-five."

"That's just it—I haven't! I've had the chance for that experience, but I've been completely unrealistic. I've acted as if that poor old farm out there were going to be a plantation again, somehow, by the grace of God, maybe. I've kept the good horses too long because of how they made me feel, when what we needed was pigs and cows and turnip greens. I've done things I can no longer afford to do, because I'm still living as if my land and my life existed in 1857 and not 1897. I've been blind. Worse, I've been stupid."

Sam was bored. "If you really think you've been stupid, then you'll change," he said, in the best no-nonsense voice he used to his children.

Nathan Grimes stared at him for a moment, then began to laugh softly. "Sam, Sam," he sighed, "and you still don't know why the next century belongs to you and not to me."

"You can have the century," said Sam. "Just give me the store and a good annual return."

Nathan got up to go. "I want you to come to a meeting over at my house one night next week," he said. "I'll let you know when. It's about building a cotton mill in Greenway."

"About who building it? And with what?"

"That's what we're going to talk about. Mr. Hobbs is coming. Can you be there?"

"Hobbs has money," said Sam. "What you need me for?"

"You've got the mood," said Nathan, smiling. "Yours is the temperament. I tell you, the next hundred years belong to you. You'll probably wind up owning the whole factory."

"I'm not going to live a hundred years," said Sam, but he was pleased. Already his mind was busy counting—how much money he had, could raise, had loaned out and could call in. "You don't really think we can get a factory here?"

"I don't know. I've been writing some letters, looking into how other towns have done it."

Just like Nathan. A study project. "Takes more than that," said Sam.

"Takes people like you, for one thing," said Nathan. He studied Sam for a long moment before he picked up his hat, smiled, shook hands.

Sam pondered that look. Sometimes I can't tell if I impress him or depress him.

He called the children. "Help me close up, and let's be heading home. Thomas, I want to talk to you. Want you to help out in the store. Think you can do it?"

"Boy, I'll be the best one! I'll be the best one you could get!" called Thomas, running down the aisle. "Hey, Esther, did you hear that?"

But she was leaning into the large pane of glass at the front of the store, her cheeks distended with red candies, looking at something far away.

Chapter

5

NOVEMBER 20, 1897, was to be Esther's thirteenth birthday. She had talked about it since the middle of summer and made both her brothers nervous.

Thirteen, she said, was the Judas age. An unlucky time, it was the year of insanity. Childhood ended abruptly on one night and a new life began the very next morning. It was like being born, she predicted, and one would be brand new, and delicate, and awkward. Subject to sickness, she said darkly, and craziness and death.

About ten days before her birthday, Mildred Allen took Esther upstairs to the big bedroom and closed the door. For an hour the boys could hear the serious murmuring of their voices, and now and again Esther cried out and seemed to be protesting.

"What's it about?" whispered David. They were sitting at the head of the stairs, trying to hear.

"Being thirteen," said Thomas in a hollow voice, for he was already twelve. He gave a shudder. "Mama's warning her."

"Warning about what?"

"The dangers." Thomas swallowed hard. "All the dangers."

When Esther finally came out, she looked different. Thomas couldn't decide whether she was shocked or angry.

He sidled up to her. "What did Mama tell you?"

"Oh, hush," snapped Esther.

"You may as well tell, since it's my turn next. I'm already twelve."

Without warning, she wheeled around and thumped him in the ribs with her fist. "You don't know anything about anything," she hissed.

Angry, then. He waited till his mother had followed Esther downstairs and then he peeped into the bedroom. There was a Bible open on the bed, of course, because Mildred said any serious talk should be started on the basis of the Good Book. He tiptoed over and looked into the pages for some clue. It was open from Psalm 49 to the early part of Psalm 55, and he knew he would never narrow that down.

". . . dark saying upon the harp . . ." he skimmed, thinking of Esther's hosannas and timbrels. ". . . beauty shall consume in the grave" might deal with Esther's games in the cemetery. He was hopeful about the verse which began, "Thou sittest and speakest against thy brother." But there was nothing about birthdays that he could see.

David tugged at his arm. "What does it say?"

"It says to trust in God, what do you think?" answered Thomas.

But as the days passed, the two boys saw that Esther had been right. She was truly into the Judas age, and into it a week before her time. She was moody, irritable. No longer would she climb in trees with them or race to the bottom of the pasture hill, and sometimes she sat in a porch rocker like an old lady and said nothing for hours at a time.

"Is she crazy yet?" asked David.

"She's something," Thomas brooded.

"It's only November fourteenth!"

"I know that."

"Will she be like this all the time till she's fourteen?"

"She may get worse."

Esther, passing by just then, said in a cool voice that David's ears were dirty and Thomas had tracked mud on the hall floor.

"How can she get worse!" sighed David.

The two of them set grasshoppers leaping in her room, and knotted every sleeve hanging from the nail inside her door. Into the toes of her shoes they put sand and sharp stones and cockleburs.

They waited, then, for a wave of temper to turn her back into someone they understood.

But all she did, by the time they had worked down to the prickly burs, was lie on her bed and cry. Esther never cried.

Then they decided she was wasting away of consumption, with no one to tell.

Thomas went back to the Bible again and studied those same Psalms.

"I'm happy to see you taking more interest in Scripture," Mildred Allen told him approvingly.

"Yessum." The words rose now to his eye like homing birds. "God will redeem my soul from the power of the grave . . . soul is precious, and it ceaseth forever . . . like the beasts that perish. The terrors of death are fallen upon me . . ."

He pushed the book from him, breathing hard. Then he rushed downstairs, grabbed David by the arm and dragged him off into the pasture. "Our sister is dying," he moaned. "Come on! Pick up your feet! She's really dying!"

"Before her birthday?" puffed David. He had been carving a chunk of wood into a doorstop for her present.

"Those trips to the graveyard! That Nora Lafferty!"

"You want that doorstop?"

"Is that all you can think about when your own sister is going to be cut down like a flower?"

David burst into tears. "We'll never get through the mirror!"

"Grandfather lying up there in bed when all the time Esther—" His throat filled up and would not let the words get by.

David said enviously, "She'll get to fly though. Don't they get wings?" A terrible thought struck him. "Will Esther get wings if she doesn't finish the catechism?"

Thomas said he thought everybody baptized had a right to wings.

Now the two of them began their grieving for Esther. They followed her, their faces rapt. Thomas brought her bits of cedar to tuck inside her pillowcase, and promised sassafras and sweet shrub and honeysuckle in the spring. ("So she'll hang on," he said to David.

"Don't bother me," said David. "I'll never get this doorstop done in time.")

Her birthday was still four days off, and time was fermenting within her. That morning she was late downstairs; the boys were already at breakfast. She stopped in the kitchen doorway. Her face was as white as a china cup.

"Mother . . ." she said, and raised one arm carefully to rub her eyebrows.

Mildred hurried to her. "Esther?"

Esther nodded her head. "I hate it," she said. "I just hate it."

Helplessly Mildred patted her hand. "It's not always so bad, dear. Later, when you're more accustomed—"

"I'll never be accustomed."

Mildred smiled. "Yes, you will." She smoothed her hand down Esther's long black hair. "Everybody does."

"I'm not everybody. Let me alone." She wandered into the parlor, where Mildred had put holly branches into bowls, and the boys could see her picking off the scarlet berries and rolling them in her palms.

David began to whimper. "What's wrong with Esther?"

"She's tired," said Mildred briskly. "Let her be."

Thomas said slowly, "She just got out of bed," and David moaned to him, "Why is Mother smiling? Thomas? Why is that?"

Thomas said in a louder voice, "She just got out of bed!"

Esther turned on him a look of pure venom and marched back into the kitchen and poured a whole handful of holly berries into his milk. She laid the tip of her forefinger between his eyebrows. "I hate you," she said levelly.

"That's enough," warned her mother.

"I do, I hate him. I hate them all. I hate David in advance. I hate Papa. I hate Rutledge and Uncle Silas and Mr. Hobbs and Nathan Grimes and Dr. Newton and Preacher Holt and—"

"Esther, I said that would do." Mildred slapped the kitchen table. She knew her religion. You hated the deed but never the doer, or even whoever you thought might be the doer. "There's no excuse for this, Esther!"

Esther began to laugh and to fling her hair around. "Oh, you're right! No, there's no excuse at all for this! None at all!" She ran from them through the parlor and up the stairs.

Mildred touched her throat. "Ah, Esther," she said to the empty air.

"What's the matter with her?" David cried again.

Mildred shook her head. "Never mind, boys. She doesn't mean it."

Thomas said flatly, "She means it."

"No, no, why I remember—" Mildred caught herself and said instead. "You two won't even remember this! Not when you need to. Not when you have daughters of your own!" She began to wipe the table angrily.

David tried to be generous. "Esther's hated me lots of times," he put in, "but not for long."

"I will too remember!" Thomas vowed. "I'll remember Esther till I die! Till she dies and I die!"

To his surprise, his mother burst out laughing. "You don't even know what to remember," she chortled, and turned to follow Esther. "Tell Miss Eliza your sister isn't feeling well today."

Thomas ran after her. He felt very old and very responsible. He cocked his head and—with an air of conspiracy—said, "Shall I say she's coughing with a bad chest?"

Mildred put her head down onto the banister and seemed almost to be snickering. "Oh, tell her that by all means, Thomas!"

She went upstairs, making an odd, gasping sound.

I am the eldest son, he thought. I will work in the store. When this is all over, I will be a comfort to my mother.

He felt indescribably noble.

David was right behind him when he walked onto the front porch, which, unfortunately, faced the wrong way for him to look into the rising sun.

"Is it true then?" breathed David.

"You heard your mama." He was terse. "Not feeling well. Tell Miss Eliza. Bad chest."

"It's true," said David, choking.

"Think of Mama telling her it wouldn't be so bad when she got accustomed. Think of that." His voice broke. He knew suddenly he was about to cry as loudly as his little brother.

"What can we do?"

Thomas reached over and shook him fiercely. "Nothing!" he shouted. "Don't you know that yet? Nothing!"

He vaulted the railing into the yard. David, sniffling, climbed after him.

"Come on!" yelled Thomas.

David stumbled when he hit the ground but followed after, still crying and asking breathlessly, "What for, Thomas? What for?"

And Thomas showed him. Together they rushed forth into the yard and woods and pasture, breaking off the blackberry canes (that they might not bear again when Esther should be gone), kicking nuts onto stony places lest they root and grow, tearing their hands as they pulled up trumpet creeper and passion flower, which must not bloom another season—making gray and barren the world in which they would be recalling her.

Very late that night, Thomas woke abruptly in his bed. The stillness was terrible. He felt as if doom had been lowered upon him like a glass bell and that by reaching out he could touch the cold sides of it.

Then he saw Esther. She was sitting on the foot of his bed. She had drawn up her legs and wound her arms about them and, leaning forward, had laid her cheek against one knee. Perhaps she had been there motionless for a long time, fixing his face in her mind for eternity.

It was too dark to show, he knew, but still he shot her a look of knowing rapture. "Esther," he said. He kept his voice soft and warm. "My sister Esther."

"You sure do snore," she said, and yawned.

"I do not."

"Like a hog."

He remembered the shadow of death was upon her. "You ought to be in bed. You ought to be saving your strength."

She mumbled so that he could barely understand her. "All I ever hear in this house is Save. I want to hear Spend. I want to hear Give. I want to hear Waste."

It smote him to the heart. "Name it," said Thomas, sitting up. "Anything. You shall have anything."

"You must be sick."

"No, but I wish it was me. I'd rather it was me!" The words were not out of his mouth before he knew what a lie that was. Yet it *felt* true when he spoke it. If he could only keep talking and stop thinking, all that was good in him might rise up and blot the other out. "Esther," he rushed on, "I want you to talk to me. You can say anything. Because I already know. Esther, I know what's wrong with you."

"You couldn't." She narrowed her eyes and studied his face.

"I tell you I know. I understand."

Esther shook her head. "Listen," she said intensely, "I don't even think Papa knows. I don't think boys and men are allowed to know."

"What's that?"

"I wouldn't be the first to let it out for anything," said Esther staunchly, and burst into tears.

"Don't do that, Esther!" Thomas put out his hand to her. She slapped at it.

"Do you think," she sobbed, "that if every woman since Eve has gone in silence, I'd be the one to tell?"

"What are you talking about?"

Now Esther really broke into a moan, which she buried in the quilts. "Oh, Thomas, Thomas, I'm *bleeding!*"

Thomas jumped out of bed and made his sister lie down in his place, too horrified to answer. He saw no blood. The age of insanity, he thought suddenly, and he stared at his poor mad sister who was not going to make it over the chasm to fourteen. "You rest," he said vaguely. Should he call Mother? Would Esther be locked in a jail and fed grits and water all day long? Or was it consumption after all?

"Coughing up blood?" he stammered. "Something like that?"

"*All* of us bleed," said Esther irrationally.

"Go to sleep," he ordered. How could he think while she was raving?

But then Esther began to ramble on—about Mama and Aunt Rosa and having babies and once a month—until he stood gaping. The story seemed to go on and on. Could anyone, even Esther, have a madness which reached so far? Half the world was in on the conspiracy she described! From all Esther said, even Miss Eliza Tilley—so free with poetry and spelling and discipline—was full of scarlet secrets!

"I don't believe it," he finally managed to stammer.

Her hand disappeared beneath the covers and when it came out again, the tip of one finger showed a smear of red. He bent forward and moved her hand into a shaft of moonlight to be sure. Then he dropped it hastily and leaned against the bed, sickened. "Oh, Esther!" he cried.

"Thomas, you mustn't tell. You mustn't ever say I told you. Why, you're the only *boy* in the world that even knows about it!"

"I don't feel good," said Thomas weakly.

Esther rapped him sharply on the head with her knuckles. "You don't feel good?" She was furious. "Who do you think you are? Will you ever have a baby?" She got out of bed, looking very purposeful, as if she might have one then and there by way of demonstration.

"I wouldn't want to."

"So there you are! Maybe I wouldn't want to either! Nobody asked me what I wanted. I wouldn't bleed like this for all the babies in the world! But who asked me that?"

"What did Mama say?"

"She said I'd get used to it." Esther gave a harsh laugh. "She said everybody gets used to it."

"You mean Mama . . . ?"

"Yes, Mama! And sooner or later your prissy-clean Nellie Grimes! And Ellie Faye down in the kitchen! Don't you understand anything?"

"No," he whispered.

Esther looked grim. "Well, I do. I understand somebody blundered, that's what."

"Somebody who?"

"Somebody God, that's who! You can't tell me that whoever worked out the stars and the days and nights and seasons couldn't have thought up some better way than this!"

Thomas said automatically that Esther mustn't even think such things. He was chilled.

"Take your choice then—blunder or meanness! What difference does it make?"

"Esther," he said in a trembling voice, "if you don't hush, you might get turned to a pillar of salt right here and now."

She flung up both hands. "What else then? Either you're so mad at Eve you curse people that aren't even in sight yet, or else you're so busy making oceans and mountains you can't be bothered to fix the women right." She stomped back and forth in the room. "Anybody that would work out a whole rainbow just for promises and then wouldn't stop long enough to—"

"Esther," said Thomas uneasily, "I'd rather you turn to salt some other place. In the hall maybe. But don't stand here at my bed saying you don't believe in God."

"Oh, I believe in Him," said Esther wearily. "I just don't like Him much."

Thomas turned his back. "How long . . ." He cleared his throat. "How long will you . . . ?"

"Nearly a week," said Esther.

"A whole week."

"You realize," she snarled, "that with sleeping and bleeding, half my life is gone? There's not any time for anything! Not anything!"

Thomas could think of no good answer to that except, "We

thought you were dying of consumption. David and me. We were . . . we were sorry."

"Well, thanks a bucketful," said Esther.

In spite of himself, a nervous giggle rose in his throat. "Some birthday present, eh, Esther?"

She didn't laugh. "I'm going back to bed. Don't you tell David. He's little." She gave a long, windy sigh. "Let him measure his trees and his pine cones."

"What will I tell him then?"

Now she did laugh, high and shrill. "Tell him the angels troubled the waters in the Katsewa River! Tell him I bathed and was healed! Tell him prayer can do anything!"

"You keep that up and a week won't be anything. God might punish you."

Esther nodded sagely. "I thought of that. Remember that woman in the New Testament, the one with the bloody flux?" She shuddered. "Isn't that the ugliest thing you ever heard of—a bloody flux?" Abruptly she curtsied in her white nightgown and tipped her fingers from her eyebrow toward the moonlit window. "Scuse *me!*" she said merrily.

As she was going out the door, Thomas called, "You say your prayers tonight," but Esther said she wouldn't; she would not; she never would.

The first thing Thomas did when she had gone was drag the quilts down and search his bed for stains. He hated the very thought of lying in the same place.

Finally he climbed into bed and lay in a stiff line on the far side. Life began to come back into his cold feet, and as he curled up reluctantly and began to sense the approach of sleep, he had an awful vision of bloody women. They paraded redly across the wall of his room and dripped onto the floor: the preacher's wife, the women in neighboring houses. His stomach moved and shrank. Had Cleopatra? Mrs. George Washington? Queen Victoria? And last of all, with a sense of brushing the edge of Hell, he thought of the Virgin Mary.

He had intended to pray for his sister. But just as she might have defaced his bed, she had somehow managed to stain his thinking. Father, I am sorry, he prayed frantically. I am sorry.

But he was not sorry. He did not repent one honeysuckle vine, one dying seed, one shredded berry bush.

Chapter

❧ 6 ☙

IT SEEMED THAT YEAR, 1897, as if a Judas age had come over the whole state of North Carolina. Progress couldn't decide whether to go or stay. One century was almost ending and one century was coming; and that little war brewing over so-called Cuban independence couldn't compare with the tales of uncles and grandfathers who had fought in a real one, and who gathered every summer in their tight gray uniforms to picnic at the burying grounds. There they drank persimmon beer and whiskey and cider, heard a few speeches and started off conversations about McKinley that filtered straight back down the Presidency to Lincoln and veered off hastily to Lee.

In one of the eastern counties that year, a Negro man committed a series of murders and set off rumors which came rippling westward over the tops of tobacco, cotton, pines. He was caught and lynched in Sumter. There were a lot of lynchings in North Carolina that year; and Richmond County put a Negro on its board of education who could not read or write.

At the University, trustees voted to admit women. The lieutenant governor of the state was arrested. And in July, a crowd of angry people stormed the ice factory at Wilmington because there was no ice to put into the glass or around the dead fish—when else an ice famine, but in Esther's thirteenth year? Earthquake—in Winston; fire —in Lumberton. Signs and portents.

68

In Stone County cotton was cheap, but the prices at Hobbs Dry Goods Store were high. Land was also cheap, but few could buy it. Most of the people living around Greenway were poor, and some few were making money at last who were, by nature, best suited to owning no more than a jug of corn on Saturday night.

The town of Greenway was not much bigger than when Sam Allen first had seen it twenty-seven years before. It had grown up near the Katsewa River, where a water mill, now no longer used, had been the first building. There was one street of small shops, a blacksmith, a woodworking shop, one cotton gin, the Greenway Academy, three churches, Dr. Newton's office, and one dentist. The nearest newspaper was published once a week in Stoneville, where the courthouse was.

The railroad had come to Greenway about 1880. The forty-saw cotton gin, fed by hand, could produce four or five bales a day to load the train. Passengers did not use the railroad much. Politicians came through; a few boys went away to school; and an occasional woman rode the train to reach her dying mother's bed in time.

It was a country town. Farmers brought to it cotton and some tobacco, and rode home looking grim on their wagons which had brakes made out of worn-out shoes. Their faces, Esther said, were like the apple slices Mildred dried on a sunlit roof—dark, dry, drained of both tart and sweet.

In other parts of the South, and in some parts of North Carolina, there had been a stronger tradition of The Great; but in Stone County there were never any real plantations and few slaves. There were the "best" families, like that of Nathan Grimes, but they'd never been cruel overlords. Such as they had left after the war, they shared; and so of course grew poorer while certain dirt farmers would not give so much as a grain of wheat away and, grain by grain, had begun to own a little more.

In Greenway, the Negro population by 1897 was larger than before the war. Negroes came to work on those growing wheat-grain-by-wheat-grain farms, or to stand in line to work for Mr. Grimes, where there were still old clothes and Christmas baskets to be had.

This certain Mr. Dirt Farmer, soon as he turned over a few of his acres for a colored man to work, he'd come to Greenway strutting; he'd drop in noisy change when the plate passed at the church of the foot-washing Baptists; he'd talk Populist. Those who were still scrabbling along might listen to him with respect; didn't he have a sharecropper now? Mightn't he know? Even if he was still boiling shelled corn in ashes to get hominy and drinking coffee made from parched okra seed, he had an air of confidence. Things were getting better. The government would help; the Grange would help; and cotton was going up.

When things did not go to suit him, he grumbled in the streets. He went to the post-office shelves in the rear of the dry-goods store to hear his letters read aloud to him, and stayed to win contests aiming squirts of tobacco juice and to tell other farmers what they were doing wrong. Sometimes outside the polls he would stride into a circle of talking men and slap some backs before he yelled, "I'm going in and vote against them all!"

But in Greenway, at least, he didn't want his world to change— only his spot within it. What he wanted was the world to be fundamentally as he had always known it, only turned hindside before. He didn't want to rise in it financially, still as his plain old self, and thus humble those better families; he wanted to be *in* those families. He wanted the mere acquisition of land and property to perform the same miracle his church was promising, to get him born again; to get him born a second time into the same system, but at the other end.

The few times he was not talking, Mr. Dirt Farmer watched from his eye corners when Nathan Grimes passed him in the street. He measured the man's gait and the width of his smile and turned his own head at that angle to see how it would feel to his neck. He wanted, then, not the halfway measure that the poor should be made rich, but that it be swapping time on the seesaw and his turn—money or not—to walk like that and be watched like this, by somebody else.

Grimes, he would think, is as poor as I am now. Maybe I've already got more than he's got. Why doesn't it show more?

How come on him it looks so temporary and so unimportant?

Who is it cramped my life in such a little room?

"You won't promise to put up any money," said Mildred uneasily.

"How do I know what I'll promise? I don't know anything about it yet!"

Frowning, Mildred shook her head. "One of Nathan's grandfathers was going to grow mulberry trees and ship in silkworms, you know. And there's some story about some Grimes wanting to mine copper out near the river before the war; nothing came of that either."

"I know all that. It's not the same," said Sam gruffly, for he feared it might be. The Grimeses had a penchant for unworkable ideas. Nathan's father had hoped to make the Katsewa River navigable, at least for small barges, between Greenway and the South Carolina line. Hopeless. Sam hardened his jaw and raised his voice.

"The plan as I understand it is to raise at least a hundred thousand dollars ourselves, and promise to hold off taxes on the mill till it's made a good start. Nathan says he'll give the land to the corporation outright. A big parcel out by the river."

"That mining land?"

"What difference does that make?"

"Just seems like a bad sign. I don't think there's a hundred thousand dollars for six counties on either side."

"Some people keep their money secret," said Sam with a certain personal satisfaction. "Besides, Nathan says he can work something out, ways to pay off securities a little bit every month. I'll know more after tonight's meeting."

"Cotton mill. I'll believe it when I see it," Mildred said.

In the front room, Sam fed the fire and lit his pipe with one of the tapers Esther rolled from newspaper strips and kept in a jar on the mantelpiece.

"I'm going to settle it with Nathan to ride Esther home from school, starting tomorrow," he called back to the kitchen.

"He won't mind?"

Sam laughed. "Somebody new to listen to him? He won't mind. Nellie's to stay in town with her aunt the next few weeks. Time she learned how to make fruitcakes, Nathan says."

Mildred came to the doorway. "Time Esther learned, but last year, remember, she put the shells in the batter instead of the walnuts. I don't know what to do with that girl."

"Be firm," said Sam absently. Daughters, he felt, were not really his concern. He checked his watch against the mantle clock, with its painted lilies on the glass door, before he went out under a star-speckled sky and started the three-mile ride to Nathan's house.

Already he was beginning to think tonight's meeting would be a waste of time. What he saw on the way did not encourage him.

Fields on both sides of the road lay empty in the dark, and not just because it was November. Some had not been planted the spring before and anybody could buy that land at four dollars an acre and sharecrop it out—*if* he had the four dollars, *if* he could advance that tenant fifty to a hundred fifty dollars at the year's start, or stand good for it at the store so the cropper could draw against his credit.

It took, they sometimes said, thirteen months a year to tenant-farm, and all of them fell between spring and Christmas.

Cotton into the ground in March and corn in April, if you could afford corn. Plow around cotton in May, whenever spring rains allowed, and tend to the early grains. By August the cotton would be standing tall in the heat, topped with red-and-white flowers like hibiscus, and there'd be corn and fodder to lay by. Time to dig sweet potatoes, and after that the backbreaking job of picking the white boll. The pickers, if you could hire or give birth to enough of them, began in the fields at the first light of day before the dew had a chance to dry—for dew on the cotton added weight, and pay was made by weight.

If we get this mill, thought Sam, there'll be more cotton farming and more skinny men coming in the store to mumble about drought or storms or sick babies.

Of course Nathan says a mill will help everybody, even those women with cheekbones like arrowheads and eyes pulled in deep behind.

Sam wasn't sure about that. There were people in Stone County so discouraged that if the Lord rained down manna overnight they wouldn't trust it enough to stoop over. Sam was not exactly sympathetic; he was just wary. He didn't want that spirit to be contagious.

And it was contagious. Some days he couldn't wash off the smell of their fear. They'd be in and out of the store all day, too tired to sweat; and it got to where when he called a mortgage in, he was shouting the news of foreclosure into their still faces. They looked so deaf, those people. Deaf to good news as well as bad, for all he knew.

Sam turned the mare into the curving drive to Nathan's house. Once it had been made of sand, dredged from the river bottom and hauled on wagons to spread on the clay like sugar icing; and Nathan's wife, now dead, had edged it round with yellow buttercups, which came up every spring. Between the drive and the main road stood a small brick building which had been used as a law office by Nathan's father and his grandfather. The house beyond was made of brick with a portland-cement finish. A porch and balcony ran along its back width.

"You're the first!" called Nathan, emerging from behind one of the four columns on the front. A Negro man led the mare away. "Come in by the fire. Want to talk to you before Hobbs gets here."

In the front sitting room, Sam stood with his back to the hearth. "Just what I need," he said, taking the glass of whiskey Nathan brought him. "Cold out."

"I wanted to talk to you," said Nathan abruptly. "I want you to see this thing the way I see it. What a mill can mean to the people living around here. No need to say these things to Winkler Hobbs. What's it cost and what'll it earn—that's all he cares."

"You go asking somebody to put up money and what you expect them to care about?" said Sam.

"But beyond the profit to be made, Sam, there's so much good can come from this thing."

Sam nodded. "More money in people's pockets. More cotton grown at better prices."

"And not only that. Decent work for everybody who can't find work now."

"Everybody?" said Sam uneasily.

"Look at the people in Stone County who can't farm because they can't even buy a mule! Sitting on useless land or borrowed land or rented land, and not improving. Their children growing up and not improving. Planting a little garden to can from and picking enough blackberries and shooting enough squirrels and rabbits to get through the winters!"

Sam decided he would have to come straight out with it. "Nathan, you talking about white people?"

"I'm talking about everybody. There's no high number of Nigras in this county, not like they have down east. Why wouldn't a mill make work for them too?"

"No, sir," said Sam flatly. "No, sir, it'll never work; and if you want Winkler Hobbs to put his money behind this mill, you swallow down that talk. The blacks can grow cotton; nobody begrudges them that. Just leave it there."

"Sam, this isn't some outlandish thing. Before the war, slaves and free whites worked a cotton mill in Athens, Georgia; and no trouble."

"Slaves, you said. Big difference, slaves. Before the war, you said."

"And in Columbia, South Carolina! They did it at the Saluda mill in Columbia!"

"How long ago?"

There was no answer.

"Come on, Nathan. A long time."

"In eighteen forty," he finally said.

"Eight years before I was born," mused Sam. He lifted the glass. "Here's to time, which now and again goes forward." He turned and looked into the fire. His enthusiasm for the evening had now entirely gone. It would turn into another angry night of talk, and everybody would know some story worse than the one before about rape and theft, or funnier about how the night raiders had come and Jimbo had been scared to death and blurted out this or that. Winkler Hobbs had nearly died of stroke and fury already once this year, when North Carolina sent George White—a Negro—to Congress. Now Nathan was going to kill him sure, this very night in this very room, and there went the cotton mill straight along to the funeral parlor with his corpse.

And if Winkler Hobbs dies on this very rug, he thought, I might inherit the store first thing Monday morning.

He squinted at Nathan, who knew for sure what Hobbs had put into his will. "Nathan," he sighed, "the trouble with you is that the world is all in your head. Don't make trouble with this thing."

"Let me at that fire!" called Lloyd Morrison, president of the Bank of Greenway, as he came from the hall flapping out of his coat and reaching to warmth. "Nathan. Sam. Thought I was late."

While the other two were talking, Sam took occasion to pour himself another drink. He did not like Morrison, who had, for all practical purposes, married the bank when he wed Amy Sue Rogers. No money sense, really, Sam thought. Just counts it. Bleached white hands from sitting in dark rooms counting other people's money. Like the people Jesus ran out of the temple.

Now Winkler Hobbs, his weight on a cane, lurched into the room. He moved in a left-and-forward way, the left leg always carrying him slightly sideways and off course and the other leg compensating. "A legacy my stroke left me," Hobbs called it; much as if the stroke had perished under the strength of the Hobbs will power while he had survived, an heir and beneficiary.

"Evening, banker. Hello, Sam," said Mr. Hobbs. "How's that girl of yours, Nathan?" Without waiting for an answer, he made a crooked descent into a chair and began insisting in a loud voice that they get on with it; it was cold outside; it would be a colder ride home.

"Dr. Newton's upstairs," said Nathan. "Came in earlier and wanted to sleep an hour."

"Let the man sleep," grumbled Hobbs. "He's got no money. People pay him off in eggs and fatback."

"I have here," said Nathan, "a list of others to whom I've spoken about a factory. Those who think they could help us out are marked." He passed the sheets around.

Hobbs and Morrison barely glanced at the list, but Sam read the names carefully, repeating them in his mind. The man who owned the newspaper in Stoneville. Carter, said to be a heavy investor in railroads across the state. Weaver, of the General Assembly. Men from neighboring counties of Iredell and Davie, Rowan and Catawba. Men of substance.

Sam looked up from the list and into the flames in Nathan's fireplace. It was an old fireplace, surviving from an earlier Grimes house which had burned to the ground in 1809.

"Through with that?" asked Nathan.

Was the tone impatient? Sam handed him the paper. Nathan's front door locks with a six-inch key, he thought, and I'm a storekeeper from someplace in Kentucky.

Nathan had now begun to address the men in his best jury-speech manner.

". . . have also written a number of letters to get us more general information. . . . Don't think there's any need to go into the entire history of the textile industry in the South; however . . ."

Here we go, thought Sam. Right into it.

". . . we all know North Carolina was the only Southern state with the obligation to clothe her own Confederate soldiers. . . . I understand from a Raleigh friend there were about thirty-nine cotton and nine woolen mills in the state at that time."

"Before Sherman started burning," grunted Winkler Hobbs.

Sam edged away. Nobody needs a door key that big. Some men ain't got six inches where it really counts.

". . . Nowadays four or five cotton factories are being built in this state every year. I think it's safe to say that wherever a mill comes, prosperity follows. Greenway is long overdue some prosperity."

Banker Morrison, who was already prosperous, cried a theatrical "Hear! Hear!"

"Less enthusiasm, Nathan, and more facts," Hobbs said dryly.

"Cost. Return. Time. Machinery. Workers."

A look of distaste flickered on Nathan's face so briefly that his smile didn't even change size. "I understand floor plans and drawings of a standard brick building may be had from certain of the machinery manufacturers," he said coolly.

"Free?" chirped Morrison.

"As a service to encourage sales. They expect terms of half cash with the balance in one year, or sometimes a quarter cash and balance in two years."

From Hobbs: "How much cash are we talking about?"

"New machinery runs between six and ten dollars a spindle. I have one letter saying the average mill, complete with looms, can be built and outfitted for sixteen to eighteen dollars a spindle. Of course, we'd want to get other opinions on that."

"At least seventy-five thousand for a plant, you think? Five thousand spindles or thereabouts?"

"A proper capitalization—" Morrison began with a frown.

Hobbs interrupted. "I know that. I know that." He waved his cane. "Did you look into the possibility of paying for machinery in common stocks?"

"Some firms will take stock as partial payment, but the big ones don't like to do so. It's acceptable under the state corporation laws, of course. I think we'd be wise to avoid it."

"I'm interested in what we can do, not what we should do," Hobbs grunted.

Nathan said stiffly the transaction was machinery at list price and stocks at par value. "If you find a manufacturer who's willing," he couldn't resist adding.

Morrison, to whom financial trends formed cycles more real than winter and spring, frowned. Sam could almost watch history ripple across his face as if it had been water—depression 1883, revival five or six years later; another drop in 1893. The years rolled beyond this year and this night in the year, and his countenance went blank. Morrison was always pretending that he made predictions, but really he hated to run the risk of taking yesterday to tomorrow. He pretended he could do this, with his judicious "All this reminds me of eighteen sixty-five, when wheat was fifty dollars a bushel," but he was never really comparing. He was only slipping away from the uncertain tomorrow into a yesterday which had safely congealed behind him and was now solid—like that bird in the hand opposed to whatever might flutter in next week's bushes.

Nathan now began talking of how the Greenway Manufacturing Company would look—a basement, two other stories. The basement to be used for a machine shop.

"Right at first, couldn't we just build a basement and one other floor?" asked Morrison. "And then add on after profits . . ."

Nobody seemed to be listening. Carding and drawing would be done on first floor, spinning and finishing work above. With a pitched roof there could be a storage attic.

Hobbs seemed restive. This kind of detail he preferred to leave to underlings. "I think we've done all we can for the first meeting," he said abruptly.

Morrison said shouldn't they come to some actual agreement?

"Or," said Nathan with a sharp glance at Winkler Hobbs, "make some specific commitment?"

Hobbs ignored them both. "Have Bob Shelton put a piece in his Stoneville paper. Meeting of Greenway Betterment Association, or whatever you want to call it. Plans laid to organize a cotton factory for Greenway."

"Meeting of what?" said Sam, coming suddenly to life.

"Get people talking about a mill. Get people counting their money. Start them thinking in terms of next year's crop."

Sam wondered what money was left in Greenway to count. Had it not largely slipped through invisible funnels to Winkler Hobbs—the way a bin of grain will sift mysteriously, moving and rumbling with unseen life, all the while it is trickling away through unseen holes? Well, I own a few of them holes. I got a little of that spilling.

"Get some quotations from the machinery people," said Hobbs. "I'll go to Boston to meet with them when it's time."

Now, from his tone, Nathan Grimes had become an underling. Sam saw the muscles under each of Nathan's cheekbones leap and harden.

See how you like it, being pressed down till you lay in Hobbs's pocket like a watch! thought Sam. And then, abruptly, he didn't like it himself.

And without taking time to think about it, and in the middle of something else Hobbs was saying, Sam walked rapidly across the room and took Nathan's hand and said in a loud voice, "Good of you to have us over tonight, Nathan, and give us a chance to share in this fine idea of yours." His smiling mouth was a crowd of teeth.

"Thank you, Sam," said Nathan, and nearly broke his fingers.

"I'll be hearing from you then. Banker. Mr. Hobbs. Hope we can all do business," said Sam heartily.

But once he had left them and the cold air outdoors had washed across his face, his silly voice rang in his own ears. They must be laughing at him even now—and Nathan with the others. Imitating him, perhaps, mocking him in his role of store clerk who dipped out seed corn and went up on his ladder to fetch tonics and poison-oak salve.

"He means well," Nathan would offer. Him and his damn door key.

"Getting too big for his britches," from Hobbs.

And now, relieved that Sam Allen had gone at last and required no more of their politeness, Hobbs and Morrison and Nathan Grimes might be really discussing the factory in dollars and cents, writing down figures. Signing their names.

It seemed to Sam a long ride home.

His house was dark. Inside the front door Sam stopped at the foot of the stairs and listened to the small noises—the cracks and pops from the walls and floor, Angus Mackey's life going in and out his throat with a rumbling sound, a cough somewhere.

From the upstairs bedroom Mildred called, "Sam? Is that you?"

He almost answered her: No, and I don't know how he got here using my name, with me on the way to the edge of the sea.

"Sam?"

He mounted the stairs. "Go to sleep," he said. "It's only me."

Chapter

❦ 7 ❧

THE BARE WILLOW TREES sagged along Black Creek. Mildred, who was hunched in the buggy seat against December winds, caught herself leaning forward and drooping down like the willows. She watched the road at that point where the buggy wheel rolled off it, and the earth seemed like flowing liquid passing under her in the opposite direction.

It was two weeks before Christmas. Mildred had left home early this morning, carrying a fried chicken in a small sack, to visit Rosa.

She had heard nothing from her sister since Angus Mackey's heart attack. So, when she topped the rise from which one could usually glimpse smoke from the Bennett chimneys, she drew the horse in, stood in the buggy and squinted into the clear sky. Oh, Lord, she thought, and laid on the whip.

The Bennett place, sixty acres of scrub pines and red gullies, had a look of abandonment. Dead limbs had been two seasons in the fruit trees; barbed wire lay on the ground like string along the pasture fence. Lacy caterpillar webs hung in wild cherry trees each spring. Near the house itself, spiraea and yellow-bell bushes had become a hedge of matted winter twigs, and the crepe myrtle struggled under a tent of dried honeysuckle vine.

Mildred tried the gatepost, saw how it rocked in the earth, and tied the horse to a low limb of a white-oak tree. The third tread on the porch steps was gone entirely. By the front door was a small pile of stones, used—she knew—to throw at mockingbirds in season. Mockingbirds, which nested in the tangled bushes near the house and sang late into the summer nights, made Rosa nervous. This little heap of rocks was left over from last year's songs.

There was no answer to Mildred's knock. "Rosa? Rosa, you in there?" She tried to see through the long glass pane beside the door. "Rosa? Oh, Rosa."

Mildred took one of the stones from the pile and banged it sharply against the front door. Nothing. She pushed, rattled the knob, looked through both front windows into empty rooms.

Then she walked around back, driving before her a mildly uneasy chicken, and entered the kitchen. The house was very still and no fires were burning. Rosa's kitchen was so clean Mildred opened the doors to every safe and found nothing to eat—not one cold biscuit or half a pie, not so much as an opened jam jar. Mildred looked at the small cloth sack in which she had brought fried chicken. Absently she tied it onto her waist belt as she moved into the other rooms.

There was no one in the dusty parlor or the hall, or inside the deep closet underneath the stairs. The upper rooms were also empty, and had not been swept—judged Mildred—for a week or more.

Now she was really worried. Out back again, she hollered down into the well, although ten strong men could never have stuffed Rosa down that narrow opening. She called into the tool shed and the hen roost. "Rosa? You out here, Rosa?"

Then she saw Silas coming from the barn with his hand held up. He waved her back.

Mildred cupped her hands to her mouth. "Silas? Is Rosa down there?" Again he waved his hand around in the air.

When he was closer he began to call, "Don't go down there."

She stood on tiptoe. "Down where? What's wrong with Rosa?"

"She's down there digging." Silas plumped onto one of the big molasses vats which had been dragged into the weeds to rust away. "She's been digging all day. And for days before that she's been planning to dig. Sitting in the house looking down the hill and thinking about it."

"In the orchard?"

Silas nodded. "Claims she's been dreaming nights about a box of silver candlesticks, buried when people thought Sherman was coming through. Three silver candlesticks, she says, and two brass, and a chunk of hard money in the toe of an old wool sock."

"Oh, Silas," Mildred said in despair. This might mean Rosa was headed into another of her spells.

"All of it locked in a black tin box. She's got so many holes in that orchard, one good rain will float the trees away."

Mildred shaded her eyes but the orchard was behind the barn. She saw no sign of her sister. "Nobody owned this place but Bennetts in the war. Didn't you tell her that? Didn't you tell her none of your family buried any box?"

"What good would that do?"

"She'll wear herself out, digging all day in this cold weather, and the dirt wet and heavy." Mildred started down the path.

"She made it up about the dream," said Silas heavily. "I know she made it up. She knows I know it. Hate to say anything."

Mildred turned to look back at him.

"It's her babies she's digging for. Little bits of things without as much bone as a bird has. She thinks I'd worry if I knew that was what she was really after."

Mildred laid her hand on her throat. "What on earth for?"

"For that old colored woman that claims the power. You know. Miss Bethesda Lee Michael."

Mildred knew. Miss Bethesda Lee Michael—eighty-odd years old and named for the archangel—lived in a little shack built out over the Katsewa River, one overhanging porch nailed precariously onto a huge tree limb. Bethesda Lee's powders and potions were said to ease childbirth, fetch lovers, find lost watches and maim enemies.

"When did she start going to see Miss Bethesda?"

"Right after the old man took sick."

"Is she . . . Silas, is she . . ."

"No. She isn't and she wasn't. But she thinks a little dust from one of them . . . one of them things I buried—" He brought his fist suddenly down onto the metal molasses vat with a terrible clang.

Mildred jumped and shivered.

Silas got himself under control. "In a little pouch, she says, hung on a string around her neck. And Rosa's to wear it when. . . ." He bent over and pulled up a brown grass blade and ran it through his teeth. "She's to wear it at night."

Mildred closed her eyes and asked the Lord Jesus to look down on them this very instant and do something *sensible*, like breaking off the handle of Rosa's shovel. "You go to the house," she said. "I'll bring her in."

"She won't come. I been trying."

"I'll whip her home with a thornbush if I have to," snapped Mildred, and she pressed her mouth into a thin line and set off trotting past the barn and downhill into the apple orchard.

From a distance Rosa looked like some giant buzzard flapping under the trees. She had on a black cloak and wore a red spotted apron underneath. She was down, Mildred saw, on her large haunches, poking the earth with a crooked stick.

Wet as a rat in all this mud, thought Mildred. She began to run and call her sister's name.

Rosa glanced behind her, then sat on the ground and waved. "Hey, Mildred!" she called happily.

"I've come to help you, Rosa."

Rosa gave a gay laugh. "I've looked and looked for the candlesticks. I dreamed them right here. I tried to make Silas help."

Mildred knelt by her. "No candlesticks here, Rosa. No box."

Rosa held out her hand. "What you think this could be?"

Mildred turned the tip of her tongue back into her own throat for a minute and held it there, rigid. Then she said, as gently as she could, "It's a worm, Rosa. Smashed on the shovel, I guess. You must be digging down pretty deep to hit worms in this cold weather." She turned her face aside and held out a handkerchief. "Clean it off your hand now, and let's go to the house."

Obediently Rosa wiped her fingers and then studied the blade of the shovel lying by her side. "I guess that's it," she said to herself, but she did not stand up.

Mildred moved the shovel with her foot. "I've brought something special to eat," she said, "and I want to tell you all about how Papa is. Let's go in and make a fire. I'm about to freeze."

"Papa will be so disappointed," said Rosa absently. She reached for something white that gleamed in the earth. "You think that's a rock?" she asked.

"It's a rock," said Mildred. "Come on inside. You'll feel better after you eat something. I can tell from your kitchen you've not had—" The thought which came suddenly into her mind nearly caused her stomach to roll over. She laid her hand on the sack of fried chicken she wore tied to her belt. Jesus, she prayed, You could save me all this. Jesus, it wouldn't be right for me to do that.

"You go on in," said Rosa. "I dreamed it so clear—the candlesticks and the money. All in a black box."

Mildred turned her back and worked her fingers into the sack and onto the pieces of chicken, cold now, and greasy. She moved past the drumsticks, wings, and at last slipped a forefinger into the cavity of breast and began to pluck at one of the tiny ribs.

Rosa talked on about the candlesticks but Mildred, pacing nervously while she probed inside the sack, barely heard. She pulled out pinches of meat, skin, brown flour crust, and at last a few fragments of bone and gristle. These she laid in the palm of her left hand, fighting her nausea. The largest piece looked so much like cooked chicken that she did the only thing she could think of—slipped it between her teeth and cleaned it down to the white. After that was done she bent over and spat for a long time, trying not to gag.

"This weather's nearly making me sick," she gasped to Rosa, her voice pleading. "Just listen to me cough and wheeze."

"You go on in," said Rosa again. "I'll dig a little more. It must be here."

Mildred began to walk back and forth, looking into first one hole and then another that Rosa had dug. Some places the smaller roots of apple trees had been laid bare, and bits had been broken off and pulled up, cleaned and examined.

Mildred stooped by one of these holes, closed her eyes briefly and laid down the little handful of chicken litter onto a heap of red earth. She did not look at it again. She kept her back to Rosa.

"Why, what's this?" she said, staring straight ahead to the pine forest. Rosa said nothing.

"How strange," Mildred murmured. "It almost looks like bone. Very small bone."

Rosa, with grunts and heavy breathing, got to her feet and came to stand over her, looking down.

"I wonder what that was?" said Mildred. She stood up and began brushing at her skirt. Rosa's gaze was fixed on the earth.

"I'm going to the house," said Mildred crisply, "and if you've got any sense you'll come in too." She moved away a few steps. Rosa was bending from the waist. Mildred could hear her sister breathe.

Mildred turned and began to walk rapidly away, her footsteps firm. "The Bennetts," she said loudly, "never owned any silver candlesticks. Silas could have told you that." From the corner of her eye she saw Rosa lean down, pick something off the ground and hold it to her cheek. You see that, Jesus? Have a little mercy! Mildred's eyes ran over with sudden tears.

"Wait for me, Mildred! Wait for me! I'm coming!"

She waited stiffly until Rosa came, tucking something inside her apron pocket.

Silas walked down from the barn to meet them on the path, moving a bit loosely in his shoes, so that Mildred guessed he had been watching from the loft and drinking a little in his nervousness.

"You give it up, Rosa?" he was saying with an uneasy laugh.

Rosa looked very placid and very dignified. "You might have told me," she said from a great distance, "that ya'll didn't own any candlesticks." Her husband shrugged.

Between the barn and the Bennett house, Mildred fell back a few steps to walk by Silas and, when he looked away, to drop a sack of chicken into the ditch.

"I don't know how you do it," Silas whispered, his eyes on his wife's back.

Mildred was suddenly furious with him, thinking about Rosa and how Miss Bethesda Lee Michael could sew anything into a little cloth and make a spell out of it.

"Silas," she hissed, "don't you dare sell off a single one of my sister's hen eggs to get your whiskey!"

Silas Bennett dropped his head. "I wouldn't do that," he whispered back. "Why are you saying that to me?"

Mildred thought of her sister wearing that magic pouch to make her fruitful. "I'm only warning you it wouldn't be decent," she said. "It wouldn't be a bit decent."

Esther's eyes were as wide as teacups.

"Now don't be foolish," Mildred said irritably. She was sitting on her back steps, honing the big knife against a rock. Rutledge had already sharpened it twice at the grindstone, but still its edge didn't suit her.

"I won't," said Esther tensely.

"Yes, you will. You will because that's the way you are," her mother grumbled.

They were going to the hog killing at Nathan's house. Nathan had two colored women to make lard and sausage, but lacking a wife, he needed somebody to be in charge. Besides, he said, Nellie ought to learn these things. Time was, no Grimes did more than look on and give orders, but these days everybody should learn these things and he would give Mildred a ham for her trouble.

Mildred had told him they'd be glad to come. Ellie Faye and Rutledge too.

"Esther," she said now, "if you're to be sick this year, you run down in the woods. Last winter was a terrible mess."

"I'll not be sick," said Esther faintly.

For a while there was no sound except the scraping of her knife against the stone. "We need the ham," Mildred said to herself.

"I'll not eat any of that ham. All that blood. All that hair scraped off and dropped just anywhere. The way they dip that hog and it hangs up naked. Last year they put the insides in a big pile and they smoked on the ground—"

"Steamed," said Mildred.

"David stuck broom straws in them."

Her mother sighed. "Will you do what I told you and think about ham gravy in the mornings? Think about side meat in the beans? Just look at it in your mind already *cooked*."

"I'd rather eat chicken any day."

Mildred said shortly she had no taste for chicken meat these days, no taste at all.

"Thomas gets to stay at the store and help Papa. Clean work. Oh, Mama, is there going to be souse?"

"If you could do as much as you can ask!" sighed Mildred. "Esther, you wear me out, talking things to death before they even get here." Shaking her head, she carried the sharpened knife inside to wash.

"That isn't fair," hissed Esther to the toe of her own shoe. Why, if I talked half the things that are in my head . . . if I let loose even part of the questions that are always on the boil up there!

When Mildred came back to pour a pail of water off the porch, Esther could not help blurting out, "Mama, you don't even know me at all! I'm all inside! I'm underneath!"

"Who isn't?" said her mother lightly. "Now go find David and tell him while we're gone he's not to set one foot outside this house."

"Please let me stay here with Grandfather. Please, Mama! The way that blood runs out when they hang up the pig—"

"Carcass. Hang up the carcass. Your trouble is thinking with the wrong words."

"David wants to go so bad. He even wants to scrape the bristles off."

"Esther, the whole point is to teach you how to run your own kitchen someday. Nellie will be there. She's willing to learn. She's going to salt down meat right alongside the rest of us."

"David's been studying the hairs on his arm all morning, Mama. He thinks a pig's grow out of his skin different."

"Oh, Lord," said Mildred crossly.

"And he wants a bladder to blow up. Oh, Mama, take David instead of me. Grandfather would rather have me with him than David—you know that." Seeing her mother hesitate, she put both hands onto her stomach and pressed hard. She let out a soft, high moan. "I'm sick already from thinking. What if I get sick right in the sausage this year? Oh, I can smell that fat boiling now. If I have to stir that fat with a stick, I'll fall right in the pot. I know it."

Mildred slammed down her bucket and hollered into the air for David to come on if he wanted to slaughter hogs. She slapped both hands to her hips. "Esther, you could talk the ears right off the dead, and when you get grown, no man will have you! Can't cook, won't work and never stop talking! When I was your age, I was running a whole house and my mama was under her tombstone!"

David came running. She sent him to tell Grandfather. "What will become of you I'll never know, but when your hair is white you'll likely blame me. You'll look back, Esther, and know I should have made you do things. That's the reward I'll get." The tip of Mildred's nose turned red.

Esther tried to hug her around the waist but Mildred knocked her hands away. "Want everything changed to suit you. And you not willing to change to suit one thing that already is. Esther, this world was here before you came. Hogs going to be killed long after both of us have died!"

"I love you, Mama," said Esther.

"Much good that is! You'll love me when you've got neither husband nor house nor child, and don't even know how to stir up a soup for yourself!" She slammed the door behind her into the kitchen. "Ellie Faye, let's get going. Rutledge has been in that wagon waiting ever since the rooster crowed." Her voice rose even louder. "David? You *coming?*"

Mildred walked rapidly across the porch and past her daughter, her head held high, banged her heels down the steps and climbed up into the wagon, which was loaded with pots and rags and small bags of sage and dried peppers. Ellie Faye, carrying a pan of sharp knives and ladles and strainers, came behind. Last of all David ran out, still working an arm into his coat. Esther leaned up against a porch post, watching.

David fell into the wagon. "Rutledge, let me drive. Please, Rutledge."

Mildred turned. "Come here, Esther."

Esther stood by the wagon.

"You look after your grandfather. That's one thing you're good at, tending the sick."

"Yessum."

Mildred leaned from her seat and laid a cool forefinger on Esther's face. "I was good at that too. That's how I met your father. He was hurt, and Mr. Hobbs sent for me to look after him."

"I didn't know that," said Esther.

Mildred gave a soft grunt of satisfaction. "Forty-'leven things you don't know yet, young lady," she said. "Rutledge, drive on. And David, you sit still."

When they were out of sight, Esther carried a glass of buttermilk upstairs to Angus Mackey. He was in his usual chair by the window, waving at the empty place where the wagon had disappeared. At the sound of the door he wheeled around, embarrassed to be caught flapping his hand at nothing.

"Left you here, huh?" he barked. "I never was lucky."

"Well, I am," said Esther, setting down the milk, "because I sure didn't want to go to that hog killing."

"I like a good hog killing. Not with guns though. Cain Evers used to run right into the pen and stick a knife over the heart. Let the hog bleed its own self, he always said."

"Drink your milk."

"Some folks whack a hog in the head with the blunt end of the ax blade. I've seen hogs hung up to be bled like that and they'd turn out still living, and start to flop around on the chain."

"Don't tell me," groaned Esther, rolling her eyes. "Mama said take that buttermilk for your strength. She thought you looked poor this morning."

"I don't want no buttermilk. My stomach's sour enough today."

Esther lay down across his bed, which smelled like . . . like cold biscuit crumbs, she guessed. "I'll never get married, Grandfather."

He snickered. "Hoo, I reckon not."

She rolled onto her stomach and looked at him. "Mama said so again today. She said nobody would have me."

"She tell you how come?"

"Because I can't do one single married-woman thing!" Esther balled her fist and hit the bedcovers. "My bread never rises and all the jars of peaches I put up last year blew up half a cellar shelf. You remember that."

Grandfather said grimly he sure did remember; he thought at the time he'd been shot in the head.

"I ruined that sampler I was making. Kept sticking the needle in my finger so many times you couldn't tell what was blood and what was roses."

"And sewed it to your skirt," he agreed, nodding.

"And hog killing makes my food come back up. Last year was just awful, the time I got sick."

"You leaned over Nathan's well and let fly, as I remember."

"I don't know any other girls like me," she sighed.

After a little thought, Grandfather suggested that she marry a rich man.

"You know of one?"

"No."

"Drink your buttermilk."

He drained the glass and rolled it in his hands. "Might be one up North."

"Not doing me any good way up there." Esther closed her eyes. "I do want to love somebody. What if I just got old and died and never did?"

"Your trouble," he said, "is more apt to be with narrowing down. Settling on one."

"He won't settle on me—Mama already said it."

Angus Mackey was beginning to feel sleepy. "What is it," he said through a yawn, "you'd like to do best of all when you got growed up? If you could have things all your way."

She covered her eyes with her hands, thinking. "I'd be a man to start off, very strong and very handsome. And rich. I'd own big buildings." She moved one hand in the air to show: Strong. Tall. Big Building. "And I'd marry a princess from across the ocean, and she wouldn't be able to cook either, but I'd be the kind of man who wouldn't care. And she would be beautiful and have a lot of sons. In the summers we'd move to an island and pick fruit off the trees. He'd always want to know what I was thinking and I wouldn't even mind telling—I mean, *I'd* always want to know what *she* was thinking, and she could trust me. I'd like everything about her. I'd like all the things other people thought were faults. I—Grandfather?"

Angus Mackey had dozed off in his chair, his head down awkwardly into one shoulder.

"Oh, Grandfather, come on to bed if you're going to sleep!"

He snuffled in a great breath through his mouth.

"You'll fall out on the floor if I leave you like that." Esther patted his cheek to wake him; then, curious at the cool limpness of his skin, she let her fingers rest. She took up one of his cheek folds and rolled it between thumb and forefinger.

He woke with a start and eyed her. She thought of crawdads watching from the mud. "I'll help you to bed now," she said softly, knowing he was half dreaming still.

"Don't want to move," he said sleepily.

Esther dragged his chair to the bed. Its four legs made a screaming sound as they scraped across the floor. He was lighter than she thought. "Ease in now."

Grandfather stared dead ahead into his bureau drawers. "I am watching out this window," he said flatly.

"There's not a window there. Come on. I'll help you."

"Hell and damn if you will," he spat, opening his eyes wide for the first time and striking out wildly with the palms of his hands. She turned back the bedcovers.

"Get in then, and I'll stir your fire. You want anything?"

"I want to live forever," he growled. He got up from his chair and half stumbled onto the bed. "You ought never move a man that's still asleep."

Esther yanked the quilts around him.

"If you ever do marry," he droned, already sinking away into comfort, "don't ever bother your man till he's woke himself all the way up. Half asleep is awful. He's liable to kill you."

"All men ain't like you, Grandfather," she said softly.

"Nor all girls like you, praise God," he muttered, and began to snore.

Esther put a log into his fireplace and sat by the bed awhile, watching him sleep. Tired or not, he usually walked around his own room, and she did not know what to make of his sudden weakness. Half asleep, he said. Maybe so. She laid her head on his chest as she had seen Dr. Newton do, but what could you tell from that? He was taking air in and letting it out; his heart throbbed on and on; his ribs squeaked like an old gate and buttermilk was burbling in his stomach. She laid her hand on his forehead and then on her own and felt no difference.

For a while longer she watched him before she went downstairs. The house was too quiet and too empty; she walked from window to window, looking out. The world looked like a dry husk. No wonder we have Christmas in December, she thought, when it's all straw and clay and you can look on through the empty trees forever without finding a single leaf. Until at last there's one green cedar tree on the hillside and—well, you *need* it, that's all! You have to go out there and cut it down and bring it home.

The parlor clock said 11:30.

She opened the jar of blackberries Mildred had set out on the table and poured them into a bowl with sugar. Grandfather liked a lot of sugar. There was cold cornbread. She crumbled a chunk into a glass, poured sweet milk to the brim, and stuck in a teaspoon. All this she put on a platter and carried to Angus Mackey's room.

He was awake, but when Esther bent over to tell him about the food, his eyes seemed strange. It was as if the vision in them had dropped deep into his skull. She thought of rocks settling in the silty bottoms of pools. "Grandfather?" she said softly. He pulled his eyelids down, drew with an effort all his seeing power to the surface, and then looked at her. She saw that his neck had got hard from strain.

"It's time to eat," she said.

He whispered, "That buttermilk has poisoned me."

"Are you really sick?"

He struggled to a sitting position in the bed. "I got gas all the way to my chin," he said. "What's that to eat?"

She put the platter on the table by his bed but he insisted on getting into his chair again. "And don't you help."

She stood back while he got to his feet and slid the chair up to the table. He seemed to be steady, she thought. He's just complaining like he always does.

"Eating in bed kills people," he was saying. "The organs get lined up wrong. Up and down, that's the way it ought to be." He began slurping the cornbread and milk. "I've got the teeth of a young man, you ever notice that?"

She nodded. "I put plenty of sugar on the berries."

He paused, let the spoon slide down into the milk and rubbed his chest.

"Grandfather, are you breathing hard?"

"I got gas, I said." He started on the blackberries. "Your Mama told you to throw out feed for the chickens. You done that yet?"

"Chickens can wait. You keep sucking in your air so strong. Does something hurt you?"

"Your talking hurts me. Go feed the hens."

Uneasy now, Esther ran all the way outside, into the granary, where she grabbed handfuls of cracked wheat and corn grains out of a sack and slung them wide into the yard. "Here chick chick chick chick!" she screeched, already running for the house again.

She was panting when she got back to Angus Mackey's room and could not find him in it. The empty chair was overturned. She saw he had eaten about half the blackberries and vomited on the floor.

Something seemed to be crushing her throat. She screamed, "Grandfather? Grandfather, where are you?" She searched all through the room, even inside the wardrobe, under the bed. Grunting, she pushed the window up and looked out onto the porch roof, calling for him.

"Grandfather!"

At the far corner of the hall, where it was dark, she found him sitting on the floor. His suspenders had fallen down around his arms.

"Come to bed," she said, the words trembling in her mouth. "You ought not be out here in the cold."

He gasped, stiffened, and held his mouth open wide. His shoulders came forward so she saw how the suspenders had fallen, and his chest drove in as if it had been stepped on. The next minute he was breathing almost normally.

"You're sick," said Esther. She was shaking.

"I got to coughing. Brought it all up. Couldn't stand to look at it."

Esther got behind him and put her hands under his armpits and wound them back around his bony shoulders. "Go limp," she said, "and I'll drag you."

"Looked like blood," he muttered.

She began to back down the hall, pulling him as rapidly as she could. "Soon as I get you to bed," she puffed. She stopped herself. The mare was in Greenway and both mules at Nathan's house; she could not ride for help. Besides, Grandfather might get up again and go headfirst down the steps. "You'll soon feel better," she finished. "And I'll stay with you. I'll stay right here."

She dragged him into his room and to the other side of the bed, away from the puddle souring on the floor. She sat on the edge of the bed and left him sitting on the floor, leaning back between her legs.

"Grandfather," she said, blowing for her own breath as loudly as he. "I'll heave you up here in just a minute."

"It sure don't smell like blood," he said. "I can get in bed myself." But he sat still, resting against her.

Esther pulled hard but she could not lift him to the height of the bed. She bit her teeth together and drove her breath down and lifted as strongly as she could. It was not enough. She rested again, panting.

"You should of gone to the hog killing," said Angus Mackey. "Back off. I'll get in myself."

"No, you just hang loose. I can do it." She worked him out a little further from the bed and edged her feet beneath him until he was nearly sitting on the tops of her shoes, his back sagging against her two legs. Now Esther leaned forward, ran her arms under his and clasped them together on his chest. She could feel it working and pumping.

"I'm going to pull back," she said, "and bring my feet and legs up at the same time, and we'll go rolling into bed together."

"I ain't paralyzed," he grumbled.

She dropped herself back, swung up her feet and legs and rolled left, carrying his body on her body into the feather mattress. He went easily into its softness and lay doubled up on his left side like a child. Esther got loose from him and climbed shakily off the bed. She took off his shoes.

Again he was jerking for air. Perhaps she had crushed his ribs, yanking him that way. Esther straightened him out, rolled him onto his back and moved both pillows under his head and shoulders the way you did for croup. Somebody was moaning in the room.

She discovered it was herself. "Grandfather, don't die, because I don't know what to do for you or how to help you . . . No more good to you than David would have been. Ah, don't die, Grandfather, don't die with only me here and not knowing how to help you. Please, Grandfather!"

He began to breathe deeply, if unevenly, and seemed to be asleep. She touched his face. Maybe a nightshirt would be better than his tight collar and those suspenders in the way. She found a torn one in a drawer, chunked up the fire and tried to get him out of his shirt. The arms wouldn't go and the old man was too limp to help. Esther got sewing scissors from her mother's room and began to saw the sleeves jaggedly from around his upper arms. She pulled them down his wrists and over the crooked fingers. From collar to shoulder she cut straight across and folded the two fronts back and cut them from him at the sides. The rest of the shirt she left lying under him. Anything was better than just sitting here, counting the breaths he took.

The nightshirt went over his head. He did no more than shake himself slightly when it passed across his face. She was able to get his arms into those ample sleeves well enough. She pulled the nightshirt down in front. Most of the back was still bunched at the nape of his neck and she left it there in a wad. The fragments of his cut shirt—for no good reason—she threw into the fire, buttons and all.

"How's that, Grandfather?" she asked his empty face. He said something in his sleep about the baby. The baby was always crying.

His pants were not so difficult, with the suspenders down already. Her fingers were awkward on the buttons but after that she could work the trousers down his thin hips without much effort, and pull from the cuffs till they were off. Esther hung them on a nail behind the door.

The long underwear she left. For one minute she stared at the bulge he made in its front and eyed the rip along his groin where something dark could be nearly seen. Then she pulled the nightshirt down as far as it would go and covered him up.

She waited by his bed. There was sand inside her mouth and under her eyelids and behind her tongue. For an hour he slept, talking sometimes. He was young now, she decided, and talking to his wife. My grandmother. Virginia Grace Collins Mackey. Fodder he mentioned once, and a spotted calf. And that baby.

I guess that's Mama or Aunt Rosa crying inside his head, thought Esther.

She cleaned up the mess he had spit out on the floor, using a handsome embroidered spread that was on his bureau. She burned that too.

When he did not get any better or any worse, she could not stand the waiting. Down to the kitchen she went, and climbed on a chair and took Sam Allen's shotgun off its rack above the door. The shells were in a cotton bag hung on a nail beneath the stairs. Esther loaded the gun as she had seen her father do, stood out under the chinaberry tree in the front yard and fired it toward Nathan's house.

The gun whanged back against her and knocked her to the ground. Her ears were ringing from its blast and her shoulder must have broken off at the roots. Esther laid her face onto the cold grass and cried. Who would hear that noise or, if they heard it, give it a minute's thought? She got up, sniffling, and blew her nose into her skirt. Loading the gun again, she shot straight into the winter sun. This time she got quickly off the ground, holding her shoulder raised with her chin pressed in against the hurt. She left the gun on the ground where it had fallen and hurried upstairs again.

Grandfather was sitting up, his eyes wide and his jaw hanging. "Was them your peaches blowing up?"

Esther burst into tears.

Angus Mackey, smiling, lay back against his pillows. "Not everybody puts up peaches and has them keep," he said. "I remember when Virginia . . . that was before she got so strong on Bible reading . . ."

"You get some sleep." Esther choked. "They'll soon be home. Rutledge will ride for Dr. Newton."

Grandfather said happily that last time the doctor had given him whiskey.

"Whiskey? Are you sure? Is any left?"

"If there was, your Mama locked it up someplace."

Esther ran down the hall into Thomas' room and peered out his window into the chinaberry tree. The jar was shining against the brown limb. She bounced downstairs two treads at a time, ran from the house, found a hoe in the barn loft. On the porch roof, she stood on her toe tips to catch the limb and draw it slowly downward. The ribbon was likely rotten from being out in the weather. She eased her hands up the hoe handle until she could reach the bottom of Silas' jar and then wind her hand around the neck. Sure enough, the ribbon broke when she jerked sharply at it.

Then she couldn't unscrew the top. Esther sat on the roof and braced the bottle between her legs and twisted the lid, banged its edge, grabbed a handful of her skirt to wrench it again.

At last it turned free and she carried the jar carefully in both hands, like an offering. Angus Mackey was lying quietly with his eyes shut. His skin was white. Esther moved the jug back and forth under his nose.

"Drink some," she ordered. "Grandfather? Take some of this."

He squinted at her. "My feet feels funny."

Esther looked under the quilts. "They're a little swollen, that's all. Take a few swallows."

He had a coughing spell, then swallowed down a little of the whiskey. "That stuff would melt door hinges," he said.

"A little more and then rest awhile."

"I got to pee."

Esther put her hand over her eyes and leaned briefly into the bedpost. "Is there a pot under the bed? No, never mind." She rubbed her forehead, back and forth. Then from Mildred's room she brought back the large china pitcher out of the big bowl on the washstand. It bore a painted wreath of babies' breath and a smattering of butterflies.

She sat him up in bed and pushed the fat pitcher underneath the quilts. "Can you do it your own self?"

"I ain't dead yet," he growled. "You prop my back."

She heard the stream hitting the pitcher before he began to heave again and croak for air. She eased him back and lifted the quilt. The fat-bellied pitcher had turned on its side but little had spilled. Esther poured it into the pot beneath his bed. He was wheezing.

"Take some more whiskey," she said. She was almost angry. "I said for you to drink this whiskey!"

He did not seem to hear.

Downstairs the clock said no more than 2:30. Esther opened its glass doors and stared at the pendulum to make sure it was really swinging left and right. It would be dark before anybody came.

Numbly she went out front and loaded the gun again. Somebody might hear. Or a bonfire . . . She looked aimlessly around at the fields, wet from last night's rain. She raised the shotgun to her aching shoulder. I'm apt to kill him from the noise, she thought. And the gun was suddenly so heavy to her arm she could hardly get it back down again and lay it on the bottom step.

She went back inside to her grandfather. He was lying as she had left him, eyes closed, except that he had his right hand in the air and seemed to be motioning with it. "Come on to bed, Virginia, and let that baby cry," he said distinctly. His hand wavered on his wrist-bone as if only a thread were holding it there.

"It's all right," said Esther automatically. "Everything's all right."

For a while he was quiet except for the spasms when he fought to get his breath. His face grew white and whiter, and then gray. He would not drink any more of the whiskey. His mouth hung open, so she had a clear view of all the teeth he was so proud of.

"Virginia?" he called once. "I never meant to make you mad! Come on to bed!"

Esther leaned over him and his groping right hand closed on her shallow breast. "Ah," he said, and left it there. He choked again, and his clutching fingers hurt her. The tears ran out of Esther's eyes and down her nose and smeared around her mouth.

"Virginia?"

She managed to get it out. "I'm right here. I'll stay right here."

It was nearly dark before Rutledge drove the wagon home. When Mildred saw Esther huddled on the front steps, holding a shotgun across her lap, she jumped to the ground while the wheels were still rolling.

"Esther!" she screamed.

"Dead," said Esther dully.

Mildred took the shotgun. "Are you sure?"

"Yes."

Mildred stooped and wound an arm about her shoulders. "I'm sorry it had to be this way, Esther, and you here alone."

The others had come forward and were now standing in a group around the steps. David stared toward the window of his grandfather's room. Mildred handed the gun to Rutledge, who balanced it atop the ham. She patted Esther and started slowly into the house. "Jesus have mercy," said Ellie Faye, and she whimpered into her dark, cupped hand.

To Esther, David whispered, "Did you pray with him?"

"I was too busy," Esther said, staring straight ahead.

He wondered about the mud on her face and what looked like berry stains across her dress. "You praying now?"

"I'm too tired," she said numbly.

Mildred had left the front door open to the cold night air and they could hear her sobbing in Angus Mackey's room.

David could not think of anything else to tell his sister's ghostly face. Finally, in a strained voice, he said, "You should have gone to the hog killing."

"Yes," was all she said.

By the next evening the coffin had been carefully placed in the parlor on an east-west line, and Sam and Silas sat near it in the growing dark. The silence bothered Sam. Rosa had stopped the mantel clock, its hands marking the time of Angus Mackey's death. Worse, she had turned every mirror and picture in the house to face the wall, and draped everything in the old man's room with sheets.

Sam walked to the fireplace now and squinted into the glass panel of the silent clock, trying to examine by reflection a small boil growing by his nose. He pressed it, almost enjoying the pain.

Without turning, he asked, "Sure you can spare the time to sit up tonight?"

"It's all right," said Silas, who never did have an ear for sarcasm.

The women and children were upstairs. Rosa might even be sleeping—Mildred had given her a strong dose of toothache remedy. Thomas and David were doubtless lying stiff and wakeful, waiting for Grandfather to cough or hit the wall. Esther . . . well, you never could tell about Esther.

Too quiet in here. Sam said, "You sit up when your father died?"

Silas said he had. "We owned a lot of cats."

It was common knowledge cats were drawn to corpses and—if not discovered—would rake their claws under the cold eyelids. Sam, who was already feeling contrary, put no stock in these stories. He marched now to the front door, flung it open and called in a tenor voice, "Here, kitty! Kitty kitty! Here kitty kitty kitty."

"Don't do that," said Silas.

"It's all a damn lie. And they don't suck breath from babies either. Here, kitty!"

From upstairs Mildred called out, "Sam? Sam, what's the matter?"

"Nothing," he called back, slamming the door.

"No need to worry the women," Silas said.

Sam dragged at his chair and perched on it for the tenth time. Without noticing, he had been drawing it farther and farther away all night from Angus Mackey's coffin, until now he sat on the other side of the room, in a circle of lamplight. Silas had not once been on his feet, yet he—too—had scraped and walked his chair across the parlor floor.

Once more Sam got up, this time to fetch whiskey and two glasses from the kitchen. "Don't need to beg you, I reckon," he grunted, passing one filled glass to Silas.

Silas grinned but hesitated. "We oughta say something."

"Merry Christmas," Sam suggested. It was December 17.

Silas shook his head. "Drinking with a dead man . . . oughtn't we say something?"

Sam edged his chair even farther into the light. "Suit yourself," he said, already drinking.

Silas got to his feet and held the glass uneasily toward the casket. He glanced at Sam. "To . . ." he began. "Drink to . . ."

Sam shook his watch to one ear. "Now *this* one's stopped. Won't know the time all night."

In a rush Silas said, "Name of the Father, Son and Holy Ghost, Amen. You forgot to wind it." He sipped, let out a happy sigh.

Sam wound the watch, guessing at the time. "Nobody but you and me to sit up with Angus Mackey, and he never liked either one."

Silas giggled. "Run me off his place with a pitchfork when I was courting Rosa."

"She wasn't but fifteen," said Sam, suddenly thinking of Esther asleep upstairs.

"He never run you off like that."

"It was different with Mildred." Sam didn't want to go into all that. "Rosa's taking this hard. It might set her back."

"It might," said Silas. "Want to play some cards?"

Sam shook his head. Silas turned his wooden chair down on the floor, tipped it so the backrest formed a slope, and padded that with a series of cushions. Then he sat on the rug, located his glass between his legs and reclined against the chair back. "Going to be a long night," he said. "Just because we can't sleep don't mean we can't get comfortable."

The man who fell asleep on a death watch, it was said, would be the next to die. "You are full of tall tales tonight," said Sam. "Next thing I know, you'll have Miss Bethesda out here putting flour on the doorstep so he won't come back from the graveyard." He waited, hoping Silas would tell him about the charm Miss Bethesda had made for Rosa.

But all Silas said was, "Rosa wanted to have that done, but I told her you wouldn't stand for it." He yawned.

Sam stepped to the coffin and peered through the gray veiling which hung from the open lid like a mosquito netting. "Funny thing," said Sam softly, "An hour after a man dies he still looks like himself. Six or seven hours and he quits it." He thought this might be the real death—the slow removal which did not even begin until after the last heartbeat. It was hard to believe this shell of a face had ever let out a swear, or seen that flowerpots became an ambush. Nor could Sam picture that thin line of a mouth ever opened to warn him. . . .

Yet it had, once. In 1874, when Sam had been courting Mildred Mackey half a year, the old man had come to the dry-goods store. "Case you aim to marry my daughter, there's something you ought to know. And if you're not aiming to marry her, I better hear it now."

In that instant Sam decided. He had known her only six months; he did not even remember the young girl who had tended his bruised head the day he came to Greenway. Mildred told him about it; but he never did remember. Now he was twenty-six. There had been women—but not very many and not often enough.

"I'm going to marry her," Sam said to Angus Mackey.

"Then you better get Mildred to tell you about her mama. And her little sister."

That very night Sam had asked about it. Mildred, her face white, paced by the parlor table and at last laid her hand flat on the large Bible. "Mama was a Christian woman," she said, as if she were swearing it in court.

"That's what Mr. Mackey wants you to tell me?"

Mildred slapped the Bible's binding. "She did what it says in here! Papa doesn't, and I don't, and God doesn't ask everybody! If God asked Mama, it's not our business. We're not supposed to understand all His ways."

Sam wanted to know just what it was that God had required of Virginia Grace Collins Mackey.

"You read what it says here in the Bible. Jesus fasted for forty days. John fasted many times. David and Samuel fasted and even put ashes on their heads."

Sam stared at her.

She let out a long sigh. "It's just that Mama fasted a lot. In the name of Jesus. And that's all."

He thought about that. At last he asked, "How much is a lot?"

Mildred was talking rapidly now. "Sometimes she cut herself and offered the pain to Jesus—but all this was private. It was the way she prayed! Just like fasting was the way she worshiped! And all of it private. In church she was just like anybody."

"Cut herself," Sam repeated.

Mildred had begun to pace again. "She'd been fasting six days when she took that last fever. So of course she was weak. And then she wouldn't let me feed her anything—well, the fever was high and she was forgetful. She didn't remember how long she'd been fasting, you understand. She thought she'd just started. So she didn't eat and she didn't take water and finally she died."

Sam jumped to his feet. "Your mama starved herself to death?"

Now Mildred was crying. "It was the fever that killed her—the fever—but she was weaker than usual. I'm trying to explain why she was weak. Maybe God planned it that way. Maybe it was a holy death."

Slowly Sam lowered himself into the chair. "And your sister Rosa?"

"Rosa's not strong. That's all Papa meant. She's ten years old now, and she's outgrowing all that."

"All what? Does Rosa fast and—and cut herself?"

"Of course not." Mildred sounded almost scornful. "She's never been very strong. She used to take sick . . . when she had these spells"—Mildred cleared her throat—"she got stiff. Sometimes she fell down—"

"Rosa has *fits?*"

"Papa had no right to say anything! I said she used to. Now that's over; she doesn't do that anymore. It's just that sometimes she gets quiet and won't move or say anything—but that doesn't happen often. Maybe two three times a year. I know things sometimes run in families, but with Rosa it's run out—and Sam? Sam, I'm fine! I'm healthy! I swear it."

Sam looked glumly at his shoes, thinking that you could never tell about anybody. Look at Ernestine Foxx. . . .

"Papa said you wanted me to marry you."

Still he said nothing.

"Our children will be all right. We'll wait awhile; we won't have any children until you're certain Rosa is growing up and turning out all right. We won't start a family till that's proved to you."

"Wait?" said Sam, frowning.

Mildred stopped her nervous marching and hurried back to the Bible, flipped through its pages and copied out a reference. "Read this later," she said, holding the folded note to him.

When Sam reached for it his hand grazed her hip. He let it rest against her skirt. He thought about how well Mildred could cook, and how she had been keeping house ever since her mother died of whatever it was. He remembered the clean odor she had, soap and starch and vanilla. He said, "I don't care about your family. We've gone together for months and it's you I want to marry. I don't think there's anything to worry about. Let's get married, Mildred. And soon."

Was it his imagination, or did she shift her weight so the curve of her body brushed his palm?

"Yes," she said.

At her answer Sam got to his feet so hastily that he crumpled the Biblical note she had written and thrust it into a pocket, out of his way. He kissed her carefully on one cheek, but his arms were already pulling her firmly against him and he could not help the way his upper body turned left and right to rub himself against her breasts.

Two days later he found the paper while he was looking through his pockets for something else. It said "Genesis 38:9," and Sam carried it across Hobbs Dry Goods Store to the shelf of Bibles and found the verse. The reference was to Onan, son of Judah, who was told to make a woman conceive but disobeyed by spilling his seed onto the ground.

"Damn it to hell," Sam whispered among the Bibles.

In 1874 Sam Allen was married to Mildred Mackey. Rosa—then ten—lived in their home four years while Angus Mackey tended his farm alone. Then, having learned all Mildred could teach her about running a house, Rosa at fourteen went home to care for her father.

By that time, Sam and Mildred had passed through a series of quarrels. Sam had finally balked about Onan's method. Mildred had evaded, grown ill, quilted at night until he was sound asleep, taken overnight visits with the sick in the neighborhood.

Still, he might have got a child out of her the year Rosa went home to live with her father had Silas Bennett not come courting at Angus Mackey's house. It was not long before there were complaints that Rosa was acting queer again. Her father said she was worse than ever.

"It's love, that's all," Sam protested, for he knew Mildred would not soften in his bed if she thought they might produce a child with Rosa's streak of strange behavior.

"Maybe Papa was right," said Mildred, "Maybe there's something that runs in this family in spite of everything you can do."

In 1878, Rosa ran away to marry Silas. Angus Mackey blamed Sam for it. "It's all your fault!" he swore. "Four years she lived in your house and you ruint her! Turned her against her own papa. Got her ready to run off with the first scalawag that asked her!"

In 1881—they had been married seven years—Mildred Allen lost her first baby when it was five months along. Sam had a lot more Scripture shook at him when Esther was born in 1884; they'd been married ten years then.

"What have we done?" said Mildred sadly. "Marrying hasn't helped Rosa. She still has her spells." She read Sam how the sins of the fathers were visited on the third and fourth generations.

But Esther was so pretty and so alert that even Angus Mackey said she was a treasure; no child had ever exceeded her. So Thomas followed in 1885, and David five years later.

And nothing wrong with any of them! Sam thought now, looking into Angus Mackey's coffin. Esther may be flighty and hard to handle, but she'll be all right. Thomas had never given anybody a minute's trouble. David was a little lazy and kept to himself too much, but nothing important.

Turning, Sam found that Silas had helped himself to more of the whiskey and finally fallen asleep leaning back on his upturned chair. His legs sprawled widely on the floor.

I guess that means he'll be the next to die, thought Sam. And though he put no stock in such things, it was still a relief to think he might outlive Silas Bennett, and maybe last long enough to grow rich off Nathan's cotton mill.

He turned back to the coffin. *I wish you could have lived long enough to see me get rich, you old—*

For the first time Sam realized he was going to miss Angus Mackey. In the silent room he felt suddenly lonely and he shook Silas by the shoulder.

"Bad enough sitting with one corpse, much less two!" he said.

Silas said fuzzily he hadn't been asleep at all. "I was lying here thinking." Sam didn't ask him what about.

Chapter

8

WINKLER HOBBS could not attend the funeral.

He was in Boston December 18, 1897, studying diagrams and specifications brought to him from machine shops in Massachusetts and Rhode Island. He was reading over proposals from commissions houses in Baltimore, Philadelphia and New York—all hoping to serve as outlet for the finished goods to be made in a Greenway cotton mill.

Nathan was in court that week, but he left long enough to come to the Presbyterian church and hear Preacher Holt read somberly from the last chapter of Ecclesiastes, about man going to his long home. Miss Tilley dismissed the Academy for the day and all the students, wearing black crepe armbands, sat in a group and sang "When the Roll Is Called Up Yonder," and "Abide with Me."

Nellie looks sadder than I do, Esther thought.

They buried Angus Mackey not thirty feet away from the tomb of Nora Lafferty. The monument, a standard model hand-carved in Stoneville, was a large pair of hearts suitable for husband-wife interments, and now the stonecutter had added sunken inscription letters on the second heart:

ROBERT ANGUS MACKEY

June 4, 1820—Dec. 17, 1897

Safe Into The Haven Guide

The new words looked scraped and raw. In the twin heart alongside, time and weather had already darkened the first inscription:

VIRGINIA GRACE COLLINS MACKEY
Gone To Jesus
1828—1863

From the church the casket was carried to the graveyard in a wagon, but the mourners walked, the preacher leading and the black-garbed family hunched together near the front. Aunt Rosa had the grief-stricken staggers and two of the church elders had to brace her elbows and drive her forward, one wide step at a time. Silas Bennett walked with the children and let the others tend her.

Rosa wanted the casket opened at the grave for one last look, but the others wouldn't hear of it. Preacher Holt caught Rosa's two hands in his own and forced her to fold them together. He held them like that while he made his final prayer about believers being caught up in the air when Jesus came. Then he lifted the first handful of clay and broke it in his fingers and cast it into the grave.

Esther looked back once while the procession was filing out. She knew the two colored men who were shoveling shut the grave—Rutledge was one and Big Jube Jackson, who worked at the dry-goods store, was helping. The cemetery itself felt strange to her, as if she had never been in this place before or seen the shapes of these trees. The two men with their shovels might have been digging potatoes or making fence holes for all she could tell.

I don't think I'll come here anymore, she thought.

Only David Allen had any heart for Christmas that year.

David wanted a knife in the worst way. He would make whistles with it, peel arrows, chip pine knots, scrape his name into fences. He would flip it easily off his wrist till it stood quivering in the earth, skin squirrels, gouge splinters, slice apples and trim pencils. He would cut off his own toenails and save the parings in his pocket. He would open snakebites for sucking, stick hogs, and stab enemies from one end of Stone County to the other.

At the very least, he thought during the funeral, he might get Grandfather's old knife, even if the blade was nicked.

He jerked at his mother's arm outside the graveyard. "What happened to his knife?"

"David, don't bother me now," she said, shaking loose and stuffing a cloth against her mouth.

Nobody understands me but the niggers, David fumed. He ran out of the procession and back to the graveyard and sat on one of the tombstones while Rutledge and Big Jube covered up his grandfather. At sundown, Sam had to come looking for him. And Rosa—wailing that the grief of a child was the purest grief—broke down all over again.

For several weeks, David had been worrying about the ways of white people and the unlikelihood that he would get a knife this Christmas. The two things now were tangled in his mind.

It had begun just before Thanksgiving in the Allen corncrib.

He and Little Jube Jackson, Ellie Faye's six-year-old nephew, were sitting inside the corncrib making the hard ears rumble and settle like stones, riding the avalanche. Little Jube was the only boy near David's age for miles.

"What kind of name is Jube?"

"Jube is Jubilee." He slipped a corn grain into his mouth, showing his large front teeth. "If you ever get lost without water, you slide a rock under your tongue like this. Keeps your spit coming."

There was no accounting for how Jube knew so much. "Jubilee? Is that your daddy's whole name too?" Big Jube was the man who climbed up once a week to wash the front sign at the dry-goods store.

"That's it."

"Funny name," said David.

"When I get grown, my little boy will have that name."

David didn't think that much of it. "What for?"

"My daddy was born right after the slaves got freed and his daddy named him for the Day of Jubilee. Only my daddy says Jubilee Day didn't really come and when he was three years old his daddy carried him into the church and laid him right on the pulpit and swore that name would keep handed down and handed down till it was here."

"That's really something," sighed David. He thought about Samuel being carried off to the Lord's House when he was too little to know better. "Was there a sign? Did the Lord say anything?"

"I reckon not," said Little Jube. He spat out the corn seed.

Waiting for Jubilee. It struck David this might not be much different from waiting for Messiah in the old days, and he asked Jube about that.

"Jesus ain't Jubilee," said Jube. "My daddy say Jesus helps but He don't cure."

"Cure sickness? Of course he cures sickness. Anybody knows that."

"Sickness ain't what my daddy means."

The next time David Allen was in the store he sidled up to Big Jube and whispered, "How you going to know when it's Jubilee Day?"

And Jube, who was big and dark and could make a fist the size of a tree stump, said softly, "We'll both know, boy." It sounded almost like a threat.

"What happens on Jubilee?"

"Joy," said Big Jube.

"A party?"

Jube nodded. "Singing. Laughing. Like a party."

"What if they have Jubilee and nobody comes?"

Jube made one of his famous wide fists and struck himself lightly in the head as if he had never thought of such a thing. "That," said Big Jube, "would be pitiful."

David thought about it. He pictured people marching off to Jubilee as if it were a place, a Canaan or Jerusalem; and they walked all in pairs the way Noah had taken life into the ark—Big Jube with Little Jube, and Mother and Father, and Esther and Thomas, and Rosa and Silas—With a caught breath, David said, "Have you got to go to Jubilee two by two?"

"Nawsir." Jube grinned. "You go all by all. How's that?"

All by all, David marveled. He thought that was the prettiest thing he ever heard.

Around Thanksgiving, David took to hanging around Ellie Faye in the kitchen until she nearly lost her sense.

"It's not so cold outside. You go and play."

"I'd rather sit and look at you." In this house, he was thinking, things seemed to break down two by two and he was always left out. Thomas, right now, was with Father at the store. Mama and Esther were sewing on a dress. Grandfather was extra, but he slept so much. Yessir, at Jubilee he was going to walk right beside Ellie Faye if there was any dividing up at all.

Ellie Faye plucked nervously at her apron. "Don't watch me, boy."

"Ellie Faye, hold out your arm. I want to touch your arm."

She put it forth cautiously. "Arms is arms."

David had thought somehow the skin might tickle his fingertips like velvet. Or even be slightly slick, like the nose of a calf. But it was just an arm, and he took his finger back and rubbed his own arm.

"Ellie Faye, tell me what you do when you go home from here."

Ellie Faye sighed. "Wash clothes. Cook supper. Sweep floors. What you think I do?"

"Ellie, if you shaved off your head, would it grow back like that?"

She was alarmed. "Who's going to shave my head?"

"Your head is like moss," he said.

She put a wary hand up there to see if that was true.

"Ellie Faye, tell me about your children."

She pronounced it "chu-run." Her chu-run, she said, was Gabriella, and Tildy, Mary Sue, Robert Paul, Sarah Anne and Halliburton.

I'll walk with them, thought David happily, and it'll be crowded. "None of yours named Jubilee?"

"That's my brother's family. You know all that. And tomorrow I'm sure going to bring Little Jube with me to give you something to do. You are in my way."

"You beat your children, Ellie Faye?"

"They need it, I beat 'em. Sure. Is that what's ailing you? You get a beating?"

Shaking his head, he began to walk around the kitchen, getting under her feet. "Ellie Faye, you like to work?"

"Nobody asked me what I liked."

"I'm asking you. You like it?"

"I like to eat," she said. "You must not like it much, from the looks of that woodbox."

He carried in a load of stovewood just to obligate her, so she would have to talk to him.

"What your children want for Christmas? What's Gabriella want?"

"She want a big, pretty doll." Ellie Faye's voice dropped and she looked out the kitchen window. David got up to see what was there but it was only the same twisted apple tree, dead since September.

"And Halliburton?"

"Oh, Halliburton's little. A sling shot will do him." Ellie Faye began trimming the edge around her pie pan. Lacy ropes of dough fell curving onto the board. David lifted one and drooped it worm fashion into his mouth.

"Raw dough makes your insides stick together."

"What you all do at Christmas?"

She thought a minute. "We might have firecrackers. There'll be a jug maybe. I speck Pless will sing—"

"A Christmas party! You're going to have a party!"

She made a horse's noise in her nostrils.

"At home, Mama reads St. Luke. We never have firecrackers."

Ellie Faye pointed out he might have raisin cake, a Christmas tree, perhaps even a real orange. David looked these over in his mind. And he could see, too, how those three stockings would be hung on Christmas Eve. Thomas and Esther would have their stockings side by side, hanging down the same length, and his own stubby one would be alone off to one side.

"I want a knife," he said grimly. A knife would just fit inside his stocking. And its handle would be bone—bone from a—a buffalo's head. From an eagle's breast. The rib of a tiger. He'd even take Grandfather's knife if that was the best there was.

"Maybe you will," said Ellie Faye.

And when he took that knife from his stocking Christmas morning, he would run straight to the woods and wherever he found two things growing he would cut one down. David chopped his arm cruelly into the moist air of the kitchen.

"Mind what you're doing!"

That's what he would do with his fine, bone-handled Christmas knife!

And soon every tree in the county would bear his initials—D.A., he would carve in their trunks, D.A., da-da-da. . . . The letters babbled baby fashion in his mind and embarrassed him. Very well, he would scratch out his whole name instead, even if that took longer —DAVID ALLEN. He dug into space, gouging the letters on a shaft of pale sunlight coming through the window.

"People want lots of things never come true," warned Ellie Faye.

"This knife is coming true."

She said nothing.

"It is! It is! I'll bring it all the way to your house to show you the day after Christmas!"

She slid the pie inside the stove but she never said a word.

"And I'll show it to Tildy, and Gabriella, and Mary Sue. And Robert Paul and that other girl and Hallibut."

"Halibut is fish. Halli*burton*," she said scornfully. Then she laughed. Now that he thought of it, Ellie Faye was always doing that —she'd fuss and smile. David wondered if this happened whenever she beat her children, this softening of a blow while it was already coming down.

I like the way she does that! I'd like to know how to do that!

All the time from that day to Christmas he looked for other things to like in Ellie Faye, and in Big Jube and Little Jube, and Rutledge and deaf old Cabiliah Henderson. It seemed to David only colored people treated him right.

"How you today?" they'd say to him softly on the street. Catch his father saying something that polite to a boy just seven years old!

Or, "Cold enough for you?" Had Thomas ever cared?

And David knew in his heart that if he got no knife on Christmas, he was going to run off to the niggers, where all his life he would be asked how he was feeling and if he thought it was apt to snow. And there he would help pop off the firecrackers, or sing with Pless and his guitar, and it would be Jubilee. They would be all together, and Christmas would be Jubilee.

Then Angus Mackey died. It happened on the very day David had seen new marvels committed with a knife blade. All the way riding home from Nathan's hog killing, he talked about his need for a pocket knife. Had Mama seen how easy they slit the skin of that hog? Took out the spare ribs? Cut off the side meat?

"I never meant to be so late," was all his mother said. "I don't like Esther there by herself past dark."

"I could look after Esther if I had a knife," he babbled. "I could fight people off. I could snap off her sewing thread so she'd never use her teeth."

"A little faster, Rutledge," Mildred said.

"Rutledge, you think I'll get a knife for Christmas?"

Rutledge grinned. "Can't never tell about that," he said.

Now it was Christmas Eve, and David still couldn't tell.

He asked Thomas. Thomas said Father was investing some money in a cotton mill and there might not be much of a Christmas this year. "And the casket—that cost money," Thomas said.

David wanted to talk about knives, not money. He asked Esther what she thought his chances were.

"You've got to understand everybody feels bad about Grandfather," she said gently. "It doesn't seem much like Christmas."

On Christmas Eve, David sat by the front window with one cheek flattened against the cold glass. The stars were so thick in the sky they looked as if they had been spread on with a knife.

There was that knife again.

Esther called to him. "Come help with the tree."

Thomas was stringing holly berries. "You can't get David to do any work."

Yes you could, thought David, You just don't ask me right.

Mildred came from the kitchen to examine the cedar they had hung with popcorn and berries and sweet-gum balls rolled in sugar grains. Even her skirts were aromatic, from the baking; when they billowed and swung, there rose odors of cinnamon, ginger, clove, nutmeg, brown sugar.

"David, why aren't you helping?" she began briskly.

He knew how to distract his mother. "There's the biggest star up there. Like Bethlehem."

"Let me see." She stooped beside him and the spice swelled his lungs. He looked at her sideways. Her cheeks were raw where Ellie Faye's were toasted. Ellie Faye had been warmed up and turned brown.

Mildred tapped one finger on the glass. "I see the one you mean. There. Over the pine."

David nodded absently.

"The wise men traveled a long way watching a star like that. And the shepherds—"

"Mother, am I going to get a knife?"

She was jolted down from Heaven. "Christmas," she said coldly, "isn't just for getting."

"But am I?"

"Perhaps when you're old enough."

"I'm old!" he cried, and when she did not answer he blurted that he was every bit as old as Thomas.

"David, don't lie."

"I am! As old as Thomas! I'm just as big! I'm as good as Thomas is!"

"Boys who lie get nothing but stones and ashes in their Christmas stockings." Mildred swept off, stirring the air about her into a whirlwind of tangy smells. David put his forehead against the window as if he might press through it into darkness. Stones and ashes. Maybe he should go, right now, down the road in the dark and under that starry pine to Little Jube's cabin, where, he was sure, guitars were being strummed.

Esther's hand fell lightly on his shoulder. "Come look at the Christmas tree," she said. "It's right pretty." She patted him once.

He shook away from her just as—it seemed to him—the distant pine jostled its needles in the wind to dislodge its sticky star. Esther, hurt, drew back. And the star drifted slightly westward in the night, leaving the tree dark from tip to root. Dark.

"David's always pouting," said Thomas sensibly. "Just let him pout."

"I don't," he said.

"You'll never be old as I am."

"That's one good thing," growled David.

He was the first one downstairs on Christmas morning.

He was in such a hurry that he caught his bare toe on the first step and had to grab at the banister to stop his fall. He thought his elbow was coming out of its socket.

He still had hope when he saw the bulging stocking. Something long was in it, something slender, something with a handle.

"Oh, glory!" he yelled at the top of his lungs, grabbing so hard that he tore the stocking on the nail. He sat on the floor and poured it out between his legs. Then, disbelieving, shook it and ran his hand inside and poked out the heel and toe.

There was only a slingshot—like Halliburton's, he thought. And one spinning top with a silver rim. There was also a small metal bank in the shape of a soldier, into which he could put all the money he didn't earn by not being Thomas and not working at the store.

Esther was careful not to look at him. For Christmas she had got a set of paints and brushes, suitable for decorating china plates, and some ribbons and hair combs and a necklace of jet and amber beads.

Even the paints would have been better. If David had paints, he might draw sad faces onto onions, or paint the edges of all their windows blue—to keep out evil spirits, as Little Jube said. If he had been given Esther's paints he could have covered over his own skin until it grew rich and brown and gleaming.

But David had barely turned his bitter face aside from Esther's gifts when he saw the knife.

Thomas had got a knife. A huge knife, a grand knife, a knife for men. Its handle glistened with strength, like a jawbone some Samson might use to slash through armies. And when it was open, light lay lovingly along the blade. The glow from its edge struck David in both eyes and started tears.

Esther whispered to him. "What's the matter, David?"

"Slingshot flew back in my eye." I bet I don't tell the truth one day a week.

His mother was smoothing with one finger the lace collar Aunt Rosa had tatted for her Sunday dress. And Thomas, silent, pressed the sharp blade into the pad of one finger. David could feel it. He stuck his own finger into his mouth and sucked.

"Try out the top for us, David," his mother said.

Oh, he tried to be silent. He choked back the stone which lay so solidly behind his tongue, but it came rolling out along a string of broken words.

"You already had a knife! It isn't fair! It isn't fair, you already had one."

"David?" His father came to stand above him. He was folding a new neck scarf longways in his hands until it looked like a rope, or a whip.

I must keep quiet, David thought, and instantly he screamed, "That's why you got Thomas a knife! You knew I wanted one! You always know what I want and you never do! You never do!"

Mildred now put down the collar and rose from her own chair. "What's all this? Do what?"

Sam Allen said in a cold voice, "David, I'm ashamed of you. Now that's enough."

"It isn't fair!" David threw the useless metal bank and the head broke off its shoulders as cleanly as if it had been cut with Thomas' marvelous knife. It rolled away on the floor. Goliath's head must have toppled that way for some luckier David, he thought, and threw down the slingshot too.

"This is no way to act on Christmas Day," his mother said.

"You're to go upstairs and stay there all day and eat cold cornbread while the rest of us are having Christmas dinner." His father sounded very angry.

Esther, almost to herself, breathed, "Ah, David." And Thomas said David could have his other knife, the little one. "I planned to give it to you anyway. It can be a Christmas present."

"I wouldn't have it!" David yelled. "I wouldn't cut butter with your old knife! I wouldn't scrape off my shoes!" To his father, "And I don't want any dinner! I wouldn't eat one bite of it!"

Sam thundered his name again but David was running from the room and up the stairs. He heard his mother say wearily, "It's impossible to please that boy."

It's not, he told the quilts and mattress underneath his face. It's not. It's not impossible. It's not.

It was early morning but still dark.

Thomas, fat with food and the ownership of knives, slept like a pig. David eased his feet carefully onto the cold floor, never taking his eyes from his brother's sleeping face.

Sleep with your mouth open like that, a spider might crawl in, he thought.

He dressed as quietly as he could, wadded some extra underwear into a roll and bound it with his knotted string—the one he used to measure trees.

The new knife lay on a table by the bed. David thought about taking it with him. Then he decided: No. They'd expect me to do that.

He did have an aching desire to touch the dappled handle only once, to run one finger down that length, but if he couldn't steal it, he mustn't touch it either. So he only looked at it, letting his eye run along one side and then return.

He made his bed (They always say I'm lazy), and on the counterpane arranged neatly all the gifts he had received for Christmas, so they would know he rejected them all. He hesitated longest with the soldier bank, not liking its broken look. Finally he placed the body alongside the slingshot and the spinning top, and rested the broken head on the table next to his brother's knife. That should be clear enough.

He climbed over the windowsill, slithered down the sloping porch roof and into the chinaberry tree. Chainy-berries, Little Jube called them, because his sisters strung them into chains and wore them round their necks till the stink got bad.

I could sit in this chainy-berry tree all day. They'd walk around under me calling, "David! David!" And I wouldn't move. I wouldn't let out a rattle. I'd just listen to them.

Once he was outside the fence, David wanted to let out a yell that would shake creation, but he was afraid they could still hear him and would sit upright in all their beds.

Not yet.

He started to run, hoping to warm his tingling feet. The cold wind seemed to break in the center of his face and slide by icily on either side. As if my nose were a knife, cutting the wind. As if I were a fine long knife with a handle of bull's horn and a blade to stay honed forever.

When he thought he had run far enough, David stopped and climbed up the bank alongside the road. Little sticks of frost which sprang up at night like forests of tiny white trees were crunching under his feet. He looked back at the house.

David yelled. He yelled back at all the Allens, paired off by his departure and evened up. At Mother and Father, at Esther and Thomas where they lay so neatly in their beds. He yelled no word, no name—just a roar which started at his navel and swelled up until every vessel along his throat had turned to wire and his face burned from the heat of that exploding voice. Steam floated from his mouth.

Still they slept on. David jogged ahead, out of breath from his great noise.

He passed a row of black and silent shacks. Colored people live there, he thought.

It was like a song. Colored People Live There!

He broke out laughing. A thin dog came out from under one house to watch him going by.

Far off he heard a little trumpet sound. That's a nigger rooster! thought David, and he went on running and laughing.

Under a barbed-wire fence he went, across a field still lumpy from last year's furrows. Ahead of him ran a narrow westward road with three houses along it. David could see the third one, where Little Jube lived. The road itself ran all the way to the Katsewa River and gave way to footpaths which stopped at the doorstep of Miss Bethesda Lee Michael, who could catch fish with pieces of red flannel on her hook. In front of one yard a crooked sign still said dimly: WORMS. CRICKETS. MINNERS.

David began to run to Little Jube's house.

At the edge of its bare yard he stopped and stared. The porch was empty, the house still. Only a trickle of smoke oozed slowly from the chimney.

I thought they'd all be out here waiting for me. I thought when I came down the road, Little Jube would begin to shout. I thought Ellie Faye would be over here frying my breakfast.

He almost tiptoed into the yard. Maybe they'd given him up. Slowly he walked to the slanting front steps and sat on the bottom one. It was still early.

David slid both hands into his armpits. He was cold.

Behind him Little Jube's mother opened the door. "Who's out there?" she said.

He didn't turn, knowing they might want time to get the celebration lined up in the doorway. "Good morning, Vinnie." He looked thoughtfully into the gray sky.

She came out, bending around and forward to see his face. She was wrapped in an old quilt and bits of stuffing fell from her like handfuls of snow. Her feet were bare.

"Your feet'll get cold."

She was frowning. "Is that the Allen boy? The little one? Mr. Sam's boy?"

"My name is David."

She stood there, indecisive, and made some careful adjustments to the folds of the quilt. "Mighty early," she ventured, and eyed him. When he did not answer, she clutched the quilt tighter and came a little closer. "Think I'll sit down."

"It's your steps."

She sat. She cleared out her throat. "What you doing here? Come to see Little Jube?"

"That's right."

"He's not up yet."

"I'll wait on him."

Vinnie caught a thread from the quilt, pulled it out and began to wind it on a finger. "Hope ya'll had a good Christmas?"

At last David turned his head. He gave her one long and bleak stare, then looked again into the horizon.

"It sure is early," she said again. She had folded her feet under her as she sat; now she took one out and held it tightly in her hand. David tried not to stare, although it was nearly as big as his father's foot. The sole was tan and pink except for a peppering of sand and splinters. Vinnie said her feet were about to freeze right off. "I'll go on in."

"Go on," he said.

She stood, frowning down at him. "I'll tell Little Jube you're here."

David said soberly, "Merry Christmas, Vinnie."

She stopped to think that over. "Sure," she agreed, and went inside the house.

In no time, the window behind him was full of grinning faces. One of the boys took the cardboard from two frames to see better. Jube mashed his face against the remaining glass. Looks like a toad, thought David. And what were they laughing at? He heard the deep voice of Big Jube and the giggling stopped.

Now the house behind him was full of movement. Under his rump, the board on which he sat vibrated sharply. Vinnie's big feet must be stamping the inner floors.

It was not Little Jube who came out next but his father, yelling back over one shoulder, "And I mean fast."

"Good morning!" he said hastily to David. He showed his teeth. "Trust you feelin' well?"

"Where's Little Jube?"

"He'll be out when he eats his mush. You off on a trip?"

David said yes. In a way.

Jube looked uneasy. "Not going down to the river in this weather!"

"How much has he got to eat?"

"He'll be right along. How's Mr. Sam and your mama? Everybody at your house getting up mighty early the day after Christmas."

"They're still asleep."

Without moving, Big Jube raised his voice to a roar. "Vinnie! Is Jacob doing what I said?"

"He's doing it!"

Now Big Jube seemed to relax. "You mad at your mama and daddy?"

"What for?" David began to walk around on the porch, sometimes holding a post and swinging out over the yard. He was very cold.

"It's just no weather to be going down to the Katsewa River. Even the fish ain't home." Jube laughed but David did not. "Even Miss

Bethesda Lee Michael has hauled up her porch ladder and stopped counting on company till it thaws."

"I ain't going to see *her*," said David, but now that her name had been mentioned he gave it some thought. It didn't look as if Jube understood why he was here, or Vinnie, and maybe not even Ellie Faye. "You got a knife, Big Jube?"

"Sure I have."

David swung out and around the edge and onto the porch again. They could have asked him to come inside. He was about to freeze.

"Why don't you tell me what it is you want with Little Jube so early in the morning?"

"I've quit telling people what I want." David sighed. If I go round this post another time, I'll be sick, he thought. "Could I have some breakfast?"

"You want mush?"

"Anything." At last he would be called in by the hearth. He would be able to explain things better then, while it was warm and the firelight was hitting their faces.

"I'll get it."

Big Jube was inside a long time. He came back carrying a chipped dish of cornmeal mush with a central lake of molasses and one tablespoon. Steam rose from the bowl, but the first bite David took was already lukewarm and hard in his throat. He smiled and nodded, and kept spooning up mush and sorghum until they flowed to the back of his tongue and formed a dam, larger and larger. He tried to swallow the mass in small sections so Jube would not notice.

"You musta been hungry," said Jube. David could only nod.

They sat together in what David felt was companionship, Jube staring up the road, David swallowing so hard his eyes were smarting. He could hear his heart. No. That was no heartbeat.

He sat straighter. Jube, too, had grown alert and now peered more closely up that road. It seemed to David the mush had muffled his voice. "What's that?" He cleared his throat. "Jube, what's that I hear?"

"Eat your mush, child."

David put his bowl on the porch and rose to his feet. "I hear it," he whispered. He shook Jube's sleeve. "I hear it coming."

"Little Jube's getting his britches on right now," said Jube absently, straining forward to the sound.

Away up the road came a bouncing blur, and the thudding sounds were not heart but hoofs. David could not believe it.

"Is that a horse?"

"Can't never tell," said Big Jube, just the way Rutledge had answered him when he asked about the knife.

"You sent for my father," he breathed. "You sent Jacob to tell him I was here." He backed away and when his foot hit the bowl of mush he kicked it furiously into the yard.

"*You sent for my father!*" he screamed, and pulled away from Big Jube's hand, jumped off the porch and hit the ground, running down the road toward the Katsewa River.

Jube was calling something. Then David could only hear the pounding—his feet, his pulse, the coming of his father's mare down the road behind him. He ran, hopelessly, the way one runs in dreams.

"Stop where you are, David," called his father.

At that he lowered his head and floundered off the road and tried to go straight through a dry blackberry thicket. The next minute he thought the mare had kicked him skyward. He was flung out and up for what seemed like a vast distance, and then laid heavily over the mare like a sack of meal, or a corpse being carried off the battlefield.

David lay panting where his father had scooped him up and put him. He felt the mare slow and turn, then gallop along the road toward home.

Sam Allen did not speak. David closed his eyes and prayed to die there, folded over that saddle, so he might really be delivered home a casualty. But of course he did not die, merely bounced along, the blood rushing and singing in his head, tears sliding from his eyes and into his brows and hair and at last in slow streaks onto the heaving mare.

Chapter
❧ 9 ❧

ESTHER ROLLED AROUND in bed for the hundredth time, looking for the one spot which was warm and comfortable. No use. It wasn't there.

When I was little, she thought, I didn't just fall asleep; I got into bed and sleep came falling down on me. She felt sad for those lost, black nights. In fact, she was often sad of late, and sometimes she wondered if it were possible to be homesick two ways at once: for her little-girl days and grown-woman days. Any days but the ones I'm having now.

She sat upright and listened. It was a squirrel she heard or maybe a mouse, eating its way in and out the walls.

She had lain down and started to play a word game to put herself to sleep when the distant mouse began raising a window in the next room. Esther rolled quickly out of bed and crawled on her hands and knees to her own window. She could see nothing on the porch roof but a shadow of a chinaberry limb.

Then the widest part of the shadow moved. Esther watched it inch its way toward her. When it flattened itself against the edge of her window, she yanked up the pane as fast as she could and popped her head out. "What you doing?" she said in a loud whisper.

David nearly fell off the roof. He dropped to his hands and knees and scrabbled frantically at the shingles.

Esther leaned farther out. "I said what are you doing?"

He flapped his hand at her: Back. Go back. She put the stick under the window and sat round-shouldered in it, dangling her feet into the cold night air. "You might as well come in here and tell me," she said, "because if you don't I'm going to yell. I'm going to yell so loud Cabiliah Henderson will hear it on the other side of the county."

He made hand movements. She backed inside again and waited until he had crawled across the sill. Together they put the window down.

David made himself small. He leaned against the wall and let his head hang down.

"Well, say something."

He didn't.

Esther let out a gusty sigh. "You're going to do it again? Just last week you got that bad whipping, and you're running away again tonight?"

"It looked like a good time," he mumbled.

She knew why that was; Thomas was at the dry-goods store helping count stock after Christmas, and both he and their father would sleep in town tonight. "What is it at Little Jube's house that's worth two whippings?"

"I ain't going there."

"Where then? Come on. I won't tell."

He said it grudgingly. "Ellie Faye's maybe. Maybe even Miss Bethesda Lee Michael's. Someplace."

"What have they got that's worth two whippings?"

He flopped his shoulders. He did not even know.

"It's better than lying here awake all night," she said after a minute's thought. "Turn your back."

"What for?"

Esther said she wasn't about to go tracking off to Ellie Faye's in nothing but a flannel nightgown. "Turn your back."

"You can't go! You can't go with me!"

"Go get me some clothes out of Thomas' drawer," she ordered, and when he continued to stand with his mouth open, she peeled off the gown to a camisole and long drawers. He saw it was no good arguing. Out the window he went again, took pants and a shirt from the bureau, and crossed the roof to her room. He hung them in the window.

After she had dressed, Esther wound her long plait around her head in a coil and stuffed it under a woolen cap. David leaned in to watch. "You look like a boy."

"I'm supposed to." She climbed out beside him. "Ease down this window. We'll be back before anyone knows we're gone."

"I'm not coming back."

Esther put her hand on his shoulder. "You'd let your own sister walk home in the dark by herself? In spite of the Ghost?"

The Ghost lay in wait along all Stone County roads between white houses and colored houses. It was because of the Ghost that colored help could not be asked to work after sundown, when they might meet Him walking home.

David said doubtfully he might walk Esther back at least, just to see she was safe. "But I'm not coming. You understand that. I might see you back, no more."

"That's good enough," said Esther, and swung out behind him into the moon-flecked tree.

When they hit the ground, David said, "Run," and set off head-long between the gateposts and down the dusty road. There was nothing for Esther to do but come pounding after him. She ran as fast as she could. Her young breasts bounced against her ribs and after a while she took both hands and cupped them there. She had a feeling they might fall, the way a cake will collapse in the oven.

When David slowed, she panted up behind him and grabbed his arm. "Enough of that," she wheezed.

He scowled. "I told you not to come."

All the way between the Allen house and Ellie Faye's, Esther was slapped by briers which never even grew there in the daytime. Her jump over one ditch was short, so the edge fell in upon her and she rolled to the bottom and tangled her foot in honeysuckle, brown now, and tough as wire.

She was puffing. "Let's go ask Miss Bethesda Lee Michael what kind of fool would run across the countryside in the middle of the night."

"You're slowing me down," said David.

At Ellie Faye's they crouched behind a small woodshed. Along the porch of the cabin, gnarled tubes up one side showed where wisteria would be blooming in the spring. There were hens roosting in the low branches of one tree; these had already flown off and clattered their wings in the air and nearly scared Esther to death.

She sat on the ground and leaned back against the woodshed and caught her breath. "We're here," she said. "Now what?"

David said he couldn't see a thing. "There's a lamp lit, but I don't see anybody."

She didn't even look. "I don't know what you expected."

"You hear any singing?"

"Not a song."

He sat beside her and said he didn't know what to think. "You'd think there'd be some singing."

Esther yawned.

"I've been watching them," David went on. "Colored people are nicer than we are. They're softer."

Esther nodded. "They're hungrier too. They sleep under newspapers in the wintertime. The only meat they get is catfish and possum. They don't go to school."

"That's right," he said in approval. "No school. And they live longer and have more children. And sing better." He stood up and took another look at Ellie Faye's cabin. "I see somebody now. What's her husband's name?"

"Feimster."

"I see Feimster walking around and walking around."

"Well," said Esther drowsily, "that was surely worth coming all this way to see. That is the finest thing I ever heard."

"And all the time they say something nice to me. Big Jube does, and Ellie Faye and Rutledge."

"That's because you're white," said Esther. "It's got nothing to do with you."

He was so angry he leaned down and hit her in the shoulder. "Don't you say that."

"All right. What's he doing now?" Esther got up beside him, rubbing her shoulder, and took a look around the woodshed at the lighted window. Ellie Faye, her eyes closed, was leaning against the far wall of the room. Feimster was walking back and forth in front of her just the way David said.

"Is Ellie Faye saying prayers?"

"I don't think so," said Esther. Both of them jumped when

Feimster began to make a rhythmic singsong noise. He waved his arm as he marched through the lighted space and back again. Ellie Faye did not move or open her eyes.

"The singing's started!" crowed David. "Let's go inside. It's a party."

"It's not a party," Esther said.

"I want to go in and sing too."

"No," she said. "Wait."

Inside, Ellie Faye had begun slowly to shake her head from side to side. She looked at Feimster. She spoke a word.

"I told you not to come with me," David hissed.

"Be still," said Esther.

Feimster poured out of a fruit jar into a cup, held his nose and took a quick gulp.

David knew all about that. "I bet that's medicine. Ellie Faye says her husband has the aggravates. Worst on Saturday nights, she says."

"It's not medicine."

David watched Feimster fill the cup a second time. "It sure must stink," he said.

"Drag over that chopping block so I can see better," said Esther.

Muttering, David worked the heavy chunk of wood by rocking it from side to side until it was at the corner of the woodshed and Esther could stand on it. "If we're not going inside, we might as well go home."

Feimster eased the cup to his other hand. Ellie Faye had closed her eyes again and he began to reach toward her slowly through the air. He had stopped singing. Suddenly his hand leaped the remaining space and fastened on her wrist. Her eyes flew open. Now they could hear her.

"No!" she yelled. "No! I already told you, no!"

"There," said Esther, turning to look down at him from the chopping block. "Seems to me they fuss as much as white people."

"Who's that?" said David.

A little boy—maybe Halliburton—appeared in the space they could see through the window. Feimster picked him up and carried him someplace, probably out of the room. Yes, a door banged. Out of the room. They could not see Feimster for a while.

Ellie Faye was pointing at the place where the boy had been, still shaking her head. "I don't want no baby!" she yelled once or twice, and said some other things they could not hear.

Feimster loomed up and hit her on the side of the face.

Softly Esther said, "We better go home." She didn't move.

"He can't hit Ellie Faye!"

Feimster grabbed Ellie Faye by the shoulders and shook her. She had her eyes shut again. When he stopped shaking, she seemed to be loose and limp against the wall. He touched the back of his fingers to the spot where he had struck her. Then he turned his hand over and rubbed it there, around and around.

"We ought to go," whispered Esther, staring.

Feimster let his hand come down to her throat.

David started forward. "He's going to choke her!"

"Hush up," said Esther, and held him back.

The hand came farther down and he eased it around Ellie Faye's waist. Now Ellie Faye opened her eyes and stared out over her husband's shoulder in such a fixed way that Esther thought for a minute she had seen them there, behind the woodshed. Feimster leaned into her.

Then, very slowly, Ellie Faye raised a broad hand and laid it on the back of his head, spreading the fingers wide. She pulled back slightly, at least her shoulders pulled back, and yet the man and the woman seemed to draw closer together.

"I can't see so good now," David complained.

The two inside the room had turned slightly, and Esther could see clearly when Feimster pulled down the front of Ellie Faye's dress just far enough until one breast rose up and toppled forth. It was full and round, but suspended strangely from her open collar, so that it seemed to be growing from near the center. Feimster took the palm of his right hand and rotated it lightly on the tip. Watching them, Esther clutched at herself through her brother's shirt. She could not get hold of half a handful.

Then Feimster slipped both hands up under the breast and raised it until Ellie Faye seemed to be going up on her toes, and he crouched and fixed his mouth onto the nipple. Against the dark skin, his dark fingers were kneading and drawing.

Ellie Faye touched his shoulders, then his neck, and at last the back of his head, which she pulled tightly to her. Something soft was said. They moved out of the lamplight and into the corner of the room.

Esther rose up taller on the chopping block. "Now I can't see," she grumbled.

David was angry. "He hit Ellie Faye. First he hit her and then he bit her with his teeth."

"There's a bed over there," said Esther.

"She should have hit him back. I'm going to hit Feimster for Ellie Faye."

"No you're not," she said absently. She strained upward. "I can see them. When they move, I can see them."

Without a chopping block to stand on, David was not tall enough to see anything. He began to fidget and feel cold. "Is the party over?"

Esther, peering into the shadows of the room, did not answer.

"I said, is the party over?"

"I guess," she snapped.

"It never even got started." He was disgusted with them all. "We might as well go home."

"In a minute," Esther said.

David kicked at a tree root. "I thought it would be happy. I thought all of them would be happy."

"Maybe they are."

"I didn't know he'd hit her."

"Lots you don't know."

He yanked at her. "Esther, let's go."

"In a minute, I said. You wait right here."

"Where you going?"

"Just you wait here." She stepped down carefully, trying not to rustle the wood chips. "Move this block back where you found it."

Complaining, he began to tussle with the heavy chopping block.

Esther ran lightly across the yard to the window, crouched below it, then eased up to eye level. At first she could not get located in the room. Then she saw Ellie Faye lying on her back on a sagging bed. Her dress, which buttoned all the way down, had been opened and laid back like a set of double doors. For some reason, Esther thought about Grandfather's shirt and how she had cut it away from him on both sides. Esther ran her eye thoughtfully along Ellie Faye, comparing that body to her own.

Then Feimster, wearing only his blue shirt, came around from the foot of the bed and sat on its edge. The footboard was of metal in an ornate if rusty design. It was like watching through the mesh of a kitchen strainer. Feimster sat on the edge and leaned forward slightly, as if to look in his wife's face. Esther could not see where he was putting his hands. He got up on his knees beside Ellie Faye.

When David tapped her lightly between the shoulder blades, Esther was so shocked that she threw herself backward from the window. The fall knocked all the breath from under her ribs and, for an instant, she saw the starry sky swirl and come down for her like a cyclone of fire. Her chest was an empty eggshell before she sucked in a desperate mouthful of air and pain.

She crawled away after David to the woodshed. In its shadow she blinked back the tears. "I ought to kill you," she gasped. "I ought to kill you right here."

"I got cold," he said. "Are you hurt?"

She took in a few more ragged breaths. "I won't even answer that."

Someone turned down the lamp inside the cabin. It faded, flickered once, and the window went dark.

"See there? I told you it was over," said David. "We might as well go home."

She got painfully to her feet. "I thought you were going to move in with Ellie Faye."

"Come on."

In silence they crossed the field, stepped on barbwire to hold it down while they straddled across, and began the slow walk home.

"At least Father doesn't hit Mama," David said finally. He whirled around to keep himself warm. He did a few hops and skips. "I thought it would be happy."

"Maybe it is," said Esther.

"How come you're so quiet? You mad? I didn't mean to make you fall down like that."

"I'm thinking," Esther said.

A dog went by them in the far ditch, growling. She thought it might be Feimster's dog, who should have been home biting strangers all this time.

"I sure never did see anything like tonight," said David. "I never expected that. Did you?"

When they were at a safe distance, the dog sat down in the road and barked.

"Esther, did you? They really are different from us, but I don't know all the ways yet. Really different. You think so?"

"I wonder," Esther said.

"You got the back of that shirt dirty. I don't know what Thomas will think." He brushed at it. "I guess I really surprised you, coming up behind you at that window."

"David," said Esther, "lately I've been having one surprise right after the other."

When the heaviest of the spring rains were over late in April, they broke ground on Nathan's land to the west of town, along the Katsewa River, for Greenway Manufacturing Company.

A steam-operated mill with 5,600 ring spindles, it was to make brown sheetings, shirtings and drills; and capital stock had been set at $100,000. Much of this sum still existed only in pledges covered by advances from the Bank of Greenway and a nervous Lloyd Morrison, who couldn't help feeling farm loans at high interest were a better investment.

Mr. Morrison went every morning to the site and looked sternly into the red clay as if he might find predictions written there. He walked the length and width of the projected walls and stared skyward, inspecting the future roof. If a beaver appeared at the water's edge he heaved a clod at it angrily, for in its presence he saw the threat—how the mill would fail and the river would rise up and cover it, and vines would creep over the foundations and choke out the railroad spur with fox grapes. Every buzzard flapping overhead was a blot on his hopes.

The day before Nathan officially lifted the first spade of earth, the Yankee came to town. The machinery people in New England had sent him. "To help you get started," their representative said politely; and although Winkler Hobbs raised his voice and poured more bourbon and shook his head until it seemed about to fall off and roll away, the northerners had their way.

The Yankee would oversee construction and installing of machinery, would advise on standard housing for the workers, would hire and train and manage the mill for at least a year—his salary paid by Greenway investors.

"At the end of that time, you may feel like promoting some local man to management," said the machinery salesman to Mr. Hobbs in a soothing voice. "But so long as your terms with us amount to credit on your part and a calculated risk on ours, you understand our position."

Nathan didn't like it, paying a high wage to a stranger none of them had chosen. "And starting now, before the mill even exists, while all our money is going out and there isn't a cent of profit. Raises our costs beyond reason!"

Hobbs played the jury-word trick back on Nathan. "Reason? You talk about reason? Just use your reason a minute and you'll see why we need this man. Who here can do what the Yankee can do? Can you? Can I? How many mills has John Lucas built or any of those fools working for him he calls carpenters? Do you know how far apart machinery ought to be set, or how to operate it? Do you know how many people we need to handle each stage of the manufacture? Does Sam Allen? Does Dr. Newton? Lloyd Morrison?"

"I know I don't," drawled Sam. "But neither do I know enough to judge what the man does, whether it's good or poor. What if he's a ruffian or an idiot? Seems to me from that paper you signed, we have to keep him on and like it."

"If you read carefully," said Hobbs with sarcasm, "you'll see that if he doesn't suit us we can appeal to the foundry. I told you that. They send down an inspector to survey the work and hear our complaints."

Nathan pulled out his watch. "Time to go meet the train."

They said good-bye to Mr. Hobbs and left him on his front porch behind the boxwood hedges, hollering for Katie to come put cornbread on the steps. He liked to sit on his porch and watch the blue jays swoop out of the maple to attack the crumbs. Each bird seemed to feel he had to kill the bread before he could eat it, and the way they whacked the cornbread against a tree limb never failed to make Hobbs chuckle.

"I didn't mean to be so rough on Hobbs," said Nathan as they walked down the street in the warm sunshine. "It's natural the machinery people want us to succeed in this thing. They'll send us a good man."

"I guess so. It's just that Hobbs is getting old. I'm not sure," said Sam thoughtfully, "he can't be outsmarted. He's become right forgetful. Never comes into the store anymore."

Nathan tapped him on the back. "Good thing you're an honest man, Sam."

"Good thing," he repeated.

"I've been wanting to talk to you about Esther."

Sam was alert. "Not giving you any trouble, is she?"

"No, no, quite the contrary. I've enjoyed having her ride with me in the afternoons. She's quite a different girl from my Nellie."

Sam made a face.

"I mean that comparison to be in Esther's favor. She's got a real head on her shoulders. Expresses herself well too. And she's independent."

"Too independent."

"She'll settle down when she marries if—and that's a big if—she marries some man she can respect."

"Who you got in mind?"

"It's not who. It's what. I think you ought to send Esther over to State Normal School in Greensboro. Let her become a teacher maybe."

Sam said he couldn't see the good of that.

"Greensboro's a growing town, a lot different from here. She might meet somebody more—more suitable. A college teacher, for instance, would be right in her line." Nathan did not say what he really thought: that already Esther's wings ached to be tried and she was growing up faster than many girls. Just last week, riding in that buggy through the twilight, he had quoted a rolling bit of Shakespeare to Esther, and had the uncomfortable feeling she might kiss him on the mouth from gratitude.

"A college teacher!" Sam snorted. "I'd sooner have one of them Keever boys from down Snow Creek instead of some fellow that never dirtied his hands except on book dust. No, sir, it'll take a real man to handle Esther. She's got a stubborn streak wider than she is." Sam was sorry he'd referred to "streaks" of any kind. It sounded like Angus Mackey, warning him some flaws ran in families. And Esther wasn't like that. . . .

Nathan cleared his throat. "She's curious about everything. She wants life to hurry up and happen. You wouldn't really want Esther tangled up with some wild boy just because she got curious and didn't have anything better to do."

Sam stopped in the middle of the street. "What you mean by that?"

"I mean no more than I said—that Esther's got a good mind and would do well at State Normal School."

They were now crossing the railroad yard to the depot building.

Sam said doubtfully, "She don't get near the good marks Nellie does."

"That's her stubborn streak again. She won't concentrate on being another Eliza Tilley, not even for a few hours a day and not even to get good marks. For somebody else, some really remarkable teacher, Esther would do remarkable work."

The train pulled in and stopped on a cushion of steam. Sam said he would think it over. "Thomas wants to go to the University, you know. Might be a lawyer." He looked at Nathan hopefully. Of the three children, Thomas was his own favorite, the one for whom he foresaw a real future. If Nathan would take him into his law practice, now . . .

Nathan pointed to the only passenger stepping down. "That must be our man. What do you think?"

"Too young."

Nathan looked at a slip of paper he was carrying. "Twenty-five, it says here. Henry Maxwell Carson." He led the way to where the stranger waited and introduced himself and Sam. Carson was a tall, lean man with long legs which seemed to be searching for his waist, and long arms which seemed to be searching for his shoulders. His hands were large and long-fingered, and wrapped themselves in a handshake that was uncomfortably firm. "Max Carson," he said with a nod. He did not smile.

Sam leaned forward, trying not to stare. At first he thought the man had a hole low in one cheek. Then he saw it was a dark scar, smaller than a penny and nearly as round.

"We break ground tomorrow, I understand," said Carson, who had still not bothered to smile and now was talking business before they had even finished saying hello. "I hope that means actual work can begin in the afternoon. Digging foundations. Moving in materials. Unless you've done that already."

"No, no, we haven't done that. About tomorrow, I don't know . . ." said Nathan doubtfully.

"Ground's pretty wet," Sam offered. He was wondering about that scar. A pointed stick, jabbed right through the cheek and into the mouth, might leave a place like that. He studied the man. The eyes were blue, almost gray, and the hair was brown and seemed to fall down in his way. Outdoors a lot—you could tell that from his skin.

"Let's get your satchel over to the hotel first," said Nathan. "Then we can have a drink and talk things over."

"I don't drink," Max Carson said.

Sam and Nathan swapped a glance, after which Nathan said quickly, "That's the hotel right over there," and picked up Carson's bag.

"I'll take that," said the Yankee, and removed it from Nathan's hand without waiting for the customary polite insistence. The three men crossed the street to Greenway's only hotel, Governor House, built in 1879 by Winkler Hobbs. The name on its swinging sign was a reminder that the county had been named for David Stone, governor of North Carolina from 1808 to 1810. Nathan started to mention these interesting historical facts, but he had a feeling they would make Max Carson impatient.

Sam did not go to the desk with the other two but stopped a colored boy in the lobby and ordered some whiskey and two glasses. He wasn't about to talk serious business in any bone-dry condition.

As he followed them upstairs he could hear Nathan.

"Several good boardinghouses here if you prefer. Some people don't like it here, right next to the railroad. The train makes a lot of noise."

"I like trains," Carson said.

Well, he don't talk much, Sam thought. *I don't drink. I like trains.* Likely he had his mouth wide open when whatever it was went through that jaw. Might make a man cautious.

Inside the hotel room, Carson opened windows while the other two stood and watched. He didn't seem to hear Nathan explain that the colored boy would tend to all that.

The whiskey came. While Sam was pouring a pair of drinks, Carson opened the closet and threw his satchel in unopened. Sam pulled up two straight chairs.

"Now, Mr. Grimes," said Carson, turning from the closet, "I have all your letters to my company and I believe everything is clear. Tomorrow you turn the first spade of earth and we begin. Where do I find this John Lucas, the local builder?"

"He'll be out there," said Nathan. "We plan quite a ceremony."

"I mean now," Max Carson said, sitting on the edge of the bed.

Nathan lowered his drink untasted. "Why I don't . . . Sam, where you think Lucas would be this time of day?"

Sam glared at him. Lucas might be anywhere. He might be fishing. He might be having a jaw tooth pulled. He might be home in bed getting over last night's drinking. "He's in Stoneville for the day, recording a deed at the courthouse," Sam lied.

Nathan spread his hands.

"I did want him along today when we looked over the land."

"Today! No need to rush out there today, when we'll all be out at eleven o'clock tomorrow for the ceremony!" Nathan protested. "I mean, there's certainly not that much to see. I've already described the parcel in a letter to your company."

Sam, who had not even finished half his drink, did not relish a long ride to the Katsewa River. "I couldn't go at all today," he said hurriedly. "There's nobody minding the store but my son Thomas."

"I won't keep you then," said Carson, getting off the bed and extending his hand. "Thank you again for meeting the train."

Nathan fumbled with the glass in his right hand, finally set it on the chair behind him as he got to his feet. "Ah . . . yes." he said. Their handshake was quick.

"And I'll see you tomorrow, Mr. Allen?"

Sam drained his glass in a few quick gulps before he got to his feet. The shaking of hands seemed to carry both him and Nathan all the way across the room and through the doorway into the hall.

"Very businesslike," said Nathan as the door closed firmly behind them.

"It seemed like a mighty short time between hello and good-bye." Sam looked at his fingers. "He's got big hands. And where do you think he got that funny scar?"

"I think he put his tongue through there," said Nathan irritably.

They were halfway down the stairs when Sam remembered the whiskey. "Hey, I left my jar in there! He's just the kind of fool to empty it right out the window."

"If you hurry," said Nathan, "you might get out to the street in time to catch it in your hat."

"Hell," muttered Sam, "I'm not going to like that fellow."

Max Carson had not the least interest in being liked. It was a good thing too. The first week he was there it grew plain nobody in Greenway could do anything fast enough to suit him. The speeches at the groundbreaking were too long; the wagons were slow and the mules were lazy. A road to the mill site should have been finished weeks before. Even the Katsewa River ought to be moving more rapidly to make more water power. Carson swore he never heard so much silence betwen ax blows when a tree was chopped, or saw men take so long to eat one potato and a chunk of bread.

"If this was the wild West," one of the workmen complained, "Max Carson wouldn't be satisfied till he could stand in front of a mirror and beat hisself to the draw."

There was other talk about him. He was twenty-five and still not married, but nobody could get him to hold still long enough to be introduced to any of the girls who would have been just perfect for him.

Most important of his flaws, he was a Yankee. Some local talk held that Carson's daddy had been a white officer attached to the 54th Massachusetts regiment of the Union Army, that same regiment of Negro troops which attacked Charleston Harbor. Young Carson might even secretly have a colored wife—you couldn't tell about Yankees— and that would explain his lack of interest in some of the finest young ladies to be found anywhere.

That's what the women said. But the men who knew him decided the Yankee just didn't have the time for women; he hardly slept at all, much less with anybody.

None of this bothered Henry Maxwell Carson, who arrived at the mill site every morning at sunrise, in time to see that every one of that day's nails were driven straight. He had set up an old table under a maple tree and from this temporary office he was always tearing forth —as the workmen said—with his hands full of pictures and his mouth full of hurry-up.

Gradually the railroad cars began to roll in along the spur, carrying brick, metal piping, lumber, opaque window glass and flat tin roofing. At first the wide area for the mill and the mill village looked as though some giant foot had stepped down heavily; it was a field of raw stumps and fallen trees. When the logs were chained up and dragged to one side to be sawed, the field became pockmarked with excavations large and small—the main building, the office, the superintendent's house, the store, the lyceum, and rows of rectangular holes outlined in string where the workers' houses would face each other across a narrow street.

When Nathan rode out to see Sam Allen on a Sunday afternoon early in May, he admitted he'd have to give the Yankee credit. "He's doing a fine job. And he's already put out printed handbills all the way into South Carolina, looking for workers."

"I thought you were the one so strong on local work for local people," said Sam mildly.

"I am, but you need some experience to mix with inexperience. And you need a foreman in each department who's able to train the others. Tomorrow they start on the underpinnings for the houses. And the company store. You know there's to be a store?"

"Yes, and I think Winkler Hobbs has got soft in the head, setting up an extra little store way out there instead of making everybody trade in Greenway," said Sam.

Nathan explained it was because of the scrip. Every two weeks the mill would pay off in scrip and Hobbs wanted it cashed at his own store. "He says by the time they ride all the way to Greenway, there are other places to spend it, but if they go first to his store, that bill gets settled first and something new is bought."

"I don't know why we keep calling it a company store," said Sam. "Nobody owns a splinter of it but Winkler Hobbs."

"The location and all," said Nathan vaguely. They both knew the exclusive store outlet had been a condition of Hobbs's investing in the mill.

"Wonder who he'll get to run the place. Better get Max Carson to add that to one of his handbills. Store clerk wanted."

Nathan looked more and more uncomfortable. "Here's a sample of the scrip."

Sam looked at the little slip of paper.

NORTH CAROLINA
The Proprietors of
Greenway Manufacturing Company
Agree to Pay the Bearer on Demand
ONE DOLLAR
In Current Money

While Sam was examining it and rolling it in his fingers, Nathan said softly, "Hobbs expects you to run the store."

"Using this scrip, it looks to me Hobbs will just keep cashing in these papers at the mill and taking out every piece of money he ever put in," Sam was saying. He almost thought he had imagined Nathan's words until he looked up. "Me? What was that?"

"That's right."

"You must have misunderstood him." Sam shook his head. "If I had to run back and forth between two locations, Hobbs would have to hire at least two extra clerks so somebody would be in each store all the time. He's never going to do anything like that."

"It's you who misunderstand. Hobbs expects you to run the mill store. And that's all." Nathan took back the scrip and spent a long time getting it folded just right before he slipped it into his watch pocket.

"He *what*?"

"Wants you to run the mill store and nothing else. Called me out of church this morning to explain it all and sent me out here to tell you."

Sam got control of himself with an effort. "And the dry-goods store uptown?"

"He's got somebody in mind to handle that."

The two men had been sitting in the front yard, drinking cool tea off a table Rutledge had made when the oak was cut down by nailing a boarded surface on the stump. Sam now leaned forward in his chair and poured his tea onto the ground, more to allow himself a deliberate action of some kind than anything else. He watched the liquid make a dusty pool and lie on the hard-packed surface like rain on a rooster's back. "Now who could that be?" said Sam softly to himself. "Who could run the store for Winkler Hobbs after I've done it all these years?"

"I'm sorry about this, Sam. I told him you wouldn't like it."

Sam put his glass down for fear he might crush it in his hand. "I hope he's at least raised my pay. It's a lot farther from here to the village than it is into Greenway. I'll be gone so much I'll never see this house in the daytime except for Sundays."

"There's more," said Nathan. Sam looked at him in disbelief. "More. Hobbs thinks this kind of store needs closer supervision. Needs a man who sees and knows each customer. Needs to open earlier in the day and stay open later than the Greenway store. He expects you to move down there to the village."

Sam jumped to his feet and the overturned chair struck the ground. The next minute it went flying through the air. It came down with a crash in the center of the yellow-bell bush by the gate, and the cushion flew off toward the house.

"Wants me to move down there? Pick up and go just like that, because Winkler Hobbs thinks it would help his business?" Nathan leaped up and put his hands out in front of him, palms pushing the air; and Sam reached over and took Nathan's chair and gave it a sling over the banister onto the front porch. "The damned old skinflint! Thinks he can just pick me up and set me down like I was a tomato plant that would bear for him and bear for him!"

"Sam."

"Just tell me to move? The hell he can! Put my family down there among strangers just on his say-so, and live in one of those houses no bigger than a chicken coop—"

"It's a special house," said Nathan quickly. "Just like the superintendent's. Two stories. I've made a drawing here of how the rooms are laid out—"

"You carry that picture right out to Winkler Hobbs's privy. You can even stay out there and help him use it to good advantage; you do the rest of his dirty work! But as for me, I quit; and you tell him that."

"No rent for the house," said Nathan. "You could crop-out this place here."

Sam laughed wildly. "No rent? No *rent!* I tell you, Winkler Hobbs has got a heart like a hickory nut. You better get along home, Nathan, and the next time you see that old man, you just mention to him that I quit and quit good. I won't even open up his damn store tomorrow."

"What will you do then?"

"Do? I'll sit back and wait for this mill to make me some money, that's what! I'll do some fishing. And ever' so often I'll go into Hobbs Dry Goods Store and spit on his floor, that's what!"

"Sam, you begged and borrowed and scraped to put a little money into this mill. If you quit Hobbs now, what have you got put back to live on? Would you try to farm this place? Or get work in the mill itself, and live in the village anyway?"

"Hell, no, there's other towns than this one, other stores. I'm not tied here. You want to know the truth, Nathan, I don't like this town worth a damn. I don't even like this state. If Hobbs won't go dropping any barrel of nails on me this time, I'll move on out; go someplace where a man can get ahead."

"That still sounds like moving your family among strangers to me," Nathan pointed out. "And it still doesn't say what you live on while you're picking out a new job in a new town—you, and Mildred, and Esther, and—"

"Shut up," said Sam. "I know that." He felt abruptly tired out, and he dragged the chair out of the flowering bush and sat on it backward, straddling the seat and letting his arms and chin rest atop the back. "That son of a bitch," he said softly.

Nathan dropped a hand on his shoulder. "I had some idea it would be better coming from me than from Hobbs, but I was wrong. There wasn't any way to make it better."

"Ah, me," Sam sighed. He made the chair rock from its front legs to its back legs. "Tell me this one thing, Nathan. Did you argue? Did you stand up for me?"

After a pause Nathan said of course he had.

"I'm not sure," said Sam slowly. He continued the rhythmic jerking back and forth. "I'm just not sure you did."

"I told Hobbs you wouldn't like this a bit. And Sam, you know how sorry I am—"

"I know both those things, yes. I aint sure about the other." He stopped the rocking and looked up at Nathan. "I like to watch the way you do that thing with your face, Nathan; I've seen you pull it on juries. Around the eyes and down the jaw it just gets cooler and stiffer. Reminds me of beef gravy. I've seen you do it when it was so and when it wasn't so, and it's got so I can't tell the difference."

"I'd better go," said Nathan.

"Not yet you ain't." Sam grabbed his arm. "I never asked you before but you better tell me now. That old man's will. Who gets the store when Winkler Hobbs dies?"

"A nephew. The same one who's coming to run the store in Greenway."

Sam dropped the arm. "That old man ain't got no nephew. I'm as close to family as he's got!"

"He's got a nephew. George Trumble from Fayetteville." Nathan marched rapidly away and untied his horse from the gatepost and climbed into the carriage. Sam followed.

In a flat voice pushed out between tight teeth, Sam said, "I'll skin him."

"What's that?"

His voice got louder and louder. "I said I'd skin him. I'll skin that old man! I'll cheat him!"

"You couldn't do that."

"You watch it get done. I'm going to rob that old man blind."

"Sam, I know how you feel—"

"And he'll make me a rich man. What I couldn't get one way, I'm going to take another. I want you to watch it, Nathan. I'm going to skin Winkler Hobbs till the bones show through."

Mildred leaned out an upstairs window. "Ask Nathan to stay to supper," she called.

Sam whispered, "Just you watch it." Then he bellowed, "Nathan can't stay!" and slapped his hand hard onto the horse's rump. Mildred waved from the window but Nathan seemed too busy with the reins to notice.

"He sure is in a hurry," she called. "Did I hear some yelling out here?"

Sam picked up the paper with its drawing of the house to be built in the village. Two stories, painted gray. A porch with a banister. Four fireplaces. Located next to the store itself, and at the end of a long street of smaller houses, with the superintendent's house behind it and the mill building to the right.

"Mildred, come here," he said. "I want to show you something."

A late cold snap had delayed the spring and struck down most of the peaches while they were still hidden in their blossoms. Not until late April that year did the dogwoods break open white in the piney woods, and the purple clusters of bloom run up the stems of flowering judas. The ends of the red maple twigs opened little pale strings of bloom, but these waited a long time and grew limp before the first leaves pushed them aside; and the acorns clung late to the oak trees. Then the last acorn in its shallow cup and the last leftover leaf from the previous season disappeared in a single night, and the willow branches grew feathery from half a day's sunlight.

None of the Allens noticed the thickness of springtime the May Sunday they drove over to see the raw bones of the mill and the mill village. While Sam tied the horses, Mildred and the three children walked aimlessly up and down the hard strip of dirt which was not even a street yet, and studied the stacks of lumber promised to walls and floors.

Mildred was very pale. "Here?" she asked. "Our house will be here?"

Sam studied his chart of the village layout. "That's it."

"They didn't leave a thing. Not a blade of grass. Not even a honey-suckle root," she complained. "Think how hot the summers will be."

"The woods are close," said Sam without much enthusiasm. "We ought to get some breeze off the river."

"Mosquitoes," said Mildred glumly. "We'll get clouds of mos-quitoes. And there'll be snakes on that bank and snapping turtles." She stamped her heel into the ground. "Maybe nothing grew here to begin with. It's hard as stone."

Sam said, "You promised me not to look on the dark side. You're the one said we had to make the best of things."

She was still kicking the earth and did not seem to hear. "Land that won't grow grass sure won't grow people," she said to herself.

"What happened to last night, and you swearing all things worked together for good, to them that loved God?" Sam hollered.

Thomas thought it was time to be helpful. "You won't have to ride far in the evening to get home. Just walk across the yard, Father, and you'll be home for supper."

"I'll never get to see Rosa, moving way over there," sighed Mildred.

Esther had walked away from the others and was staring at the out-line of the mill. "That's big," she said. "I never saw anything so big. Father, who's that man under the tree? There, at the table.'

"That's Max Carson," Sam said. "That's the Yankee. I told you he didn't know Sunday from any other day."

"Aren't we going to speak to him?"

Mildred had turned her face aside. "Let's go. We'll be getting up at daybreak on Sundays to get to church on time. And where's my well?"

Sam told Esther the Yankee didn't like interruptions. "There's to be a central pump for everybody. Right about yonder."

"A pump? I carry my water from a pump with all these other people?" Here Mildred waved a hand across the rows of woodpiles as if behind each one she could glimpse someone inferior. "Let's go," she said again.

"I hear there's to be a tall smokestack and a loud whistle."

"Esther, don't talk about it," Mildred snapped. "I want to go home."

Back in the carriage, nobody said a word. David leaned over one side and let the rolling wheel brush his fingertip. When one finger grew hot and began to throb, he replaced it with another. Esther had laid her head back against the seat to watch the sky unroll above her like a long blue banner. Sam grumbled at the horses; and Thomas wiped at his shoes with an old rag he had found under the seat. Mildred neither said nor did anything. She stared straight ahead. As soon as they were home she went upstairs and lay across the bed and stared up through the ceiling.

"Mama, can I get you anything?" Esther called.

"There's nothing to get,' said Mildred.

Sam went to the back steps and began to whittle on a piece of white pine. David sat with him awhile, but the sight of a knife beyond his reach was too much for him. He edged to the pasture fence, to the sumac thicket, and at last ran off down along the creek to the place where Mildred dug clay for whitewash. He dipped his fingers in the mud and covored his face with triangles and pale crosses.

Esther and Thomas went into the kitchen to eat tea cakes.

"I don't see how Mr. Hobbs could do such a thing to us," Thomas said. He bit into one of the cookies, which were much like biscuit except they were browner and a little sweet.

"Because he's an old bastard. That's what Father calls him. A crooked old bastard."

"You better talk soft," said Thomas.

"I don't think it's going to be so bad, living at the mill. At least we'll have neighbors."

"You know what kind of people they'll be!"

Esther thought of Grandfather dying in the upstairs bedroom while she pointed a shotgun at the sky. "Sometimes you're glad to have anybody," she said. "At least David will have some boys near his own age."

"The mill boys will be working in the mill. Anyway, David would rather be off by himself. You know how he is."

"I do," said Esther, "but you don't. I thought I heard something." She glanced out the back door but Sam Allen had walked toward the barn, cutting his stick to pieces as he went. "I thought I heard a dog barking somewhere near. Is David outside?"

"Don't you remember? David's mad 'cause Mama wouldn't let him go off to the baptizing with Ellie Faye. Little Jube and Halliburton are getting baptized in the river today."

"Seems like I did hear something." Esther wandered into the parlor and looked out that window, then to the glass panel in the front door. She turned suddenly and bolted up the stairs, calling out, "Mama? Mama!"

Thomas got to the hall as they were coming down the steps, but he couldn't see anything outside worth yelling about. Mildred said, "Thomas, go fetch your father. Now." She looked out the front door. "He must have stopped to rest by the roadside. Hurry up, Thomas."

Thomas ran to the barn. Sam had been brushing tangles from the mane and tail of his mare but when Thomas said somebody was coming and Mama looked worried, he let the brush fall right into the straw and hurried to the house.

"What is it, Mildred?"

She waved at the door, which now stood open to the afternoon sun.

"I don't see anybody."

"Down in the ditch, resting. It's Uncle Henderson. Cabiliah Henderson." She added, although there was no need, "Papa's friend who used to come—"

"I see him. He missed his winter visit."

"That's because we got word to him by Ellie Faye that Papa was sick. Sam, you think maybe he doesn't know—hasn't heard that Papa . . ."

"I doubt he does. Living all the way across the county. And you know how hard it is to make him understand things. Probably thinks the old man had a winter cold." Sam took out a handkerchief and wiped his forehead. "I meant to send Big Jube down to get him for the funeral but it clean slipped my mind."

"He's getting up," said Esther. "He's coming in."

They huddled there as if all of them had done some wrong, and watched the aged Negro man get painfully to his feet, waver up the side of the ditch to the road again, and head for their gate. He had a sack with a hole poked through one corner and slid up his arm to the shoulder; in this he had probably carried some lunch for the long walk from the other side of Greenway.

Mildred was flustered. "Sam, you'll—you'll just have to explain to him."

"Explain to him how?" growled Sam.

The old man leaned on their gate a minute and looked up into a tulip tree where a redbird was calling.

"Does he hear that?" Esther whispered.

"No," said Sam.

"Papa said once Cabiliah sort of felt the air move when certain sounds were made. I guess that could be one of them." Mildred's face was whiter now than it had been when they rode home in the buggy from the mill village.

"He sees it, that's all," said Sam. "It's red and he sees it." He hunched his shoulders once or twice and then went out into the front yard to meet the old man. The others could see him bending his head toward the deaf mute, touching the shoulder where the sack of food was hung, waving his hands at great speed to make his message visible to the eye.

It was terrible to watch. Cabiliah Henderson looked at him incuriously, the way a robin who has been surveying the ground for worms will suddenly spot a human form and give it a one-eyed examination. Sam flapped his arms around. *He's dead. Angus Mackey died. Before Christmas. Dead.*

Calibiah Henderson rolled up his eyes slightly to take in Sam's height; he flicked them here and there to follow the flying hands. He adjusted the sack and scratched himself briefly in the crotch, all without taking his eyes from Sam and his motions.

Then, with a quick nod of his head, he walked past Sam toward the house and sat upon a low step and crossed his legs, lifting the right one with his hands and placing it atop the left until he was comfortable. Sam came after him, talking in a very loud voice. Cabiliah raised one pink-palmed hand to the air politely, to show he would wait until Angus Mackey had finished whatever he was doing and came out to sit with him as usual. This past September, the two friends had sat together on this very porch, in the days of tobacco market and copper persimmons and daisies beginning to shatter in the fields.

Mildred turned her back and moved down the hall to the parlor door. "I can't bear it," she whispered.

Thomas swallowed. "How long you think he'll wait?"

Mildred's voice caught. "He'll sit there till dark and never know why Papa doesn't come out."

Sam still stood helplessly where the old man had left him, his noisy hands dangling now at his sides. He motioned to the others.

"You go out there," said Thomas to his sister.

"No. You. It's best for the men to do it."

This time Thomas did not want to be classed with the men. "You're the oldest," he said.

Before he could even get up his arm, Esther reached out and slapped him in the face. "I was with Grandfather!" she cried. "Wasn't that enough?"

Mildred caught hold of her. "That won't help," she said. "We must be quiet and think."

Sam crossed the yard, hesitated at the foot of the porch steps. Again the old man nodded to him and waved his hand gently in the air. Sam stepped by him carefully and came into the front hall and closed the door behind him.

Mildred was leaning into the doorsill of the parlor, facing a piece of wall halfway between two chromo pictures: one of a jaybird, one of a woman with very long hair who clung to a cross in a stormy sea. Sam touched her between the shoulder blades, very carefully. "He doesn't understand."

Mildred jerked away from his touch.

"He won't go home. He just can't understand me. He thinks your papa is a little late, that's all, busy with something, not dressed, something like that. He's going to be sitting out there when the moon comes up."

Still she said nothing.

"Mildred, he's not going home."

Her voice was muffled. "Surely he'll leave when he waits and waits and no one comes. He never had to wait more than five minutes . . . before. Papa used to be able to feel it, the week Cabiliah would walk over. The weather would warm up, or something. He'd start looking for him. And inside a few days that old man would come staggering down the hill—remember how Papa would stand up?" Mildred reached over one shoulder and caught hold of Sam's hand where he had left it resting on her back. "Remember how he'd hold onto the post on the porch and stand up to wave? Cabiliah couldn't hear him yell, you know, so Papa would start waving when the old man was no bigger than his finger down the road. When he got closer, Papa would wave the chair cushion up and down." She let out a long breath that she had been holding. "Up and down."

Sam turned. "Thomas . . ."

"He'll never understand me."

"I suppose not." He squeezed Mildred's hand. "Nothing to do then but leave him out there until—"

At this, Esther said furiously, "I can't stand it I can't stand it I can't stand it!" All the others seemed to be in her way as she pushed through the doorway and ran into the middle of the parlor floor, shaking her head over and over. "At least I can go out and sit with him. I can't stand this," she swore. "I'll take him something."

"What?" said Mildred.

"Something," said Esther. She flew off to the kitchen for a tea cake soft enough for his gums and a cup of lukewarm coffee. Grandfather and Cabiliah Henderson had taken a great interest in each other's mouths—Grandfather thrusting forth his upper jaw so Cabiliah could run an appreciative finger over those hard teeth before, with a soundless chuckle, he pointed into his own empty mouth. Sometimes, while the two men watched a horseman pass and then examined each particle of dust as it settled behind his journey, Grandfather Angus Mackey had scraped apple pulp with a dull knife into a saucer until there was nothing left but the core; and Calibiah had then eaten the pulp, daintily, pinching up bits between thumb and forefinger and holding each morsel a long time inside his cheek.

Esther passed through the parlor now with the fat cookie and the coffee cup.

From the parlor window they watched her. Cabiliah seemed delighted with the food and sucked for a long time on the cookie, and then took up the last remaining crumbs out of his palm with the tip of his tongue. He blew a whirlpool into the coffee cup, took a long drink, broke a stem off the rosebush and stirred the sugar out of the bottom and drank again. Esther sat on the step at his side and seemed to be talking at great length.

"I tell you, he can't hear a word she says," Sam grumbled.

"That doesn't matter," Mildred said.

Whatever she said that Cabiliah couldn't hear, he once leaned forward and clapped his hands together. All of them jumped, and Esther nearly fell off the steps.

After a while Esther carried the cup and saucer back to the kitchen. As she passed the others at their post by the window, she said nothing; her face seemed to be hung in a taut smile as if it were some sort of spasm, and her eyes were very bright. She passed them a second time returning, carrying a whole plateful of tea cakes, which she poured into Cabiliah's sack. Then she looked at her mother and father and brother, over Cabiliah's head, and sat down once more and began talking and smiling and moving her hands in the air. Now and again the old man would bob his head forward. Sometimes he looked uneasily behind him at the closed front door.

Inside, Mildred said softly, "He'll soon be chilly out there when the sun gets low. At his age. And he's walked so far."

Sam felt he had been accused. "What can I do? I told him the old man was dead. I told him and told him. I made motions and shouted. What do you think I can do?"

"Oh, hush," said Mildred. "I'm not even talking to you."

The day wore on. It seemed to pass distantly behind the two panes of glass—one the windowpane through which Esther and Uncle Cabiliah Henderson could be seen, and one the glass panel in the mantel clock where time was going by.

Mildred went back to the kitchen and set out the remains of Sunday dinner, but nobody could eat. Thomas carried a biscuit with blackberry jelly into the parlor, but as he stood watching Esther and Cabiliah, he absently crumbled it all onto the floor in a little pile.

At last the old man rose and bowed to Esther slightly. He reached into his sack and took one of the tea cakes and pointed to it and nodded his head, and rested his hand for an instant on her dark hair. Then he edged down the steps and, without looking back, started his slow walk across the yard to the road.

Esther started after him, stopped at the foot of the stairs and laid the back of her right hand against her mouth. Then she turned and ran inside to the others. "He thinks—Oh, Mother—he just thinks Grandfather won't come and sit with him anymore! He thinks Grandfather must be angry about something! He thinks he just won't come. . . ."

"There's no way of telling what Cabiliah thinks," Sam stated reasonably.

But Mildred had begun to move briskly, patting her hair, and she gave Thomas a sharp push in the back of his neck. "Go fetch that man. Esther, unbolt your grandfather's room. Hurry up. He's not got that many steps to waste."

Sam asked, more to get things straight than anything else, "You're bringing him right in? You're bringing a nigger in the front door?"

"Yes," she said. "I am."

Thomas ran up to Cabiliah and caught hold of him by the elbow, turning him gently. The old man cocked his head to one side and waited. Thomas pulled his hand through the air to motion him in. Cabiliah nodded. With much effort, the two got up the front steps, the old man pulling along the rail.

Mildred went to meet them. She took Uncle Henderson's tiny arm and led him in, over the wide oaken boards of the hall, to the stairs, where she thrust a pointing hand upward. Again Cabiliah nodded, took a deep breath and began the climb.

"Prob'ly he thinks Grandfather's still sick, after all," said Esther to nobody. They all followed up the stairs.

Mildred led him to Grandfather's bedroom door, lifted the wooden arm latch, and threw the door wide. She stood back, and he went in.

In the middle of the room, Cabiliah stopped in his tracks and looked thoughtfully upon the empty bed. None of them spoke. Esther was breathing so lightly she thought her lungs must be shrunken, and Thomas, she saw, was walking on his toes.

Mildred opened the wooden clothes bin to show how little was left. She took the tortoise-shell box off the dresser and flicked up its lid to let Cabiliah see the pocket watch lying there with its hands stopped. He had not moved; and she stepped in front of him and closed both her eyes and crossed her hands upon her breast.

Then Cabiliah understood, and a tiny warped sound came out of his throat. He hobbled to the bed and placed his palm flat on the pillow, then flat on the mattress at the place where Angus Mackey's feet would have lain. Then he turned and half fell across the room to the mirror, cupped both his hands on the cold glass around an image which was not there, and laid one index finger swiftly on the handle of each drawer. He was still making that choked noise, something like a bullfrog and something like a bleeding dog.

From the mirror he turned to go; the Allens, who had stood transfixed while he laid his hand on this place and that, now stumbled back on each other out of his way, and he came to the doorway and stooped down and spread the fingers of both hands out upon the sill.

The others were motionless wherever they had stopped. Mildred was still in her place with her hands folded upon her heart and her eyes now pulled wide open; Sam and Esther and Thomas had fallen back from the doorway over chairs and the bureau and were bent at odd angles against the furniture. They waited, frozen, unable to tell blessing from curse, and Cabiliah Henderson had been puffing and twisting on the threshold for some time before Mildred realized he had got down and could not get up again. His bones had bent and then gone hard, so that over his acts of requiem there fell suddenly the aspect of the ridiculous; and the grief and the rheumatism were so mixed that none of them knew whether to laugh or cry. Mildred leaped forward and slipped her arm around him. Sam came to the other side. Together they stretched him up again into the shape of a dark grasshopper. He did not nod his thanks this time; he did not look into their faces nor into any face, but stumbled down the hall and scuttled along the stair rail and flung himself out the front door. Through the yard in a half-running crouch he went, and as he passed he extended one thin arm into the lowest branch of the chinaberry tree, which showered him with wrinkled and bitter pellets. His sack of food slid down his arm and fell behind him; he kicked free of it.

Mildred started after him down the steep stairs, then stopped midway and sank down. She caught hold of one of the banister posts and pulled on it: one two three one two three one two three. Rocking back and forth, she watched him as he slipped out the gate and began his uneven journey home. Like a hoptoad, he leaped, paused and then seemed to slide. Her fingers on the wood were white and no longer young. "I cannot bear it!" Mildred said harshly, yanking at the banister one two three, one two three.

And the others, who were still huddled at the door of Angus Mackey's room, held still without going to her, knowing that none of them would be able to bear it, whatever it was.

Chapter
❧ 10 ❧

By August more than half the thirty-five mill houses had been completed, and some of the families were already living in them and eking out a living on odd jobs until the mill was finished.

All that summer, strangers were coming to Greenway to walk up and down the future streets of the mill village, looking over the small frame houses, each set on a half-acre lot and backed up by a row of narrow wooden privies spaced behind every other dwelling.

The typical house had a front edging of fence, four steps to a wide porch without a railing, and a front door which opened into a skimpy hall, a living room to the left and two sleeping rooms to the right. At the back were the kitchen, pantry and a small porch behind a crisscross lattice. Atop a sharply peaked tin roof, two chimneys served the front-room fireplace and a stove flue in the back. Each room had a single long window except the kitchen, which had two. The houses stood on brick pillars two feet off the red clay.

Greenway Manufacturing Company had set its rent at fifty cents per room per week, with a kitchen or unfinished shed counting half a room. Behind each house there was space for a small garden, and some of the earliest families had set up chicken yards or knocked together a sty for fattening a pair of pigs they brought with them from wherever the came. A few martin poles with their swinging hollow gourds had sprung up in the back corners of the lots.

149

The village looked raw and ugly. Blazing sun fell straight down, now that the trees were gone, and cracked the earth in so many crazed patterns that the houses seemed perched above tiny, perpetual earthquakes. The garden sometimes had to be broken with mattocks and there were places where a mule could drag a plow blade along without making a shallow scratch; but the men and women seemed to manage, and sent their children to drag home buckets of leaf mold from the woods and stable manure from nearby farms. This they dug in among the clods to lay over till the following spring.

The late spring had become a quick summer. Barely had it grown warm before it turned hot, and the scant rains failed to settle the powdery dust or raise the river's level. The unpainted boards of the houses popped and crackled in the heat and sweated out streaks of resin. Here and there a few tufts of stubborn grass lay in the yards like wisps of straw. When the mill opened for work (some said that would be by October, at least) the privies would be limed once a week and the houses and grounds would receive regular inspection; but now odors hung rank in the air and flies blackened watermelon rinds thrown off into nearby woods.

The Allen house was one of the first to be finished, because Hobbs wanted Sam to move as soon as possible and hurry along the building of the store. By August it was ready, but Mildred wouldn't even go look at it, much less move into it. She developed a series of summer complaints and headaches, all of which left her unfit for packing, and the end of July she fell down the back steps and twisted her ankle and wrenched her knee.

Esther sometimes rode with her father to inspect the work. Thomas was still working at the store and David was too much trouble. She liked the cool ride down the narrow road which ran like a tunnel through the woods, but she never got used to the shock of coming out of that greenness and having her eyes shrink up in the sudden light which bleached the framing of half-finished houses as if it were bone. The sun's rays off the sheets of tin roofing seemed to fall into her face like a volley of shattered glass.

The road came abruptly out of the forest and ran through the center of the twenty-acre site. Twenty houses faced each other across it, and the Allen house stood at the very end. Two stories high, it had been painted in gray and dark green; and although it was new, Esther thought of something on which moss and lichen had been allowed to grow. Beside it men were hammering inside the skeleton of what would become the store, and beyond it they were just raising the first-floor walls of the superintendent's house. Eventually the road would loop in front of the mill and go between a second double row of houses; these were now no more than isolated brick underpinnings, like dwarfs' chimneys.

"Go see if they got the shelves up in the pantry," Sam Allen said.

Esther hopped out of the buggy and he reminded her again to step down lightly, like a girl instead of a jackrabbit. She balanced along two boards left to bridge some puddle which had not been there since April, and climbed the six steps to the left side of the front porch. On her right, a three-paned bay window with dark-green trim bellied forth. The second story was topped by an angled roof, with gables, and in the upper front were set two widely separated egg-shaped windows like a pair of startled eyes.

Inside the house, Esther's feet were like horses' hoofs. She drummed them on the floor and sounded a few halloos and hoys; then, delighted with the echo, she began to sing. Each tone came back to her ear in a series of rising and falling globes of sound until she laughed aloud and did a rattling toe dance down the bare hall.

As she came whirling by, one of the doors flew open and a man with a hole in one cheek scowled out at her. "What do you think you're doing?" he barked.

She flattened herself against the wall across from him.

"You've already been told to stay in your own yards and keep away from this end of the street," he said. "That's in the rules. Didn't you read the rules?" He frowned. "Can you read?"

The song Esther had been singing was stuck in her throat. She finished swallowing it down, drew herself tall, and then put out a finger and shook it in the air. "What are you doing in my house?" she demanded. She hoped he would not notice that her whole hand was trembling.

Max Carson had no sympathy for mill girls who put on airs. He had moved his work inside to get away from the gnats and now this noisy girl—sixteen, he judged her—had come onto private property to play games like a child and shake her finger like a queen.

"That's enough out of you," he said brusquely. "Don't you know better than to wander in empty houses by yourself? Doesn't your mother tell you anything?"

Her curiosity got the best of her. "Tell me what?"

Carson said he had work to do, and turned and went back inside the room, banging the door shut behind him. Before the echo had died out of the hall, Esther turned the knob and marched in at his heels. A table covered with papers, rulers and rolled-up charts was against the lone window and the man turned from it to stare at her.

"Who said you could use this room?" she said sharply, "and how in the world did you get a hole in your face like that?"

He grabbed her by the shoulders and shook them with an upward movement. It made her feel her neck was growing out of her ribs. "I told you to get home," he said, glaring, and bent his head and thrust his mouth hard upon her mouth. It was more like a blow than a kiss, a striking of dry lips upon dry lips, and he pulled back quickly and gave her another jerk. "Now get yourself home before you find yourself in real trouble," he growled. "Some days a hundred men are in and out of here, and some are drunk and some are plain mean." He let go her arms and pulled his chair back to the table and began to study a column of figures.

Esther blinked a few times. She ran her fingertips in an oval around her mouth. "There's not so much to that," she said half to herself.

Without turning, he stamped his foot on the floor. "I said go home."

Esther was determined not to run. She reached behind her for the door and opened it slowly. "I think," she said, "that somebody shot you in the face," and then darted out and gave the door a great slam. When she heard no sound of the chair sliding back or his footsteps crossing the room, she stopped in her headlong flight down the hall and tiptoed back, eased the knob around gently and inched the door open the width of her hand. The man was still working at his table. She yelled through the crack, "And no wonder!"

Esther yanked at the door and took off running. Between the pounding of her shoes and the multiplying echoes and the wild pumping of her heart, she felt as if she might be outrunning a stampede; and she burst into the sunlight with her dark hair laid out in the air behind her like a fan. She vaulted the porch railing, hit the hard earth with a thud that loosened both her knees, and hurried to where Sam Allen was talking to one of the workmen about shelves and a ramp for rolling barrels.

Sam did not look at her but he did say, "I told you to quit jumping off things like a billy goat. You never going to grow up?"

"Jackrabbit," Esther panted. "You said jackrabbit."

She could see nothing at the long window of the room where the man was working at his table, but she thought there was at least a chance he might be standing there and looking out. While her father went on talking, Esther wheeled toward the window and thrust her thumbs inside her jaws to pull her mouth out of shape, and with forefingers dug into her lower lids, made her eyes sag as if they were going to topple out of her face. She stuck her tongue out as far as it would go and wagged it from side to side between her bared teeth. After she had completed the ugliest face ever seen in any of Miss Eliza Tilley's classes, she shook her fist into space for good measure.

Then she turned back in time to give her father a pleasant smile.

"We've just got to go ahead and move in," he was saying, half to himself and half to Esther. "I've got stock to order and I want to make sure they get shelves in all the different sizes I need." Now he gave her his full attention. "You think the house is ready? Can you tell your mother everything is ready?"

"Yes," she said.

"No need to put things off," Sam said morosely.

She pulled at his sleeves. "Why is it nothing is ever the way you think it's going to be?"

Absently he patted her hand. "It won't really be so bad down here," he said. "Give me a little time, and I'm going to own this store. And I'll hire me some fool to work for wages, and I'll move us right into Greenway and build a house so big its shadow will always be in Winkler Hobbs's front yard. Morning and noon, I'll shade his house, and the young men that come courting you will be from big places. Important places. Not like Greenway."

Esther was not paying attention. She had taken the tip of her tongue and drawn a warm, damp outline of her upper lip, then raised her forearm and pressed a kiss heavily into it. The downy hair touched her nose and the taste of her skin was like twigs and salt. It sure was funny what people saw in kissing.

Esther jerked her arm down and shot a quick glance at the window of their new house as she followed her father. She hoped that man hadn't seen her nuzzling her own self and thinking things through. At first she intended to send him a second fierce face with her fingers waggling like ears atop her head for decoration, but it didn't seem worth the effort and, besides, her stomach felt funny. It felt as if it had begun to soften from the inside and might any minute melt and be no further use to her.

In October the machinery began to arrive, though the mill was nowhere near finished, and people had bits of it waiting all over town—long rows of cartons in the cotton gin and the warehouse by the depot, big barrels blocking the aisles of both dry-goods stores, in Greenway and the mill village. There was a crate in Max Carson's room at Governor House and people said Winkler Hobbs's dining room was full of spinning frames, and a boxcar full of something sat alone at the end of the railroad spur.

The first week in October, the Allens moved into their new house in the mill village.

Mildred vowed she still wasn't up to the work of moving. Lifting the crates of dishes would twist her backbone, she said, and undo all the healing. But Sam said he had rented out the farm to a widow woman with three grown sons, and hired two wagons to carry all they owned to the new place. "So it's tomorrow. We move tomorrow."

Mildred went into the pantry and had a good cry and a good prayer. "Lord Jesus," she said, "they are taking me off to Egypt."

The next morning the two wagons were in front of the gate and Mildred had all the quilts folded and stacked so they could tear the beds apart first. She stayed in the kitchen, crying, and wrapped her good dishes in flannel rags and nested them one upon the other inside a pickle barrel. She had tied a wet rag around her forehead like a turban, to ease *that* ache, and from time to time as she was packing she poured half a teacup of vinegar-water over her head. When the last loaded wagon drew up in front of the green-gray house with Mildred riding atop it in the porch rocker, she jerked the wet head rag across her eyes and they watered all over her rigid face.

She pulled her mouth in until it was no wider than a scratch. "Now I know how Satan felt when they threw him out of Heaven," she said to Sam.

He was so irritated he nearly tossed her box of jam jars onto the front porch. "Mildred, you've grumbled for years about that other house. There were never enough shelves to suit you, and the fireplaces didn't draw, and the roof kept leaking. And you said it was so far from town that in the winters you never saw a living soul."

Her mouth stayed shrunken. "I didn't know when I was well off," she said.

David asked to go visit those boys they had passed, the third house back, but his mother shook her head. "You're not to play with them. You're not to go to school where they go. You're not even to see them. I can do that much." She climbed painfully out of the wagon, stretched forth her chin and marched inside.

To the right of the Allen house, the mill's shell was already up and men on scaffolding that looked no more substantial than spiderwebs worked furiously to finish the walls and roof it in against coming bad weather. Mildred was surrounded by so many hammer blows she felt it would be like living inside a thundercloud, and the whining of the saws made the ends of her teeth tingle with discomfort. The first thing she did was hurry from room to room, closing all the windows which Sam and Rutledge and Big Jube had taken such care to open.

That first week, Mildred stayed entirely inside the house. She would not even walk out to the clothesline Sam had strung for her in the back, but dried her things on a rope she tied from post to post along the porch. She quarreled about Thomas working in *this* store, in *this* place; and when Sam insisted, she rolled her eyes to Heaven as if to make sure God noticed what a hard heart Pharaoh had. She would not let Esther get any more fresh air than could be coaxed in an upstairs window. And she hung thick curtains on all the windows on the mill side of the house, and kept them tightly drawn so that by crossing the hallway one could move from daylight to dark at any hour of the day.

The second week, a place had been found for everything and everything had been duly put in it; and Ellie Faye began to get on Mildred's nerves. She ventured across the yard to the mill store. Sam was not there. The knot of men standing around the door were laughing and rocking back and forth.

I'd hate to know what *that* was about, thought Mildred as she hurried home.

Another day she walked al the way through the mill village, dressed in her Sunday clothes with her scalp damp under the black bonnet. Children as tall as her hip squatted in some of the yards wearing nothing but strips of cloth knotted at their loins like savages, stripping skin from baked sweet potatoes and throwing it over the fences into the street. A few had shirts and a few of the shirts had sleeves. It seemed to Mildred all their teeth were slimy and tapered down to points.

The men and women were no better. The men were pale, long and rank as weeds, with shoulders which had come forward and seemed to enfold their ribs. The women sometimes took spoons or dry sticks and scraped up clay out of their back yards and ate it. Others chewed green twigs till they resembled brushes, dipped these in snuff and painted their gums the color of mud and tucked more powder into their cheeks and the pockets of their lips. They looked like chipmunks with their lumpy faces under small, bright eyes.

After that one inspection, Mildred did not want to walk again in the village. Sometimes she would go out through her own back yard and into the woods, partly to get away from the noise of the builders and partly to rest her eyes on scarlet and yellow leaves and dark earth. If she found a clearing, she was apt to begin pacing in it absently and talking aloud her worries about Esther, worries which she sometimes threw forth in the form of prayers and psalms.

"The shadow of a mighty rock within a weary land," she would sometimes implore the underside of the maple leaves. The rock she sought was strength to tell Esther about men, and especially strength to warn her about the men in the mill village.

Mildred had already been to the Scriptures, seeking a passage to illustrate what these men were like. The closest she could find—in Second Samuel—was the story of Amnon and Tamar, which wouldn't do at all. Amnon and Tamar were brother and sister; no need to stir up trouble that wasn't even thought of!

"I know even the Devil can quote pieces of Scripture to suit his own ends," prayed Mildred aloud among the trees, "but could I just use a piece of that one and leave out the brother and sister?"

The wind moved high among the branches but she couldn't read an answer in it. If she could have that one verse and use it in all conscience, she might be able to show Esther what certain men desired and for how brief a time. "Then Amnon hated her exceedingly," the Scripture said, "so that the hatred wherewith he hated her was greater than the love wherewith he had loved her. And Amnon said unto her, Arise, be gone."

No, it did not seem right to use the end of that story without its beginning, and since Esther had two brothers of her own, those sleeping dogs had better be let lie.

"Lord Jesus," said Mildred softly, "the only thing else I can think of is the woman taken in adultery, and if You remember, You forgave that one."

Other times she would try to recreate what Esther might be thinking by looking back down the long perspective of herself to recall what questions had once rattled in her own head. Why, thought Mildred, even when I was a bride I used to lie as stiff as a hoe handle while Sam was sleeping, for fear I might roll in my own sleep and somehow drop a hand on his private place, or twist in a dream and wound him with my knee.

And I was no older than Esther when I would think how strangely men were made; what an inconvenience it must be! (She did not, of course, say any of this aloud—even to God.) I couldn't see why it didn't hurt them when they straddled a horse, or how the fat boys could sit on the top of fences without being pinched, and I wondered if boys bounced and rubbed against their clothes when they went running down the hills.

Even if Esther wouldn't be fourteen until next month, she looked older, seemed older; and maybe even now she was wondering how they were made and studying those spindly mill men when they propped one foot on a rail and pulled their trousers tight. "Lord Jesus," sighed Mildred into the open air, "You might have offered me something more substantial than Mary Magdalene."

Sometimes her thoughts flowed like a dirge. Oh, I could tell her! I could tell her things! I could tell her being a girl is worse than any of their inconvenience. I could say how a girl is something to be opened—by a man or a child. By herself once a month, just to keep in practice. Oh, I could tell her, Mildred thought; but in truth she couldn't tell her anything of the sort.

She had not been able to tell her own sister, even after she knew Rosa was slipping out to meet Silas Bennett and he was putting his hand on her in the dark.

And yet, thought Mildred, if I'd talked about that—about men, about women—she might have waited to marry him! But no, I talked to her about Mama. I told Rosa there was a family weakness and she had some of it. I told her that was why Sam and I had put off having children of our own. . . .

"Because of me?" Rosa had gasped, and then pulled free before Mildred could answer. "Well, don't you wait a minute longer! Because Silas Bennett wants me just like I am, and we're going to have a dozen children! There's nothing wrong with me, not a thing. You're making it all up!" Rosa ran crying to her room and the next night Silas lifted her out of her bedroom window and took her to Stoneville and married her.

That youthful elopement in 1878 explained why Rosa—still only thirty-four—had been married to Silas for nineteen years. Each year had been a childless one, but nobody could claim Rosa Mackey Bennett had ever fasted like her mama.

Soon Esther would be as old as Rosa had been then; and maybe some boy would be touching her and guiding her hand until she, too, would touch, would draw back at the unexpected fullness, return, linger, stroke. . . .

Mildred snapped off that thought as if it were a dry twig. *Years I worried my children might not be normal and in good health; now I'm scared to death they are!*

Well, Jesus, she said silently, it is in Your hands.

One windy afternoon when they had been living in the house a month, Max Carson banged on the front door and asked leave to bring a hurt man inside.

"They've gone for the doctor," he said, "but this is the closest house and we hate to move him far."

"Bring him in," said Mildred. "Use the front bedroom."

The workman had been rolling a wheelbarrow piled high with bricks down a high board ramp, had slipped and gone over, pulling the heavy load onto his chest. Carson and the others had roped two shorter boards together and eased him onto it as gently as they could; now they carried him down the hall and deposited him, boards and all, on what had been Angus Mackey's bed. Blood from his nostrils had run down both cheeks and clotted in the folds of his ears. He looked like a dead man, but a frothy bubbling issued from his nose and when they laid him on the bed he made a bleating sound.

Mildred took one look and sent Ellie Faye to get a basin of water and some cloths. "Has he got family?"

"One brother, and I'm here," said one of the men who had carried him in.

Mildred nodded. "You stay then, and the others can wait on the porch."

It was useless to clean the hurt man's face; as quick as blood was wiped a new bubble broke onto his upper lip and made a streak on his skin. "Don't you worry," said Mildred to the brother. "Dr. Newton is coming."

"Yes, ma'am," he said.

There was a rap on the bedroom door. "You wanted more cloths?"

"Bring them in, Esther."

The door did not open. Mildred frowned, blotted the newest stain and then went to the door. "Why didn't you bring them in?"

Esther turned her face aside. "I can hear him breathe all the way out here. I don't want to hear anybody else breathe like that."

"Nobody does," said Mildred shortly. "Things happen." She took the clean rags and closed the door.

After Dr. Newton had arrived and made a brief examination, he said the man was as good as dead. "I'm sorry, son," he told the brother, "but it's no good to lie about it. His chest is crushed. What he sucks in now is mostly his own blood."

The brother closed his eyes and nodded. Then he said, "Can't you give him something? Let him go out easy?"

Mildred left while Dr. Newton was saying he would do all he could. In the hall, Esther was seated on a stool watching the bedroom door. "Is he going to die?" she asked.

"Yes." Mildred called out the front door for Mr. Carson. The young man with the hole in his face came inside, nodded while she told him what Dr. Newton said.

"I was afraid of that."

She had a glimpse of Esther swaying on the stool. Over one shoulder she said, "Esther? You going to be sick?"

"No," said Esther in a high voice. "Isn't it funny that only hogs make me sick and not people?"

"Don't talk," said Mildred. "You feel worse when you talk." To Mr. Carson she suggested it might be well to bring a wagon round, so the two brothers could be driven to Greenway when . . . when it was time. "And if you think . . . if it seems the brother will need a little whiskey during the trip, I think my husband—"

"We'll supply the whiskey," Max Carson said. "You've been very kind."

Mildred looked at the ceiling. "Once in my life," she said to it quietly, "I'd like to let go and fall right to pieces. Just once I'd like to faint at the sight of blood instead of being too busy to notice it." She kept her gaze up. "You hear me, Esther?"

"I hear you."

When Mildred had gone back into the room with the dying man, Carson continued to stand by the door. He called softly down the hall to Esther, "I'm sorry for what happened that day."

"Well, this is a poor time for it," said Esther.

"I know it is. Excuse me." He went to make arrangements for the wagon.

By eight o'clock that night the man had died. The life went down in him like a light that fades by imperceptible degrees—there was less blood, less movement, less warmth, less breathing, less color; and finally nothing at all but a deserted trunk and limbs getting cooler and cooler.

Dr. Newton weighted his eyes while Mildred wiped away the last thin stain. At first they tried crossing his arms on his chest, but this had been so driven in by the load of bricks that his hands had the look of being carried in some basket. Mildred was even tempted to stuff some rags into his shirt and fill him out again for his brother's sake.

"How old do you think he was?" she whispered to Dr. Newton.

"Twenty-two," he guessed. "Maybe just twenty."

The men who had carried him into the house now carried him out again on the same boards, all but the brother, who stood off to one side and looked at the floor. They slid the corpse into a wagon and covered it first with a blanket, then with a sheet of oilskin from the dry-goods store in case it should rain before they got to Greenway.

Max Carson, hat in hand, came back to thank them again before they left. "I'll get the blanket back to you," he said.

"No, no, don't bring it back," said Mildred hastily. "I don't want it."

By now Sam had come in from the store. He walked out to the wagon with Carson, saying a death on the job was always a bad sign and made the other men uneasy.

"It's a wonder this is only the first one," Carson said. "Not many of these men ever worked on anything this big or this long. I don't think some of them ever worked on anything at all except pasture fences."

"Farm boys," Sam admitted.

"Even experienced men have accidents sometimes. Farm boys . . . well . . ." He looked up and saw Esther's blazing eyes fixed on him. "My appreciation to your wife and daughter," he said again, and climbed into the wagon beside the brother and took the reins.

Esther watched the wagon rolling slowly away from them, down the street. People had come out onto the porches of some of the mill houses to see it pass, some with candles and some with kerosene lamps.

She said bitterly to her father, "Doesn't he ever think about anything but this mill?"

"That's his job."

After the wagon passed each house, the watching people would turn aside and carry their lights indoors, so that by simply rolling down the street its shadow seemed to snuff out two rows of winking fires. At last there were no fires at all and very little moon, and the dark shape of the wagon blended with darker shapes and fell out of sight in the blackness of the forest.

They turned and went into the house.

Mildred and Dr. Newton were sitting on the stiff parlor chairs, and Dr. Newton had his bag in his lap as if he were about to go.

"But is it really true?" Mildred was saying. "All those other times . . ."

"I'm sure of it. On a night like this, I'm glad to be bringing good news to somebody," said the doctor with a tired grunt. "Sam, I was just telling your wife I saw Rosa Bennett this morning. And Esther, I figure you'll have a little cousin this summer. Early in June."

Sam looked embarrassed and said he was glad to hear it. Esther said nothing.

"And you say Rosa seems all right? You think this time . . ."

"I think just what I said—that you will be an aunt before the middle of next June, and Silas Bennett will be a father at last," said Dr. Newton, nodding. He thanked them all once more for their help before he unhitched his own buggy and started the ride to Greenway. Riding in the same ruts, Esther thought.

"I'm tired," said Esther. "Night, Father."

Mildred walked upstairs with her, chattering at every tread. "Isn't it wonderful that Rosa may finally have the child she's wanted for so long? Nineteen years! And to hear about it on a night like this! Esther, I tell you it's really true that in the midst of death we are in life, just like the Bible says."

"It's the other way around," said Esther. "I'm sure it says we are in death . . . of life in death."

"I know my Scripture, young lady."

While Esther brushed out her long, dark hair, Mildred walked up and down the room. "Sunday we must all go see them. I'll bake Rosa a cake; she loves cake. And we need to start a present for the baby—we could crochet a shawl. I'll make the dark circles and you make the light ones, and when we join it all together, it will be something special from the two of us. Esther, what do you think?"

"You know I can't crochet. It always turns into knots."

"We'll knit it then, in squares. Anybody can knit."

"I can't purl. It feels too backward."

Mildred was exasperated. "Then we'll knit it in garter stitch. No purling at all. How about that?"

"Oh, all right," said Esther impatiently. "All *right*."

"Esther, you're growing up," Mildred began, and shifted quickly to, "You have such nice hair. Mine used to be like that before it began to gray."

"You can sit on yours."

"I don't know why people say that as if it were some sort of accomplishment. Who in the world wants to sit on her own hair? Sometimes after a woman has a baby, her hair gets thin—did you know that? Pieces comb right out."

"I don't guess the baby cares; no more than he's got."

Mildred decided to come at it another way. "Did I tell you Rosa's been seeing Miss Bethesda Lee Michael? She had her throw a spell to help her have this baby, and now I guess she'll give credit to the magic. As if magic had anything to do with it. I say, Esther, what makes women have babies is not magic." She eyed her daughter, waiting.

"Someday I'd like to see that Miss Bethesda Lee Michael."

"June, Dr. Newton says. That's a nice month for a baby. Not as hot as it gets later in the summer. A woman can feel very heavy and very hot near the end."

Esther slipped on her nightgown and tied the neck ribbon. "Are they going to drive that wagon all the way to Greenway as slow as they went through the village? How long you think it will take them to get there, driving that slow?"

Mildred, who had been pacing around the room, practically dragging, she thought, Rosa's future baby back and forth across the floor, now stopped and put her hands on her hips and said in a cross voice, "Esther, isn't there anything you want to ask me?"

"Yes. I want to know if Dr. Newton gave that man something to help him die quicker. I heard his brother ask."

Mildred thought: I could just as well have used that story about Amnon and Tamar. She said crisply, "Good night, Esther. Sleep well."

"I didn't think you'd tell me," Esther said.

After that Mildred decided to postpone the long conversation she needed to have with Esther about men. Somehow, when the Lord was ready, He would open up a way for her.

"Lord Jesus," she prayed, "I want you to know I am just standing by."

"It was nearly Christmas before the mill was ready to start. The mayors of Montbury and Stoneville were to join Greenway's mayor, Lloyd Morrison, in a series of speeches appropriate to the day, and Coite Reece—oldest local Confederate veteran—had been invited to say a few words about rising from the ashes. It was the wrong season for a picnic, but only with reluctance did Nathan Grimes give up his plans for a county-wide barbecue. No one person could buy that much pork and nobody else was willing to donate it, even one pig at a time.

So it was set that the speakers would mount to a wagon in the mill yard and talk from there, and a crowd of townspeople and mill workers would warm themselves by scattered bonfires during the ceremony. Sam Allen expected to sell a great deal of whiskey to supplement those bonfires, and Big Jubilee Jackson had been out of the store for weeks getting it made at the large still which he worked for Sam on something like a sharecropper basis.

Although the day was clear and bright and Miss Eliza had closed the Academy, Mildred refused to let the children go.

"They could at least hear the speeches," Sam said mildly.

"They will not go."

Thomas said Uncle Silas would be there.

"That's different. Silas is to be working in the mill. None of us has any business there."

"And Father's going," said Esther. "And Mr. Grimes said he was even going to bring Nellie. He said he wanted her to remember the day the cotton factory got brought to the cotton—isn't that pretty? It's in his speech."

"Little Jube gets to go. Ellie Faye said she was going to walk the whole way over so Halliburton could hear the machinery run," David put in.

"We will not go," Mildred said.

Sam shrugged at them and put on his hat. Esther said, "I wanted to see the boiler room where Uncle Silas will be working."

"Well, you won't," snapped Mildred.

Sam was ready to leave. "You heard your mother. No farther than your own front porch. Mildred, I may be late."

The three walked with him as far as the porch, where David climbed up on the banister rail and balanced this way and that, trying to get the best view of the speakers' wagon. "Nothing," he pronounced. "Nothing but the fires. We won't be able to hear a word."

"We'll hear Coite Reece," said Thomas. "He always gives a Rebel yell. At least he says it's a Rebel yell."

They sat in a line on the railing and swung their legs to the outside so they were facing the mill. Thomas reached across David to poke his sister and recite in singsong, "Three little niggers, sitting in a row; one in the middle is black as a crow."

"Don't say that!" David got up and banged his brother in the chest. "Don't you ever say that!" Thomas had to grab hold to keep from falling into the yard. He waited till David had settled down and turned his back; then he pinched him, hard.

Esther pointed to the wagon. "Wouldn't you think they'd have hung a sheet in front? There's not even a flag."

People had begun to arrive for the ceremony, most of them having walked only a few doors from their own houses. Some came from Greenway in buggies and carriages and wagons, and certain farm boys rode over on the family mule. Nearly all the women and children were from the village itself. Of the city people, many were businessmen carrying leaflets about their services; the undertaker was handing out black-edged cards, and the barber was shaking hands in the crowds; and the blacksmith started out introducing himself to everybody until he counted up who owned most of the horseflesh and saw it wasn't the mill people.

Some waved at the Allen children as they passed the house going to the mill. Preacher Holt spoke, and the foot-washing preacher pulled off his hat and swept it nearly to the dirt, and Nathan Grimes rode his horse up to the fence to say he was sorry they couldn't come.

"How's your father?" he said. "I've not seen much of Sam lately." He sounded wistful.

"He's fine," they all said at different speeds.

Dr. Newton waved to them and Mr. Winkler Hobbs made some sort of threatening gesture with his cane as he was rolled all the way up to the speakers' wagon and lifted off by two Negro men and propped up in a special armchair. Hobbs was so tightly bound in scarves and coats and mufflers that Esther thought of swaddling clothes.

"They're late starting," Thomas said. "The fires will all burn down."

Esther was bored. "Couldn't we sing something?"

David took a knife out of his pocket and began thumping it into the boards of the porch, trying to make the blade flash into a crack. Thomas said, "When you going to be through with that knife! When I said you could borrow it, I never meant forever."

"Soon," grunted David. "Soon."

"Let me see how it's coming," Esther said, holding out her hand. He shook his head. "I keep messing it up."

"Oh, let me see. I thought you'd be nearly done by now."

"I used the wrong wood." David took a grimy object from his pocket and blew away dust, lint, crumbs. He wiped it on his pants. "See?"

Esther examined the small figure between her thumb and forefinger. "This is pretty good, especially around the face where you had to carve so small. Thomas, look at this."

But David was shaking his head. "While I was working my fingers kept getting hot and wet and the whole color changed. Now the wood's red. It looks like an Indian."

Thomas returned the miniature infant after a brief glance. "I told you to use holly. Holly woods stays nice and white."

"I don't want it white."

"What about dogwood? Doesn't that turn kind of pink? Like skin?"

"I don't want pink."

"Think you're so smart," grunted Thomas.

"Who's that?" asked Esther suddenly. She threw one hand to the side of her face and seemed to be hiding behind it.

"It's just Mr. Max Carson."

Esther began to tug at her skirt. "Is he coming over here? Thomas, look that way and tell me if he's coming over here."

"Of course not. He's going right out to the wagon."

Esther lifted the ends of her hair and pushed at them aimlessly. Then she raised her head slowly and looked at the wagon. Carson had his back turned and, in the crowd, she could only see his neck and one shoulder. She wiped her mouth on the back of one wrist.

David was still looking at the small baby with the outsized belly he had whittled and smoothed down. "Next time I'm going to get wood from a persimmon," he announced. "They say it has a dark heartwood. The man at the sawmill promised he'd look out for me."

Esther stared. "Does Mama know you've been as far away as the sawmill?"

"I didn't go. Max Carson asked him for me."

"And how did you get to know Mr. Carson?"

"I was out cutting wood one day. Willow sticks. You know, back when I thought I might put this baby in some kind of cradle you could see through. And Max Carson had been out in the woods. He was— Well, Esther, you know it was a long time before they got the privies built at the mill. People had to use the woods."

"Never mind all that," said Esther, but her eyes slid away and looked across the crowd toward the wagon. She could see Max Carson's head.

"He asked what I was doing and I told him. And that's when he said persimmon wood was like ebony. And you need a real old tree to get the heartwood, so the man at the sawmill would have to find me one and cut it. They make bobbins out of persimmon wood—did you know that?"

"There's Uncle Silas," said Thomas, waving.

"Is he drunk?"

"He looks all right. I heard Papa saying if Uncle Silas got drunk on the job after he put in a good word for him, he was going to carry him out to the still and drown him in the mash."

"You mean mash him?" said David.

"No, he doesn't mean that. I sure would like to see that boiler room. Is Uncle Silas really going to be in charge?"

"How can you drown him and mash him? And where's Aunt Rosa?"

"The baby," said Esther impatiently. "All she does is lie home in bed and moon and make that baby."

The speeches had begun. Since they could hear none of the words, Esther stood up on the rail and moved her arms in an imitation of the gestures, pounded the air, spread her hands skyward, hammered a fist into her palm. Thomas said she ought to get down before she fell down. She jumped to the porch onto one foot and whirled around, then began to incorporate the hand movements of the speakers into a slow dance. She did not even notice when Coite Reece gave his Rebel yell and stepped down into a scattering of applause.

But Mildred, glancing out the front window, witnessed the dancing and came out onto the porch and caught hold of Esther by the earlobe. "You stop that wiggling!" Mildred gave the ear several sharp tugs.

Esther backed away, cocking her head to one side. She felt all her brains had been pulled off center. Thomas said, "They're all going inside now."

"Mama, let us go see!" David begged.

"You heard me."

The crowd had begun to straggle inside the mill, through the huge metal door which slid on a special track. Men and women, young boys with legs so long they seemed joined to the armpits, irritable children, here and there a sleeping baby folded over a shoulder, all moved across the yard and shuffled inside and then— probably to demonstrate how it worked—the big sliding door was closed. There's a story about that, thought Esther, leaning forward. The children all went inside the mountain.

Now the mill yard was empty except for the orange spots of low fire, and the village looked empty too—as if that gaping mill door had somehow sucked all the life inside it, swept clean the streets, and not missed so much as a single spider.

"Now what?" asked Mildred. She looked off toward the woods, where most of the visitors had tied their horses. Mildred never looked at the mill when she could help it.

"More speeches," Thomas said. "There's a telegram from the Governor somebody's going to read."

"You could have let us hear *that*," said Esther. "From the Governor."

"I could send telegrams too, if I was way off in Raleigh," Mildred snapped. "I could write down how this was a joyous occasion."

Then there came a strange sound, a slow, straining groan which spread to a growl and at last rose to a roar. Under that long stream of noise ran a series of rhythmic whacks and rumbles. Mildred grabbed hold of Esther as though the force of the noise might fling her down. David leaped into the yard and spread wide his arms. "The mill! They've started the mill!"

"Machinery!" yelled Thomas. "They're running all the new machinery!"

Mildred clapped both her hands to her ears. She understood for the first time what the Book of Revelations had meant by the Beast, now that she heard Him roaring. "Children!" she screamed. "You come inside."

"It's not so bad, Mama. You'll get used to it," Thomas said.

Esther moved her hand in the throbbing air. "You could dance to that."

Mildred stamped her foot. "Come in" she shrieked. "*Come away from it!*" They followed her indoors, Esther last and walking backwards.

"Oh," moaned Mildred, "it shakes the house! The windows rattle!" Thomas and Esther looked at each other and Thomas shook his head. Mildred flew ahead of them into the parlor and began to holler for rags to stuff around the window cracks. She kept her hands to her ears and sometimes, as if she were holding a gourd, she shook her head from side to side to rid it of that whirring.

"Esther, I said go get rags for these windows!"

"I'm going, Mama."

The soles of Mildred's feet were prickly with vibrations rising from the floor. "You feel that?" she cried out softly, and lifted her right shoe and shook it. "Can't you feel that?" She threw herself into a rocker but still the trembling came through the boards and climbed up the chair rungs and ran out twanging onto her skin. She heard her dishes skitter on their shelves.

"Here I am Mama. See? I'm putting them in now." Esther bent

down and began to work the cloth in with a kitchen knife against the window sash.

It wasn't going to do any good, Mildred could tell that. All these weeks she had waited for those endless hammers to be stilled, not knowing they were getting her ready for this. She leaned over in her chair and put her face into her knees, folding both arms over her head. She sat that way, crying, the whole afternoon.

PART II

Thomas

❧⟨⟩❧

JANUARY, 1899—DECEMBER, 1899

Chapter

❧ 11 ❧

THE SECOND TERM at Greenway Academy began in January. Thomas didn't want to leave the store long enough to go; he wanted to attend the lyceum with that handful of mill children whose families could spare them for a shift. Mildred wouldn't hear of it.

"We may live here," she said, "but we're not buried here."

"Besides," his father added, "you can't go off to the University next year with a mill-village education."

"I'd rather stay here and work in the store."

All three of them went back to the Academy, but Thomas spent the afternoons and early evenings with his father in the mill store. At supper, Thomas would sometimes lie about whether he had washed his hands so he could later curl up in bed and hold them to his face and reconstruct the store by the smells embedded in his skin. The barrels of sugar, molasses and beef in brine, the rows of tobacco cans, the glass jars of candy, the tin scoops used for dipping out meal and flour, the dark drum of kerosene—all left their memory along his damp fingers.

In the store, he was no longer Esther's sensible brother. He was not the older boy responsible for keeping David out of mud and trouble. In the store, Thomas was the one who knew how to measure the sheeting, cloth, trimmings; how to find every color of O.N.T.

thread; he knew which medicines were best for which ailments and how to take off a tin cuspidor or a chamber pot without the whole tower crashing down.

When he was in the store, Thomas often counted out money to men four times his age who could not count their own, and at the back post office he wrote letters or read incoming ones aloud to some of the mill hands. The men called him by name. Some asked his opinion on politics or cases in the county court. In front of him they talked about money, about the foreman who cheated everybody, the potato beetles, the best hunting dogs they ever knew, about their women and other men's women; and often they compared their bunions and ruptures and remembered fist fights.

"I don't see why I have to keep on with school," Thomas complained to his father. "I learn more here, with you."

"When you're my age, I want you to be someplace else," grunted Sam. "There's more to learn than this."

Esther was not allowed in the store at all. That suited Thomas fine. Behind him stretched years and years of Esther drawing her silly circle within another circle, winning all the games, making up the best stories; but here was a line she could not cross. "Esther thinks her mark is on everything," he said once to David, "but the store is mine."

"I thought it was Father's," David said.

"You and Esther think you get everything. She's the biggest and you're the baby, and I'm tired of it. You hear me, David? I'm tired of it!"

"It wasn't me got a knife for Christmas."

One cold January day, Sam and Big Jube rode to the still to see how the mash was working. It was not the first time Thomas had been left entirely in charge. As soon as they were out of sight, he walked up and down the aisles and let his hands brush against the edges of the counters. He studied his face in the bottom of a snuff tin and tried to see if he looked older than his thirteen and a half years. When Max Carson came in for rope, nails and a bucket, Thomas got the order together with a series of high-elbowed flourishes. "Anything else?" he asked in his best casual voice.

"That's all."

Thomas wrote out the charge in the ledger book. "I'd like to work for the mill someday," he said airily.

"Plenty younger than you over there right now," said Carson.

Thomas had not meant ordinary labor. He tightened his mouth and finished the notation.

"How's your sister?" Max Carson said.

"She's fine."

"Older than you are, isn't she?"

"Not much," said Thomas between gritted teeth.

Max Carson shook his head a few times and said he would have thought her older. "Sixteen? Seventeen?"

"She won't be fifteen until November. I'll be fourteen this summer." Thomas rubbed his hairline. He was getting a headache.

Max Carson looked surprised, said something about the climate, and picked up his bucket and left. As soon as he was out the door, Thomas rushed back to the shiny snuff tin and studied his face again. He was still looking at it when the bell rattled above the door and a little girl who looked about eleven or twelve came into the store, dangling her baby brother at the end of one arm. She headed straight for the gumdrop jar. "Look at that," she whispered. "Look at the colors."

Thomas hurried behind the candy counter. "How many?" His father had warned him not to leave mill children anywhere near the candy. Some of them would steal anything. One little boy had tried to get away with a whole ax slid up one trouser leg and his hand in the pocket hanging onto it.

"Nothing," said the little girl. "I just come in out of the cold." She rubbed the red tip of her nose and pointed to the jar. "Winkie, you see?"

"You can't hang around here."

"Winkie and me got two gumdrops Christmas. Didn't we, Winkie?"

"Just two?"

"There's eight of us children. The oldest ones got more. I had the red ones. Winkie, what kind did you get?"

Winkie began to cry.

"If you don't want anything, go along home," said Thomas.

"It's cold at home." She spread the fingers of her right hand into a gaping comb and ran it back through her straw-colored hair. "Winkie and me got cold."

"Don't be telling me. Go tell your mama."

"This is her shift. And Papa's in the bed. We take turns with the bed." Now she shifted her attention to the red-striped candy sticks. "How much is one of them?"

"Two for a penny," Thomas said. "You got a penny?"

"I only asked about one."

"I can't sell you just one. You have to buy a penny's worth of something." He shook his head. "There's nothing smaller than a penny—don't you know that?"

The baby brother, who might have been two years old, cried louder and began to kick the counter till all the jars rattled. Thomas leaned down toward him. "Stop that! You want to break something?"

"Listen," said the little girl intensely. "If you give me some pennies, I'll let you see something. I'll let you see me."

"I see you already. Make him stop that."

She jerked the baby's arm so hard it lifted him slightly off the floor.

"Now hush." She laid her head down on one side on the counter-top. "You know what I mean." She smiled.

"Get up from there," said Thomas, not very strongly.

She straightened with a stretch. "Ah, you know what I mean." She patted the front of her skirt with her free hand. "Four pennies. No, five. I'll let you see for five pennies."

Thomas stared at the place she had put her hand. She rubbed it back and forth a few times. He gave an uneasy look around the empty store, shifted from one foot to the other, and finally said he couldn't leave. "There's nobody else here," he said in a low voice.

"You got a storeroom, ain't you? In the back?" She let go the baby's hand and he promptly sat upon the oiled floor and began to pick at splinters. "Where the curtains hang?"

Thomas said she ought to be ashamed of herself. He scrubbed the back of his neck. "Besides, I don't have any money."

"Oh." She dragged her little brother to the iron stove and stood with her back to it. "It's hot," she told him. "Keep your hands off."

Thomas followed her, clearing his throat. "You do this much?"

"Sometimes," she said.

"What's your name?"

"You can't have my name," she said scornfully. "I ain't selling that."

"And what if your daddy comes in?"

"I told you he's asleep. Looky there, Winkie." She pointed to a glass case full of spectacles, knives, razors, soap and brushes. "Let him try them on."

"The glasses? He might break them."

She sighed and stooped to her little brother. "Anyhow, they make things look real big. I'll show you someday."

"I could give you candy. In place of the money, I could give you some candy," said Thomas in a rising voice.

The girl sauntered to a table and fingered a pair of work shoes tied together by thick tan laces. "Winkie, you reckon your feet will ever get that big?"

Thomas half ran to the candy counter and laid out four peppermint sticks in a neat row. He glanced at her. She had taken down one of the shoes and was measuring it on the floor against the baby's little foot. He added four gumdrops and a heap of cinnamon red-hots. She took up the shoe and looked inside it.

"All right," she said abruptly. Her little brother held out his hands and began to whimper for the shoes. She hit him in the ear. "I'll carry it in my pocket."

"Not yet," said Thomas. "You can have the candy after, not before."

A sly smile came over her face. "I'm not very hungry," she said lightly. "Winkie, are you hungry?" The boy burrowed his face into her leg.

"It's all the same to me," said Thomas, trying to hide his desperation. "You can't be much to see."

She shrugged her shoulders and led the way toward the back of the store, pulling on her brother's arm. Thomas hurried after her. "What about him?"

"Winkie don't know nothin'." Halfway through the curtained doorway, she stopped and wrapped herself in the black cloth until only her pale face was showing. "Listen," she said, "I sold you nothing but a look. Touching costs more."

His throat was shrunken. He could hardly talk. "How much more?"

"Not today," she said.

"But how much more? Just so I'll know."

She shook her head and disappeared behind the curtain.

Thomas took one last nervous look around and pushed his way through the curtain folds, which nearly suffocated him. The storeroom, stacked high with crates and barrels, had only one high window. In the dim light, he could not tell much about her except that her hair was pale in color and she would not come to his chin. She had already pulled up her skirt and begun knotting it in some fashion around her waist, out of the way. She gave a quick look at the room.

"The way it is back here," she said, "you'll have to get down on the floor."

"On the floor? I will not!" cried Thomas. He stuck his head back through the curtains to make certain no one had come in and heard him.

"No chairs," said the girl, "and not hardly a wall to lean on." She waved one limp hand at all the bins and boxes. Then she untied the string of her drawers and let them fall. "I don't see any other way." She stepped out, tucked the drawers in a wad beneath one of the skirt knots at her waist and parted her legs. "Seems to me you'll have to take your look from down there," she said, and fluffed up her hair. "You stay still, Winkie."

Thomas had begun to tremble at the whiteness of her skin, which seemed ghostly in the half light of the storeroom. She looked as if there were no more substance to her than a square of pale silk which could be folded up and carried in a walnut shell. "Oh, Lord," he breathed. "How much is touching?"

"We finished talking about that. Nothing but a look," she said. "Winkie, don't you bother a thing!"

"Can't you even let go his hand?"

"And have him fall in a pickle barrel or something worse? Hurry up," she said irritably. "It's cold back here."

Thomas took the baby's hand and pulled him to the side of the room where light came in one thin ribbon from the high window. "Now watch the dust float up and down," he ordered. "Stay right here."

"F' goodness sakes," the girl said in disgust.

Thomas lowered himself to a sitting position on the floor in front of her and studied what he could see at eye level. She was very thin; the navel would not have held his little finger, and her stomach sloped down to a little hill with a line in it. "How old are you?" he asked, gulping.

"You done?"

"Hold still, hold still!" He leaped up quickly and ran to the curtains and peered through. The store looked foreign. He could not remember which shelf was for cough medicine and which held axle grease. "Nobody's out there."

"Somebody will be if you take all day."

This time he bolted across the room and scrambled down and lay upon his back and slid across the floor until his shoulders were almost even with the toes of her spread shoes. He stared upward. "It's awful dark back here," he complained.

She nudged him with her foot. "I'm getting cold, I truly am."

He could make out no real details except that the line continued for some distance, and he caught hold of her ankles with his hands. "Hold still," he hissed. "Couldn't you come closer?"

"We never talked about closer. That's enough now. I want my candy." The little boy, as if on cue, began to grumble and twist from side to side.

"Let me go get a lamp. It won't take a minute." He clung to her ankles and tried to raise his head slightly off the floor for a better view. She turned her toes in and caught the skin on each side of his neck and stepped down in a pair of hard pinches.

"We never talked about lamps," she said, then kicked her right foot loose from his fingers and stepped deftly back. Before he could get to his feet she had her drawers yanked up about her waist.

"I'll give you lots more candy," he begged. "Just let me go bring a lamp."

She loosened her skirt and let it fall, brushing at the wrinkles. "Honey pot," she said to her brother, "we going to have us some candy." Without looking at Thomas, she whirled through the curtains so rapidly they billowed back behind, and the two-year-old had to run to keep up.

Thomas ran too; but she was already at the candy counter, scraping off her pile of sweets into one hand. She stuck one peppermint stick deep inside her mouth and balanced another behind her ear.

"Will you come back again?" called Thomas. She was already opening the door, jamming a gumdrop into her brother's mouth.

"Don't bite me, you devil," she said.

"You coming back?"

Halfway through the door, she stopped and looked him up and down. "I might," she said, and caught Winkie's wrist and pulled him out behind her.

After that Thomas begrudged every minute he spent riding back and forth to Greenway with Esther and David, every hour they sat listening to Miss Eliza Tilley's precepts. Who knew when the girl would have another sweet tooth strong enough to grant him lamps and touching? Thomas was at the store early in the mornings; he had to be driven out to school by force; and as soon as he got home in the afternoons, he leaped out of the buggy and hit the ground running to see if she had come. When he and his father locked up in the evenings, Thomas would slide his eyes up and down the night streets, watching. Sometimes, just from the effort of staring, his head would buzz and begin to ache.

"Yessir, Thomas," his father would sometimes say as they crossed the yard home, "I like your attitude. Hard work and long hours— I tell you, they pay off. We're going to own this store before long."

Thomas barely heard him. His eye seemed to bounce from one lighted window to the next all the way between the store and the edge of the forest. He wondered which window was hers.

It was hoped that Greenway Manufacturing Company would be nearly paid for by the summer of 1899. Already there was money in Greenway pockets, which—Sam Allen said—had been empty so long the linings had stuck together.

One hundred thousand dollars in stock in the mill had been issued, subscribed by a variety of Stone County people at either a dollar a week for two years or fifty cents weekly for four. Many of the workers themselves, as well as local cotton farmers, had pooled their small resources to own stock jointly.

Now the mill was keeping one hundred employees busy at about five thousand spindles and two hundred looms from six in the morning till six-thirty at night, and every turn of every wheel ate into indebtedness. There was hope that by 1900 nearly half the machinery would be paid off, and in 1901 and 1902, everything in the mill would be free and clear. It might be possible, then, to add incandescent electric lights, with a dynamo to be driven by a waterwheel in the Katsewa.

"If it goes like it's going now," Sam would say to Thomas when they were closing the store at night, "that mill will be making a profit of anywhere between fifteen and thirty per cent. With that and my profits out of this store, we'll buy your mother her house in Greenway."

Thomas didn't quite understand how Sam, who was on salary, could be making any profit at the store. Sam had several times explained that not all the store's merchandise was the property of Winkler Hobbs.

"Some things are all mine, and the profit off those things is mine," he said. Often he laughed when he said this, and struck himself in the leg.

Thomas was trying to cultivate a businessman's mind. "Mr. Hobbs didn't buy all these things? You paid the wholesale price yourself for some, and you sell them at a retail price, and it's your difference?"

"That's right," said Sam. He walked up and down the store aisles, smiling into his own shoulder. "That's exactly right. Sometimes it seems just like a bonus. A bonus for long and faithful service."

"I'm surprised Mr. Hobbs lets you go into business for yourself in his own store."

Sam did not answer.

Often Thomas would see receipts which showed that certain things had actually been purchased for resale by Sam Allen, dry-goods merchant. He soon learned, too, that there were two sets of books; items which sold well were apt to dwindle out of Hobbs's inventory and Hobbs's books and appear on Sam's own. In effect it was like running two stores at once—one for Winkler Hobbs, which did a tolerable amount of business and was always showing a small but steady improvement, and an invisible one for Sam Allen, which was flourishing. If there was any spurt of increased business, it seemed to show up only in the Allen ledger, while the Hobbs store held even and only inched ahead. The whiskey business was also Sam's, conducted out of the storeroom to men who came in coughing and asking about slippery-ellum tea. Sometimes, too, Sam made direct loans to millworkers and their families, on which they paid and paid, week after week, when they cashed in their scrip at his store.

"Mr. Hobbs used to come in the store uptown every day or two," Thomas said. He and his father were going over the day's receipts. "I haven't seen him since the day they started the mill. Is he sick again?"

"Yes," said Sam, and dropped that grin toward his shoulder. "Sick as a dog."

"Is he going to die?"

"Not for a while, I hope. He got a chest cold out here the day the mill opened. They've put him in bed till spring. I hear his mind is failing."

"That's too bad."

"I see him every week or so, take him the books and the records from the bank. He trusts me. Even if he was well, he wouldn't ride all the way out here to see a man he trusted."

"How about his nephew? The one running the uptown store?"

Sam almost tittered. "Oh, he came once or twice. That road through the woods, you know, is pretty lonely. Somebody knocked him off his horse once and took a sack of money he was bringing down here for change. The second time he swore he was shot at out of the bushes; I told him it was likely somebody hunting squirrels."

"That's too bad," said Thomas again.

That January Sam bought himself a watch on a gold chain and a walking stick; he traded the mare for a spirited chestnut marked in the face with an irregular white streak, like spilled milk; and Rutledge drove the Allen children to the Academy in a new rubber-tired buggy.

The middle of that month Sam took out the tallest ladder from the storeroom and stretched twine in a long line high along the ceiling the length of the store. Then he set Thomas and Big Jube Jackson to moving stock around, pausing every so often to stop them in their tracks while he sighted along the twine. It was strung so high above the lamps that unless you knew just where to look, it became another crack between the ceiling boards.

"That's right," Sam said, pointing out items to be moved. "The sheep right there. And yonder the goats." Then he consulted a list he was carrying and moved to another aisle and began to order everything shifted there.

At last the store had been rearranged entirely to his satisfaction and now it could be seen that most of the real buying took place in one half of it, while the joking and checker games were held in the other half. And every time Sam Allen passed under that unseen ceiling string he lifted one foot for a high step, as if he were crossing a barrier made for his leg only.

Even with this new arrangement, it seemed Sam wanted certain items switched back and forth from one week to the other. This was a great nuisance to Jubilee Jackson, who did most of the heavy lifting. He said to Thomas, "Your daddy likes things neat, damn if he don't."

"Just hand me the ladder," Thomas puffed.

He was high atop that ladder, taking things from Jube's huge hands and placing them on the far shelf, the day the girl came in. For weeks he had been watching for the high-low shape of a straw-haired girl who had a small boy swinging from her right hand; so he nearly didn't recognize her when she walked into the store alone, headed straight for his father and held out an oil can with a little spout. "My mama wants kerosene for the lamps, and she says add it to this week's charge."

At the sound of that nasal voice, Thomas grabbed hold of the shelf and screwed his head around as far as it would go.

"You watch that," called Big Jube. "You going to come down right in my face."

"Who's that?" Thomas whispered.

"Some little girl wants oil. I'm handing it to you. You going to take it?"

Thomas grabbed a double handful of bottles and slammed them blindly onto the shelf. "Listen when she gives the name for the charge. I got to find out her name."

"Oh, it's like that, is it?" chuckled Jube. He turned and studied the girl. "Ain't she a mite young?" He handed up a box of burn salve and Thomas began to line the jars. Jube poked him in the leg. "Let me see, was it Dowdy she said? Or could it be Towson? Come to think of it, I think she asked your daddy to charge it to the Moody family."

Already the girl was carrying her tin of kerosene down the aisle to the front door, giving no sign she had seen Thomas atop the ladder. She drew abreast of them, beyond; then she twisted around on one foot and stuck out her tongue at Thomas. Instantly he turned his own face to the back of the store (where, unfortunately, there was nothing to see but those billowing dark curtains) so he would not have to watch her amble out the door.

Jube leaned into the ladder, laughing silently. "It's a real sweet case; I can see that!" he wheezed.

"Shut up."

"Now smooth your feathers; I caught her name. She told your daddy to set it down for Dowdy. Fletcher Dowdy."

Thomas would not even glance at him. "You gonna hand me that stuff or am I just here for decoration? It's hot up here. Makes my head hurt."

Big Jube shrugged his shoulders and heaved up a whole box of shoe blacking, lamp wicks and liniment. "Sort it out yourself, you in such a big hurry," he growled.

The first chance he got that afternoon, Thomas dragged out the ledger which listed all families who lived in the mill village, the houses they were assigned, how much coal and wood they were expected to need, and the record of rent paid. There was a page for Fletcher Dowdy. Married to Obedience Dowdy. House Number Four. The children, five of whom worked in the mill along with their parents, were listed as Ernest, Rachel Blessing, Mary Sue, Clyde, Dalton, Zelda, Kelly Marvin and Christine. No ages were given, but since the first five were listed as workers, Thomas thought Winkie had to be Kelly Marvin, which meant the girl was either Zelda or Christine Dowdy.

Thomas looked across the counters and practiced in his mind the firm manner he would take with her next time. *Now, Christine Dowdy,* he would begin, surprising her with his knowledge of her name, *Now, Christine, I'm ready to trade.* He would look down at her in his best storekeeper manner and Christine would jerk her head to the east and west and measure how far it was to the door, but he would be standing in the way with a handful of candy sticks. Yes, she was surely Christine, he thought, and he might get off a scornful "Teeny" or so, just to separate the buyers from the sellers and the older from the young.

Thomas leaned back into the wall and held the mill book over his chest and smiled up into the farthest kerosene lamp. *All right, Teeny. Do this. Now do that. Now move here. Hold still. That's fine. No, you hold the lamp yourself and swing it a little to the right. And stop that sniveling.*

At his elbow Jube said suddenly, "You taken up talking to yourself?"

Thomas flung the book halfway across the store. "Don't you come up on me like that without any warning!" he spluttered. "Look what you made me do!"

"You do beat all," said Big Jube mildly. He picked up the book and wiped it on his leg. "It ain't tore. Show me that Dowdy."

Thomas was tired of finding new words for Jube. He spelled the name aloud.

"What page is that?" asked Jube, turning over the sheets with great care. Thomas wrote the number 5 in the shelf dust; Jube studied the shape of that figure and began to look for it in the book. "I got it. Hey, Thomas, what's this one?" He touched the word with his yellow nail.

"That's Obedience," said Thomas. "His wife is named Obedience."

"Runs pretty long," said Big Jube. He moved his mouth to the sound of the word. "You got time to copy this one out?"

"I'll do it before we close up tonight."

"Be fine," said Big Jube softly. "Obedience. I declare, that's a long word for minding. Obedience." He grinned at Thomas and passed the ledger to him. "Maybe I can do something for you sometime. Maybe I can help you get that Dowdy girl to be your sweetheart."

"Christine. Her name's Christine." Thomas narrowed his mouth and eyes. "I wouldn't have her on a gold plate," he said in a hard voice.

Jube looked admiring. "Hey, could I have that one too? Would you write that down for me this evening, Thomas? Gold plate. That is the prettiest thing. Obedience. Gold plate."

"This is a store, not a school," grumbled Thomas, but he knew he would write the words onto wrapping paper for Big Jubilee Jackson to carry home at suppertime as presents to his children.

Big Jube could read and write—in his own way.

His daddy, a slave on a large farm near Warrenton in eastern North Carolina, had stolen in 1859 a hymnal from the Presbyterian church to teach himself to read.

The slaves had already learned their hymns by rote; now, by matching a memorized word with the way it appeared in print, Jube's daddy accumulated a family dictionary. He copied out his words onto slips of paper, repeating each one over and over until the shape of it was in his mind the same way some trees in winter are always oaks and some are always maples. The words had an outline, too, like a tracery of twigs in a gray sky. When he was sure he had one learned, he filed it with the others in boxes and crocks and jars according to the opening letter. There was no consecutive order, since he had never learned the alphabet.

Still, Big Jube's daddy kept all the A-words in the A-jars, and during the evenings he would take a few at random and empty them onto a table and recite the words to his children as he showed them the papers: JESUS. JORDAN. BLOOD. CROSS. SWEET. LOST. ROLL.

The children squatted around him in the firelight, awed at this mystery, while he—like Pandora—unleashed one power after another, honoring that power with a husky, slightly reverent voice. In whispers they repeated after him. They passed the torn slips of paper from hand to hand, as if they were sharing holy wafers in a church.

"When it comes to you, talk it aloud," he would say, and while the light from off the hearth flecked their fingertips with gold, they breathed the mysterious sounds: CROWN. STAND. LORD. GLORY. EYES. FOUNTAIN.

All of them liked that word—fountain. FOWN-TAN. It made a little song in the throat. A pity there was so little chance to use it.

Big Jube inherited these jars of language from his daddy. They sat now in his house as they had in that other cabin, helter-skelter on a thick ledge stuck in between two unchinked logs, and braced.

The number of containers had grown; some of the letters were now represented by several jars, and all were full and running over; for Big Jube sought out written words the way collectors seek fine butterflies. His job at the store gave him a daily supply of specimens: SUGAR. FLOUR. PICKLES. COFFEE. SHOE BLACK. WICK. SNUFF.

He copied, too, all the words from the signs along the Greenway streets: LIVERY. STABLE. GREENWAY. HOTEL. STORE. GOVERNOR.

Some evenings he was so excited by his new words that he would begin hollering them aloud as soon as he came into the yard. "Hey, get this, you young'uns: OBEDIENCE and GOLD PLATE! I got 'em right here in my hand. Did you ever hear the like? GOLD PLATE! OBEDIENCE!"

He kept all the J-words in a tall green jar, because J was his letter and he liked the murky look of the colored glass. Like MOSS, he would think, making the word soft and cool in his mind. Like S-L-I-M-E, stretching it slickery and wet. Like DEEP WATER, and when he thought that, the words went down forever in a bottomless pool.

He stored his own name in the green jar. JUBE. JUBILEE. JACKSON. JUNE. JESUS. JUDAS.

JEWEL. Sometimes, late at night, he would whisper that one aloud in his bed. "The JOO-ELL is in the FOWN-TAN." He felt he was minting silver with his mouth. His shoulders would jerk involuntarily at the sound of those shining words, as if he were having a nervous chill.

On winter nights he made Little Jube study. He would dump out five or six jars of words on the table and mix them up with his wide, dark hand.

"Sort them out by letters, and read as you go," he'd growl. And then he'd stare into the fire and listen to the hesitant treble of his son's voice, his heart swollen and heavy on his ribs.

"LINCOLN," Little Jube would read politely. "SLAVE. SHAVE. HAIRCUT. FOR. RENT. NOTIONS. SALVE. SALE. FIRST. BAPTIST. PRAY. GREENWAY. FREEDOM. FIFTY. CENTS. CHURCH."

"You hear yourself?" Big Jube would whisper. "You listening?"

"HILL. SUFFER. STORMY. EVERLASTING."

"Not so fast," he interrupted. "That's a long time you're reading there."

"EVER," said Little Jube carefully, "LASTING."

"That's better. Now, Vinnie. You."

His wife shuffled and moved one shoulder in a circular motion. "Aw, Jube, not me. They all look the same to me."

"Then write it," he'd order, holding out a torn paper and one of the stub pencils he got out of the store trash when Sam Allen threw them out.

She wrote it. "VINNIE," she scrawled with care and concentration, the V arcing halfway off the edge. She munched on the back edge of her tongue. "MRS. JUBILEE JACKSON, JR." she finally got written.

Big Jube would study that signature, frowning but content. "That's it, then." Looking up fiercely, he would demand of his children, "And what's your last name?"

They fairly leaped up and down and shouted it at him. "Jackson! Jackson!"

"Don't you forget it when everybody else do."

When Thomas first went to work for the dry-goods store, he knew nothing of Big Jube and his writing. Now and again Jube would ask him some roundabout question. "They ought to mark these things," he'd say slyly.

"Beans, Jube? Anybody can see it's beans."

He would level the bin of dried beans and thrust in the scoop at a neat vertical. "And how would you write that out?"

Thomas spelled it for him slowly and, when he looked disappointed, spelled more deliberately the second time. At this, Jube would stomp away muttering about skipping past letters and getting down to the words in the first place.

It was David who told Thomas about the jars.

"It's as bad as going to school," he said. "Night after night, Little Jube says, they read the papers out of the jars."

"Waste of time," said Thomas. "What good's it going to do them?"

Privately David thought it was insurance for Jubilee, so that when it came they would all be able at one stroke to learn the words to all the fine new songs. "I think it's good," he said. "I gave him everything in my blue-back speller."

"You did?"

"Sure. I took a whole week and didn't listen to a word Miss Eliza said and wrote down everything. Big Jube nearly had a conniption. It was 'sassafras' he liked best of all, as I remember. He had them reading 'sassafras' for nigh onto three nights."

After that, Thomas started writing everything down and leaving scraps of paper (sometimes illustrated for clarity) where Big Jube could find them and slide them into his pockets slicker than lard. Sam complained he used up half the brown wrapping paper just writing on it, and not even writing close together but spread out, so it was fit for tearing into jar-size pieces.

Thomas never talked to Jube about his reading. He'd walk through the store, eyeing Jube as he tapped his pencil here and there. "Ham," he might mutter, and if interest flicked across Jube's face he'd write it down and sketch a pig's haunch suspended on a chain.

Once he said, "Grits," and Jube—without thinking—blurted, "I already got grits." So he didn't write that one down.

But he did list the numbers one to twenty, reading them aloud to himself so Jube could tell their order, and sometimes he would send Jube home with newspapers and catalogues, "to wrap things in."

"Vinnie can sure use these," Jube would crow, already probing the new gifts with a greedy finger, looking for names that went with the pictures. CORSET. SLIPPER. FUNERAL. MULE. REUNION.

Thomas said to David, "I wouldn't tell anybody about the jars with the words in them, or about you giving him what was inside your speller. You might get Jube's family in trouble. Somebody would say he was getting uppity, forgetting his place."

"I never thought of that," said David.

"You just leave the new words to me." For Thomas was already turning in his head some way he could make Big Jube grateful to him. Big Jube could mind the store a little while the day he took Christine Dowdy down by the river. There might be lots of things Big Jube could do. Thomas would think of them.

He wrote on a little paper and repeated it aloud: "WORM." Jube looked over his shoulder. "That word even *looks* like it's crawling," he whispered.

"OWNERSHIP," Thomas spoke and wrote down. "TERRITORY. POWER."

"Tell me something with a color in it," Jube said huskily. "Like that gold plate."

"Like cherries? And violets? Rainbows?"

"That's a nice one. Let's see that rainbows."

Thomas wrote it and left it lying on the counter, but when he walked away he was still repeating under his breath, "Ownership, territory. Power."

Twice more in January the Dowdy girl came into the mill store and never looked at Thomas. In fact, she kept her eyeballs rolled upward so high it made Sam Allen nervous. The second time she came, he volunteered to her that the string up there was a dividing line, and helped him keep track of the stock.

"What string?" was all she said.

The first time she came, Thomas was just getting home from school and Rutledge had stopped the buggy halfway between the store and the Allen house. Thomas had raised his foot to step onto the small ledge and out of the buggy when he saw the Dowdy girl entering the store, and he stepped straight out into the air and fell on his knees in the clay street. He was so afraid she would turn and see him there, bent like some worshiper, that he threw himself entirely under the buggy and rolled onto his back and pretended to be examining the front wheel.

Esther climbed down very carefully, gathered her skirts about her and stooped to look at him through the spokes. "I'd like to know what you're doing."

His voice was muffled. "There's something broke."

"If Rutledge rolls on ahead, it's going to be you," she said.

"Hold up, Rutledge! Don't you move this thing!"

Rutledge leaned out of the seat and shook his head. "Did he say what he's doing down there in the dirt?"

A girl's voice called to them suddenly from the door to the mill store. "He just naturally likes to lay down and look up," it said merrily.

"Who was that?" Esther turned to see, but the girl had gone.

The second time the Dowdy girl came into the store, Thomas had been helping Big Jube roll a barrel up the back ramp and into the storeroom. They got it in with difficulty, and turned it upright in a row of others. Thomas rested his elbows on its top and had opened his mouth to ask what was inside that weighed so much, when he saw the girl's round face between the curtains. It looked like a single white button sewed on a dark coat, and appeared so suddenly he thought he might be imagining it.

"Yes, ma'am?" said Jube. "You looking for something?"

"No." She did not look at Thomas. He straightened up very slowly from the barrel and even rose slightly on tiptoes to loom into her vision.

"Sure you're not looking for something?" he asked, not smiling.

She made a little grin and shook her head. Then, very gradually, she closed the two curtains over her face.

He hurried into the store after her. "Christine? Wait a minute, Christine!"

She had begun to laugh and walk faster.

"Christine Dowdy, wait a minute!"

She stopped at the door and moved it back and forth a few times to hear the bell jangle. "I ain't Christine," she chortled. "My name is Zelda." The door slammed behind her.

Big Jube had come up quietly behind him. "Seems to me," he said softly, "that none of your seeds is coming up."

"That is the ugliest girl I ever saw," snapped Thomas.

Jube allowed himself to smile. "Maybe I better fetch you a love charm from Miss Bethesda Lee Michael."

Thomas was furious. He yelled, "I ain't as dumb as some niggers I know!" and saw Big Jube jerk his head back as if someone had hit him in the mouth with a hoe handle.

"That's all right," said Jube quietly. His upper lip had laid itself back across his teeth of its own accord. He lifted one hand and pressed the palm into his mouth. "I'll get that other barrel," he managed to say.

As the day wore on, Thomas thought about what Jube had said. He finally drove himself to ask whether Big Jube himself had ever been to see Miss Bethesda.

"No," said Jube shortly.

"Lots of people do. You know people that go see her?"

"Some."

He saw that Big Jube had closed himself up like a fist. "I'm sorry for what I said this afternoon." Still the big man did not look at him. "It just slipped out, Jube. You know I don't feel that way."

Big Jube could not keep the bitterness from his voice. "Dumb niggers don't know nuthin," he said, and spat out the back door.

"Jube, I didn't mean it. I'm sorry." Thomas put his hand on Jube's shoulder, which he did not like to do. He was not like David, and saw in the black man not a mystery but a usefulness. The white did not touch the black, he believed, except in emergencies or when they were too little to know better. And women, of course. Now and again, he had gathered from conversations in the store, a woman in the dark had no color at all.

"I really am sorry," he repeated, and let his hand fall.

Big Jube nodded his head. "It was the little girl caused it," he said, and seemed to relax.

"I hear Miss Bethesda won't see everybody that comes to her. Turns them away."

"She say she got the power; she can pick and chose."

"Does it depend on money?"

"Sometimes," said Big Jube. "Other times she takes a like or a not-like to somebody soon as they set foot in her yard. Sometimes she goes by who took 'em over. Miss Rosa, now, was took over by my wife, Vinnie. Vinnie can't hardly pick blackberries without checking with Miss Bethesda."

"Is that so?" mused Thomas. "I didn't know you all knew the old lady that well."

Jube put in a chew of tobacco. "Vinnie claims Miss Bethesda can pick up a Bible . . . you lay your right hand on the front cover and your left hand on the back cover. First she says a few things, and after that, for as long as you keep your hands without moving, it turns into the book of your life."

"What do you mean, book of your life?"

"You just hold your hands flat on those covers and Miss Bethesda manages to open it, even upside down or sideways, and she can read out of your life as long as you haven't moved. Sometimes she opens to what's already happened; sometimes she don't. It all depends. Of course, if you move even the least littlest bit, all she gets is Chronicles or St. Paul."

Thomas was disappointed. "Is that all she does? Tricks with the Bible?"

"Oh, she does lots of things if you're willing to believe in it."

"Tell me."

"She can make you a love packet. Or put a curse on somebody or fix up a dry cow. They claim she can make toenails grow in or out, depending on how she feels about it. Or she could read your cornbread if you don't like the thing with the Bible. Vinnie's good at holding her hands still and letting Miss Bethesda read her life, and that's cheaper than the cornbread."

"How's that done?"

"You bring your own cornbread—you got to make it yourself from the meal right up through the rising in the stove. If somebody else even pours the milk in, it tells you a lie. You carry the whole panful down to her, break off one chunk and take a bite. Then you crumble the rest of your chunk and throw it over your head on the ground. She reads how it falls on the ground."

"Can she read past or future in the crumbs?"

"Like them toenails, depending on how she feels, I reckon. I don't believe in none of this, but Vinnie— Lord! Before every baby come, she was over there every day getting the cord straightened and cutting the pains and laying down every tooth in the baby's mouth."

Thomas was not interested in Vinnie's childbirths. "After she reads the crumbs on the ground, is there something you do with the rest of the cornbread cake?"

"Hoo! I should swear you do! You give it to Miss Bethesda, that's what, and if it's sad cornbread, that turns out to make a sad story throwed out in her yard, I hear."

Thomas had to laugh. "Funny what some people believe," he said. "Funny."

Thomas walked to the door and stood looking out the front window down the street of the mill village. House Number Four. Fletcher and Obedience Dowdy. Zelda Dowdy. Winkie. The idea was in his mind as a fish is in the water, now deep, now shallow, now moving out of sight.

He said softly, "Jube, there is no limit to the different things you know."

Big Jube got cautious and uneasy. "I don't know much, Mr. Thomas," he said hastily, eyeing him. "How could I know much?"

"Jube, I want you to tell me lots of things. I want you to tell me everything. Everything." Thomas leaned forward and with his fingernail wrote the word on the dusty windowpane: EVERYTHING.

Jube leaned forward, his eyes shining. "Now that," he said, "is some word. That is a mouthful."

Thomas moved his hand in a series of quick stabs at the glass. "And how's this one?" He scratched in tall letters: JERUSALEM. "Isn't that a word? Jerusalem? You like that?"

Jube said reverently it sure did put EVERYTHING to shame.

Above them both Thomas scrawled out REVELATIONS and read it several times by syllables.

"Oh," sighed Jube. "Don't tell me again what it is. Just let me look at it from one end to the other."

"And Jube," said Thomas softly, "I know lots more. I bet I know a thousand words." He wrote in the dusty glass: THOUSAND, and Jube said that came out two letters less than EVERYTHING, which must be just about right.

In the days that followed, Thomas was almost sorry he had encouraged Big Jube to share his knowledge. As it turned out, Jube had other education beyond reading, an assortment of facts and views for which Thomas was unprepared.

"Nigra named Thomas Day used to make cabinets, furniture," Jube might volunteer while the two of them were putting up coal in twenty-five-pound tow sacks. "Had white men working for him."

Thomas would straighten up, shocked. "Now I never heard any such thing. Jube, where'd you hear that?"

"It's a fact. Right here in North Carolina. Time of the war."

Or again he'd ask if Thomas knew that in the Wilmington race riots of 1898, eleven colored men had been killed and twenty-five wounded?

Now Thomas was irritated. "The papers said only eight men killed, and three or four white men were hurt."

"Papers!" sneered Jube. "Who owns them papers?"

Perhaps this education had come from Jube's daddy, too, along with the words in their glass jars, for the Jacksons were militant in their racial pride—militant, but careful who knew it. At first Thomas answered him lightly, trying to joke because he needed Big Jube's loyalty, but sometimes the arguments grew sharp.

Thomas would ask him, half joking, if black skin wasn't the telltale mark God set on Cain for his sin of murder? And Jube would come back without a quiver and claim that the black man was one of the lost tribes of Israel.

Or—when things were really turning to argument—Thomas might quote from some of the speeches he'd heard. He'd tell Jube the Negroes had degraded Craven County (where Wilmington was located), had sent a Negro to the Legislature who was a convicted felon. Then he'd grow dramatic and recall the claims made in the last governor's campaign. "Remember!" he'd quote with a wide sweep of his arm. "Remember, it took Spain eight hundred years to expel the Moors!"

Jube straightened up. "What's that? What Spain? What Moors?" He threw the two sacks of coal easily across one shoulder as if he might march right off to Spain and settle that thing.

Thomas really didn't know much about it. "Spain's a country," he said lamely, "and the Moors were colored."

"You write that down." Jube dropped the coal. "Write down them words."

Thomas put the two words on more of Sam Allen's brown wrapping paper—SPAIN. MOORS—while Jube stood over him suspiciously as if he might scribble the wrong thing just to confuse him.

Then, some days later, Jube would confound him by asking in a very casual voice if it was true that Othello was a Moor in a play by William Shakespeare? Thomas had to go straight to Nathan Grimes to find out if that was so; and it was.

And so, gradually, Thomas began to learn that the Negro in Stone County had not only its Conjur Woman; had not only an occasional individual "born to rest" whom he supported in a lazy existence; but he also had his Educated Man—somewhere. Thomas believed that somehow Jube was able to contact some anonymous black in some other place, an Educated Man, whose knowledge was some racial fund and who was always on call like a doctor.

Somehow the word would go out, maybe scratched on wrapping

paper from the store, with the message, "Answer me this," and it would be carried forth by . . . by . . . by whom? By migrants and bums and peddlers and beggars and wanderers. And then slowly it would come back, perhaps on paper but more likely memorized, transferred from tongue to tongue and borne like the torch of Marathon.

Sometimes the reply which came back to Thomas was interesting without having anything to do with the question. It was as though the unknown source of knowledge had found himself out of stock on this particular matter, but had offered Jube something else as a substitute.

For example, once Thomas told Jube the African had held a quarter of the earth for three hundred years and made no progress, and folks said now there were cannibals among the black folk in Haiti.

And back, after days and days, came the word, across whatever route, that in 1898, ninety-two Negroes were lynched in the South by white men, and them civilized.

Thomas did not like the drift things had taken between him and Big Jube; he did not like these long discussions; he did not like being given information he did not care to own. But patiently he listened when Jube talked, and often he smiled when Jube brought him some triumphant answer to yesterday's question. He could afford to do this the way Sam Allen could do business in the store: it was wholesale investment toward retail profit.

Because Big Jube was going to fix it, sooner or later, so he could see Miss Bethesda Lee Michael, and Miss Bethesda was going to fix it so he could see Zelda Dowdy; and he and Zelda were going to fix it so he could see everything. He smiled over the word just as Jube had smiled. Everything. EVERYTHING.

Chapter

❧ 12 ❧

THE SOUND OF THE MILL had become like the sound of his own heart, Thomas thought. He could hear it only by taking thought.

David's mind was always separated from his body and roaming elsewhere, so he did not hear the noise of the mill or anything else, least of all his own name when he was called. As for Esther, she found it like living with a drumbeat which could be altered to fit any occasion—thumping war chant, harvest celebration.

But for Mildred Allen, the noise ran through her in a long echo day and night. Often her bones ached, she said, and the words on the Bible page seemed to shake loose from the paper and flow together, humming.

She did not allow any of the three children to set foot inside the mill. She said it might "take hold" of them; by that she meant either some metal arm might grab them by the hair and draw them into a crushing death, or they might look around and somehow find it all marvelous.

Still, they formed some idea of how it must look inside the mill and what took place behind those walls. Thomas heard the men talking in the store. Esther sat at her bedroom window and watched Max Carson pass in the mill yard, and saw what the mill took into itself and what it gave up again. David carved two tiny men and a bale of cotton out of some thread spools, tacked them together into a group, and dipped them in soup until they were orange and sticky, the color of the mill walls.

"That's good!" Esther exclaimed when she saw it.

"No, it's not," he said, and threw it straightaway into the Katsewa River.

They could not help learning something about the mill, living right next door. Raw cotton, some 1,200 pounds a day, went first to the picker room, which was cut off from the main mill by a fire wall. Here several bales, each weighing five hundred pounds and held together by seven dark iron bands, were broken open and mixed together, the cotton fluffed up, the last seeds and dirt removed. At last the pickers would take a long fleece and wind it into a roll for the carding machines. This was called scutching.

(Esther loved the obscure threat she heard in that obscure word. To be scutched was to be . . . well . . . squished, squelched, scrooched. It meant some total change. All the people Esther didn't like deserved a scutching.)

All three Allens had seen women carding at their spinning wheels in Greenway homes, so they knew that the cards—revolving flats— continued the cleaning of the cotton and made the fibers lay more parallel along fine, stubby wires.

These fibers then would be brushed and drawn into compressed slivers, like swatches of an old woman's long hair combed out for bed. These slivers would also be combed, stretched out long, until each strand was fine and even. Then they were sent to the roving frames to be thinned and reduced in diameter and pulled out even further in length, and given a slight twist.

(Esther liked, too, that title: slubbing frame. To be both scutched and slubbed—what could be more final?)

At last, on the ring spindles, the cotton strand would be further twisted and wound onto bobbins and made ready for the loom. When Esther heard the throbbing of the mill she thought first of the bobbins; she could somehow hear the small noise they would make flying around and around, going forever faster. Sometimes in her own room she would listen to the general noise until she could pick out what must be the tiny whir they made; and she would turn as fast as she could until everything ran blurring in a whirlpool around her eyes and she had to slump down on the floor and wait for the world to put itself together again.

From Silas, who ran the boiler room, they learned that the mill ceilings were a blur of unending motion, crossed and recrossed by ropes and pulleys leading from the tower and dust flue, through which belts carried power from the engines to the line shafts on each floor. It made Thomas remember his father's long string, hung above the interior of the mill store, which never moved at all.

Most doors inside the mill were like the big one at the front, made of iron, and clanking shut like something at the mouth of an old dungeon. Some of the inner doors were two layers of matchboards covered with tinplate and hung on sloping rails. These, said Uncle Silas, squealed when they scraped shut the way a hog squeals at the butchering; and after that Esther could pick out the rare squeal which crept into the mill's standard noises. In fact, with practice, she and Thomas and David were able to hear it all: the roar, the clank, the squeal, the purr of the moving belt, and the bobbins forever turning.

The mill was lighted by oil lamps hung on the walls. When summer came and the air grew hot and dry, experienced workers said water would be poured on the floors to add moisture to the air, and to keep the cotton fibers pliable and soft. "And sweat?" they sighed to Thomas. "You don't know nothing about sweat till you work in a mill with a wet floor in August. I've knowed the water level to rise half a inch just from people sweating!"

"That can't be so," breathed Thomas, wondering.

Every morning the women in their long-sleeved dresses and big white aprons came down the street of the mill village and were eaten up by the mill's huge mouth. Watching them, Esther thought she would just as soon be going where they went, as riding all the way to Greenway to listen to Miss Eliza Tilley tell her Pretty Is as Pretty Does. The men who worked in the mill dressed as if they were going forth to plant corn or thresh wheat. The look on their faces as they walked down the street was still a farmer look; they peered skyward for rain clouds and predicted the date of the last frost, then vanished inside the mill, where no weather was strong enough to reach them.

Uncle Silas Bennett was in charge of the boiler room only because Sam had got him the job before the mill opened that summer. Mildred said that would be the finest gift they could find for Rosa's coming baby.

Sam said, "It ain't going to be much of a gift for the cotton mill."

"That's all Silas needs, steady work. Responsibility. Regular wages. Promise me you'll talk to Max Carson."

"Lie to Max Carson, you mean." Sometimes that hole in Carson's face looked like a third eye, one that could see right through you. "Who wants a drunk in the boiler room?"

"But this is going to straighten him out. Rosa says he's already better, now that a baby's really coming. And this baby is going to change everything." If it's all right, she thought. If it's healthy and normal, that might be all my sister needs. There mustn't be anything wrong with that baby!

Sam threw up his hands. "I know that's what Rosa says, but I thought you had better sense."

For all that, he had lied to Max Carson. My brother-in-law. Good man. Hard times like the rest of us. Farm that won't bear. Dependable fellow.

And Max Carson had trained Silas himself and told him all about the compound condensing Corliss engine and its four hundred horsepower.

"Four hundred horses," muttered Silas. "The South could have used four hundred extra horses."

Carson blinked, but he was not about to get into that old war. He explained all about the boilers, the gauges, the vital feeding of four tons of coal during each eleven-hour day. In fact, he told Silas far more than Silas cared to know. In the heat of the little room, Silas felt a glaze forming on his skin, baking onto the surface of both eyes, closing his ears against all this information. By the time it had hardened all the way down the tube of his throat, he knew he had never been so thirsty in his entire life.

"That's about it," said Max Carson with satisfaction.

"It sure is." As soon as Carson had gone, Silas called in the two men who were to help him in the boiler room: Jester Sneed, the colored boy; and a white man named Claude Rickert, whose wife was a doffer and whose oldest boy swept out lint from the mill floor. To Rickert he said, "Suppose you look over the coal pile."

"This one?"

"Naw. The big one outside."

Rickert started out, then stopped to stare at him. "What am I looking for?"

"Coal, of course," said Silas, giving him a hard look. "You some kind of damn troublemaker?"

Jester gave a little snicker. "Want me to go help him?"

"No," said Silas as soon as Rickert was outside. "You go straight over the mill store and speak personal to Sam Allen and buy me a jar of whiskey. I am tired out from learning things."

Jester held out his hand.

"You tell him to charge it. Silas Bennett. I'm in his family."

Jester shook his head. "That Allen man, he don't charge *no* whiskey. He wouldn't give credit to Jesus Christ."

Silas fished out a little money. "A pint then, and if you hurry you can have a swaller."

After that, Silas came into the boiler room at the proper time every morning and looked at the pressure reading with an air of surprise. There was something other-worldly and unbelievable that he, Silas Bennett, should be standing here in this man-made place, already awash with his own sweat and suffused with the stink of himself, to read a message sent him by heat and water. It was hard to credit. Max Carson had told a lot of things, but not how to credit a crazy thing like that.

Usually Silas thought that over for a while, and then went scrabbling into the back of the coal pile for his jug, which he could now buy regularly with his regular wages. He would lie on the dark lumps, drinking and musing, thinking how unlikely it was that a gauge could tell the truth. When Sneed and Rickert came in to work, he would call out for one of them to see how the pressure was. Did they need more coal? Was everything all right? In this way, Silas managed to do nothing at all.

The colored boy, Jester Sneed, was quarrelsome. Claude Rickert didn't have sense enough to quarrel. Silas thought a lot about them both while he rested on the coal pile. Could he, by taking care, cause brains to swell spongelike in Rickert's tow-topped skull? Or would all his smiles and handshakes make young Sneed turn slightly friendly, or ease one portion of his suspicion?

"No," he said aloud with relief. As usual there was nothing at all Silas could do. He took a blazing swallow. Them boilers was the damnedest things.

The other thing he worried about was the coal dust. He was not worried about washing, but about what it would do over a period of years to drink in the dust and breathe in the dust. Would his stomach blacken on the inside? Would his lungs turn the color of ashes, then tree trunks, then mourning? Some night would it all filter through so that, when he came to wash, the inside black would have met the outside black and fused into a coating no soap could touch? Well, there was nothing a man could do but drink. That ought to thin the color down, like water thrown into the gravy.

Every day at noon, Silas took dinner at the Allen house. Often he arrived from the mill singing, and when he had eaten all the meat from a chicken leg, he might bang the bone absently against the edge of his plate. The rhythm he made was that of the mill. They could all feel how he kept time to the throbbing of those next-door machines. Thomas and Esther and David fixed their eyes on him instead of their own plates, and unconsciously Esther would take in morsels to the beat of that thumping until eating became like a dance.

Usually Mildred carried her plate to the pantry, where she ate off her breadboard. "I will not eat my meals to his tune," she would say if asked. "And Rosa carrying his baby. It makes me sick."

"At least he doesn't eat much," Esther said.

"Eat! Hah! His stomach is full when he gets here, and not with chicken dumplin's!"

Rosa wanted very much to move to the mill village and fix dinner for Silas herself, as soon as more houses were added. Mildred had already warned her against it.

"But I get lonely out there on the farm. Sometimes it's late when Silas gets home from work. Sometimes it's already dark."

"Gets dark here too."

"I'm so afraid the baby will come when he's not home."

Mildred made an irritated noise. "Rosa, this is January! The baby's not due till June! You're hardly showing yet!"

"I wish I lived close to your house. You're always so good when people are sick or babies are coming. If you were there, I know everything would be all right."

"It's going to be all right anyway," said Mildred kindly. "And I do promise to come if I can."

"Is Sam satisfied with Silas at the mill? Mildred, is he doing a good job?"

Mildred patted her sister on the shoulder. She tried to keep her voice light. "It's not blown up yet," she said.

"I want you to bear in mind, whatever happens, this won't my idea."

"You been telling me that all the way over here." Thomas carried the gun high above his head as if he were fording some waist-deep stream, though actually he and Big Jube were only wading through prickly brown underbrush and dried berry canes alongside the riverbank.

Jube, who was walking behind, said, "I wish you'd point that thing down."

"Taking it with us was your plan. The hunting trip was your idea," said Thomas sarcastically. "Might even see a coon or possum, that's what you told my father. And how it would do me good anyhow to try shooting at night. It's not me thought up a hunting trip. You're the one got me toting this thing over half of creation." As an afterthought he said, "Besides, it's not loaded."

Jube dodged a twanging bare limb. "You tole me think of some reason and I thought of some reason. And the graveyard is full of men was carrying unloaded guns. Don't slap them things at me."

For a while they crackled through the leaves and brittle weed stalks without talking. It had been payday at the mill and heavy trade at the store. Both were tired. Then Jube puffed, "Don't you let Miss Bethesda catch sight of any gun, I warn you. And how come you walking so fast?"

"I'm cold." But he was not. He was warm with excitement. After this night, he thought, I will understand everything.

Jude shook his head back and forth. "If your mama and daddy knew this . . . if they thought Jubilee Jackson was the cause . . ."

"They wouldn't care," lied Thomas.

The two pushed on in the dark, snagging their clothes on twigs and thorns. Had they come from Jube's house or the other Negro cabins, there would have been well-worn paths leading to Miss Bethesda Lee Michael's house, but striking out downriver from the mill, they were making their own, parallel to the running water. Above them, the moon barely slipped away from one cloud before it was tangled in another. The thin light came and went.

"How much farther?"

"Fifteen, twenty minutes," said Jube. "I never come this way before. You still got your cornbread?"

Thomas patted the sack on his shoulder.

Jube said he hoped Vinnie never knew the true reason she'd been asked to make that slab of cornbread. "If she thought we was set forth this night to fool Miss Bethesda . . ." He shook his head and whistled.

"Fooling Miss Bethesda might get a spell thrown on us, but we already said we don't believe in Miss Bethesda's spells. You not getting scared, are you, Jube?"

"Scared of Vinnie's yelling. Not anybody's spell." He stopped Thomas with one hand. "We're getting close."

Thomas could see no change in the woods before them. "Straight ahead?"

"That's right. What I don't see is why you want to talk to that old lady if you don't believe in nothing she says."

"I always wanted to know what she looked like." Thomas had taken only a few more steps when Jube stopped him again, grabbing a handful of cloth between his shoulder blades. "Look yonder. There it is," breathed Jube.

Thomas could see nothing but darkness and more trees. "Look where?"

"Straight on."

It was hard to see Miss Bethesda's house because she had built it up in the trees—built it by herself, people said, unless you could count the spirits that flickered in and out the woods helping. Some had gone by like lightning bugs and some like buzzards and some held down in the shape of bumblebees, to fix Miss Bethesda a monkey house by the river, people said.

At this one spot alongside the Katsewa, the same trees that had watched Daniel Boone march by still stood. Swamp oak and willow, sour gum and poplar, like pillars which now held up a whole field of stars, made a widespread grove. Their limbs were thick as ordinary trunks, and the roots drove down below the river as far as the crowns thrust up to the sky. Even in drought the river fed the grove, bringing down particles off granite and limestone and rusty shale, carrying the remnant of rotted leaves and powdery stem pith. The surface roots of one sweet-gum tree had grown through the riverbank in crooks and tangles, and young sucker trees coming off those roots had made that slope a thicket, then a living wall.

Miss Bethesda Lee Michael's house was built on the lowest and thickest and oldest tree limbs, from six to ten feet off the ground, depending on which way the floor sloped. Her house appeared to be only one suspended room, its floor lashed and nailed to the trees. There were wide cracks between the boards, which in wintertime she stopped up with river mud, then carpeted with mats woven from the long stems of cattails growing nearby. A wide shelf or ramp led to a rickety porch which overhung the flowing water. This followed a tree limb so faithfully that it dipped down and then sloped up again like a hollow in an old bed, and looked as if it was not strong enough to support a squirrel. The porch stuck out dangerously above the thicket of sweet-gum suckers, some of which were already coming up between the crooked boards and might—just by growing—carry the whole thing skyward.

Thomas had heard so much about Miss Bethesda's house it seemed to him he knew where every knothole was. Actually the moon was smothering again inside the clouds and there was little to see but two black box shapes, hung in the tree limbs like something stuck on a web.

"You coming with me?" asked Thomas, clearing out his throat uneasily.

"Just to speak," said Big Jube. "Just as much as we planned."

Out of the woods they came and into the cavelike space under the four largest trees. In summertime, thought Thomas, when all these giants filled up with leaves, no sunlight would be able to reach this place. He thought of the powdery earth under the old Allen house and stooped to touch the surface here, but it was hard and damp and slimy.

"Miss Bethesda Lee Michael!" Big Jube called, suddenly thundering in the winter night.

"What's that?" said a little raspy voice from above their heads.

They jumped. For someone who did not believe a word Miss Bethesda had ever said, Jube became nervous. Thomas could hear his uneven breathing.

"Speak out," hissed Thomas.

Cautiously Jube said to the dark, "Somebody's out here."

Thomas let out a grunt. "Now that's something smart to say," he complained softly. "She knows somebody's out here."

Not a leaf rustled. Finally Jube said again, "It's Mr. Thomas Allen, Sam Allen's boy. Wants to talk to you."

Still there was silence.

"I'm Jubilee Jackson!" he called. He turned his face upward to catch what little moonlight there was.

"Him that's with Vinnie?"

"Yessum."

Above them the old lady hacked out her throat and spit into the darkness. Thomas pulled himself in, uncertain whether he ought to dodge to the left or right.

"Good God A'mighty," he heard Jube mutter.

"She hit you?" Thomas whispered.

"She never misses."

"Well, ask her again."

"Ask her yourself," said Big Jube, wiping the back of his neck on his coat sleeve.

"I know about you, Jubilee Jackson!" called Miss Bethesda out of the black. "Going to end in vi-lents. I already told Vinnie."

The way she said it—"vi-lents"—Jube's death sounded like a bunch of little woodland flowers. Jube tried again, "This boy's brought cornbread."

"He ain't old enough to bake decent cornbread."

Thomas decided it was time to speak up. "I been practicing!" he called up toward the treetops. He could hardly tell, this close, where the tree left off and the little hanging house began.

"How old?"

"It's fresh, Miss Bethesda. Baked this morning."

She sent forth a little cackle. "Not the cornbread. How old for you?"

"Oh," he said foolishly. He stretched it a little. "I'm fourteen."

There was more silence after that, so long that Jube turned to go and motioned Thomas to give up and follow. Then the old lady said out of the darkness, "If you're fourteen, it's love; and I don't like to give love readings in the winter." She sounded quarrelsome.

"It ain't love," said Thomas.

In a minute Miss Bethesda's ladder—a haphazard rope-and-chain affair with green branches woven in for steps—fell down before them. Now that it had swooped down from the darkness like some unexpected snake, Thomas could not make up his mind to climb it.

Jube pushed at him. "Well, go on, boy. That's what you wanted."

"You say you can't wait for me?"

"I tole you that when we set out. I got to get home. I only said I'd bring you and speak out for you."

"It's mighty dark," said Thomas.

"We talked about that and how all you need do is follow the river back. That's why we come the hard way, so you could find your way home with no trouble."

"All right, all right."

Jube turned to go and Thomas pulled uneasily at the ladder with one hand. "I'm coming up!" he announced loudly, more to convince himself than anything else.

Jube's arm flew out of the dark and clutched his elbow. "For Jesus' sake put down that gun," he whispered hoarsely. "She see that gun, she might fly straight up."

Thomas could not decide where to leave the gun so it would be easy to find again in the dark, and at last he laid it flat on the ground where the ladder touched. "I warned you about that gun when we started out," Jube was saying.

"It's down. I'll see you at the store tomorrow."

Still Jube lingered. "Now don't make her mad. And you see me tomorrow, you mind we walked around and didn't see one sign of life and I walked you back to your house." Jube began edging away. "You tell your daddy we never shot at nothing."

"I'll remember."

Slowly Thomas began to climb the ladder. It swayed and seemed to be bending under his foot. He had the feeling that whenever he reached the top the last green limb would break, and he would come down through the whole row of shattering footholds, land on his own gun and shoot himself to death. He stopped and clung to the ladder.

"Jube?" he called very softly. There was no answer. He hung there, midway between the deep shadows of ground and floor, and looked around to the four walls of the forest. He could hear the sound of the Katsewa River sliding past, but could no longer tell whether it was behind him or before.

"You stuck?" somebody said from over his head.

"I'm coming." Just then the moon struggled out of a long cloud and he could see above him a jutting floor and a black opening. Something rattled over his head. His throat clogged up. "What's that noise?"

"Bracelets."

He took a deep breath and climbed. At the top a hand which looked too small to hold a sparrow came out of the dark and grabbed onto one of his. "Lift yourself over," somebody said. Thomas braced his other hand and lower arm flat on the floor and pulled himself up until he was lying with only his legs hung into space. Then he dragged them over and swung around to a sitting position. "Miss Bethesda?" he said after he had panted a few times.

She jangled a thin arm at him. "The blacksmith makes bracelets for me. Out of barrel staves. I cured his daughter's fainting spells one time."

"Yes, ma'am," Thomas said politely.

"Just say what you want." Miss Bethesda's voice was thin and scratchy. She was supposed to be ninety years old but Thomas could not tell much about her in the dark, just the small dark shape she made squatting near him on the floor. "Say what you want," scraped the voice again. "I don't get nothing much done these days but sleep and prophecy. Tonight I feel more like sleepin'."

"Want me to light a lamp for you?"

"If you got oil, we could. If it's my oil you're being so free with— no. Just say what you want."

Thomas could not think of any easy way to put it. "I got to talk awhile first," he blurted.

"They all say that. I tell you, talking just gets in my way."

"But I want more than one thing. I brought cornbread and pepper-mints and a slab of bacon. Big Jube said that was right."

"Three things gets three things." The moon now broke entirely free into a wide patch of open sky, and struck down on a slant so Thomas could see half her face. The cheeks had been squeezed down by age to slight bone and a dry layer of skin. Her mouth was tucked under as if all the lower teeth were gone. She wore her gray hair cut short and woolly.

"First I want my future read," he said automatically.

"That's one."

"And I want a girl to do something particular when I tell her to."

"No love in the wintertime, I told you that. It's like green leaves when the sap's down. Too much effort."

"It ain't love," said Thomas again.

Miss Bethesda Lee Michael seemed to be laughing silently. She rattled an arm of iron bands, swiped the back of one hand across her mouth.

"And most of all I want . . . I want . . ." Thomas could not think of any word for it.

"Money?" suggested Miss Bethesda. When he did not speak she began to run down her catalogue. "Curse throwed? Curse lifted? Warts cured? Find something that's lost? Straighten a bone?" She grew impatient. "What is it then?"

"Do the other two first. Let me think about the third."

"Just my luck, it's that third one attached to the slab of bacon," Miss Bethesda grumbled to herself. She threw out both her small hands and the bracelets made a sound of chains. He saw that every joint in her fingers was overlaid with a wad of gristle. "Your trouble is, you don't believe. You want to see whether you believe enough after the first two to ask about the third."

"I do believe, I do!" he muttered hastily, for Jube had warned him Miss Bethesda could not abide being disbelieved.

She let out a scraping sigh. "Cornbread calls for light," she said, and disappeared inside the blackness of the open doorway where they had been sitting. He could hear her knotty hands moving along wood, carefully. A shelf, he thought, on which she kept her lamp. The bracelets barely clinked against one another.

He called to her, "How you keep warm up here in the wintertime?" He had seen no sign of fire. "That wind off the river's cold."

"I do what animals got sense enough to do. I go to bed. Pull down the cover twice a day, reach out and eat, go back to bed. That's how Methus'lah got so old."

"I didn't know that."

"Not many do." She had lit a lantern, which gave off an ugly smell. He saw her more clearly now, bent above it. Her upper lip was the only plump thing left in her, the last place where any moisture was stored, and it swelled out and overhung her chin. She was no taller than he, and turned inward at each end in the shape of a quarter moon. He caught a quick glimpse of the bare room— a pallet against one wall, a pile of tins and cracked dishes, and something square hung up at eye level. She carried the lantern to the doorway and the dark poured back into the room behind her.

"What was that I saw hanging on the wall?"

"A picture," she snapped. "You think I'm ignorant? You think I don't know what belongs to hang on walls?"

"No, ma'am. What kind of picture?"

She thrust the lantern toward him on the end of one arm and pursed her mouth. "You don't look fourteen."

He leaned away. "Pew-ee! What you burning in that lantern?"

Miss Bethesda looked at it without much interest. "I forget. Grease, I expect. For a cornbread throwin', we better move along this way. You come behind and come slow; there's no sides to this part." She raised the lantern and tottered ahead.

Thomas followed her up a slight incline which seemed to be part board, part raw tree trunk. It ran like a ramp to the porch (or dock, or pier) of Miss Bethesda Lee Michael's house. Through the cracks under his shoes he could see the pale, slightly shiny surface of the Katsewa River. There were no railings here either, and the floor dipped downhill and uphill again, leaving a place where rainwater would have puddled if the floor had ever been chinked. Thomas was not sure whether the porch had been built this way, to fit the tree's contour and dip into a hollow like that in a much-used bed, or whether it was sagging from their weight.

"Is this apt to fall?" he managed to ask.

Miss Bethesda let out a high giggle. "I don't know. I ain't read the book of my own life lately." She sat on the boards and shook with laughter. "I ain't been throwin' any of my own cornbread!" Giggling again, she snuffled air into her nose. "That's really something. Well, come on. Sit down."

He sat in front of her and crossed his legs Indian fashion. She set the lamp to one side. Through his trousers Thomas could feel the cool river going by, passing under, sending up damp.

"Let's see that corn cake."

Thomas pulled the bag off his shoulder and slipped the yellow bread into the light. He held it to her but she swayed back, her bracelets rattling. "No, no! I mustn't touch it yet. Just hold steady in the light." Miss Bethesda leaned over the square of bread, turned her head to one side to examine its brown edges. "Is it burned on the bottom?"

"No, ma'am."

"You bake it yourself?"

"Early this morning," he lied.

She put her face nearly against its surface and sniffed noisily. Satisfied, she drew back and warmed her right palm over the lantern before laying it flat across her eyes. "Now break off a corner chunk and take one bite," she ordered. She parted her fingers to peer at him through the slit. "Not too big a chunk," she added sharply.

Thomas broke off a triangle, filled his mouth and chewed. Vinnie had baked good cornbread but he could not remember ever tasting anything so dry in his life and he wondered if he would be able to get it swallowed down. He thought about the flowing river, cold and wet. The bread grew hard and lumpy along his teeth.

"You swallowed yet?"

He made some kind of noise, straining to force it down his throat. It fell into his stomach like a file. "It's gone," he said hoarsely.

"Crumble the rest of your piece."

"Big or little?"

"It's your future," Miss Bethesda said from behind her hand. "You crumble it like it ought to be."

After thinking that over, and remembering that the cracks in the porch were wide and he would be chiefly feeding catfish in the river below, Thomas broke the bread into large pieces and cupped them in both hands. "All right," he said.

Miss Bethesda rubbed her forehead and took down her hand. "Too dark to throw," she said. "You shake it in both hands and then drop it right here, on the floor between us."

Thomas let crumbs spill into the circle of light. She glanced at them once and looked away, beyond his shoulder. "You're careful, I see. Big pieces. It figures."

He said nothing.

Still with her eyes fixed past him in the dark, Miss Bethesda began warming her right hand again over the lantern. Then she passed it, palm down, over the crumbled bread. She said a few things in some foreign language. Then she sat staring at the bits of cornbread.

"Well," she said after a while, "that wasn't hardly worth your trip."

Nervously he asked what she meant by that.

She shook her fuzzy head. "That is the nearest nothing I ever saw," she murmured.

"Tell me what it is. Just tell me."

She threw up that right hand as if it were some rag and let it hang, limp-wristed, over the bread fragments. The metal rings settled around her elbow. "Well, you going to grow up all right and live a long time. You won't ever want to marry but one girl, and that's the one you'll marry. You going to die of old age right here in this county."

Thomas drew back, more horrified than if she had told him of some bloody death. "And that's *all?*"

She rolled her eyes up to him. "There's money," she offered.

"This girl, does she love me?"

Again the flap of the right hand. "That would be in *her* cornbread."

"Do I love her then?"

"I reckon," she said, not very convincingly.

"Do I fight anybody? Do I take long trips? Am I in a war?"

"Naw," she said, almost with boredom. "You just worry is all."

He grew more and more desperate. "Well, tell me something else."

"There ain't no more."

"Of course there is! A whole handful of big cornbread crumbs like that! Big Jube says sometimes you can talk a whole hour. Just tell me something else you see."

She leaned forward abruptly, scraped the edge of one hand across the pile of crumbs and forced them down between the boards. They tinkled into the passing river. "I said that was all. What was the second thing you wanted?"

Thomas banged his fist on the floor until he thought he would bring the whole house down. "You old nigger woman!" he yelled. "You didn't give me half what was in there!"

"I give you all of it. The second thing?"

He was trembling. "I don't believe you."

"No need to fool with the second thing," she said agreeably, and began to unfold her legs and loosen her shoulders. "The ladder's yon way." She picked up her lantern.

"I might as well hear the other things."

She looked at his sullen face. "Don't put yourself out on my account," she said.

"I'll hear the others."

Miss Bethesda slid the lantern to one side until its light shone mostly on Thomas. She settled herself again in the shadows. "Some girl, you said."

"I want her to do what I tell her."

Miss Bethesda snorted. "Everybody wants that."

"I want it so she can't help herself."

"What's her name?"

Thomas was surprised. "Jube said you didn't usually need names."

"When you want control, I got to have names. I got to have something has touched that person. The nearest to the heart it has touched that person, the better off we are."

"Her name is Zelda. Zelda Dowdy."

Miss Bethesda spit into the palm of her hand, yanked something out of her hair, dipped it into the spittle and held it forth. "Write her name on the floor," she said. "Here in the light."

He saw it was a feather she was holding, out of some blue-colored bird. Perhaps a jay. She had wet the soft tip, making it a brush rather than a pen. Thomas tried to control his face as he stuck the tip into the spittle in her pale palm again, wrote on the floor, wet it, wrote once more. "It's going to be dried off before I get to the end," he said.

"Don't matter."

He finished the name. Already the Z was fading. Miss Bethesda took the blue feather from him and poked it into her hair, near the crown. He saw suddenly several others standing there in a small rosette among her fuzzy hair, lost from the wings of redbirds and thrushes.

"You got anything has touched this person?"

Jube had not prepared Thomas for this. He started to shake his head. Then he held out his own two hands. "I touched her."

Lines sprang up above Miss Bethesda's eyes. "How old you say you was? Fourteen? And how old is this Miss Zelda?"

"I don't know."

She continued to stare at his extended hands. "Touched her where?"

He was tempted to improve it with lies. "On the ankles," he finally admitted.

Miss Bethesda's overlapping lip curled up in a smile. "That's right far from the heart," she said. "I reckon you didn't think it was close enough either."

"That's all I've got," said Thomas, remembering the candy jar, the work shoes, the back-room curtains. "Just my hands."

"It ought to serve," said Miss Bethesda. She reached across and took his hands between hers. The movement was unexpected; the cool touch of her palms was a shock to his skin. "Don't move," she said. She began rubbing his hands between her stringy ones in such a way that his own palms scraped against each other. He could feel every mound and pad and wrinkle. In contrast to the rest of his body, his fingers began to warm and then to tingle and at last to sting. He shifted from one hip to the other. "I said hold still," ordered Miss Bethesda.

His hands were hot. She pressed them down where he had written Zelda's name and his heated flesh sucked up the last fleck of moisture off the floor.

"Now. Can you get a hair out of her head?"

He pictured himself leaning from the store ladder, yanking. "I guess I can."

She reached inside her clothes and pulled out a long thong which hung from her neck nearly to the waist. Strung along it at intervals, like jewels, were oddly shaped bags of leather and flannel. She began to work along the bags as if she were telling a rosary, discarding and fingering around until at last she reached one tied shut with blue sewing thread. "This is it," she said, and worked loose the knot. "Take this, and get a hair from the girl's head. A fresh hair; you can't use one that just falls out. You got to put the hair into this bag yourself, in pitch dark. One look inside breaks the power. Then you wear the bag around your neck."

"How long?" To Thomas the bag looked no different from the one Aunt Rosa had used to make herself a baby.

"However long it takes," said Miss Bethesda. "Depends on her stubbornness how long it takes the spell to wear her down."

"And it will work?" Her jerky nod loosed one of the feathers from her hair. It floated gently down, hung on one shoulder, drifted away in the dark.

"I reckon you don't believe that either."

"I don't know," he said thoughtfully. He rolled the little bag in his fingers. It was lumpy, as if there were small stones or rotted teeth inside. "Why couldn't I do this all by myself? Write out her name with a feather and rub my own hands and fill up my own bag?"

" 'Cause you ain't got the power."

He continued to feel the little bag. There was something long and hard on one side. A nail? A locust thorn? "Suppose I change my mind and want a new spell? Or just suppose Zelda herself comes to you and wants a spell thrown against my spell. What happens then?"

"So long as I do it, the last spell's always the strongest. If it's two spells laid on by two different people, then you get to see which one's got the strongest power. You got to travel east a long way to find as strong a spell as mine."

She sounded very proud. Thomas said, "You can't throw a spell so strong you can't break it?"

"What kind of crazy talk is that? Does God make a river so wide He can't jump across it?"

Thomas stared. "I don't know. Does He?"

Miss Bethesda Lee Michael looked disgusted. "You told me the solemn truth. You ain't a day over fourteen," she said.

He passed her the remainder of his cornbread, along with a little sack of peppermints. "Suppose," he said slowly, "the spell on Zelda Dowdy works so fine I get in the habit of it. Suppose I come back someday and I want a bag that covers not one person but two?" David and Esther loomed up suddenly in his mind.

"I can do that." She nodded, gumming one of the candies and rolling it in her empty lower jaw.

"Maybe I want to control three. Or five. Maybe I even got my eye on ten or fifteen."

"Now hold up," she said. "Fifteen different people, no kin by blood to one another?"

"Just talking, you understand. Yes. Fifteen."

"I wouldn't do that if I could."

He measured her, thinking. "You can't do it then. I figured that must be so or else you'd have taken the control of people all to yourself, and not be living out here like a monkey."

Miss Bethesda bristled. "Like a whut?"

Thomas was now talking mostly to himself. "That's what I told Big Jube all along—anybody had real power wouldn't need to sell it. He'd just use it for himself. Throw spells on who he didn't like and love charms on the rest. Find all the lost pocket watches and keep them. He wouldn't be doing what you do. He'd have a lot of money and other people would be doing all his work."

She fixed him with a cold stare. "You come not believing then? And Jubilee Jackson with you?"

"I was right all along. And I was going to ask you this third thing . . . I don't know . . . I was going to ask to have some kind of power."

"Some kind of power," she repeated.

"I didn't care what kind. Some people are favored; anybody can see that. Things come easy. Maybe I didn't want anything more than that, to have things come easy."

She had not moved. Her dark face had not altered in any way and the lump of candy was still traveling behind her lip, but he saw from the thin strips of her eyes that she had grown very angry. The bracelets on one arm quivered like the rattles on a snake.

"That was the third thing," finished Thomas lamely.

"That was it," she said in a flat tone. She began to sway back and forth. "You wanted to buy the power for one little slab of bacon."

He did not like the way her face had stiffened, the candy making a little lump on one side, the overhanging lip tensed as if any minute it might turn back in a snarl. "Look," he began uneasily, "I never meant to make you mad. I'm going to wear the bag around my neck. I'm going to put the hair inside."

"Don't trouble yourself," she cooed, swaying.

Her soft voice scared him. "I'll come another time," he said nervously, "and talk about that other thing. You can have the bacon anyway."

"Keep your old bacon," she said, almost sweetly.

"No, no!" Thomas pulled the meat out of his sack and thrust it into the circle of light. "It's nice and lean. You see?"

She stopped rocking and leaned near the meat. The bracelets pinged down in order to her wrist, one-two-three. He expected her to smell it the way she had sniffed the cornbread, and he had almost begun to smile when she made a great whooshing noise and blew the lantern out.

The blackness was shocking. The moon, which he had not missed, now seemed to have vanished entirely from the sky, taking every star with it. The darkness against his eyeballs was like a solid wall. He froze; the smile hardened around his teeth. "What'd you do that for?" he whispered. She couldn't be more than two feet away but his eyes—unused to the night—could no longer pick out even her pale mound of hair.

Out of the dark she laughed, and from the sound he knew that she had moved to one side without even a rustle. "What you know about power?" she said from the void. "Maybe you come down here only because I called for you. Maybe all the time you was on the end of my string."

He began stealthily to get his legs under him in a crouch. "I'll just leave this bacon," he said as hopefully as he could. "Here on the floor."

He heard the clank of her iron bracelets from a different place. "I never told you all your future said. I don't aim to tell you. And you won't ever get a sore inside your mouth without asking if it's mine."

Carefully Thomas got to his feet. "What was it you didn't tell?" He heard one of her shoes scratch on the floor. "You better tell me now," he said huskily, and eased toward that noise.

"You pore little white boy!" She mocked him from off to his right. "Come here full of I-want and going home full of ain't-got." She cackled. "My power's that I don't want. Everybody comes wanting but me. I am just here!" She screamed that last word a second time. "*Here!*"

He jumped in that direction. There was nothing but air. "Hand me that light," he said through gritted teeth, "and I am going home."

"You use your own light!" she crowed, from off to his left this time. "You burn that piece of bacon meat. And I am growing a new brier every place you set your foot. I am laying down rocks for you to fall on."

"You *nothing but a crazy old nigger woman!*" he yelled.

Out of the dark, with no warning, Miss Bethesda Lee Michael suddenly blew a blob of spit, which smacked him just above the eyebrow. "There's my curse on you and I heard it hit!" she snickered.

Thomas lunged across the porch, half stumbling where the floor sloped up, and his hand, which was sweeping outward like a pole, struck her. She grunted; he heard her heel come down hard. Then the bare hint of her shadowed form swung back from him, swayed outward, seemed to pause in midair the way Thomas had hung waiting on the ladder. But now there was no ladder, no railing, no wall. He saw her arms flung out like sticks to claw the empty air; there was a squeaking noise and the arm bracelets banged together. She fell backward very slowly over the edge and into the Katsewa River.

Thomas dropped to his knees, crawled carefully to the end of the porch and called her name. "Miss Bethesda?" He could see no ripples and no bubbles, only the sheen of the water. He grabbed hold of the edges of the boards and gripped his fingers tight to stop them from shaking. "*Miss Bethesda!*" he called again, desperately. His voice rolled up and down the river, and the pines on the far bank began to sing in a sudden wind. He closed his eyes and, slowly, began to tap his forehead over and over against the cold wood. "Miss Bethesda," he whispered. The evergreen needles whined.

Thomas leaped to his feet, ran back to the still warm lantern. He felt around for its handle, scrabbled his fingers across the floor until they found the cornbread, bacon, candies. One by one he slung them all into the night, the lantern last of all, and counted the splashes as they fell into the moving river.

On his hands and knees, the left hand guided by the edge, he crawled carefully along the narrow ramp, fumbled his way to the black hole of the open door, and slapped around until he found the ladder. Over the side he dropped it, threw himself upon it and took a few steps, then let go and plunged into the blackness. His feet slid on the damp moss and he sat down heavily. The jar went up his spine like a blow traveling along fence pickets. He heaved for breath.

The swinging ladder kept tapping his shoulder like some warning hand. He threw it from him irritably at first, and it vanished in the dark and then whipped back and struck him in the neck. Thomas stood, puffing, caught the ladder and rolled it up as high as his shoulder, then tossed it toward the ledge above. It bounced on the edge and unrolled down to him again. Sobbing, he wound it up, threw it with all his strength. Again it curled down with a kind of grace, like the frond of a spring fern. He slung it up, was hit on the chin by one of the falling chains as it came back. His eyes watered. Carefully then, he began to toss it underhanded, getting a rhythm in his arm. It caught and held, one section sticking out over the edge beyond his reach.

Then he remembered his gun and muddied his fingers trying to find it. He began to batter the earth this way and that. When his hand finally hit the icy barrel, he screamed aloud. He jerked the gun before his face and bit hard into the stock, waiting for his own echo to end.

Holding the gun by its barrel, Thomas began to run alongside the river. It was flowing south while he plunged north; the contrary motion pulled at his eye and made him feel sick and dizzy. He thought of Miss Bethesda, washing away from him.

He exploded through the woods, racing head on into twigs and scrubby vines, striking his face against cedar twigs and spiderwebs. His body was one giant heart cutting this thunderous swath through thickets and underbrush.

And the flight was just what she had promised; every place he set his pounding feet there sprang up briers and stones; thorns leaped out of the darkness to strike him and every tree leaned over and smote him as he plunged wildly by, dragging the gun at his heels. While he ran Thomas tried to scrub off his face where Miss Bethesda had spit upon him, but his sticky eyebrow had already matted, and he thought he would carry it on his forehead forever, like the wet signature of Cain.

Chapter
⊷§ 13 §⊷

"How'd you get along with Miss Bethesda?"

"All right," said Thomas. He broke out into a cold sweat.

Jube waited for him to say something more. "She give you any help?"

"This bag." Thomas pulled it out of his shirt. He would not look at Jube.

"You didn't make her mad?"

Thomas jumped. "Of course not. Everything was fine. Fine. She waved good-bye when I left."

Jube said that didn't sound much like Miss Bethesda Lee Michael.

Thomas looked up, at last, to watch Jube's back as he walked away. He had not looked Jube directly in the face since that trek night before last through the woods. He doubted he would ever be able to do so. For two days his stomach had been filled with hard stones. The inside of his throat was cold and greasy. Nothing would go down it but soup or milk, and he did not know whether the rash along his forearms was guilt or poison ivy. His eyelids ached. The ten fingers hung on his hands like lumps of iron; his heavy feet could hardly be lifted up and set down again. He had bolted so often to the family privy that his belly was sore, and his trousers chafed where he felt flabby and gaping-open.

Hourly he expected the alarm to sound, expected Jube to report

Vinnie said Miss Bethesda was nowhere to be seen. When that did not happen, he began to wait for Miss Bethesda herself; he would be in the storeroom, perhaps, and she would come in dripping with river water and call for him by name. Several times already Thomas had heard a voice which might have been hers, had frozen with his hands on a flour sack while his stomach plummeted and his heart swelled. Bloated and throbbing, he waited each time until Sam stuck his head through the curtains and told him to hurry up and bring out a peck of sweet potatoes.

That evening Jube scared him half to death. They had been sweeping the oiled floor, each taking an aisle, when Jube sidled up. "There's trouble this week," he said from one corner of his mouth, "among my people."

Thomas sagged weakly onto his broom. "Trouble?"

"I hear the Klan is riding."

"Oh, said Thomas, relieved, and began briskly to swipe at the dirty boards. He had a hopeful idea. "Maybe they'll get Miss Bethesda."

Jube looked puzzled. "What they want with that old lady?"

"You never can tell. If she just disappears some night, I bet that'll be why."

Jube said he would sooner try to pull wild onions out of a garden patch than try to kill Miss Bethesda.

"Might be easier than you think," said Thomas in a hollow voice.

But the next night when the Klan did ride across Stone County, it wanted—not the witch woman in the trees by the river—but Jubilee Jackson.

When Thomas first heard the white-robed men had dragged Jube down to the river to kill him, he thought that, too, might be partly his fault. Someone must have seen him writing new words on wrapping paper, or had overheard their arguments in the storeroom about the Moors and the Wilmington riot.

Nobody ever knew for certain why they came for Jube, riding up white and ghostly in front of his cabin to ask for a drink of well water and adding with the usual chuckle, "Just rode up from Hell and I'm mighty dry."

Maybe it was the way he swung his way home from work in the evenings (for Jube was not afraid of the Ghost or the dark), singing to all the pine trees in a bold voice, "My only sin is in my skin. . . ."

Or perhaps someone had heard him speak proudly of George

White, the state's Negro representative, and the bill White had introduced in Washington that January to make lynching a federal offense.

Or maybe some farmer stopped a Negro stranger on the road and asked, "What's that you're saying over and over to yourself while you walk?" And maybe the stranger recited it for him: "Slaves used to work for the Cape Fear and Deep River Navigational Company." That would have bewildered any Stone County farmer. "What you saying that for?"

"It's for Jubilee Jackson. I'm carrying it to him."

Surely no one but Thomas could have heard Big Jube quoting from the speech Booker Washington made at the Harvard commencement.

Or did they get him for that heresy he once volunteered, unasked, while he was holding Nathan Grimes's horse and overheard Nathan and four other whites talking about Jeffersonian democracy? "Easy for Thomas Jefferson to sit back and think pretty thoughts," Jube blurted to their startled faces, "when three generations of my people did all his work for him, so he had enough extra time to think about freedom."

Even Nathan, at that, sucked in his breath sharply and said, "Jube, that will do!" and hastily told the others with spread palms that he could vouch for Jube.

I don't need no vouching, Jube thought hotly, but he chewed his tongue until it had quieted down in his mouth and he led the horse away from the white men and stood under a sycamore, staring off at a low evening cloud the color of cream.

Maybe it came not from one act but an accumulation, a clinking of evidence like the growing heap of thirty coins of betrayal; but the Klan got word of Jube. Even in Stone County, where most of the Klan members were the young men who didn't have ladies to spark in the evenings and were thus especially concerned about female virtue, somebody marked Jube down. He had to be attended to.

The Klan was not strong in Greenway and Stoneville. It had not been a steady, continuing force anywhere in North Carolina, but had flared up and petered out, like brushfire.

At the end of the Civil War, there were 350,000 freedmen and 650,000 whites in the state. Thad Stevens and Charles Sumner wanted to see that Negroes had—and used—the ballot to help build a strong Republican party. In the first registration under this new arrangement, nineteen counties registered a Negro majority.

That's when the Klan sprang up, like a toadstool in rainy season, in 1867. It grew strong and open in Orange, Chatham, Alamance counties; but became more secretive after one Negro Republican office holder and a government detective enforcing anti-mask laws were murdered in 1870. Caswell and Alamance came under military law.

Now the chief Klan activities moved from the east, with its heavy Negro population, and into the middle of the state. In 1871, the Federal Grand Jury at Raleigh indicted 981 people for KKK acts. The Klan was in the piedmont, though many a night's ride was put off because a man had corn to shuck or fox to hunt, or it was his poker night.

When the Democrats finally regained political control, they swore the state had to be saved from niggers and Republicans. They seemed to be saving it and things were smooth as silk till Republicans and Populists united after the panic of 1873.

"Nigger control again," was the grumble among the state's Democrats. Even Nathan Grimes turned pale.

And maybe there Jube ran afoul. He liked to boast that of the four Negroes from North Carolina who served fourteen years in the U.S. House of Representatives, three had been to college—which was more than many of their fellow politicians could say.

Jube also liked the way the 1896 election turned out. Bryan carried the state for President; Republican Dan Russell became Governor, and in the eastern cities Negroes became postmasters, school-board members, policemen, aldermen and justices of the peace.

"Fine old places like New Bern, Wilmington, Greenville!" Winkler Hobbs would groan. "I know how Jesus felt when He saw the temple jammed with moneychangers!"

So, in 1898, the Red Shirts revived Klan methods except that they often wore no masks, and the Klan itself appeared again. In Wilmington, six hundred armed white citizens burned down the newspaper building where Negro editor A. L. Manley had written unpopular editorials. After the riots, colored officials left Wilmington on every train. Thomas and Jube had argued about the casualties in these riots—how many black, how many white.

And after Wilmington, night riders in small communities carried forth small rebels and hung them by wrists and ankles onto fences to make them recite: "Niggers is human donkeys. Mate with a horse and you get a mule."

Then, when the leather belt was laid across the dark back, the victim would be made to bray and bray and bray.

"We never lynched anybody in our town," local Klansmen were saying in little hollows and valleys and railroad depots. "We never had to."

There were not only beatings intended to encourage moral behavior in black and white alike, but the riders would stop off at some houses just to frighten.

"Reach me a dipper that well water!"

It would be handed up, quaking, to the shrouded horseman.

"Best water I've drunk since I was killed at Shiloh," would come the standard quip, or Fredericksburg, or Chicamauga, or some other place.

The week before the Klan came for Big Jube, David had been deviling Ellie Faye and Rutledge. With pokeberry juice and a hen's feather he took to painting KKK in unbelievable places for them to discover. He drew the warning in tiny blood-red letters right where Rutledge always tied the buggy at the hitching post. He painted the sinister sign at the mouth of the sack in which Ellie Faye toted home her share of the day's food, wrote on the ax handle, and once—the supreme joke—on the worn sole of Rutledge's upturned shoe while he was snoozing behind the woodshed.

Whenever Rutledge found one of these warning signs, he would leap straight into the air and squawk. He came down, crouching, to stare about him in terror. He always refused to touch the object which had been mysteriously marked.

This meant that even though it was January, he flung his shoes into the field and went home barefoot, borrowed an ax from the mill superintendent next door, and made Ellie Faye tote food in a bag made from his shirt with the sleeves looped round like handles.

Often David would call his brother Thomas when Rutledge was about to find another mark. The two would hide and watch.

Thomas came reluctantly; he said his stomach hurt; he didn't feel good. But when he saw Rutledge leap up and swallow down his scream, snap his head around with eyeballs the size of coffee cups, something delicious would stir in him. To get so much reaction out of pokeberry juice and three initials made him feel—he could hardly describe it—made him feel not the size of the scrawl but the size of Rutledge's terror. In that moment, Thomas would feel as big as Rutledge's fear, as vast, as nameless. If it were possible, he would have run from his hiding place straight back along the Katsewa River and hollered up at Miss Bethesda's house: *"That's it! That's what I want!"*

Maybe she would have come out and hit him with her ladder. Maybe she would have spit on him from the tree. Maybe she would have been there. Maybe. Thomas did not go to see.

Sometime after midnight on the night of January 27, 1899, the Ku Klux Klan came for Jubilee Jackson. There were only six.

(Later Thomas said once to Jube, "Not many would come," but Jube turned on him such a burning look that he never mentioned the Klan again. Or words or reading. Or Miss Bethesda.)

Waking slowly in his bed, Jube heard the thump of horse hoofs in his yard. Maybe he knew. Maybe he said to sleeping Vinnie in that bitter voice he had, "That jewel is now in the fountain for sure!"

Maybe he said nothing. Vinnie lay still, asleep or acting like sleep. Jube rustled out of bed, moving aside the quilt and the linings of newspaper. Something loud was said from outside. He took his shirt and overalls off the foot of the bed and put them on.

The rhythm of the hoofs was now lost, and there was only an occasional thud as the men sat their horses and waited. "You, Jube! Come out!" somebody called.

He put his hand on Vinnie's stomach. "Lay still," he whispered. Above the covers she opened one vacant eye. "Don't you move," he hissed. He patted her, and the newspapers crackled.

He went to the porch. There were six of them sitting whitely on their horses. He thought: Jesus didn't need but twice that many.

Aloud he said, "You want Jubilee Jackson, that's me." He shouldn't have said that. "Yessir" would have been better.

"Jackson, eh?" sneered one of the men. "You named for Stonewall?"

"Named for Andrew," Jube said.

That made the Klansman mad because he hadn't thought of it.

"We heard enough of your sass," he growled, "and we heard plenty more *about* it before we come."

There was a murmur from the other five.

"What have I done?" said Jube.

One of the men said to another, "He just can't help sassing. He just don't know how to talk respectful to a white man." He rode his horse closer to the porch. "And, brother, you see we are *white*. We are white all over."

"Yes, sir," said Jube at last. It was mighty late to work that "sir" into the conversation.

"You come down here, nigger," barked one.

"You walk ahead of these horses," said another.

If it had not been for Vinnie and the boys, Jube might have dodged back in the house. As it was, he jumped from the porch, landing lightly. "Boy, you think you're smart," growled one of the men, and he leaned off his horse and poked Jube under the shoulder blade. Maybe he would have hit him harder if someone had urged it. "You walk."

Jube walked ahead and the horses came behind him at a slow pace. Nobody said "this way" or "that way." He just walked. For the first time in his life, looking at the grays and browns and blacks of the night, Jube saw that the world was bouncing in tune to his stride. He stepped and the trees and hillsides jiggled up and down when his head moved. That seemed to him very strange. Maybe for all he knew the world had always done this, shaken when he shook, and he had never noticed. Maybe if this very minute he whirled his head to the right, a whole pasture would slide westward half a mile.

"Faster," somebody said. He walked faster and the world stepped up its vibrations.

They'll likely hit me with something from behind, then whip the horses over me at a dead gallop when I fall, he thought. *Dead* gallop, heh heh.

Still he walked. His feet were bare and very cold.

"That way," said a voice behind him. Jube nearly broke stride. Whose voice was that? Was it Mr. Hobbs's nephew from the uptown store? Or the county clerk? Somebody from the mill? Somebody he'd toted for?

He saw they were headed for the Katsewa River, which curved in just below his house and made a little beach from which small boys went fishing in the springtime. Had there been wire or chains jangling from those saddles? Jube tried to listen now and it seemed to him, sure enough, that a chorus of little death bells tinkled at his heels.

I done nothing deserves killing, Jube thought. It seemed an oversight. He was to be killed for words, tones, a way of holding the muscles in face and shoulder. Under that same payment he might well have stolen fortunes or raped white women or banged Mr. Hobbs in the crown of the head with his gaudy walking stick.

I hate to be killed so cheap, he thought, and tried to think what quick offense he could commit that would be large enough between here and the river's edge to balance off his death.

He began to sing, "My only sin is in my skin." It wasn't much, but it was all he could think of—and that seemed to him typical of his whole life, one long effort to do big acts in cramped quarters. He bellowed the song from deep in his chest.

"Shut up!" bawled the man behind him, and prodded his horse forward and kicked Jube in the small of the back. Jube did not fall down. He staggered and coughed and hacked up a wad of spittle. But that made him angry too; had he only coughed to excuse the presence of his spit? Could he not, even now, even at the last, get out of "his place"?

He spit a second time, leaving off the cough.

The damp cold rose from the river and came to meet him. They must have heavy coats under those white sheets. He thought about white, snow white, pure white, purity white. Green words in green jars. But the night they ride through is my color; and Jube thought in a flash of how he would break for the thickets and blend himself with the winter-brown trunks of trees. These six would be easy to spot riding high on their horses; they would shine in the forest like fallen stars, while his friend the earth would mask him as if he were a brown bird, and a covering of tan leaves would sift over his darker hands.

Yet he did not run. To die for doing was one thing; to die for doing nothing was an insult; but to die for running . . . He had forgotten to sing. He began again, louder.

They stopped at the river's edge. His feet were already numb.

"Now you walk in."

At first he did not feel the water grip his foot; it was so cold and his foot was so cold that he felt nothing but the clutch of it. He set his teeth and put in the second foot and the river caught and held it. Now his iced blood ran upward and carried the cold into his knees and thighs. Some places, he knew, the Katsewa was now low enough you could walk across. He hoped this was one of the places.

The night riders shoved him from behind and he fell on all fours into the freezing water. When he stood again, wetness ran streaming under the front of his overalls and down his body. It was so cold that it passed beyond coldness and burned his skin. He shook all over.

"Move out."

Jube walked to midstream. The water level was high as his loins, hung now with nothing but icicles. He walked carefully, thinking his balls might shatter like glass just from the brushing of his skin. In the center of the river he stopped and looked back at the six figures on the bank. Snowmen. Their edges had blurred and a few of them seemed to his eye to be floating slightly above their saddles.

One horseman called from the shore: "Say 'I repent of my sins.'"

"I repent of them," Jube whispered toward God. He would have prayed that anyway.

"Can't hear you!"

He roared it. "I repent of my sins!"

"Now answer us this: How much nigger blood makes a nigger?"

"One drop," called Jube, doing his catechism dutifully.

There was a muttering from the bank and several of the Klansmen put their heads together and talked something over. Then one of them called, "Say that again, and don't you sound proud of it."

"One drop makes a nigger," said Jube. There were some more rumblings and grumbles from the shore.

"Name the four races!"

Jube knew the traditional answer they wanted: white man, Indian, dog and nigger; but he said, "I know of three," and named them, leaving out the dog.

The horses milled around. "You better remember them all!" came a furious yell. But somebody said in a softer voice, "I'm cold as hell."

Jube's teeth were rattling in his head. "I know the four seasons," he offered politely, so like that unknown communal historian who gave out whatever knowledge he had in stock, altering the question to fit his answer.

Somebody threw a rock. It fell nearby and icy water splashed up shoulder high and spatters struck him across the face and eyes.

The water seemed to revive him. He yelled boldly, "I know the names of the four colored gentlemen this state sent to Washington!"

There followed a hail of stones. Somebody said to somebody else, "That is the craziest nigger I ever saw."

"Go on and shoot him."

More stones flew. "I hate to waste my shells on him."

A few of the rocks had already struck. The lead horseman rode out alongside in the water and brought his quirt across Jube's face, slicing it open from the bridge of his nose in a line down to the earlobe.

Jube blew out his lips slightly to keep blood from his mouth. It was the warmest blood in creation. He wished he could bathe in it. He wished he owned it in bottles to lay in his bed at night.

"Now you sing us a good Christian hymn to make up for that other heathen song," ordered the man with the whip. He sloshed the horse back from Jube and waited. One man on the bank said, "You want to kill him?"

"We ain't killed nobody yet. Charlie, you want to do it?"

"Don't use my name!" came the hiss.

Jube looked at the dark stain where blood had dripped from his face and a rock cut on the neck and now spread on the water's surface around his thighs. Swallowing hard, he launched into song.

"*There is a fountain filled with blood!*" he sang lustily, and each time on the word "fountain" he raised his voice till he seemed to be baying it forth like a hound.

The Klansmen were muttering and uneasy on their horses. It was not going right; he had not broken and begun pleading for his life so they might give it to him, carelessly, showing how little value it carried.

"That is the craziest nigger I ever saw," one of them said again.

"He ain't hardly *worth* killing," whined another.

There had been no killing yet by the night riders in Stone County. By some unspoken agreement, people assumed this would be reserved for known offenses against white women—if not rape, then at least suggestive insult. And here was Jubilee Jackson, who had lifted so many boxes of supplies in so many wagons for their wives. . . .

"I am froze and stuck to this horse," one Klansman said glumly. "Kill him if you want to, Charlie. Here. Use my gun."

Charlie took his own gun and whacked the other man in the back of the neck. "I told you we don't use no names!"

"You had enough?" somebody shouted to Jube.

But Jube, who by now was so cold that he thought he was probably dead already everywhere except inside his lungs, sang on. ". . . drawn from Emmanuel's vein . . ."

They whispered some more in the shadows and their horses blew and snuffled. "You just stay there awhile and think!" yelled the leader, sounding nervous in spite of himself. Jube went on singing.

The men seemed to straggle away, first one and then the other, riding apart, so that the separate gleams of their white robes faded off right and left and straight ahead. Jube watched them scatter, and as they walked their horses into the night he sang louder, hoping his voice would follow them through the trees along the river road: ". . . beneath that flood, lose *all* their guilty stain!"

He knew when the last one had gone and the last flicker of white was lost to view. He could leave the water now, wipe off his face, run home on numb feet. But still he stood freezing until the song was finished. Then he splashed weakly to the bank. His face was a sudden long streak of pain. He felt a bolt of lightning had just run down it. The hymn tune he mumbled was mostly a sob as he stumbled out of the water. He fell onto the wet sand, crying, "Lose all their guilty stain, lose all their guilty stain. And sinners washed beneath that flood . . ."

There Vinnie found him. She ran for the river as soon as she counted the sixth set of hoofbeats going past the house. They were hurrying. They must be running from something awful.

She ran barefoot to where Jube lay thrumming the remnants of his song at the river's edge. Half walking, half dragging, she got him home to wash his cuts and lay her fingers on his mouth to shush his music, and then to nurse him through the days and nights of long ascending fevers of pneumonia.

Vinnie sent word to Sam at the store that Jube was too sick to work. Sam only nodded, but David, who waited for Little Jube in the street, pulled the whole story out of him. Before it was even finished, David ran with his hand clapped over his mouth as if he might vomit, screaming for Rutledge.

"*Rutledge! Rutledge!* Where are you, Rutledge?"

Rutledge was in the back yard, building Mildred a new chicken lot. He stopped, stretched the wire around the next post and leaned on it to keep it taut. "What you want now?" he said wearily, for David had been underfoot half the morning.

"*Rutledge!*" David screamed. "It was me, Rutledge! It was me wrote the KKK sign everywhere."

Rutledge looked distressed. "Now, young David," he began softly.

"It was only me! Don't you believe that sign! They're not coming for you!"

"It's not your worry," said Rutledge. He smiled and reached out a hand to still David's wild movements.

"No, no! Don't you be afraid of it! It was only me!" In his sincerity, David jumped up and down and threw his arms about like a windmill. "I did it, Rutledge! It was for fun! It was just a joke by me and Thomas!"

Rutledge let the wire roll back to the previous post he had nailed and bent to David with a smile. "That's a kindly thing for you to say and I appreciate it," he said.

"It's not for kindly!" David screamed. "For true! It was really me!"

"You're a good boy, wanting to make me feel better. I done heard about Jube."

David was wild. "I'm not good. I'm not a bit good! And you've got to believe it was me, just me! And Rutledge, I take it back! I take the signs back!"

But Rutledge only thanked him again for his kind thought and began to stretch the chicken wire. David saw that Rutledge would continue to go home every night and lie awake waiting for masked riders to call his name from the yard and whistle their leather straps in the air about his house.

"I take back the sign," cried David again, helplessly.

"It ain't your fault."

Now David did vomit, all over himself and the coil of chicken wire and Rutledge. It was mostly milk from breakfast, and the flecks of curd speckled Rutledge's arms until they looked like one of the Plymouth Rocks he was making the hen yard for.

Rutledge was alarmed and bent forward quickly and gathered David into his arms. He carried him into the house to Mildred, who put him weeping in his bed. Thomas thought it a silly way to behave.

The next carving David made with his knife was a shapeless human figure swathed in some loose garment; and the sharp buck teeth and the thin hands he touched up with streaks of pokeberry juice and he carved it from holly wood, and it was white.

Chapter
❦ 14 ❧

Spring atoned for its slow start the previous year by bursting forth on every bare twig ahead of season. Rainy nights and sunny days made new pine cones appear like an invasion of pale-green worms high in the needled limbs. As early as March there were days when country boys took off their shirts and hung them on limbs or fence posts. Beetles dropped full grown out of the air and began to feed on the tender leaves. In the shady places, toad-frogs no bigger than a thumbnail bounced awkwardly about.

Miss Eliza Tilley came down with some springtime complaint and second term at the Academy closed early. Only Preacher Holt handed out certificates in a ceremony held on the school lawn, where the ladies could use their palm-leaf fans.

So all three Allen children were home early for summer before summer had even come. Sam took Thomas straight into the mill store from early in the morning until late at night; and Thomas grumbled his shoulders no longer felt normal unless they ached, and the calves of his legs were always so heavy they seemed ready to melt down around his feet. Esther and David were set to helping Mildred outdoors, for she had decided to transform the ugly yard into a living green wall around their house, so they could live secretly within it the way something slumbers inside a tight cocoon.

Mildred had already alerted her friends in Greenway. None of them called without bringing cuttings or roots or seeds or bulbs recently divided. These Mildred planted in holes fairly hammered into the clay.

Rose of Sharon, thrift, white spiraea, bachelor's-buttons, touch-me-not, crape myrtle, larkspur, four-o'clocks, bleeding heart and butterfly bush—Mildred planted them all; and started ivy along that front fence behind a bed of lemon verbena.

Then Mildred began to expand into surrounding woods, looking for other greenery to fill the gaps. Since it seemed God would not bend from the trees to tell her what she should do with Esther, she could at least have the benefit of those worried walks by going back now to spots where she had spied fern, or adder's-tongue, dogwood seedling and wintergreen, and holly. To Mildred it was only right that Esther should tramp through the woods with her—perspiring and fussing—and help dig locust and birch and tulip poplar and red maple, soon to be standing around that house like sentinels. Whenever the two of them could not free some deep root, Mildred tied a small yellow scarf to the trunk and Thomas and David were sent to bring the plant straight after supper on the same day, and set it where she said.

Sam had warned her to bring home no willow trees, not to this clay, where they would thirst to death.

The minute he said that, long green fronds of willow began to whip back and forth in Mildred's mind. She could see how their branches would stir at her window in the heated air which—she was certain—the mill blew forth upon the Allen house. "All right," she told him, as if it were of no importance. Already she was retracing her walks by the Katsewa, remembering where the greenest ones had grown.

Mildred was partial to the willow, that tree by the rivers of Babylon on which the Israelites had hung up their harps and wept, remembering Zion. Sometimes when she saw willows waving beside a stream, they seemed to her like the bent heads of women—any women—surrounded by drooping shafts of loosened hair.

On these trips to the woods, Esther usually walked behind, eyes rolled to Heaven. Mildred marched at a vigorous pace with a spade propped on her right shoulder. Sometimes she sang:

> "We hanged our harps
> Upon the willows
> Upon the willows
> In the midst thereof;
> In the midst thereof."

Between them they carried home not only those willow shoots which were already growing along the riverbank, but even stalks of their green branches, which would sometimes sprout if merely driven into damp ground.

Nothing Mildred planted would die, not even in that earth which was hard as mortar. Every evening David carried out his bucket and dipper and fed water patiently through the crust. Mildred watched from her kitchen and would sometimes drop her song to a whisper:

> "For there they
> That carried us away
> Captive
> Required of us a song,
> And they
> That wasted us
> Required of us mirth
> Saying sing us
> Sing us
> One of the songs of Zion. . . .
>
> How shall we sing the Lord's song
> In a strange land,
> In a strange land?
> How shall we sing the Lord's song
> In a strange land?"

If Sam was in the house he would begin to squirm and mutter how he hated that song, had always hated it. Anyway, you couldn't hang any harp on any willow; it would have to be tied or maybe plaited among the drooping stems. Soon he would be calling Thomas to come ahead; come on; there was something important to do at the store! "Let the children and womenfolk plant their bushes!" he would grumble.

It was only a lull, then, in the activities of buying and selling and digging and planting that found Thomas and Esther and David all together on the front porch of the house with nothing to do.

"It's hot," said Esther. She wiped her forehead on her skirt tail.

"I know it's hot," snapped Thomas.

"You know what Mama did this morning? Had Rutledge take the buggy all the way back to our old house and dig up half that yellow-bell bush by the gate. Rutledge says it was tangled in chinaberry roots and he nearly pulled his back out of place."

"You know how Mama is," was all Thomas said. He looked, from habit, along the village street. Six weeks he had been watching for Zelda Dowdy, who was somehow going to come to him crying, "Anything! Anything!" He had not seen her yet. She might be sick. The bag hanging from his neck had darkened and grown slick and smelled of his own body. He had not added the fresh hair.

"Go ask Papa for some candy," said David. He poked his brother. "There's nothing to do."

Thomas shook his head. "He gave me the afternoon off and if I go messing around that store he'll find me some work."

This was only partly true. What he disliked at the store these days was not the work, but Jube. The Klansmen had been unable to break that limber spirit, but neither was Jube able to unwind from a certain twist the night had put into it. Now, even while he worked alongside Thomas, Jube laughed only after he thought it over, and he took no new words home in the evenings to store inside his jars. Now, when a white man came into the store, Jube stiffened, and whatever his hand was doing became a fierce thing—the loop throttled the bag of coal or the ax on wood became some amputation. The sound of the name Charlie made Jube's nostrils quiver. Even when he smiled— and that had become rare—it was only below the pink, spongy scar, which now divided his face at an angle, and walled off any warmth from rising to his eyes.

"Besides," said Thomas flatly, "I am sick of the smell of candy."

Esther raised her hand, shielding her eyes from the sun, and gazed at the top of the mill chimney. It was built square of brick and rose almost two hundred feet. "Wouldn't you hate to fall in that?" she said to herself.

Thomas asked sensibly how anybody could fall in a chimney two hundred feet tall. But now she had mentioned it, the smoke grew darker and looked menacing. "You could be working around the top edge," he admitted unwillingly. There was a metal ladder embedded in its face to the upper rim. "Replacing a brick or something."

Esther shook her head. "I mean falling down from a long, long way. Like you do sometimes in dreams. And when you dropped down past the last cloud you'd see there was no place to land but right in that open chimney. And all the way down it would open up bigger and bigger to catch you. Like a mouth."

"You'd burn," said David. He watched the smoke. "You sure would burn up."

Esther swayed slightly, matching the way the smoke went this way and that in the warm air. "You'd get hotter and hotter falling down, and scream, and your clothes and hair would begin to smoke and give off a smell and it would take nearly forever to hit and— Who's that?" She jerked her head aside.

"It's just Max Carson. He walks behind the mill sometimes." The three of them turned from the chimney to see him head back of the boiler room, toward the river. David said he might go see Mr. Carson right now and ask him about the persimmon wood.

"I wouldn't do that," said Esther quickly. She caught hold of David. "We're going to have some candy. Thomas is going to get us some."

"I never said I was." He jerked his head away. He had been staring at her long, black hair, wondering what would happen if he stole one of those for Miss Bethesda Lee Michael's bag.

Esther frowned. "You know Mama won't let me go inside the store. Go on, Thomas. Get us something."

"Peppermint!" cried David. "I'd rather have peppermint."

"Go get him some. It won't take a minute." She smiled.

It would probably ruin the spell. She wouldn't— Thomas jumped to the ground. "Come on, David. You can carry it back in case I get stuck with some work."

As soon as Esther saw them set foot on the first stair step at the mill store, she threw herself over the banister, tramped flat in Mildred's lemon-verbena bed getting over the yard fence, and ran for the river. She skirted the big pile of coal and cinders behind the mill and took a quick glance up and down the cleared area to the river's edge. She saw no one. To the left she pushed her way through a curtain of honeysuckle and prickly greenbrier. Even here the mill was reaching out; snuff tins and papers and leftover lumber were scattered among the dead leaves. Esther ran toward the sound of water.

The way the bank dropped sharply off, she was already upon Max Carson before she could stop. He was standing in the edge of the river, barefoot. Esther tried to stop when she saw his head above the greenery, slid on the rushes along the slope and came bouncing down the muddy bank in a sitting position. She skidded to a stop before him on the damp sand.

Carson had whirled at the noise and now sloshed rapidly to where she sat, eyes closed. "Are you hurt?"

"No," she lied.

"Is somebody chasing you?"

Her eyes flew open. "That's right," she said quickly. "He's back yonder. I was scared."

"Stay here." He climbed the bank along the slick path of broken reeds she had made, and Esther could hear him thrashing about in the underbrush. She got painfully to her feet, brushed at her skirt and discovered the back was clearly imprinted in water and sand with the outline of her rear. It looked like a pair of sugar-frosted cookies which had run together in the oven. She twisted her head back, looking down. Her two hands would not be enough to cover that design. She kept them there anyway, turned her back to the water, and waited.

Max Carson looked down at her over a wall of saplings and muscadine vines. "I can't find anybody. Who was it?"

"I don't know. Never saw him before."

"How old was he?"

"Old," she said hastily. "Maybe thirty."

He smiled and slid down the bank to her. "We've never really met. I'm Maxwell Carson." He put forth his hand. Esther did not move hers from where they were spread against her skirt.

"I know who you are."

"And you're David's big sister. Miss Esther Allen."

"I know that too."

"You seem determined not to take my advice about wandering around by yourself." He gave up the handshake and made his voice severe. "The next man who kisses you may not want to stop with that."

Esther felt heat coming to her face.

"Describe him to me."

"Who?" she blurted, alarmed.

"Whoever was chasing you?"

She began to shake her head. "I was running too fast. I couldn't tell much about him. He wasn't from the village. I'm sure of that."

He cocked his head. "What you hiding back there?"

Esther pressed her hands against the wet skirt. "Nothing! Not a thing!"

Carson shrugged his shoulders, ran one hand through the hair which had fallen across his forehead. She thought he could use some fattening on his bones—a diet of biscuits and gravy. He needed a shave too. There was nothing pleasant about his looks, she thought, and he was so thin his ribs must lie in ridges. "What were you doing in the water?"

"Just loafing." He sat down now and began to brush at the soles of his bare feet. "I've stepped on something, crashing around up there." He separated two toes and began to pinch at some unseen sticker.

Esther stared, fascinated. She had never seen anything so ugly as that foot. It was long, white, bloodless; the toes looked as if they could curl around tree limbs and atop each one grew a tuft of black hair. Carson said to himself, "I've got a brier in here."

"Is it bleeding?" she whispered.

"No." He pulled his head down and tried to see into the space between his toes. The sunlight, speckling through overhanging leaves, lay on his face in such a pattern of light and dark that Esther could not tell which was the scar and which was a patch of shade.

"I'll get it later," he grunted finally.

She walked to him. "Let me."

At first he shook his head, then he stuck out his leg. "Second and third toe," he said. "Right in between."

Esther could hardly bring herself to take the foot between her two hands. It was wet to the trouser cuff. Flecks of brown leaves and dead grass blades were plastered on its top, which, she now saw, was crossed by two fat blue veins. One ran all the way into the largest toe while the second curved swollen by the ankle bone and wandered off the side of his foot. She shivered.

It was not hard to find the sticker which had slipped under the pale skin. "It's a nettle," Esther said weakly.

"A what?"

"Hold still." She pinched up the skin between thumb and forefinger. "I could do better if I didn't bite my nails," she said softly to herself.

He jerked his foot away, "*Bite* it?" he echoed.

"No, no. Will you hold still?" She pulled his foot closer, braced it above her stomach and worked at the pinch of skin. The thistle slid suddenly out and was lost somewhere in the wrinkles of her hand. "It's out. I don't know where it went, but it's out." She went on holding his foot a minute more; then, carefully, she placed it on the ground.

"Thank you," he said. He was looking up very directly into her face. The surface of her cheeks felt so alien she could not tell whether she was flushed or pale. She straightened, started to turn away and remembered that her skirt was wet.

"It'll be all right now," she said, looking beyond him into the forest.

"About this hole in my face . . ." said Max Carson softly.

She shot him a quick look of anger, looked away again. "It was just a brier. You don't have to tell me that."

"But about this hole in my face," he continued. "The way I got it—I was your age. Maybe a year older. I was sliding one night in the snow, downhill on a sled I built myself. Turned over and fell, going fast. There was a sharp stick under the snow. It went right through, right between my jaw teeth, flat across my tongue. I could feel the point of it touching the inside of my mouth on the other side."

"That's awful," said Esther, sorry she had ever asked.

"It was a stob on an old cedar tree the wind had blown down. I sawed it off the trunk with my pocket knife—took the longest time. Blood all over the snow, and my hands slick. Cedar's tough; I thought about that, talking to your brother David. I don't know why I didn't just jerk my head up and pull the thing out, but I cut it off. And it took a long time." He was still looking at her, intently. "I think somebody once told me about the barbs on Indian arrows and how you mustn't just yank them out. People do funny things when they're scared."

"Yes," said Esther. She felt sick. Maybe it was the thought of his red hands sawing away at a cedar stob. Maybe his foot had some smell to it. Something.

"I walked home with the stick through there, biting down. It didn't even hurt much—my teeth were clamped so hard half my face felt numb. It was almost a good feeling, to walk home in the night with a stake driven in my face. If I could have managed it without opening my teeth, I might even have done some singing. You won't understand that."

"I do understand it. I do" she breathed.

"It healed like this. Puckered."

"It looks all right," she said, not looking anywhere near him at all.

"It might have healed quicker and smoother if I hadn't been such a damn fool. I used to try to keep it open. Fill up my mouth with air and force it through. Blow right out that hole and make the thing bleed."

Esther felt awful. She hung her head, scrubbed uselessly at the back of her skirt. "You shouldn't have done that."

He got easily to his feet. "You asked how I got it that first time. When I thought you were somebody else. Most people don't have the nerve to ask me. I really meant to tell you then."

Something about his face, his relaxed smile, suddenly made Esther furious. "If it was because I pulled out that silly brier," she said, breathing hard, "you didn't have to tell me anything."

"How old are you?" When she did not answer, he added, "Fifteen? Like Thomas says?"

Still she said nothing. Her clothes were wet all the way through, she had decided, and there were chill bumps on her thighs. And she wouldn't be fifteen until November.

"You're going to be very pretty." Max Carson turned his head to one side and looked her carefully up and down.

Esther said shortly she was not the least bit interested in going-to-be.

"At your age, I wasn't either." Carson laughed.

"My birthday's in November."

He had untied his shoes from a nearby sapling. "All right then. You're pretty now. Is that better?" He began to put them on.

She turned now to study him, while his head was bent away from her. Skinny man. Hole in his face. Hairy feet. Crossly she told him, "People in Greenway claim you wouldn't know pretty if you saw it."

He slipped into the second shoe and laced it. "They're the ones don't know."

Esther thought then she might as well ask. "You think I look older than I am?"

"You look both." All he did was lift his head, but his look was like a heavy weight upon her. "Older and younger. Thank you for getting out the brier."

She did not know what it was about him that made her so angry. "Why didn't you just walk with that brier stuck all the way through and touching the other toe? Why didn't you bleed on the leaves? Why didn't you start singing?"

Catching hold of a small tree, he pulled himself up the bank. "All right—older!" He was laughing. "You look like an old lady of at least thirty years!"

She watched him gain the top. "You have got the ugliest feet I ever saw!" she called at his back.

She could hear only the sound they made, walking away.

Twice Thomas tried to speak to Zelda Dowdy in the store. She laughed and darted out the door. Once he saw her in her front yard with Winkie, scraping some picture into the hard dirt with a nail. Thomas ran all the way down the street, heedless of who saw, and just as he pounded near, she threw her head back, froze like some rabbit in a field. Then she bounded inside the house.

She left Winkie squatting in the dirt. He rolled his eyes to their very top to look toward Thomas without moving his head.

"Go get your sister," Thomas puffed. He was red from heat and anger. This boy with his taste for candy—was it not his fault that now Miss Bethesda Lee Michael lay at the bottom of the river? Thomas roared, "Go tell Zelda Dowdy to come out here right now!"

Winkie put forth one fat foot and scrubbed out the round face she had been drawing for him.

"Call her!" Thomas ordered. He balled his fists. "If you don't call her out right now, I'm going to hit you one."

At this the little boy scuttled for the steps, crawled to the top one and sat hugging the porch post.

It seemed to Thomas he could see Zelda watching from the front window. He shook his fist at it. "Mill people!" he said between gritted teeth. "I know what you're all like!" He turned on his heel and hurried back to the store. There was a pain in his head, just at the eyebrow; he tried to wipe it away on his sleeve.

After that, Thomas began to study the schedule of the whole Fletcher Dowdy family. He worked this out on a large sheet of brown wrapping paper, which he rolled into a tube and kept behind a picture frame in his bedroom. Here he recorded the hours Fletcher and Obedience Dowdy went to work and came home, and the regular night Fletcher walked downstreet to pitch horseshoes with Claude Rickert in House Number Two. On Saturday evenings the oldest Dowdys—Ernest, Rachel Blessing, Mary Sue, Clyde and Dalton—trooped to the lyceum, where somebody usually showed up with a fiddle, a guitar and a wagonload of cider for sale by the cup. Sometimes there was dancing. Often the mother went with them, because she was an alto and there might be songs before the party ended. Whenever Obedience Dowdy walked to the lyceum, Fletcher sat on the front steps of the house with his overall straps flapping and, until about nine o'clock, drank the whiskey he bought at Sam Allen's store. Then he went indoors and blew out all the lamps except a small one in the front-room window.

None of this, so far as Thomas could see, was going to do him one bit of good. Fletcher Dowdy was still inside the house, drunk or not, along with Zelda, Winkie and Christine, who was about eight and had something wrong with her mouth and upper lip. Christine could take water into her mouth, bend forward and blow it forth through her nostrils in twin streams. She was much in demand to entertain other mill children with her water-blowing and strangled efforts to talk, and was locked inside the house when Zelda had to leave her during the day.

Yet (Thomas convinced himself) all he wanted was one hair from Zelda Dowdy's head. In all these weeks he had not been close enough to jerk out one single yellow hair.

Because I wouldn't force her to do anything, he'd think. I'll just put the hair into the little bag in pitch dark like Miss Bethesda said, and she'll be all over me. She'll whimper. She'll tell me: "Look here. Look there. Put out your hand."

Thomas thought of asking Esther to pull the hair from the Dowdy girl's head. But Esther spent all that spring staring off at nothing. He could have pulled out a handful of her hair and she'd never have noticed.

It forced him to search for whatever it was she saw. For whole afternoons Esther would sit rapt by the window, but even though Thomas stared till his eyeballs ached, there was nothing outside but one clay street and a red-brick mill.

It got on his nerves. When he criticized her, Mildred said, "She's growing up."

"Me too!" he protested. "All the time! Every day!"

But his mother did not seem to be listening. He was so angry he eased into the parlor, where Mildred had left the shawl she was knitting for Rosa's baby, and pulled the needle out from all its stitches.

So Esther was no help to him. Thomas gave David two candy sticks to bring him one of Zelda Dowdy's hairs. "That girl there," he said, pointing her out carefully. "One hair, that's all. Bring me one hair."

David was gone half the day. When he finally came home he had a whole pocketful of hairs—none of which he remembered to offer Thomas. He carried them all to his bedroom to study: hair from a horse's tail, the mane, cow's tail, a wisp of fur caught in some bush. Spirals out of Ellie Faye's head and gleanings from all the family combs. A squirrel's bushy gray tail, a rabbit foot, a hog bristle. One tiny breast feather out of a baby chick—to examine for differences. A woolly worm, a cat whisker, a gray hair off some old lady he knew, and an assortment of pale hairs—some curly—donated by different mill girls. David had entirely forgotten Zelda Dowdy.

Thomas was so furious at this collection he grabbed up every hair and rushed downstairs and threw them all into the open fire in the back yard, where Mildred was boiling an iron pot of sheets. David ran after him, leaped furiously to his back and clawed at one ear. They fell fighting to the ground, rolled around beating each other wherever they could reach. Finally Mildred came out to where they were thrashing about and whacked them soundly with her broom.

That very night Thomas stepped from squeak to squeak on the dark stairs, crept out of the house and slipped through the shadows to where Zelda Dowdy lived. He cut an indirect line through the woods behind the row of privies. At House Number Four, he walked softly from window to window, trying to fix names to the sounds of deep breathing he could hear. He could not tell which one was Zelda.

Coming home, he was chased by a barking spotted dog. He let it run him among the trees, where he killed it with a chunk of wood to stop the noise. It was the stupid dog's fault altogether. Thomas left it there under an oak, moonlight shining in those open eyes like some secondary life. He got back to his own bed without being discovered and, automatically, began to run through prayers as he had always done. At the end he added something about the dog, but when he tried to think back on it next morning, it seemed to him he had fallen asleep without finishing that petition, or explanation, or whatever it had been.

Two nights later, after Thomas had squatted for hours back of the Dowdy house, he saw Zelda in her nightgown, picking her way to the privy in the dark. Starlight on her straight hair turned some strands to silver. He was tempted to hang her by it to some tree, like Absalom. He edged in closer to the privy and flattened himself against a side wall, breathing lightly through his mouth to limit the smell. He saw her put her bare foot on the rock which served as a step. She closed the door behind her.

Thomas pressed his eye to the nearest knothole. Nothing but a stack of torn paper. There was the sound of trickling water.

When she stepped out of the privy again he grabbed her at the waist from behind and pulled his other arm hard against her mouth. His face was full of her shaking yellow hair. Fiercely she struggled against him, and the scream she was straining to make came out moaning into his sleeve. Thomas let go her waist and slapped her over the ear, not too hard. Then his hand, which was intended to stay where it was and pluck out one hair for his magic pouch, ran amok of itself, slipped to her shoulder and under her arm, and scraped roughly down her body to cup her between the legs. He could feel all the life in him plunge swelling to his groin.

The sudden chill along his back was like a stream of cold water. So small she was . . . so slight . . . and the noise which gurgled against his arm was strange. Zelda, by now, would have driven her teeth into his bone. Thomas jerked his hold tighter, drawing her head back, and grabbed her harder through the nightgown.

Then, slowly, he eased his head around to examine her face. She was stiff now, but motionless against him except for a trembling in the throat. Her eyes were larger than an owl's.

It was Christine. With loathing, he let go of her, pushed her from him to the ground, and plunged for the woods. All the way pounding home he waited for the shrill screech and the noise of grown men shouting. Not until he was leaning weakly against his own door in his own room did Thomas remember Christine could not call out, would not even be able to tell who had grabbed her in the night.

He fell into bed with his clothes on. There was no prayer he could remember that had not already gone upward for Miss Bethesda. It seemed to Thomas he must have used up all the forgiveness God had ever allotted to his name—and it was all so unfair, because things seemed to happen of themselves! He began to sob and strike himself with his fists. At last, where his hand fell he squeezed cruelly, then less cruelly. He touched himself with gentleness, and began to stroke. Some time after that he had a dream in which Zelda Dowdy sat upon him and watched out of mocking eyes while she hurt him and hurt him and hurt him and then healed him, in a sudden and unexpected surge of warmth. His hand was wet. Half between dream and waking, he watched Zelda's face unmold; her hair became long and black; she looked like—

He rolled onto his stomach, still holding himself, and slid altogether into sleep.

Chapter

✺ 15 ✺

"SILAS! CALM DOWN! I can't even understand you!" Mildred put her hand on his arm. He was shaking. "Tell me again, slowly."

The horse on which he sat was breathing hard, but so was he. "I come for you," he panted. "Get up behind me."

It was a Sunday and Mildred had not yet taken off the black straw hat she had worn to church. She reached for it now, without thinking, and let her two hands rest on the brim. "It's Rosa?"

"It's her time and she sent me for Dr. Newton but he's over in Davie County with an outbreak of fever."

Mildred made herself take the hat off and thrust the pin neatly through the same holes. "Is she sure? This is a month early."

"Get on up here," Silas said, and leaned forward as if he might sweep her up behind him on the saddle. As thin as Silas was, such a grand gesture would have yanked him straight down to the ground. Mildred brushed his hand from her, turned instantly on her heel and started for the house. She looked back at Silas, who sat numbly in the saddle with his right hand where she had thrown it. "Don't just sit there!" she called back to him. "Go home and stay with her!" Still he had not moved by the time she reached the front door, and she turned and screamed at him impatiently. "I said get along!" Silas went.

"Ellie Faye? Call Rutledge in from the garden to hitch the buggy!"

245

"It's Miss Rosa?"

"Yes." Mildred changed shoes, added a bonnet and took a shawl from a hook in case she should be driving home after dark. Then she stood in the hallway, thinking. Should have told Silas to warm some water, make tea. Don't know how far along she is. My sewing scissors are sharper than Rosa's.

These she slipped into her pocket. "Esther?"

Esther was already at the parlor door. "I saw Uncle Silas riding off. Is it Aunt Rosa?"

"That's what he says, though it shouldn't be till June. You want . . ." She studied her daughter thoughtfully. "You want to come?"

Esther shook her head.

"Sam went to the store to open up long enough to get some laudanum for somebody's toothache. Tell him when he comes. Ellie Faye will finish the meal. You and Thomas keep an eye on David."

"Yes, ma'am."

"Ellie Faye?"

She appeared behind Esther. "It's coming around front. You want Rutledge to drive? You need me to come with you?"

"You cook and tell Rutledge to water my flowers. If I'm not back by dark, tell Sam I'll stay the night."

"Yessum. Is she bad?"

Mildred threw out her hands. "How would Silas know?" To Esther she added evenly, "Or any other man."

Rutledge held the horse until she was settled, handed her the reins and leaped back when she whipped down the mill-village street at a fast pace. Children who were out playing in the sunshine rushed to the edge of the street to see her go by. Hope I don't hit any; I don't have time . . . thought Mildred. They all looked as dirty on Sundays as they did on weekdays, she noticed, which showed the kind of raising they got. For a minute she felt encouraged, almost blissful; Esther was growing beautiful; Thomas diligent; even David was settling down. Rosa's baby had a good chance to be fine, just fine.

The thought of children threw her mind miles down the road to Rosa's house and she half stood in the buggy and whipped the horse. It raced through the narrow road cut tunnel fashion in the forest.

At the junction, where a left turn went to Greenway and a right toward Stoneville, Mildred jerked the horse right and picked up speed on a thoroughfare hardened by the hoofs of many horses. She had not gone a mile down the road when she pulled in suddenly and stared. That horse grazing at the edge of the field. Didn't it belong to Silas?

Mildred sat, indecisive, and finally called his name. "Silas? Silas Bennett? Is that you?" She was about to drive on when she spotted him at the edge of the woods, standing with his back to the road, one shoulder leaning into a pine. She stood up and shaded her eyes. "Silas!" He did not move.

"For pity's sakes!" She began to spit angry whispers to herself. Finally she tied the horse to a sapling by the road and tramped across a furrowed field to where he stood. The last fifty feet she called his name irritably, over and over, without it making any dent.

She spoke to his back and shoulders. "What on earth are you doing?" Leaving poor Rosa alone in the house at a time like this! Silas? You hear me, Silas?"

He looked back at her across his shoulder. She saw that his face was white, the wrinkles elongated. He looked frightened. Mildred gentled her voice. "Rosa will be fine," she soothed. "Don't worry."

"I ain't worried."

Looking at his pinched face, Mildred tried again to remember that Rosa had run away and married Silas Bennett against their father's wishes. It had been unbelievable at the time. She had been unable to understand it since. "We must go to her," said Mildred firmly. "She'll want you there." Heaven knows why, she thought. And she had the sinking thought that no child of Rosa and Silas Bennett's could really be just fine, any more than two wrongs can make a right.

Silas looked away from her into the woods. "I'll be along," he said.

She said sharply, "Come on *now*," the way she might have given an order to Ellie Faye. When he did not turn, she added, "Silas, she's doing this for you."

"That's not so," he mumbled. "I never asked her."

Mildred gathered a handful of his shirt and pulled on it. "Come on this minute."

"I'm coming." He followed her toward the road, dragging behind and looking back.

When Mildred paused to let Silas untie her horse from the sapling, she found he was not there at all; he had stopped entirely some twenty paces back and was bent over a stump taking something from behind it. He made movements with his coat. Then he came on to her, his chest bulging.

Mildred set her mouth, took the reins and climbed into the buggy unassisted. Not until he had drawn alongside did she snap the reins at the horse. Half standing in the moving carriage, she called back to him in a furious voice, "All you can think about is whiskey!"

She fell, jolted and angry, onto the seat. Her eyes were full of tears. All the men there must be in the world, and this was the one Rosa had wanted. She remembered the quarrels in the living room, Angus Mackey yelling that Bennett boy wasn't worth a hill of beans. And Rosa saying softly, almost in a whisper, "I never cared for beans."

Mildred whipped the horse. When the farmhouse came in sight, she saw that this time there was smoke rising from the chimney—now that it was the end of May and hot. At least I can warm up some water, she thought. At least I won't have to chop my own wood. At least I won't have to find the ax and then put an edge on it.

She began nervously to call her sister's name all the time she was throwing the lines onto a post and running to the house. The heap of stones still waited by the front door; Mildred stepped on one and nearly turned her ankle.

Damn him to Hell, she almost said; but did not, being a Christian woman.

"Rosa? Rosa!" Flexing her foot, she limped into the hall. Immediately she could hear the sound of childbirth, half cry and half grunt, coming from the front bedroom. The door was open. Through it she saw the large shape of her sister, still fully dressed, lying atop the covers with her knees up. Rosa rolled first to the left, then right. The whole bed was vibrating.

"Rosa? It's Mildred. Everything's going to be all right now."

From side to side Rosa went, making the rough noise. Mildred saw quickly that nothing in the room had been prepared. "Rosa? I'm here now. It's all right."

"It's not all right," her sister groaned. She wallowed to the other side and, for one moment, Mildred had a clear picture of a sow turning in a mudhole. She was ashamed of herself.

"It's not all right," said Rosa again. Her words came in a series of sharp explosions, matching her quick intakes of breath. "I thought you'd never come. I'm going to die—I know it."

Mildred sat by her on the bed and began to pat her on the rump. "You're going to live to be a hundred," she said soothingly.

"Anything hurts like this has to kill you. Ooh, ooh, Oogh!"

Mildred sat motionless and watched the pang reach its height. When she saw from the tendons in Rosa's neck that it was ebbing away, she walked quickly into a neighboring room and fetched a mantel clock, then twisted two towels into ropes and tied each to the headboard of the bed. "You can pull down on these if it makes you feel better, but not yet," she said crisply. "If you'll calm down, I expect we'll find you're not so far along as you think."

It was easing. "Don't fuss at me, Mildred," Rosa whined.

It made her think of all the mornings she had plaited Rosa's hair. Mildred bent and kissed her at the hairline. "I only meant to speak fast, not sharp," she said. "Think now. You have the brown paper I saved you from the store?"

"Hall wardrobe," Rosa said. She sounded drowsy.

"The clean wrappings? Blankets for the baby?"

"They're all here. Everything's in the wardrobe."

Mildred smiled. "I'll have that shawl knitted for you in another three weeks. Somehow a needle got pulled out; I lost ten rows and there's still a rough place. Now you slip out of those clothes. Where's your gown?"

It was hanging behind the bedroom door. The two women struggled to get Rosa out of her flowered dress. She was sweaty and the folds of the fabric had stuck themselves between the folds of her flesh. When it was coming over her head at last, Mildred saw the dark little pouch hanging on a leather thong. She stopped dead, muffling Rosa inside the dress.

"What are you doing with that?"

"What?" mewed Rosa in a smothered tone. She began to paw at the folds of cloth. "What's the matter? Tell me what it is!"

Mildred jerked the dress off impatiently. "That silly bag. You still have it on."

Rosa's hand flew up and grabbed it. "You never know," she said tensely. "Just let it be. I won't feel safe without it."

Mildred began shaking out the dress as if she were punishing every seam. "If I was a good Christian woman," she lectured, "I wouldn't feel safe wearing some heathen sign when I ought to be praying for God's own strength."

Rosa put up her other hand as a double shield. "You're not to touch it," she said, just the way she had once told Angus Mackey: "I never cared for beans."

"Haven't you heard the old lady's gone? Dead in the woods somewhere, I'll bet. Some hunter will step on her bones one day. But it's all the same to me." She slapped the folded dress onto a chair and the little buttons clicked against the wood. "It's not my baby. It's all the same to me."

Rosa got out of bed and worked herself into the huge gown, while Mildred built up the fire in the kitchen range and put on water kettles. "Don't get in yet," she said when she came back into the room. Quickly she ran two layers of brown paper over the sheets in the lower half of the bed, covered the floor with other papers. She helped Rosa lie down. "Draw up a quilt for now," she said.

"I'm hot."

Mildred said crossly, "Draw it up anyway!" Her sister looked like a second mattress tied in some lumpy roll. "When this is over, Rosa, I hope you'll thin yourself down a little."

"I'll work it off running after that baby," sighed Rosa. "I'll have to be up at night. I'll have to pick him up when he's learning to walk. I'll be busy doing—" She began to groan again. Mildred looked at the clock.

"When did you start, Rosa?"

Rosa did not answer until the pain had passed. "I gave Silas dinner at noontime. Just before that." She sat up in bed. "Where is Silas?"

"He was coming behind me, slow," Mildred lied. "Horse threw a shoe, I think."

"I worry about Silas."

"Time to worry about yourself."

"He spends a lot of time outside. Just sits under the trees, thinking."

Drinking, Mildred corrected silently.

"I ask him, why can't you do your thinking in the house? Away from the bees and those awful birds. Sometimes the birds make so much noise you think they've flown in through your ears. All the time I visit you in the mill village, I don't see a single bird."

Mildred snorted. "You hear that mill, don't you? It shakes the whole house."

"He could think in the house. I keep him a clean house." She punched the pillow and lay back. "Mildred, will it be long?"

"I'll take a look on the next one." She eyed the clock but the next one was slow in coming. "I could read you some Scripture." She had the passage already in mind—Isaiah 44, the first four verses. Cheerful Scripture.

"Please don't," said Rosa irritably.

"Preacher Holt asked about you at church this morning. And I saw George Trumble—the nephew that's running Hobbs Dry Goods Store uptown now. He said Mr. Hobbs was losing his mind, and half the time didn't know him from Sam."

"If it's a boy," said Rosa dreamily, "I'm going to name him after Papa. Angus Mackey Bennett."

Mildred saw the pain gathering in her, watched it compress and grow hard. She pulled the quilt down and took a quick look, but there was no outward sign of pressure. "Spread your legs a little more, Rosa," she said. Viewed from here, she thought, women are sure ugly. "You need to push?"

"I can if it would help."

"Must not be time. Want some hot tea? I'll fix some."

"It'll make me sweat," Rosa complained.

"You've got to sweat."

While the leaves steeped in the pot, Mildred washed and dried the noon dishes, throwing the water off the back porch. A light rain had started and she could hear fragments of thunder from a long way off. Ought to get the horse in, Mildred thought.

There was a sudden blur at the edge of her vision. With effort she made out Silas through the drizzle, squatting against the wire of the chicken lot and swaying with it as though the fence were a cradle of some kind. She turned away in anger. Then she remembered Rosa's face and called him. "Silas, your wife wants you!" In the fencing he rocked back and forth.

For a minute she thought he had answered and then decided he was just talking to himself, or singing in a low voice. "Silas? It's raining! Silas!"

She went back inside and carried Rosa the tea. Rosa was lying now with both hands under herself, trying to rub the small of her back. "It's getting worse," she muttered.

"It's supposed to." Mildred held the cup and Rosa took a few sips.

"Did Silas come in? I heard you call."

"He's in the kitchen," Mildred lied. "He's so worried I thought it best to keep him out of here."

Rosa smiled. Her breathing was heavy and each word came with an effort, pushed out on a gust of air. "How do I look? Do I look different in the face?"

"You're white, that's all." She carried the teacup back and Silas really was in the kitchen, bent over the range. His coat looked wet and so did the hat crushed on his head.

"Rosa asks for you," said Mildred. Sam was right; there was a certain gloom in the man's face. That had always been Sam's excuse for not hiring Silas at the dry-goods store; he would be bad for business. He did look, now, as if half his life had been spent standing around open graves.

He said, "It's started to rain." Suddenly off balance, he lurched into the wood stove and snatched back his hand. He held it limply before his face.

She knew if she asked were he hurt, Silas would answer yes; when was he not hurt? She said instead, "Drink some of this tea and then go speak to her."

"Tea," Silas repeated. He shuddered.

Mildred poured a cup. "I told her your horse threw a shoe."

He let out a sudden high laugh. "She must have thought you was an awful liar. She knew I'd gone to pick up my whiskey. I told her so."

"Just drink this."

"Is she all right?"

"I think so." Mildred pushed the cup across the table.

"Don't want tea."

She said in a hard voice, "Silas, what is it you do want?"

After a minute he lifted the cup and drained it. Must have scalded him all the way down, she thought in wonder. "I'll go in," he said, but he did not. "You never did come to the mill to see the boiler room. I wanted you to see that."

"I'm sure you're doing a fine job," Mildred said stiffly.

"I don't do nothing. I just watch." He headed for Rosa's room, snapping his fingers. To the rhythm of the mill, perhaps. Mildred stood looking into his empty cup, put a finger to the bottom. It was still hot. She slid it into the dishpan. Couldn't live ten minutes with a man like that. Makes no sense at all.

And it had been no better in the days when he came courting Rosa. Looked like a banty hen, and his front hair sticking up like a rooster comb. Rosa then had been pink-and-white, filled out but not fat, her mouth always round and slightly pursed as if she were blowing air lightly. Angus Mackey had warned her the boy would never have anything more than the old Bennett place to his name. "And, Rosa, you're not, well, strong. You need a different kind of man. You need—" Mildred could hear them now, and the way Rosa had answered sweetly, "Somebody like you, Papa?"

Mildred put on a long apron and started back to Rosa. She stopped, surprised, at the bedroom door. Silas was bending over the bed, his fingers in a cluster about his wife's chin. He kissed her on the mouth, lingering, moving his head slightly. Rosa lay motionless, her arms at her sides.

It was hardly the time for mouth-kissing and Mildred coughed and hit her heels hard coming into the room.

Still they kissed, and when he moved his face into her hair, Rosa gave a little sigh. He stayed there a minute, pressing the palm of his hand against her face so their cheeks were tight together. Then he rose and left the room without a word, stumbling slightly. Mildred drew back out of his way.

"Put my horse in the barn," she said; but she couldn't tell if he heard or not. Almost immediately Rosa screamed.

Under her hips the papers were wet. Mildred slid in a new layer as well as she could. Weakly Rosa asked if she had a boy or a girl.

"That's only the waters," Mildred said. "But it won't be long." She loosened Rosa's fingers from the edge of the feather bedding and put them onto the looped towel, twining it a few times around wrist and forearm. "You'll be wanting this."

She straightened a curtain just to give herself something to do. She had observed births before, had been in charge of one of Ellie Faye's babies, and had given birth three times herself. Still, with

Rosa, it was harder. And when Esther's time came—why, they would just have to send word to her when it was done. Mildred was not going to set foot to ground till that grandbaby began to cry.

She adjusted the tie-back at the curtain. Rosa. Baby sister. Used to plait her hair so tight it stretched her eyebrows and she went around staring at everything with a look of surprise. Used to hold her when she was dizzy and pick her up when she fell—

"Mildred! *Mildred!*"

She hurried to the bed.

"Make it stop! Mildred, make it *stop!*"

Mildred put her hand on Rosa's belly. It formed itself into a watermelon, then a mallet, and last of all a stone. "Push down on it. Rosa, push down on it. Bear hard." She repeated the words over and over, not certain Rosa could hear. She drew down Rosa's arm so it was pulling strongly against the rolled towel. "Hold your breath and push!"

But Rosa's body was already pushing down, out of her control, and soon she began to raise her shoulders by holding onto the twisted towels and press her feet into the bed. Her long cries blended with the noises of effort.

Mildred kept her hand on the hard lump and pressed gently downward, watching for the slow stretching below and the first darkness of the infant's hair.

Now there were no more words between her and Rosa. The spasms came closer together. She was lost in the waiting and watching while Rosa was lost in the swirling demands of her own body. Mildred remembered the feeling; her blood vessels constricted slightly as they recalled how it had been. After years in which the body was under control and discipline, it suddenly broke forth in childbirth; it was paramount; the mind to it became now no more than a chip on the surface of the sea. The mind might scream for rest but the body was relentless; and all the time a woman thought: I won't push down another time, she was already pushing down. All the time she wanted to halt the process, just for an instant, one pause of rest, the process carried her along upon the torrent.

Rosa slumped, cried out, and almost immediately her body slammed down another time. Hurry, up, thought Mildred, hurry up; come along! The child is turning her wrong side out! Women have to fold inward from the skull on down, flow out behind the child and be born themselves—and born new, born reversed, with the tender underside turned to the outer skin. And now, through the baby, vulnerable. Defenses lost. Left open— There! She saw it!

Mildred stifled a gasp. That was no head crowning! She kept her face away from Rosa and threw a quick glance toward the door; but what help would Silas be?

Please, Lord Jesus, she thought; and then in panic: I forgot all about praying till now! If things go wrong it might be my fault for that forgetting! She ran the prayers now through her mind in an endless thread as she took hold of the tiny foot and drew on it gently. It came forth a little, then stopped. Mildred was afraid to pull too hard.

She whispered, "Silas!" Nobody came. She could hardly hear Rosa anymore and with a shock she realized Rosa might be dead! No, when she looked up the sounds were loud as before and Rosa's body was still threshing about and the muscles were driving downward. It was her own numb ears making the silence.

Rosa! Oh, Rosa, little sister! Mildred let her fingertips explore the tiny leg as high as she could. It was slippery and reminded her of nothing so much as a crooked little stick. She could believe more in a kitten than a human being coming forth like this. At the height of the next pang she ran her fingers carefully up the underside of the small leg and entered her sister's body.

It felt strange, wet, mysterious. It was like entering a hot cavern. Timidly she touched with her fingertips, could make out no shape at all. Mildred wanted nothing more than to jerk away and to run out of the house and wipe her hand on—on a matting of honeysuckle. On a sheaf of pine straw.

She moved her fingers slightly. A hip bone, that must be; and this the back, and the other leg curled at an odd angle. She searched out what had to be the bend of the knee and, lower down, the foot. With painstaking care she drew that downward. Even her own breath sounded like the cracking of bones.

Then the two feet were out. Mildred began to work them slowly, holding both ankles and turning slightly. Her tug was gentle, slow, tentative. It seemed to her Rosa might now split like a ripe peach. She slipped her left hand underneath to support the skin.

Now, with a rush, the baby came easily up to the shoulders. She turned the slick body slightly so the arms would be downward and he came forth—for it was the boy Rosa wanted. Just at the level of the armpits the tiny body stopped.

For the first time Mildred saw that the cord curled out of sight and seemed to be bunched to one side. She slid a forefinger to the spindly neck and found it tightly looped there, and she wanted wildly to break it free like a rope or a tangled crochet thread. She could not work her finger under it at all and she suddenly screamed, "Rosa! *Now!*" and reached up to push from outside, hard; and the head dropped and she began feverishly to remove the cord from around the twisted neck.

They're all this color at first, she told herself desperately, and she whipped it around and over and he was free. Quickly she made the two ties and cut the cord with the sewing scissors she had kept in her apron pocket. Now the child was no longer a part of Rosa, but something new and alone in the world.

Mildred dipped her hand into one of the basins of water she had readied by the bed, wiped it across her apron before she ran two fingers down the infant's throat to clear it. Then, holding him up by the ankles, she spanked him once, twice across the buttocks. He hung there, silent.

She put the limp child face down on the bed and pressed and released his ribs a few times, lifted him again and spanked. Rosa's snuffling sounds seemed suddenly loud in the room. Again she put the baby down to check his throat and began pushing rhythmically on his lower chest.

I'm going to scream. I'm going to scream louder than Rosa ever did.

She put the small body into the basin of warm water. The neck looked too small to be holding the large head onto the body; it hardly seemed as thick as some frayed rope. She lifted him out and rubbed his upper body briskly with a rough towel. Again she lifted him and he hung from her hand like a stringy fruit from a tree, Again she spanked him smartly on the rear. Then, terrified, Mildred shook him lightly in the air like a kitten worrying some old rag.

She thought she heard the first gasps of air and put her ear quickly to his small mouth. It was only her own breath coming in ragged sobs and that made her think of God putting the breath of life into Adam, or St. Paul at the bedside; and quickly she laid the baby down again and began to blow into his mouth and nostrils.

Not so hard, she cautioned herself, or I'll puff him out like a child blowing into a hog's bladder to make a toy.

It seemed to Mildred everything on earth had stopped to watch her labor over this little bit of wet flesh. She felt the billion unseen observers standing round. In and out. In and wait. In and pause. In–out. In–out. The air in the room was thick with the eyes fixed upon her. Honeybees had come to hover near the windows and turtles had crawled to the foundations of the house; and the ceiling was black with robins and dragonflies and red squirrels. All the tiny things of the earth were gathered there to see her breathe in and out, and in and out, and out and in, while a thousand years went by.

It was hopeless. Never once did the breath catch and hold and come of its own accord. Still she tried, and tried again. Her irregular tears dropped between the outgoing breaths while she made his chest swell and sink. But the baby boy lay still and dark and slippery before her, cooling under her hands.

Rosa had begun to move again. The afterbirth will have to manage for itself, thought Mildred, and she warmed the child against her, rubbed his skin with the towel, blew life into him and blew it in and watched it come back, invisible and unclaimed.

At last even she was convinced that he would never breathe. Her own mouth was full of the chill of death. Mildred leaned her head into the bedpost and allowed the shaking to vibrate over her and turn her smothered moan into a rattle. The afterbirth, red and seemingly vital, lay on the papers. In the surrounding blood she saw that it was complete and methodically she gathered up the paper's edges and put it, dripping, into a basin. She began automatically to bathe and dress the dead child.

Rosa, who had been drowsing, now cried out.

"I'm here," said Mildred, trying to sound calm.

"Boy or girl?" Rosa whispered.

Mildred looked down on the small features so completely formed and so completely ended. She looked at the tiny seed of manhood. "Boy," she said.

"I said, was it a boy or a girl?"

Mildred cleared her throat and spoke more strongly. "A boy."

Rosa's face fell into soft lines. "Silas has his boy," she sighed. She was drifting again into a weary sleep.

Mildred carried the infant to the waiting cradle, out of Rosa's sight, and laid it gently down. She slid the wafer-thin pillow under the waxen head.

Again Rosa stirred. "Does he—does he have all his fingers and toes?"

"Yes," said Mildred dully.

She walked from the room, holding herself as stiff as she could for fear she might fall down and beat on the floor with both stained fists. In her mind ran one red prayer of rage. *All Mama's fasting, but You wouldn't cure Rosa, All Mama's fasting and You couldn't give back one little baby boy.* . . .

She tripped going into the kitchen and grabbed for the door's edge to keep from falling. In horror she stared down at the protruding leg before her. But this one was trouser-clad; it belonged to Silas, prone and sleeping on the floor, his battered hat laid to his head like a pillow.

Tears were streaming on Mildred's face. She grabbed for the kitchen chair but it caught and hung on a corner of the table. Finally she snatched a blue cushion off its seat and began to beat Silas about the head and face and to cry out something hissing and unintelligible. Panting, she sobbed out to him everything there was; but Silas only muttered and rolled from her blows under the cover of one forearm. The rhythm of his snores broke once or twice, but he never really woke.

Chapter

❧ 16 ❧

"IF YOU COULD just get Rosa to come stay with me awhile," said Mildred.

"She won't come." Silas put a long pickle into his mouth and sucked it. "You know she won't."

Lately Mildred had made herself sit at the table when Silas came from the boiler room to have noon dinner with the Allens. She put up with the way he staggered in, the time he leaned his elbow right into her gravy boat, and the jiggling of his right leg, which shook all three of her children along the bench until one whole side of the table seemed to be rising and falling to the tempo of machinery next door.

"Silas, she's not herself. We all understand her grief. She ought not be left out there alone during the day. At least let me send Ellie Faye."

"She keeps the doors locked," Silas said. He put the entire pickle into his mouth and began to chomp it. Mildred walked to the pantry. She stood there, munching on a biscuit, and thinking of how Rosa, distraught, had for days carried the dead infant in and out the rooms of the Bennett house. Had propped it in chairs, dressed and undressed it, pressed its cold mouth to her useless, overflowing breast. In the end Silas and Sam had taken the child from her by force and buried it near Angus Mackey in the Greenway cemetery. Rosa had been locked in a bedroom, weeping, with Ellie Faye guarding the door, while they buried the child, which by then looked like a dry corncob doll made by a clumsy brother.

Mildred marched now into the dining room and demanded in a shrill voice, "Silas, why won't you admit it? Rosa blames me because the baby didn't live! She thinks I did something, or failed to do something."

Silas had dropped his head. Now he nodded it, slowly.

Mildred's eyes began to sting. "I'd better go out there today," she managed to say.

"Don't do that," mumbled Silas.

"She's my sister. I love her."

Finally Silas met her gaze. "She thinks you took off the little bag. Miss Bethesda's little bag. She thinks while the baby was coming you took it off and then put it back on again later, when it was too late to do her any good."

Mildred recoiled. "I didn't do that. Silas, I promised her not to touch it. You've got to believe I never did. Silas, I was too busy even to think about Miss Bethesda's little magic bag!"

"That's what she thinks," said Silas. "I've got to get back to them boilers." He swung his leg over the long bench—more steadily than he had put it in, she was glad to see.

Mildred caught his sleeve. "Is it true she meets you in the road at night? Sits right out there in the dark till you come riding home?"

"I'm careful," Silas said. "At first the horse nearly ran her down. Now I'm careful."

"Dr. Newton says I did everything it was humanly possible to do. Do you tell her that, Silas?"

He shook his head. "I don't tell her nothing. We just go inside and eat and go to bed."

She thought of them picking their way to bed in the dark, the swollen woman and the rat-size man, to lie in the dark under the burden of all the mockingbirds singing. That made her ask, cautiously, "Does she talk about . . . about having other babies?"

"Not since Miss Bethesda's gone. There's nobody to make her a new bag, she says, and we buried this one without saving her so much as a fingernail."

"Go back to work," said Mildred, feeling slightly sick.

Outside Silas stopped to watch the fire brigade practice. The dozen workers had been trained by Max Carson to operate the old fire engine bought from the town of Concord. Each man drew a bonus of fifty cents a month for this work. Silas had volunteered—needing the fifty cents—but Carson turned him down.

"I hear from Sam Allen you've had troubles at your house," Carson had told him intently, "but I want you to know I won't stand drinking on the job."

"I don't blame you one little bit," Silas had said gravely. "I'll speak to Claude Rickert this very day."

He snickered now, watching them try to roll the old engine this way and that without running one of the heavy wheels across anybody's foot. This had already happened once. They wouldn't be able to put out the coals under a vat of molasses, Silas thought.

He nodded to Thomas and Esther and David, who had come out with pails and buckets to pour more water on Mildred's flowers. The fringed leaves of the larkspur were standing tall, ready to bloom along the stalk. There were green knots standing above the thorny branches of Mildred's late-blooming roses, where the pink buds would be.

Silas called to the children. "I thought Carson put up some notice about using so much water during this dry spell. Thought he said the central well was low."

"He did," said Esther, "but you know how much Mama cares about his notices. Anyway, we have to tote this water all the way from the river."

Something blazed in his head as Silas crossed the clay street and headed for the boiler room. *Water her flowers if it gets hot as hell, and let my baby die.*

Esther watched him disappear into the small brick building. "Have you noticed how he gets smaller while Aunt Rosa gets bigger and bigger? Since the baby didn't live, Silas must have taken off thirty pounds and Aunt Rosa got every one of them," she said thoughtfully.

"He's always been skinny," Thomas said. "And you're not doing your share, as usual."

Esther took up the dipper and began to feed water slowly around the base of Mildred's willow tree. David set out for the river to bring another bucketful of water.

Thomas frowned. "What's wrong with your hand?"

"Oh, nothing much," said Esther, shifting the dipper quickly to her left so that he was not even sure he had seen an even row of scratches. "Did you know David's doing a new carving? Of Big Jube's face. It's nearly as big as a cantaloupe."

"I didn't know that," said Thomas with real enthusiasm, for anything that would cheer up Big Jube these days might do him some ultimate good. "Jube can keep it to remember how he used to look before the night riders came."

"Oh, no," said Esther quickly. "David means to put the scars into it. He's been working with cotton, staining it sort of pink and packing it down. Said he might glue it along a slash in the wood."

Thomas could imagine how the pinkish cotton would look laid level against the dark wood. "What's he been using to stain it?"

"Sometimes he cuts his own finger to get a little blood. Pokeberries are too dark, he says. Cherry juice isn't bad."

"Cuts his own finger!" Thomas exclaimed.

Now Esther put her right hand, palm up, toward him. "And sometimes I let him cut mine," she said softly. He saw then the marks he had spotted before, small dark lines in the tips of all the fingers of that hand. In several places they bisected each other in the shape of miniature crosses.

"He asked me if I'd mind," said Esther quietly, looking down at her hand, "but the crosses were my own idea."

"That was a crazy thing to do," said Thomas, staring.

Esther laughed. "Now don't you start! When Mama saw them she turned white as a ghost and asked me a hundred questions. Where else was I cut, and had I been eating all my meals! I think she was scared to death, but don't ask me why. I never did make her see it was only for David and the head he was carving."

Esther said it so lightly, with a smile, that she was surprised by the angry look on Thomas' face.

"You and David," he blurted, "you sure do stick together. You'd do anything for David." He did not give her a chance to answer, but snatched up her hand and glared at the tiny scratches. "Next time you want to cut yourself for David, just let me know. I'll do it for you."

Esther said gently, "Thomas? What's the matter, Thomas?"

"Nothing," he said, flinging her hand away. "Nothing. My head hurts, that's all. I hit it. On a tree. Getting water from the river." He touched his eyebrow with one finger. "Nothing you'd care about."

"That isn't true," she said. She put her hand up as if she might touch his aching head.

"Don't touch me there!" he cried out, clapping his whole hand over his brow.

Her fingers hung in midair. "Why not?"

"You and your crazy scratches," Thomas said. "I couldn't stand to have them touch me." He wheeled from her, swung out the front gate and walked rapidly down the mill-village street, hoping to see Zelda Dowdy. He was just in the mood to see her. And he would say—Miss Bethesda's bag or not—he would say only one word to her: "Now." He would say "Now" to her between his gritting teeth and she would come.

Sometimes that summer Esther volunteered to carry extra water from the river so Mildred could wash the clothes. She did this in the secret hope Max Carson would be standing with his ugly feet in the Katsewa, and sometimes she did see him resting on the bank, or throwing rocks to make them skip and skitter.

Often he waved at her. Esther pretended not to see, not to know he was there, not to glimpse his arm breaking the air and catching the harsh light of the midsummer sun. Instead she sucked in her stomach and threw forth her breasts and walked to the river's edge with all the grace she could find; and filled the pail as if it were an act performed to music.

Leaving the river, she could not resist creating little pictures for him. She would stop and lay one hand flat against the bark of a tree, so he might notice she was sensitive to textures. She might pause and turn her head to one side to follow the song of some bird, or to watch a butterfly looping above the trumpet flowers of the tangled vines. By this she meant him somehow to know what she was like. He would see these tableaux she put on so consciously for his benefit and be able to surmise all that lay within her, mysterious and accidental.

Once Esther almost fell upon him. He was sitting to one side of the path she usually took to the water's edge. Her heart began to hit against her ribs.

"Hello, Miss Esther Allen," he said, almost sarcastically. He did not look at her.

She said, as if it were a recitation, "Hello, Mr. Maxwell Carson."

"Still watering your bushes?"

"They're Mother's bushes."

"How old are you now?" he asked, and turned his face up to read hers.

It insulted her that he did not remember. "My birthday is still in November," she said coldly, "and I'll still be fifteen."

Carson seemed to be talking mostly to himself. "I shouldn't have promised Nathan Grimes to stay this extra time," he said. "I've been here too long."

She looked at him curiously. "Don't you do anything but work? I never see you at a box supper or a picnic. You don't ever come to church."

"I don't believe in God," he said with a light laugh. "Do you?"

"Most of the time. You must like working at the mill."

"I must," he said thoughtfully. "I'll carry the water for you this time."

Esther said in a flat voice that she could carry it herself; for sometimes it still seemed to her she had to beat all the boys at Indian wrestling to establish who she was.

But he did carry it, and even stood talking with her while she ladled the water out between the neat rows of four-o'clocks. Mildred saw the two of them from her kitchen window and watched seriously as they talked and Esther, once, threw back her head and laughed. "The cuts mean nothing," Mildred whispered. "Listen to her laugh. Nothing."

I've got to teach her to laugh more quietly when she's with a man, thought Mildred. She's got to learn how to drop her eyes.

But then she saw Esther throw back her head so the line of her throat showed white and vulnerable, and laugh with the kind of merriment that made Max Carson throw forth one hand as if he might have slapped her on the knee, had she been a man. Mildred saw his right hand spring forth and hang in the air, and get pulled very slowly back.

I don't think I'll teach her anything, Mildred said to herself; and Thank you, Lord Jesus. I guess.

Pines on the rolling hills around Greenway turned orange under a blistering August sun. Each noon the trees seemed to smolder and wait just this side of flame; and gardens behind the mill houses withered while a whole line of Mildred's scarlet hollyhocks fell under fire like a charge of Redcoat soldiers.

The central well in the mill village was so low Max Carson posted someone at the village pump to check a list so no family would get more water than its share. Towheaded children carried sticks with buckets swinging on them to fetch extra water from a nearby creek and from the Katsewa River. In both places it was low water, thick water, red with clay. It had to settle before even dirty feet could be washed in it.

All over Stone County, people with dry wells were fetching water out of the creeks and branches and rivers. That may have been why a family down below Greenway waded out to look more closely at something bobbing in the shallow current, and found the body of Miss Bethesda Lee Michael—what there was left of it. An old lady dead a long time was about all Dr. Newton was willing to say. No way to tell if she had been white or colored. There were not many old ladies missing in Stone County, and none other who had worn on the right arm a series of three dark bracelets made from barrel staves by the Greenway blacksmith. These had now rusted and discolored the arm bones and their shreds of bleached flesh.

Poor old lady, the talk went, wandering off her own rickety house in the dark and into the waiting river. It became the fashion for courting couples to pick their way along the river to look at Miss Bethesda's deserted shell of a house, rotting away in the high branches of the trees, already full of crickets and squirrels and the fans of spider webs.

The news sent Rosa Bennett into a relapse. She set out walking for the mill village and by nightfall was somewhere on the Stoneville road, squatting down in its center like a boulder where Silas could not miss her. Silas brought her straightaway to the Allen house.

It was the middle of the night. The pounding on the front door woke Mildred first and Esther second; and at two different upstairs windows they looked out. A horse was standing by the yard fence, chomping on Mildred's carefully rooted ivy. On the horse's back slumped something huge and dark. Esther always remembered afterward the moment when she decided it was a dead bear tied on somebody's saddle.

But Mildred knew right away and she plunged whimpering down the stairs and did not even wait at the front door for Silas' muffled explanations. She ran out into the moonlight in her cotton gown and began to pull Rosa from the horse.

"It's all right now, Rosa," she cried softly. "You come right inside. Everything's going to be just fine."

"Stop saying that," said Rosa, like a sleepy child.

Esther watched her mother and Uncle Silas, supporting the fat woman on both sides and steering her up the walk and upon the stairs, across the porch with a terrible thumping sound, and then inside the house. From the upstairs hall Sam Allen called, "What the hell is going on?"

"Hush up your mouth," said Mildred tensely.

That's why Rosa was living with them in the Allen house when the bell began to ring. Silas still went home in the evenings to fork out feed for the cow and the two pigs and to throw grain into the chicken lot. But Rosa had been in the village since early in August, asking Mildred not to plait her hair so tight and not to tell Papa she was meeting the Bennett boy in the orchard after dark. And not to talk about Mama. Especially that.

Mildred worked very hard with Rosa. Dr. Newton was called in to give her a tonic and a sleeping draught. Preacher Holt came daily to read from the Book of Job and follow it up with St. Paul. Mildred usually repeated the pertinent things, to make sure Rosa had caught them at the time. "All things work together for good," she would recite. "*All* things, Rosa, to them that love God."

"I wish you'd stop saying that," was all Rosa could answer.

All the time the two sisters talked, the corpse of Rosa's dead baby was laid on the parlor floor between them. Rosa—larger than ever—was pregnant with that death as she had once been pregnant with that life. They never mentioned it. Rosa had not carried so much as one petunia to the graveyard. Nor did Mildred ever speak of the birth or of her efforts to save little Angus Mackey Bennett. No future children for Rosa were ever mentioned. The one loss had plugged her up. Nothing could enter her past that loss and nothing could get out.

Yet no one could claim Rosa had wasted away from grief. She ate her share; she ate Silas' share and much of the others'. Her cheeks were flushed. When Silas stopped by to see her in the evenings, after the mill closed, he was incredibly gentle, even remorseful. If he put his hand out to his bloated wife, there was something in the air it passed through that rendered him instantly sober.

That was really what Mildred hated now in him most— his ability to rise above the day's whiskey as if it were a saving stream where he could choose either to drown or to swim.

"He could stay sober all the time if he only wanted to!" she complained to Sam.

Sam shrugged. "What difference does that make?"

"But he could. You know it! We all know it!"

"It's not what he could. It's what he does."

But Mildred felt if Silas could only fail Rosa at the important times—if he had run over her blindly with his horse in the road, if he had fallen as he dismounted and landed alongside her, helpless and slobbering . . . if, even now, he would not come to the Allen house and draw forth her chin and force some wet kiss between her open lips—oh, Mildred would think, if he could fail her all the time instead of almost all, Rosa could lose him. She could let him go.

At the noon meals Mildred could not suppress her conviction that her single piece of chicken, the one spoonful of beans Silas ate at her table, were what gave him strength to sustain the one moment of tenderness to Rosa. And that moment was Rosa's entire day.

That August Mildred came to hate Silas Bennett. She fed him grudgingly. She turned away from his rattling of bones at her table. And back in the pantry she planned every day to stride in to him the way Moses had pushed his way into the presence of Pharaoh and cried out, "Let my people go!" *Let her go!*

Mildred vowed again that soon she must really do that; and she looked away from her little sister Rosa—now fat with destruction —and thought about the plagues of Egypt and the death of the first-born.

It was during one such moment, while her mind was crowded with the thought of death, that the bell next door at the mill began to ring. She and Rosa had been hanging freshly starched curtains, Rosa serving chiefly as a mammoth base on which the ends could be draped without trailing on the floor.

"What's that?" said Rosa through the curtain mesh.

Mildred stood still on her chair. "It's not quitting time." She leaned toward the window but could see nothing unusual. The bell was ringing steadily. "Let's look out front," she said.

Through the front window they could see women coming onto their porches and curious children moving to the edge of yards. Rosa plucked at her from behind. "Why would they ring the bell now?" she said, the first edge of fear sounding in her voice.

"Must be a meeting of some kind."

"Look there. At the far end."

Mildred shaded her eyes against the August sun. For a minute she thought the mill—like a real beast—was somehow breathing. The windows on the picker room seemed to be giving off puffs of vapor at intervals.

"It's smoke," whispered Rosa.

Just as she spoke, one window spit outward in shatters of glass and a man leaped through it to the ground, his leg folding up wrong under him. He lay still in the patchy grass while a great black cloud blossomed at the opening he had made and began to trickle skyward.

Now, in a rush, the street was filling up with people. They ran for the mill, screaming, from all the houses up and down the streets. The man who had been standing by the central pump with his water list caught at their passing shoulders and called out for buckets and help; but they churned by. A roar went up from their throats, crying: *Dan! Fire! Papa! George! Mother! Creasy!*

Mildred saw Sam coming from the mill store at a dead run counter to the crowd. His mouth, too, was open on a word. Mildred leaned forward into the cool glass. Was it possible—could it be that Sam Allen had called forth "*Silas! Silas!*" She shook her head to clear it of the clanging bell. It was not possible.

"Rosa! Come back here!"

But Rosa had gone rapidly out the living room and through the open door, the way a heavy wagon going downhill is helped by its own weight. Mildred saw her almost topple on the steps. She ran after.

David and Esther and Thomas had already scattered and joined in the general rush for the mill, not for one minute remembering that none of them was allowed to go farther than the Allen yard. Thomas ran most of the way alongside an old woman whose walking cane was drawn up to her chest, out of her way. It was unbelievable she could move so fast, showering bowlegged bone hairpins out of her gray hair, making no sound beyond an occasional frog-gulp for breath. He ran as fast as he could, and the old woman kept up with him.

Smoke was now rising from all over the picker section of the mill. Every crack in the building filled up with it and then loosed it into the air. The great metal doors rolled back and workers poured out like ants from holes, looking straight ahead. These called no names. They did not once look back over their shoulders. The man who had thrust himself so violently through the window lay unnoticed where he had fallen on the ground, and not a man dropped to one knee to see if he were breathing.

Thomas saw Max Carson burst out of the mill office, carrying above his head an unlikely garden hoe. From the corner of his eye, Thomas spotted a certain still area in the headlong crowd, a halt of motion. It was Esther, pausing to see Carson bolt to the mill, where he began to clang the hoe against the main metal door, drowning out the bell.

"Fire brigade!" he yelled. "Where's the damn fire brigade!"

In the crowd Esther shifted her direction and began to move toward where Carson was standing, weaving her way in and out of the hurrying people.

They might all have listened to him then, and dragged the engine out in time, had a woman not suddenly appeared at one of the long second-story windows, beating out glass ahead of her by hand as if it were dust. She stood in the ragged frame, no taller than it was, and the sight of her drove hot air into the chests of all the crowd. Her white apron moved as if all of her were gasping for breath, even the knees and thighs, all gasping. Thomas sucked in, imitating the tug of that apron, and the old grandmother at his side threw her cane vertically into the air and waved it and began to scream, "Wait! Creasy! Wait!"

Carson moved out from the mill door and threw his head back so he, too, could see what all the crowd was watching. "Stay there!" he called. "There's no fire upstairs!"

The woman shook her head.

"The steps!" somebody else yelled to her. Others took up the cry, for they had come down those steps themselves; they were safe to use. There was nothing yet but smoke in that part of the mill. "Use the steps!"

Creasy's brother pushed his way out of the crowd and waved at her like a windmill. Carson grabbed him and sent him inside the mill to bring her down. This act caused other men to detach themselves from the mass and come to Carson, who was still yelling to the girl to stay right there in the window; men were coming now to help her down!

"Creasy! Creasy!" sighed the old lady beside Thomas.

Creasy clung to the window frame by her fingers and leaned stiffly forward until she looked as if she had been crucified in a box. Glass fragments along the edge had cut her hands and blood was streaked to her wrists. Suddenly she let go, and spread her arms for the kind of glide a jay bird will make into a cherry tree. For an instant her body, her reaching arms, formed such a clean and lovely line that no one could doubt she would swoop down to them in an arc. Then, with no grace at all, she hurtled down and broke upon the ground.

She broke. Thomas heard the breaking. His breath flew up out of him, and out of Grandma, and the next one, and the next one—a traveling groan of despair.

The old woman lowered her cane to the ground and leaned on it, hard, and then began to wilt about it like a vine dying around a post. At last she lay in a round heap at its base and the cane stuck up stiffly from a pile of crumpled clothes.

But there was no time for anyone to help her. The fire brigade had formed at last. A line of bucket passers strung out to the village pump and another was forming out back between the mill and the Katsewa River. Carson ran to the boiler room. Men sent back inside the mill began opening pipes to flood the floors. The old fire engine had been pulled out of its storage shed and was now sending a small spout of water into the picker room, through the broken window. Men who had fled the mill were now returning to it, stamping out sparks and closing inner doors—for this was a slow-burning mill, which meant with luck they would be able to keep it from burning at all. The smoke from smoldering cotton was so thick no one could reach the source of the fire, but there were pointing fingers from the yard below. That fire wall—there—extending above the roof; see that? The fire won't get beyond that. Two men, looking small and unhurried, were walking about on the roof.

Somebody ran into a house—it happened to be Fletcher Dowdy's house—and came back with two flowered bedspreads and covered Creasy and her grandmother. The old lady's cane, still extended, made her shroud into a tent.

The crowd had grown silent. Those who were not working simply stared. They would stand motionless from now on, as long as the mill was burning; and wait for the final cinder to cool and the last drift of smoke to be caught up in the sky.

Thomas took his eyes away from the bundle under the gay bedspread and caught his breath when he thought he saw a tongue of flame lick around the edge of the main door into the mill. No, it was only . . . it was only . . .

He rubbed his eyes against the gathering smoke. That was not possible. Somebody thrust a bucket into his hand and he passed it, not knowing if it was full or empty, going to the mill or coming away. It was not possible; yet it had seemed to him that the skirt of Esther's scarlet dress had disappeared inside the mill.

He looked around frantically, but could not see her anywhere. Most heads and shoulders were bent as the water was hurried along. She must be somewhere in the crowd. So many were taller that she would be hard to see. There was no reason for Esther to enter a burning mill.

Thomas knew he ought to go in after her. The buckets were heavy, and each time he handed one by, he sloshed water over the side and onto his shoes; and he felt the men to his left and right were silently accusing him for the waste. He looked up defensively. It was Big Jube on his left, his dark face shining with sweat. A rivulet had dropped from Jube's forehead and run down his scar and from there hotly onto his neck; Thomas wondered if it made his old wound sting.

Thomas screamed at him, "I'm doing the best I can!" and handed him another bucket.

I ought to go see if that was Esther. For one sharp moment Thomas caught a glimpse of his future life—just as if Miss Bethesda had opened up the Bible to read it to him. To see down the years like that was something like being able to look around a corner; the edge of his brain winced at the unfamiliar effort. He saw himself next year and the year after, being a comfort to his mother. He saw himself lecturing David in the store for laziness. He saw himself standing by Esther's grave on Easter Sunday, his hands full of white flowers.

Then the image blurred; something intruded around the neat headstone which said Esther Allen, 1884–1899. He squinted against the smoke. It was the face of Zelda Dowdy, watching him from under some man's extended arm.

Thomas passed another bucket and stared at her. She was real.

She had run out into the crowd without Winkie, without Christine, without her parents or her brothers and sisters.

Jube took the next pail out of his hand without waiting for his slow movements. Thomas said to the waiting face, "Now?" He had meant to use the word as a command. It came forth begging.

Briefly her eyes blinked. Then she nodded her head. "Now," she said in that rasping voice.

Thomas backed away out of the bucket line, watching her thread her way through the arms and legs and skirts and flying hands. He backed to the edge of the crowd. She came on toward him, stood at his side in front of the dry-goods store. He pointed behind it, into the green woods. Zelda Dowdy nodded her yellow head.

Thomas followed her down the path which ran by the store, by the first privy, over a ditch toward the river. He had forgotten the burning mill. He had forgotten his sister Esther.

It was the only time Esther had ever been inside the mill.

That, and the smoky haze which lay in swirls above the wet floor, the unfamiliar smell and the heat rising up before her like a solid cube, made it seem like an alien place in which some creature must live who did not resemble man at all.

At the end of the long room, indistinct workers were moving around. They looked ghostly through the smoke. All lamps had been extinguished and heaved outdoors to break in the mill yard and spatter the ground with black streaks of kerosene. Above the layer of smoke dust motes thickened the air. Several inches of water stood on the floor.

She splashed into the first aisle. The hulks of machinery before her gleamed in the dim light. She would not have been surprised if now, in an orderly line, they pulled themselves free from the wood floor and marched outside the mill to safety.

Her wet feet were sticking to the insides of her shoes, which had begun to squeak. She looked back at the open door. Mustn't go in too far. Yet she was drawn to this foreign place and something about it was beautiful to her. She expanded her nostrils to the acrid, tangy odor of danger.

Then she shook her head. Not beautiful, no. Had these machines been running, working, sending up noise, surrounded by people and sweat and lint, it would have seemed different. Maybe I am like my mother after all—if the mill is dead it is beautiful. As soon as it stops I can imagine all the motions and see their grace and precision.

She turned to slip back out the door and into the crowd again. Then she wrinkled her brow and leaned forward to touch a piece of metal, which should have been warm as the air. It was cool, like a crock deep inside the cellar, and a thin layer of oil coated its surface like a moisture it might be giving off. She wrinkled her brow and looked more closely. How curiously it was all made: that wheel, and the cogs, and the shadow they threw wavering against the wall. Or that carding machine—the central cylinder was like a roof seen at the end of a Japanese garden in a book of geography. And there, where the spools must whirl fatter and fatter on the ring-spinning frame; had there not been that tiny strand like a spider's thread to hold it down, would not the whole mechanism rise and burst through the wall and fly off into the air?

She moved farther down the aisle. The smoke was making her cough. This one now. There was a small lever. Esther touched it with a curious finger. It must usually move in a slapping fashion, north and south, and this in turn would cause the little—

"What in the hell are you doing?"

Esther did not move, bent over an intricacy it had seemed important to understand. She had no idea what to answer. She could not remember why she had come into the mill.

Max Carson took hold of her shoulders and jerked her upright. "You answer me!"

She thought all the machinery about them had leaped suddenly to humming life. No . . . no, that was her own heart and the thrusting of her blood. Esther shook her head at him.

"You've got to get out."

Then she remembered. "I saw my father come in. He didn't come out. And I haven't seen Uncle Silas come out."

Carson pointed into the machine. "You thought they were both in there? Under that little bar? Trapped, perhaps?"

She followed his look. "No," she said. "I only wondered how it worked." Then she raised her face to look at him. He was covered with soot and grime; his shirt was torn at the shoulder and through the fabric there was a mound of muscle she could not cover, she thought, if she laid her whole hand flat against it. She balled that hand into a fist for fear it might try.

"I saw Sam Allen in the yard," said Max Carson. "He's out. He's not in here."

Lint was streaked in his brown hair. "And Uncle Silas?"

"Silas is in the boiler room where he belongs. He's safe to stay there, doing his job. I hope he's doing his job."

Esther took a step toward the door, wading in the dirty water. I only wondered how it worked, she thought again, and threw back one hand to touch for the last time the chain she sensed within the mill, the chain of one thing causing a second, turning this, tripping the next. Movement running in an orderly course. Like a river, she thought, but invented.

To her surprise, the outstretched hand was suddenly flung against her face like a rag and the very air seemed to strike her. Max Carson pulled her to him. She heard the sudden, grinding roar. Under their feet the wet floor shook itself like a dog.

"*The boiler room!*" he yelled directly into her face. She heard stones raining on the roof. "*It's the boiler room!*" His teeth were tight when he closed his mouth, as if he might growl.

Esther did not even think about Silas. Her head, pulled under Max Carson's chin, was at such an angle that her eye was fixed on the small brown scar which centered his cheek. Her hand flew up to cover it.

Carson swung her into his arms as a great wind came roaring through the mill. It brought with it the sound of people screaming. "It blew," said Carson between clenched teeth. "I fixed it so it couldn't possibly blow, and yet it blew." He began to walk, almost to run, carrying her to the door. Esther's hand dropped from his face to his shoulder and the rent in the fabric. Through slitted eyes she examined the slope of his arm.

When they had nearly reached the door, she stiffened in his arms, raised her head and looked him full in the face; then strained upward and put her mouth onto his neck and drew in deeply the taste of his skin. It was both sweet and salt; her tongue contracted before the onslaught of the taste of him. Max Carson had faltered in his stride once, but now he walked ahead. He did not look at her. Esther lay with her open mouth fixed on his flesh.

She thought: He'll believe I was young and scared and didn't know what I was doing.

And I didn't know. I don't know!

She clung to him, frightened, but not by the fire or the explosion. Her fear came from the knowledge that she had chosen, cold-bloodedly, to place her mouth upon him, that she had selected the time to do it, that—even now—she was regulating the pressure and the length of time she would remain so joined to him.

I don't know what I'm doing, I really don't, said Esther to Esther. But she almost knew.

He carried her forth into the sunlight she had forgotten was there. Esther let her head fall down against his shoulder, as if she had abruptly regained her senses. She closed her eyes, thinking he might take it for sudden weakness.

He stood her very gently on the ground. "I've got to run," he said, "and you go straight inside your house. Are you all right?" He touched her face.

"I'm all right," said Esther, lying, lying, lying.

When the fire had barely started in the picker room and Max Carson ran into the boiler room the first time, Silas Bennett had been lying half asleep behind the coal pile. Carson was yelling things and getting no answers. The colored boy, Jester Sneed, had fled at the first ringing of the bell and headed straight for the river, where, the whole time, he sat waist-deep in water and made it vibrate from his fear. Claude Rickert stayed only a little longer. He was afraid his wife was burning in the mill.

So only Silas remained. Naturally he was not afraid. He leaned back against the hard lumps of the coal and thought about what all the noises must mean and added them up: *Fire.* Somewhere a fire. When Max Carson burst in yelling the words, Silas did not even move or raise his eyelids past the halfway mark. It was fire; he had figured it out.

He saw Carson making movements with the gauges and adjusting valves. He was cursing. Silas took a long drink from his jug and released the mouthful slowly in a trickle down his throat. Fire was never a time to be too dry. They had probably already flooded the floors in the main mill and were now closing down, shutting off pipes. Carson finished his movements and went out again, calling for Silas Bennett to get in here and stay in here.

There was no place Silas wanted to go. He drank deeply and listened to the screams. Rosa had screamed like that when the baby was coming. And what good did it do? If she had laughed aloud, if she had cursed God, would it have made any difference? He took a swallow so big that it hurt his throat pushing down.

Then Silas got up very slowly, uneasily. His feet were well planted but something caused the rest of him to sway—a wind, perhaps? Had Carson left the door open? Silas leaned a little forward and a little back, trying to think what had caused him to stand at all. Jug must be empty. He shook it at his ear. Plenty. He drank again to make sure.

Then he came walking down the coal pile as if it had been some mountain, and surveyed his realm. Fire, that was it. Too bad the board of directors wouldn't give Carson the separate fire pump he'd wanted, here, in the boiler room. I could have been the difference between a fire and a disaster then. It made Silas very angry. Wouldn't let me on the fire brigade. Wouldn't put a pump in the boiler room. Silas felt that if he listened he could probably hear the splash of water in a hundred hurrying pails.

But he did not really listen. All he could really hear were the sounds which surrounded him every day—a hissing, a roar, a gurgle, the rattle of coal under his shoes, the whir of the flywheel. Everything blurred before his eyes and it seemed as if each brass fitting on the engine flew forth like some shining bird and shimmered in the air.

I could have been the difference. Silas chortled in his throat. I can still be the difference.

He stumbled out of the coal, kicking fragments out of his way, to stand where Max Carson had stood. This foot here, this foot so. He looked down at them from a great distance. No, the right one over another inch. It was important that he stand exactly where Carson had stood. He lowered his jar of whiskey and stood it precisely halfway between his shoes and then straightened up stiffly, fighting to keep his balance.

He laughed once in the face of all the equipment before him. Then, with the gauges, Silas began to change things. He ran to heave more coal onto the blaze and still more, until it was tumbling out the open door and making small blazes about his feet. He lurched again to turn the valves, tighter. He picked up bits of coal, some of them already burning, and tossed them onto the metal in a rattling hail.

It took much longer than he expected. He had time to drink another inch and a half out of the jar before the boilers blew. The roof belched upward; the bricks of the four walls separated and flew outward as if each were no heavier than a raindrop. The coal turned into flying black splinters. And everyone who had been fighting fire stopped dead in the mill yard; no one could even groan or scream; they watched the boiler room opening and moving and coming toward them in the shape of dust and flakes and little stones.

When the boiler room blew, Rosa fell down where she was and hid her face in the dirt. A gentle rain of sand fell on her, and then a warm liquid. Up ahead somebody struck by a sheet of hot water screamed.

Rosa began to drag her heavy body along the ground. Some child was whimpering, "Silas! Silas!"

One of his friends, she thought, because Mildred's wrong and he does have friends. The child went on wailing for him until she clapped a hand to her mouth and closed it up inside. It was only the baby, after all, calling out for his father.

"Hush, child," Rosa whispered. She dug her nails into the hard ground and pulled herself forward. Somebody knelt by her and put a hand between her shoulder blades. She crawled out from under it.

"Rosa!" It was Mildred leaning over her. She was crying.

Grunting, Rosa began to struggle on the ground, sat, pulled a heavy leg under her. She got to a kneeling position and hit her older sister in the mouth, putting all her two hundred pounds behind the blow. Mildred, she saw, fell backward, her face full of blood and astonishment. Got her mouth cut on the teeth, thought Rosa savagely. Got Mildred bitten by one of her own smiles.

She got awkwardly to her feet and began to run toward the ruin of the boiler room, stiff-arming whatever neck or shoulder appeared in her way. Mildred was coming behind her. Using the path I made, thought Rosa. Sam Allen, up ahead, put out two arms to break her flight. She went through them as if they had been kindling.

Now she saw that Max Carson, lowering some injured girl into the grass, was also running. He, without argument, tackled her bodily from behind. The earth fell upward into her face and bits of it gritted into one eye and blinded her with tears.

"Don't you go there!" he hissed in her ear. He sounded as if he might kill her if she went any farther to find Silas.

There was a warmth trickling inside one thigh, through the thick skirt and petticoat. She thought she might have wet her pants like common white trash. Then she feared that her child was being born, that she would be emptied out of all life right here before a crowd.

Rosa heaved herself to one side and saw that she had fallen on a jagged chunk of glass and cut herself.

"Are you hurt?"

"Not much," she said. She slapped her hand quickly over the glass to hide it from Mildred. Then she put it against her nose but she could smell nothing. She poured it from hand to hand. It caught light like a jewel.

Carson had gone on to the rubble. For the second time, Mildred knelt beside Rosa.

"This is his," Rosa whispered. "This belonged to Silas."

"No, of course not," said Mildred. "Throw it away."

"It's part of the jug he had."

"It's window glass, nothing but window glass. Throw it away, Rosa."

"I've cut myself," cried Rosa.

"We're going home now." Mildred began pulling on her shoulder. "I'll fix the cut. Give the glass to me and we'll go home."

Rosa pressed it to her breast. The edges were slashing her palm. "I'm going to save this for my baby," she said wildly. "You're not to touch it."

"All right. We're going home now. Let me help you."

It was hard to get up. Rosa felt very heavy. The sky must be pressing down, or the dust and smoke in the air had settled on her skin. "I feel so funny," she whispered. "Is it time for the baby now?"

"Come home, Rosa."

She found with surprise that Sam was at her other arm and she was being supported between them and led out of the crowd toward the house with the willow tree.

Over her head Sam said to his wife, "You're hurt."

Mildred turned aside and spit out a little blood. "Not much," she said.

"The children?"

"They'll be all right." She looked down at her sister Rosa, huge and shapeless in the black dress. One side of her face was orange from lying in the dust. The chunk of broken glass was clutched so tightly in Rosa's pudgy hand that a dozen cuts had been opened inside the palm and up the base of each finger, and redness had stained the entire hand.

It's her right hand too, thought Mildred.

Thomas did not at first know that the boiler room had blown. Atop the small girl he had been moving up and down. His teeth were clamped into her shoulder and she was crying out and beating the back of his neck with her fists. When first the earth shook and some giant roar rose from a crowd of throats, Thomas thought it was his own explosion. He felt himself come asunder and pour forth in a way that must surely drown the struggling girl pinned down against the pine needles. He flung himself off her and fell panting to one side.

Zelda Dowdy rolled away from him and drew herself into a ball. She covered her face with her arms and sobbed. "You hurt me so," she cried, shuddering. "Why did you have to hurt me so?"

Above his own hard breathing he could suddenly hear the sound of men and women screaming in pain and fear. He thought it must rise like a music out of his own blood. "I don't know," he panted. "I don't know."

Chapter

❧ 17 ❧

Now THERE WERE TWO GRAVES in the Greenway cemetery Rosa never went to see. She grew even wider and heavier, as if she were carrying both surplus lives inside her skin.

The visit with Sam and Mildred Allen became permanent.

"I've moved your things into this room," said Mildred brightly. On the other side. Away from the mill. Rosa had nothing to say.

Every morning Rosa cleaned off the shard of glass at her washstand and polished it with the tail of her petticoat and put it carefully away in a bureau drawer. The rest of the day she did nothing. When food was put before her, she ate; if yarn was placed in her hands, she wound it into a neat ball; but of her own volition—nothing.

It seemed to Sam Allen some kind of bitter justice was operating which swapped off maddening old Angus Mackey for mad Rosa Mackey Bennett. He did not like to look at her. In her bulky widow's weeds, Rosa looked as if there were room for at least three ordinary women to live inside her skirts. If she were upstairs in her room, Sam's glance returned uneasily to the ceiling, which seemed to sag wherever she was.

After the fire and explosion, Greenway Manufacturing Company closed down for repairs. When the news was first brought to Winkler Hobbs—who had just been allowed out of bed two weeks before—

he fell backward at his front door as Eli once collapsed before the temple. But Hobbs did not die. It was his second stroke and half of him was killed instantly. His right arm and right leg never moved again, but Hobbs lived on, compressed into the other half, crowded off to one side by the edge of his coming death.

At the bank Lloyd Morrison heard the news with head lowered over his polished desk. He waited there in an attitude of prayer or anguish. What he really felt was burning indigestion and a desire to vomit. This pained him—economic loss transferred swiftly to the belly—and he went straight home and lay in the darkened front bedroom with a cool cloth on his head. He knew he should be getting an estimate of damages, projecting profits and generally trying to see what kind of future the mill might have. Max Carson would do these things, he told himself. Max Carson usually did.

It was different for Nathan Grimes. Carson had stayed this long with the mill because Grimes begged him; Grimes had promised the mill would soon meet requirements of the Factory Insurance Association. He had promised outside hoses and fire pumps. He had promised to replace the night watchman, who was a relative of Lloyd Morrison's wife, and get somebody who would be certain the steam pressure was kept at fifty pounds all the time. He had even held out hopes for an elevated tank and sprinkler pipes. All he had really given Carson was an extra cask of water in the picker room and a red fire bucket hanging inside on every column in the mill.

So when he heard that the picker room was burning, Nathan Grimes rode through the August heat at a pace that nearly killed his horse. He had the feeling that if he could only get there, the fire would go out spontaneously, and most of the scattered bricks from the boiler room would fly mysteriously together. Nathan beat his horse—something he had never done—and arrived in ample time to see the crowd thin out, giving him a clear view of two fallen lumps under a pair of flowered coverlets.

With Hobbs lying in his bed speaking with half his mouth and half his brain, and Morrison's heartburn cooling behind drawn curtains, and Nathan Grimes sick with guilt, there was no one but Sam Allen left to save the mill—so Sam Allen did.

Sam dragged Morrison out of his bed, the damp rag hanging over one ear like a nightcap, and pledged a large investment for a large amount of stock.

"I didn't know you had that kind of money, Sam," stuttered Morrison.

"You know it now."

Carson was to be given a freer hand, Sam said. Fire-protection measures would be installed even before new boilers were put into their new enclosure. After the rebuilding, the mill must be viewed by an inspector, which—said Max Carson bitterly—would complete the locking of the barn behind the stolen horse.

Sam Allen was the first visitor allowed to see Hobbs following the stroke. He started straight in to tell Hobbs all about the fire, the explosion.

The old man, who could still barely speak, squirmed on his pillows.

"Three killed and one injured," said Sam relentlessly. "And one dead, mind you, in my own family." It sounded like an accusation.

Hobbs let his left hand crawl aimlessly up and down his chest.

"Max Carson says the corporation probably doesn't have enough money to start rebuilding. Most investors won't put in another cent." Sam did not tell him about his talk with Lloyd Morrison.

Hobbs nodded. It was more a waver than a nod. He spoke as rarely as he could since whenever he started ten words toward his mouth, only five or six survived the trip, and these seemed to fall forth at random.

"Morrison has already told me the bank can't lend any money," said Sam—which was true, so far as it went.

"Morrison?" croaked Hobbs. He could remember Morrison when he tried. He could remember this man too; his nephew, wasn't it? Who ran the store? Blood was thicker than water. He said aloud, "Blood."

"Even so," Sam said, "I like that store. This is my one chance to have a store of my own. I'm willing to take one located in a mill village that probably won't even have a mill. I want to buy it from you." He leaned forward. "Did you say something?"

Whatever Hobbs had launched toward speech had perished on the way. A drop of spittle grew in the corner of his mouth. He raised his good arm and searched the skull meticulously until he could find the mouth, and then its corner. He wiped it.

"I said I want to buy the store down by the mill."

Habit got the next word out. "Terms?"

"Cash," said Sam.

At first Hobbs thought he was having another stroke, but it was only surprise jerking at his face and stinging the back of his neck. He took his time sorting out four words and shaping them precisely behind his gums. Then he brought them out with pains, and laid them in the air in a neat row. "Where'd—you—get—cash?"

"I came into my rightful inheritance." He seemed to be laughing, but—Hobbs told himself—what could you tell with only one good eye? Sam couldn't be laughing. He must mean the Bennett place had brought in a sum beyond its worth.

Hobbs whispered, "Silas?"

The man was really laughing. Hobbs decided he must have really cheated somebody on the Bennett place, and he had a moment's pride that his nephew was a sharp trader. Blood sure would tell.

"Oh, not entirely," Sam said, chortling. "It's true I'm settling up Rosa's business, and investing what little may be realized from the Bennett farm and her household goods. And my former house—you remember it, Mr. Hobbs—is rented out; I have a man growing cotton on shares. But I've had other sources. Other sources." The look on his face seemed suddenly threatening. "You'd still have the other store uptown, of course." He seemed to be hissing, but what could you hear with only one good ear? "You'd still have that store to give your faithful nephew."

That was when Winkler Hobbs decided to sell the store. He seemed to see and hear so much hostility, from his own kinfolk, that he was convinced his senses were bringing him nothing but lies. He must be sicker than Dr. Newton would admit. Hobbs nodded his head; then checked the movement with his good hand to make sure it had really nodded and not shaken No.

Sam was prepared. He had brought papers, drawn not by Nathan Grimes but by some lawyer Hobbs could not remember at all. There was an inventory, which seemed scant, and a list of figures showing the original cost of the structure less its wear and tear less the anticipated repairs for damage done by flying brick. The land would remain property of the corporation. Hobbs had seldom looked at the mill store itself, merely at its image on paper; this time it was reflected so sourly he felt he was being pretty clever to get rid of it in a perilous time. Pretty clever. And from a sickbed too.

Sam pointed out a price written on the paper. It swam before

Hobbs's eyes; he could not read the numbers. He lifted some fingers in the air several times, raising the sum in hundreds of dollars. Sam said a few things. Hobbs waved some more fingers; he meant to move nine of them but could not remember how many were growing on that hand. At last Sam nodded and wrote in a new price.

"If the mill . . ." Hobbs began, meaning to say that if the mill should be closed for any length of time, "if the mill . . . you'll be ruined."

Sam took out an envelope of paper money and carefully extracted some and put it back in his pocket, making sure Hobbs saw the surplus and understood the price could have been raised further, if necessary. "I won't be ruined," said Sam.

Hobbs pressed back into his pillow and closed his eyes. He signed the paper without paying too much attention; Sam called two strangers in from the front porch to witness the scrawl he made. Hobbs felt tired and sleepy. After all, he was sick. Even a fox gets old and sick and falters in skills he has taken for granted. . . .

He stated to Sam with great effort, "And the hounds—"

Abruptly he went to sleep, pleased with his long and thorough speech of denunciation.

All the time he had been in Greenway, Max Carson had lived at Governor House, the town hotel. From his second-floor window he could see the railroad station, a gloomy building topped by a useless round tower on which years of smoke had fallen back in layers, and beyond that the rows of houses dwindling on dusty streets and shading off into woods and cornfields.

The townspeople felt very sorry for him, living uptown like that. They all told him they would never be able to stand the noise of the passing trains.

Droning crickets and throbbing frogs were what Max Carson couldn't stand. To him, a railroad engine summed up more life than the men in it or around it. He liked the smell which hung in the air after the smoke had wandered. The predictable turning over of wheel-on-track was such a pleasure to him that he sometimes thought: My eye is the shape of that wheel and the view of it fills my eye completely.

He liked, too, the sight of seared vegetation which fell away on both sides of the track. There was too much vegetation here, too much thickness of trees, too many birds and bugs under the leaves. The train went through the countryside with the cold purpose of a knife.

He missed the trains when, at the end of August, he set up a cot in the mill office and moved there to supervise repairs. In the daytime the air was full of words and hammer blows, and at night the insects buzzed and clicked out of every tree. At dawn the whole riverbank began to scream. There was nothing to do but eat and wait outside in a racket of blue jays till the laborers arrived.

Mildred was out clipping back the tips of her yellow-bell bush one morning when she saw him sitting thoughtfully before the mill. "You're interested in nature, Mr. Carson?" she called pleasantly.

"No, ma'am."

But several mornings later she saw him outdoors again while the sky was still gray, tramping around the mill yard in the meager dew.

"Do you like this time of day best, as I do?" she called again, trying to be friendly.

"I don't like it at all."

Mildred thought any man who got up in time to appreciate morning glories and a streaked sky couldn't be all bad, even if he was embarrassed to admit it. She went inside to their bedroom and sat on the edge of the bed and shook her husband's shoulder. "How is Mr. Carson eating while he lives in the mill office?"

Sam kept his eyes shut. "Same as everybody else—take a bite . . . chew—"

She shook him harder. "I mean the cooking."

Sam said Carson built a little fire in a circle of broken bricks and fried things there, mostly eggs. "I sell him the eggs."

Mildred went out of the house that minute and found Mr. Carson sitting under a maple tree, his back against its trunk. For a minute she thought he had been looking up at the window of Esther's room, but a quick turn of her head showed that those curtains were drawn.

"Will you have supper with us tonight, Mr. Carson?" It sounded like a dare.

He was surely looking at something in that part of the house. "I'd be pleased to come," he answered politely, getting to his feet almost as quickly as any Southern boy.

Mildred was proud of herself. A few meals taken in the company of a young man—despite the age difference—would do wonders. This was just what the girl needed to bring her out, calm her down, make her more tidy, cause her to become aware.

He doesn't know it, but Max Carson, she thought firmly, is going to be Rosa's salvation.

Early that morning the black dress Rosa always wore was taken off her by force. Mildred washed it, smoothed the wrinkles with her flat-iron, sewed a new ripple of lace at the throat and a row of winking red buttons down the front, like lanterns.

Her long hair had also been washed. "You've let it fade out," Mildred grumbled, and slipped a little red food coloring into the rinse basin, "just for brightening."

I'm going to be red all over, Rosa thought as she spread her damp hair with a lazy hand in the sunlight by the window. She pinched her eyelids and thumbed each eyeball. Might as well decorate there too.

She looked down into the back yard, where Esther had been sent to watch David and see he did not dirty his shirt. Rosa could see the girl pacing up and down in the yard, where the freshened dress blew darkly in the hot wind like a pirate's sail. Esther was watching the toe of each shoe appear as she paced up and down beneath the clothesline. As nervous as her mother, Rosa thought. When David slipped up and poked his sister in the ribs, she swung with a shriek, her arms thrown wide as if she might clap his face between two rushing hands or—or embrace him.

Now Mildred was taking down the dress, walking toward the house. Rosa touched her long hair. It must be the color of a sunset. It even felt warm and red, like fire, like the opening of a cut. . . . She was whimpering by the time Mildred carried in the dress.

"Shh . . . shh. How pretty you look."

"I wish you'd stop saying that." Rosa's hair swung tickling on her bare shoulders. "Has Silas come?"

Mildred tugged at her until she stood and allowed the dress to be put over her head.

Downstairs Ellie Faye covered a platter of fried chicken. She took the stalks of Queen Anne's lace, which had been soaked in indigo until they were as blue as the painted cornflowers on the furniture, and stood them upright in a cut-glass cruet. These went on the round crochet mat in the center of the table. She opened the pear preserves but left the lid on against flies until it should be time to spread them into a dish. She decided to bring another jug of cream from the cellar.

Esther, hanging by her hands, swung lazily on the clothesline. She was watching the mill.

"You'll break that!" called Ellie Faye. "David, help me lift this door."

Esther said nothing. Sighting along the clothesline, she could see Max Carson come out of the mill office and walk toward their house. She thought he looked taller than the last time. Esther laid her head sideways on the wire, although she knew it would leave a red mark along her cheek—no, *because* she knew it would leave a mark.

When Carson turned in at their house, Esther was waiting on the porch. He smiled and pointed. "It's my turn to ask what's wrong with your face. The Klan been after you too?"

He was very near. Esther swayed toward him slightly. Now, she thought. Put the finger on my face. She fixed him with a stare.

Carson hesitated and dropped his hand to his side. "Am I early?"

"Late," she muttered; but when she saw he had not heard, she shook her head. He opened the door for her. Sidelong she looked at his fingers curved at the door's edge. I could put my face there, she thought, but it isn't my turn.

Sam had planned to spend a long while in the parlor, serving wine and talking business with Maxwell Carson. The wine was from local muscadines, and bitter—not like what Nathan Grimes had shipped through Wilmington from someplace over the sea. But he reckoned without Mildred and her fears that the biscuits would pass the point where butter would dissolve within them instantly. The two men had no more than taken a first tentative swallow when she called on them to eat. Carson looked slightly relieved.

Mildred pointed out who was to sit in what chair. "I don't believe you've met Mr. Maxwell Carson. Mr. Carson, my sister, Rosa Bennett."

"Good evening, Mrs. Bennet. I was sorry about your husband."

"Lots of people were," said Rosa clearly, "but he got over it."

Carson looked past her at Esther, whose face was grave and motionless, like something cast on a coin. Mildred was saying, ". . . our three children, Esther and Thomas; and David says he's had some long talks with you about his whittling."

"It isn't whittling," said David gloomily.

Max Carson turned hastily from Esther and clapped a hand to David's shoulder. "He can make anything. I've asked him to carve something for my office. A wheel."

It was the first the Allens had heard of it. "A wheel?" said Sam in disbelief.

Carson was still thinking of the minted quality of Esther's face. "I've always said that's what belongs on American money—the wheel and not the eagle. It's much more a symbol of this country. We're going to get a round of wood sliced from the biggest tree in North Carolina. I'm going to hang it in my office."

Sam said he didn't see why a plain old real wheel wouldn't do just as well. And Esther, half to herself, said, "You shouldn't hang it. You should roll it." She could somehow picture Max Carson flicking the wooden wheel up and down the hard-baked streets of the mill village with a peeled stick. It would do him good, she thought. All he thinks about is work.

David said scornfully it wasn't a *play* wheel. "It stands for something."

"I like things real," Esther said without much interest, and turned away. They sat down to supper. She could hardly eat. It seemed to her from one minute to the next she could not guess anymore what her mouth might decide to say, or where her hand might go. Now that Max Carson sat directly across the table from her, he did not look at all the way she remembered him. It was as if she had once seen some stranger with a hole in his face and invented the rest.

"Now, Mr. Carson," Mildred began brightly when their plates were served, "Rosa asked me a number of questions about you. It made me realize how little we know you, even if you have become a recent neighbor." She laughed nervously, then laughed a second time when she saw he hadn't even smiled. She swallowed and passed the cream and sugar.

Carson turned politely to Rosa Bennett, who was seated by him. "What would you like to know?"

"It's hot in here," said Rosa. "Is something on fire?"

Sam shook his head at her. Thomas took a coughing spell. Mildred asked in a high, sweet voice where Mr. Carson had been born.

"I was born in Massachusetts, a little town called Linwood."

"Textile country," muttered Sam around a mouthful of chicken. He gave Rosa a black frown.

Carson nodded. "Linwood mills. Uxbridge. And it's near Whitinsville." He saw the blank look on Mildred's face. "They make mill machinery in Whitinsville."

"Your parents still live in Massachusetts?"

"They're both dead."

"Pass the stewed corn," said Rosa.

"My father drowned. He fell in the Linwood pond." Coming home one night, full of drink and grief, he thought; but he could hardly tell that to the widow of Silas Bennett.

Esther had been watching his face. It began to resemble more closely the man she had invented to live behind it. "And your mother?" she asked softly.

"She was sick a long time before she died. I was fourteen. It was my third year as apprentice in the machine shop." Max Carson frowned. He did not want to sound sorry for himself.

Sam seemed to sense that. "But you don't work for the Whitin Shops now."

"I've worked for different ones. They were the first. My father worked for them." He wanted to stop talking and eat, but they were all looking at him, expectant. "When I was sixteen they took me out of the shop and moved me to one of the mills—they own six up there. I worked in every department and last of all in the office. Two years later I was helping manage the smallest of the mills. Later I changed companies. And by the time I was twenty I was an agent and adviser in the southern territory."

"I don't know," said Esther. "If I had been a boy, I can think of fifty other things I'd rather have done."

Now Mildred sent a black frown down the table. Carson smiled and helped himself to the food. It was a lot better than the eggs he'd been frying.

"You like your work, I suppose," said Mildred politely. "Rosa and I have wondered."

"I like the machines."

"Machines?" said Rosa. She received a proud look from the head of the table.

"Yes, the machines. I don't want to see a single one mishandled or misunderstood. I want them to do what they were made for doing."

Mildred looked puzzled. "I don't see how anyone can like a machine."

"I don't see how anyone can help it."

Perhaps, thought Mildred as she passed the creamed potatoes rather roughly down the line, bringing Max Carson to her table was like inviting a disease. She saw the interest on the faces of her sons; and there was to be no mill in their futures! Thomas for the law or the ministry, she thought. And David, with his curious mind, would be a natural-born schoolmaster. Only Esther—usually her most susceptible child—appeared unmoved. Esther was looking seriously across the table with an unwinking stare, the way—here Mildred frowned—the way a farmer might study the form of a mule he already intends to buy. She was still uneasy about Esther anyway. Cutting her own fingers!

Mildred said crisply, "Esther, bring in some hot bread."

Rosa had begun her infernal game of making a picture in her plate from bones and breadcrumbs. Mildred could not tell what this one was, although she turned her head slightly and tried to reconstruct it right side up. Usually Rosa made faces, with clusters of vegetable hair and an edge of tomato slice for a wide red mouth. Tonight it was something square . . . a building, perhaps, and— Abruptly Rosa raked it out of shape with her fork.

Sam had seen it. He raised his voice. "You have brothers and sisters?"

"No."

Mildred took the bread from Esther and passed it. "That must have made it especially hard, losing your mother while you were still a boy." She cleared her throat for the important subject. "I do hope religion was a comfort to you."

He shook his head. Again they seemed to sit waiting around the table for him to proceed. Esther, directly across from him, was the only one who didn't seem to care what he might say. She simply watched him.

"I'm not a religious man," he added uncomfortably. "You certainly do make fine biscuits."

"Ellie Faye does that," said Mildred in a chilly tone. To her horror, Sam—perhaps from the muscadine wine—chose this moment to say, "Mildred's father wasn't much at religion either. Angus Mackey never darkened the door of a church after his wife died. Mrs. Mackey, now, she was something else again."

"He was a born-again Christian," said Mildred through clenched teeth, all the more furious because she hadn't the slightest idea where Angus Mackey was spending eternity. "He was surrounded by the love of God." She shot an anxious look at Rosa, to see if she had heard their mama named.

Sam, baffled, could not figure out just where he had gone astray. Two hours Mildred had lectured him on how Maxwell Carson was to be made comfortable at all costs. Sam said nervously, "I'm sure he was; I'm sure we all are. I just meant that the loss of somebody close—" He caught sight of Rosa's vacant face. "In times of crisis," he blundered on, "we find it difficult—"

"I know what you mean," said Carson politely.

Sam turned to him with relief. "When your own mother died, perhaps," he suggested, and left the sentence hanging.

Esther was watching him carefully, one eyebrow peaked and that corner of her mouth slightly lifted. Max Carson put down his fork. Almost dreamily he said, looking only at the table, "My mother's health broke during the first six years of my life. I was born in eighteen seventy-three; times were hard there until the eighties. My father hired out to do any kind of work."

"Hard work never hurt anybody," said Sam, and looked quickly at Mildred to see if that was all right.

"My mother sewed and did washing. She was a little woman, smaller than Esther." Now he looked full at Esther. She's not so little, he thought.

Mildred thought that an unkind thing to say in front of Rosa, whose vast weight was hanging off the chair on all sides. "More tomatoes, Rosa?" she whispered. Rosa took some tomatoes.

"Mother wore white ruffled caps all day long because her hair was quite curly and she disliked it. She was sick for eight years, coughing with consumption. She used to turn her face to cough and that little cap would tremble on her head." He let out a long breath. "It took her eight years to empty out her lungs into a handkerchief. In the winter she died. Pneumonia, consumption. We were never sure which."

It alarmed Mildred to remember that consumption ran in families, but there were worse things than consumption. She hoped Rosa was hearing all this. She slid her foot along the floor and kicked Rosa lightly in the ankle to make sure. "It's sad to lose anyone we love," she said, giving her sister a meaningful look, "but we have to believe it's all for the best."

"I wish you'd stop saying that," muttered Rosa. Sam, embarrassed, asked in a loud voice for salt and pickles. Rosa continued to eat and to munch her food for a long time, blankly, like a cow.

"Don't you agree, Mr. Carson? Perhaps that's all I mean by a religious sense. A trust that things work out for the best?" She was willing to give him every chance, since he'd lacked a mother to teach him these things.

Carson was no longer looking at her. He did not see Rosa's steady, working jaws. He met Esther's gaze as if there were some tunnel through the air between them and he were speaking only to her. "Hearing you say that," he started—and for a minute Esther thought she had spoken her thoughts aloud—"reminds me of my uncle. He thought everything worked out for the best. He had a religious turn of mind."

Mildred was glad to know there had been someone to influence that motherless boy. "Tell us about him," she said, permitting herself a smile.

"Uncle Ben was a blacksmith in Linwood. The night my mother died, he found me crying alone in the kitchen. My father had gone . . . had gone out. Uncle Ben grabbed my arm with one hand and took a jar of milk off the table with the other. He half dragged me down to the Linwood pond. Of course I didn't know that in a few more years my father would drown in it."

"Of course you didn't," Esther breathed.

"Uncle Ben held me there with my feet in the cold water, and poured all the milk into the pond and asked me now if it was gone."

Esther had laid her palms flat on the table as if she might rise. "And you said . . ."

"I said it was mixed with the water. He stirred the pond with a stick until all the whiteness disappeared. He asked me now was the milk gone?"

"But it wasn't!" Esther supplied.

"No."

Even Sam had begun to nod thoughtfully. Mildred, smiling, leaned forward and gathered Rosa's face in with her smile to make sure everyone was giving Max Carson his full attention. "Oh, that's right," she sighed, "and so sweet! What happened then?"

Carson did not take his eyes from Esther's. "I reached up and knocked the empty jar into the pond and pushed Uncle Ben in after it."

Esther released the breath she had been holding and closed her eyes. Her mouth and eyes began to crinkle at the corners.

But Mildred gasped. "Why . . . why in the world did you do that?"

Now, at last, he smiled down the table to her. "My mother," he said, "was not a quart of milk." And as if to prove it, he reached for the tumbler of milk by his plate and drained it until he could see Esther, indistinct, through the cloudy bottom of the glass.

She was shaking with laughter. She giggled so hard that Mildred finally sent her from the table.

Chapter

❧ 18 ❧

In the fall of 1899 Thomas went away to the University of North Carolina at Chapel Hill.

At first Esther was angry that he was going away to school when she was not. Nathan Grimes had talked to her about Normal and Industrial School for White Girls, opened in Greensboro eight years before. Once she even said she might become a teacher. But the day educator Charles D. McIver spoke at Stone County Courthouse on the state's need to train more women, she lost all interest in going to his school. Most of those who heard him nudged arms, nodded, breathed in when he breathed; and Miss Eliza Tilley flapped her fan rapidly and said under her breath he was "Magnetic! Just Magnetic!"

But his speech offended Esther, who called it a "medicine show" and would not go up afterward to join the press of ladies shaking his hand. It surprised Nathan Grimes. "You, of all people, should have been fired by this man. He stands for better education in this state—especially for women!"

But Esther looked cross, and as if she had made the trip all the way to Stoneville to be insulted. "Educate a woman and you educate a family," she quoted McIver sarcastically. "If I get educated I want it to be for my own sake."

Nathan explained patiently that Mr. McIver was simply using a phrase which did apply to most women. Naturally he didn't mean that *only* those women who—

"He should say what he means."

Esther went straight off to the carriage and sat alone until the others were ready to leave. Miss Eliza Tilley took hold of Nellie Grimes and Thomas Allen and introduced them to Mr. McIver as two of her best students from Greenway Academy.

Thomas slid his eye toward the carriage, hoping Esther saw this smiling handshake; but she had captured something between thumb and forefinger—perhaps a moth—and was holding it high to see the underside.

The whole family went with Thomas to the train station in Greenway to see him off to college. He was not yet fifteen but the Academy had no more to teach him. It seemed to Thomas the brisk September day belonged rightfully to him; he was leaving home for the first time. Soon he would be learning things his brother and sister could not even guess.

But on the long drive from the mill village to town, David and Esther could talk of nothing but the wheel David was carving for Maxwell Carson. The round of wood had already arrived. David wanted it lifted into the carriage so he might stroke it with his fingertips all the way to town and back; but Thomas had loaded his trunk in first and left no room.

David drew examples of wheels he might decide to carve. "Not that!" Esther might cry from time to time. "That looks like it fell off a wagon!" Or another time, "But that one's for steering ships."

Thomas was squeezed to one side. Despite the mildness of the day and the crowded buggy seats, the back of his neck was clammy. His stomach was no larger than a walnut. He had the feeling that somewhere between the mill and Greenway, Zelda Dowdy was going to rush out into the road and throw herself under the wheels.

Mildred smiled at him. "We shall all miss you, Thomas," she said gently, but before his spirits had a chance to rise she was already asking Sam if he thought Rosa would be all right in the house alone?

"This won't take long," Sam Allen said. His words hung in the air like a warning. Thomas waited for the others to hear it, to remark on how he was going out in the world. Surely they envied him! Why wouldn't Esther say she envied him?

But Esther was leaning over David's newest sketch. Very serious.

Very much involved. "Thinner, I think," she said, her hair falling forward as she nodded. "The whole rim thinner so you notice what a delicate thing this is, after all, to carry so much."

"Like a buggy wheel?"

She made a face at David and shook her head. Thomas said gruffly, "Why don't you let him alone? After all, it *is* his carving!" The words were barely out when a drooping tree limb slapped him across the mouth and he rose toward Esther with his fist clenched.

She did not notice. She turned to him then, smiling. "You must be very much excited, Thomas, going away to college like this! And yet you seem so calm!"

From his crouch Thomas slumped into his seat again. He thought he might choke. "I may come back from the University entirely changed," he told her in a sudden high voice. "I may be different when I come home again!"

She smiled again, kindly. "You couldn't change if you tried."

The insult settled in him like lead. He leaned over the side and watched the road flowing like a multicolored liquid underneath the wheel. Maybe Zelda was hiding behind some tree, her arms full of blossoms. Maybe she would toss them in his path. The blow from the tree limb made his head buzz and ring.

"Are you going to write Nellie Grimes?"

"Yes."

Mildred said Rosa seemed a little better this morning; had Sam noticed? Sam had not noticed.

"And you'll write us often?" she said to Thomas, letting her hand light on his knee and flutter off.

"I'll write home every week," he promised.

"Ah," said Esther suddenly, "I like that one much better!" She and David bent their heads above his drawing.

Thomas bit the tip of his own tongue. He looked ahead of the carriage but as far down the road as he could see, all the overhanging branches which might strike an unsuspecting passerby grew on his side, not theirs.

There were only about six hundred students at the University of North Carolina, and about equal that year-round number lived in the tree-shaded town of Chapel Hill. One of the first things Thomas saw there was the identical poplar to which William Davie in the spring of 1787 tied his horse with the comment, "Here we shall build our University." It had, for Thomas, the ring of "Upon this rock I shall build my church!"

It was his first day. Thomas was full of high resolve. With confidence he looked forth across the patches of grass and the sandy paths between buildings set down in a grove of trees. Soon it would all be familiar to him. People would know his name—his own name, and not that he was brother to one or son to another.

He set forth happily under the low-branched trees, carrying the awkward new books. Some of these limbs, he noticed, might be thick enough to hold up Miss Bethesda's floors. But quickly he told himself: No. No more of that. A new start. No more rages. No more girls like Zelda Dowdy.

Here at the University Thomas would begin his real life. Now there would be nothing crowding him or pushing at him. He began to whistle and to believe that already his true self was reaching forth like a green leaf for the sun. For he was here without brother or sister; nobody would be getting in his way; he was all alone! The thought—which had begun in triumph—ended in terror.

Thomas wheeled around, thinking he heard some familiar step at his heels. There was nothing but his stubby shadow lying in the sand.

Thomas straightened his shoulders and marched ahead, but with more effort. Right now David and Esther were probably chopping out wheels or lugging water to his mother's flowers. They were separate from him. They could not affect him anymore. He began to walk very slowly, quaking, to his first class.

By the end of the first week, Thomas was in a state of panic. These teachers were not so easily satisfied as Miss Eliza Tilley, and did not give a hoot for his good table manners or firm spiritual foundations. Thomas sat in his rented room and wrote his mother, "All is fine and the leaves are changing color."

The Latin and Greek were the only things he didn't mind. He had always done very well at memory work, and a long vocabulary or a complex declension was easy for him.

Then the classics teacher began to read aloud in English from the *Iliad* and the *Aeneid*—to encourage the students, he said. Hearing the story, they might work even harder for the skills to master these works in the original. The more he read, the more Thomas thought it was like trying to keep up with one of Esther's invented games, like standing by the tomb of Nora Lafferty, like trying to stick your fingers through a looking glass. Like learning to fly. He squinched up his eyes and tried very hard to listen to what the teacher said.

But Esther's things continued to tumble out of those pages: swift-footed Achilles, birds carrying portents and omens, Calchas and his gift of prophecy. The more Athene flashed her eyes and Zeus shook his ambrosial locks, the more Thomas thought he had somehow been dressed in Esther's clothes and locked in Esther's room. His marks in Greek dropped badly, even in vocabulary.

He wrote his mother, "I like all my teachers and all my subjects. Thank you for the winter coat as it is getting colder here."

By the end of October he was sick with headaches and William Shakespeare. At first when his forehead began to throb, Thomas explored the area with his fingers. It had come on him so suddenly he thought his brow must be bulging forth red and swollen with a visible drumming within it like the pulse in an infant's skull. The doctor at the University could not find the cause. It might be a blood condition, he said. He sent Thomas half a shelf of medicines.

Sometimes they helped. Sometimes they had barely eased the worst of it when his eyes were tripping over "intertissued robe of gold and pearl" and he recoiled from pearls in cowslips and fathers lying full fathom five with coral bones.

It was a late November afternoon. Thomas finished his letter to Nellie Grimes—describing favorably the town, the weather, the University and his course of study. He inquired after her health and her father's health and begged the favor of a reply.

Then he sat staring from the second-story window into the trees, where the last withered leaves were wasting. He thought about Zelda Dowdy. He thought about a woman he sometimes saw on the Chapel Hill streets and what it might be like to treat her like Zelda Dowdy. He thought about Esther falling into the river and how he would dive and dive to try to save her—and probably fail.

He put Nellie's letter on the desk, winced at his growing headache and swallowed a hurried dose of chloral hydrate, hoping he would be able to concentrate, for a change, on his studies.

The effect of the medicine always came over Thomas with a swoop. Now, going out the walk of the small house where he roomed, he touched the prickly limb of a cedar tree. There had been cedars in a line at Greenway Academy, though Rutledge always said cedar trees in a yard would bring on death. He wiped misfortune and resin off his fingers.

Then the medicine fell in upon him like a net and he staggered briefly and saw Esther's face in the air before him. Her features were rippling as if they had been painted on the restless air. She recited, smiling, "Not poppy, nor mandragora, nor all the drowsy syrups of the world—" Thomas thrust out a hand and cleaved her image off the wind.

The pain slacked. He began to feel better.

He nodded to Mr. Edward Graham, an instructor, and was soon overtaken by one of his classmates, Fincher Stowe. Stowe held out a package of Sweet Caporals but Thomas shook his head. ("Cigarettes are a boy's vice, not a man's," Sam Allen had always said, and Thomas was holding onto a rickety manhood by his fingernails.)

Stowe fell into step. "You been sick again?"

Thomas nodded very carefully, not wanting to stir that pain.

"You didn't miss much this morning." Stowe sighed. "We're still outside the walls of Troy. If they got a poem that long out of the Trojan War, you'd think the South could squeeze one out of ours."

Thomas only shrugged. Now that they had begun to translate, he was not doing well at all in Greek, because of the headaches. They blurred all meaning, even shape, and the marks of that alien alphabet ran loose on the page. He could feel the headache again, delicate as a needle, searching the underside of an eyebrow.

"Mr. Kestler wants to see you."

Thomas could have hit him. "Why didn't you tell me that right away?"

"I was coming to it. They're not going to send you home, are they?"

Now the headache struck like a storm. "Of course not!" he cried out. "Of course they're not going to send me home!"

"You're behind on your work."

"I've been sick. People can't help being sick." Thomas thought of going back for the chloral hydrate, in case it should be needed. "Did he say when he wanted to see me?"

"One o'clock. In his office."

The two boys parted at the post office, where Thomas bought a supply of stamps. He began to compose the letters to which they might be attached before today's sun went down. "Dear Mama, The University finds I am not doing well enough in my work to justify . . .

"Dear Father, For reasons of health it seems advisable . . .

"Dear Esther . . ." He did not even think about that one. Today Thomas was carrying one of Esther's typical letters, written in her headlong manner. Even when he read it silently his mind gave out of breath at the end of a line. Max Carson, she wrote, had been visiting the house often. David had finished the wheel, which was now mounted on the office wall at the mill. The repairs were nearly done. David was presently carving a newborn babe with large head and twiglike arms—Rosa's dead baby, no doubt. They were taking pains that Rosa should not know of it. She wrote, "The eyes will be closed and one arm curled to the body, the other out wide with fingers spread, either to receive something or maybe to strike a blow."

Thomas thought it was time for David to stop this carving foolishness and help out their father in the store. He thought it was time Esther took the local lads more seriously, and married one, and moved away. Rosa now—if it were left to him, he would put her for a week on broth and water and, as she lost that extra flesh, half her worst terrors would melt away. I could help Rosa if they'd let me. Sometimes I think I understand her; it's the others who confuse me. I could help Rosa. . . .

Having solved all this, Thomas felt calm and very capable as he knocked at Mr. Kestler's door.

"Sit down, Thomas." Kestler was a small man with a mouth bent in a permanent half smile. "How do you feel this afternoon?"

"Not too well, sir." The minute Thomas said that, it was true. He lowered himself carefully into the chair before the desk. The smell of paper and mildew and Kestler's pipe tobacco was very strong. His head began to hum and rumble like a cotton mill.

"I thought as much. Thomas, I've been talking with several of your professors and we all feel"— he paused and the sliver of a smile made a contrast to his serious eyes— "We think it might be best for your health if you were to pause in your studies."

"Pause?" Thomas heard his voice ascending. "Pause?"

"All of us feel you might in every way be better prepared for advanced work when you return to the University next year."

Father will never send me twice. He might send Esther in spite of all she said about Charles McIver. He might just wait and send David. Thomas closed his eyes against the thunder. Mr. Kestler moved a paperweight absently about. A tiny blizzard stormed under his fingertips. It looked like cornbread crumbs.

"This way," he went on, "no poor record would follow you. This could simply be looked on as . . . as a false start. You're much younger than most of our students, you know."

"False start," echoed Thomas. He shifted in his chair. For a minute it felt as if his left side were burning up with indigestion; then he realized it was only Esther's letter in his coat pocket, flaming against his ribs. "I can't do the work?"

Again Mr. Kestler agitated the snowflakes. "Your frequent ill-nesses—"

"You're sending me home?"

"Let's don't put it that way," said Mr. Kestler, shaking his head. "We simply suggest—we recommend to you that, for your own sake—"

Thomas slid a hand onto his chest on the left side, shielding his flesh from Esther's letter. "It isn't fair!" he whispered hoarsely.

"I can't hear you, Thomas."

"I said it isn't fair!"

"Under the circumstances, we feel it would be the only fair . . ." Kestler saw this was inappropriate. "Perhaps what you mean is that illness is unfair and undeserved. None of us know, Thomas, from day to day when any one of us—"

But Thomas was on his feet. "It isn't fair! Some people are favored! Admit it! Some people are favored from the beginning!"

Kestler, surprised, made motions to rise and put out a calming hand. "Young man," he began, floundering.

"You won't admit it!" Thomas yelled. He turned and bolted from the room. He went through the corridor at a half run and down the long steps of the building, walked a slow pace along the campus paths. Esther's letter hung heavy in his pocket and banged against his heart like a millstone.

November in Greenway had been quiet and uneventful except for the corn shucking at Nathan Grimes's. Even Max Carson had been persuaded to attend that—riding over with the Allens—and in spite of his clumsy city method of shucking, had found the only red ear in the pile and not known what to do with it. The others explained that a red ear grew if the man who was planting stopped in the row to cuss, and its finder was entitled to kiss a pretty girl. Carson laid a light kiss on Esther's forehead and never said a word to her the rest of the night.

Soon after that a medicine show—headed east toward tobacco-market towns—stopped for a one-night stand and set up between the mill store and the lyceum, with one colored boy to dance and two to make his music, and a lean man in a light-blue coat named Dr. Alben K. Marvel. Dr. Marvel sold hair restorer, tonic and tooth-ache drops between the first three songs, animal medicines for mange, black tongue and distemper between the next three. Then he started over. Business was brisk and the young people danced in the mill yard to the trumpet and the drum.

Mildred got so tired of hearing them fuss that after supper she said Esther and David could go listen to the music, provided they stuck together and did not venture too near.

They arrived between songs. Dr. Marvel was talking about rheumatism while his dancer moved in the crowd with different bottles the customers might weigh in their hands, shake, even remove the cap and sniff. The stage was a board affair laid across two wagon beds, with a curtained room behind it. One of the entertainers was playing a soft beat on his drum to accent Dr. Marvel's patter.

The music struck up again. The boy shuffled rhythmically out of the crowd and landed dancing on the stage. Dr Marvel vanished behind the golden draperies with their purple tassels. David inched forward and tried to see behind them.

Esther's head began to dip to the sound of the music and her knees to bend quickly in and out. She looked up and met Max Carson's eyes. He was standing at the edge of the crowd, where the torchlight barely reached. His face was amused. He waved. Esther threw up her arm in his direction. The sharp sound of the trumpet got into her bloodstream and ran through her painfully. She fixed her eyes on one of the blazing torches at the front corners of the stage as the colored boys began to sing and clap their hands.

Max Carson watched her. The long black hair was bouncing on her back and she seemed fascinated by the music and the dancer's tapping feet. Her head was high, her small nose at an arrogant angle. The white shirtwaist with its puffy sleeves obscured the line of her body.

He knew how her eyes must be now; always when Esther was absorbed these seemed to grow larger and darker in her face. He had seen them magnified many times across the Allen table. The night he bent to kiss her forehead at the corn shucking, he'd had the fancy he might fall forward into those widening eyes and go down and down.

He caught a glimpse of David, edging alongside the stage and lifting the bottom of the yellow curtain. Somebody behind it stamped a shoe alongside David's hand and he fell over himself getting his fingers out of harm's way.

Carson stood a while longer, watching Esther instead of the performance. Then he sighed, remembering the error he had to find in either orders or shipment invoices. It would be hard to work with all this music. At least the lights and the dancing were on the far side from the little office building which joined the mill.

Esther watched him go without turning her head. She pictured herself walking alongside him, arm in arm, and wearing a wide floppy hat with black-eyed Susans on the brim. She imagined how it would be for Mr. and Mrs. Maxwell Carson to climb aboard a train and set off for far places. She saw them moving into their handsome Boston home. Then she saw herself float down its staircase to one of their famous parties. In the picture she wore a low-cut gown and her breasts—now more opulent—crowded together with a cleft that caught every man's eye, and especially her husband's.

David, she saw, was right at the edge of the stage. The whirling feet were at his eye level. He looked hypnotized.

Esther turned, wriggled her way out of the crowd, walked toward the dark. Somehow she was already wearing the flowered hat; the skirt of her bell-shaped party dress swept on the ground as she floated off in the night behind Max Carson.

In the mill office, Carson was finding it hard to concentrate on the shipping forms. Neither the closed window nor the roll-down shades could keep that piercing trumpet out. He caught himself tapping his foot to match the drum.

Then there was an unexpected sound in the mill yard, near his office door. A thud? A small cry? He opened the door wide and at the edge of the yellow rectangle of light saw Esther in a twisted position on the ground.

He hurried to her. "Are you hurt?"

"No."

"Your ankle?"

"Nothing." She watched him steadily, almost coolly.

"Come in to the light to make sure. This ground is damp."

Esther let him help her across the light, which had spilled out onto the earth like a yellow carpet. Inside she stood quietly while he closed the door. She seemed to have brought in music clinging to her skirts; he could hear it now more loudly than ever.

"You don't even have a coat," he grumbled, seeing her clearly now. "And those short sleeves . . ." He stopped before he might blurt out something else about her appearance, might follow the curve down and dip in at the waist and honor it all with words. He turned and began throwing slabs into the fireplace. She would catch pneumonia. Out in the night air uncovered. His mother had died of pneumonia. "Come to the fire."

Without the slightest trace of a limp, she walked to the hearth and spread her hands. Max had squatted down to prod the coals. Without rising, he turned to look up at her. "You're not hurt at all," he said. "I bet you didn't even fall."

"I said I wasn't hurt."

It seemed best to stop looking at her face. He dropped his eyes and found he was now staring straight ahead into the folds of her green skirt. It rippled a little from the warm air off the fire. He put the poker down.

"Esther," he started, planning to be wise, to be honorable, to speak of his age and her age, remembering for an instant other girls in other rooms and none of them like her, thinking hastily of Sam and Mildred and David and his own position with the mill. . . .

"Esther," he said again. She took her outspread palms, rosy from the heat, and laid them on each side of his head. They were so warm. If they had not been so warm . . .

She touched her forefinger lightly where his cheek was puckered. "I've wanted to do that for a long time," she said, and then giggled. The laugh seemed to embarrass her. "I'm sorry," she gulped. He was not sure for which.

He said her name again, put out his arms and gathered in all of her skirt. It was hot from the fire. He put his face against it.

It seemed to him Esther moved slowly, flowed downward no quicker than soft tallow off a candle; but actually her body slid down against his so fast it was like falling. No, like jumping, she thought. Then the face in her skirt was at her waist and almost instantly against the softness of her breast so that his mouth passed over without time enough for kissing. He burrowed briefly at her neck. Her hands, still warm, pulled forward on his cheeks and his mouth was already open when it fell upon her mouth.

They moved clumsily on the floor, faces locked. Her skirt hem had hooked on somebody's shoe heel and folded under a knee. They fought its clinging folds until they were sitting, then half reclining on the floor. Esther lay on her side, turned to him, and he put his left arm over her and pressed his hand into her back to hold her tightly against him. He spread out his fingers.

She ended the kiss before he was ready, and lay back against his other arm. There was the same wide-eyed look he had seen before, damn it, as if he were a trumpet or a tree trunk or something else to which she might choose to give her full attention.

He said to her angrily, "So this is why you came."

Her eyes grew wider but she did not speak. His arm was still around her and his wide fingers low on her back. Now she drew away slightly. Max jerked his hand and pulled her back against him. He kicked into the thick skirt, trying to flex his left knee slightly at her legs. She lay against him almost limply now, the eyes close to his, her chin almost grazed by his jutting one.

The way she looks it's like an Indian, he thought irritably. She hardly ever blinks.

He made his knee cruel and in spite of the heaviness of her skirt a way was made for him. He lay now with one of her legs, fattened by all that cloth, resting atop his leg.

Into her face he said, "You came for this?"

Still she said nothing. She ran a finger curiously down his neck, over the Adam's apple. She probed, almost lazily, the little hollow at the base of his throat.

He spoke harshly. "Say you came for this!" He pressed into her back with his spread hand, slid it lower; she came in closer upon his flexed leg. The dress tore somewhere.

"I came for this," she said at last. Her voice was husky and a little frightened.

He kissed her again as if he were making a new bruise. The open fire at his back had heated the length of him until it was painful. He rolled slightly away from the fire, pushing her onto her back, slipping his hand up and hurting her breast with it, letting go her mouth and then claiming it again.

He lay upon her now. She was still looking at him but the eyes had contracted and seemed darker. Her face was more slack. She kept her lips slightly parted, but whether to receive his kiss or to expel her rapid breath he did not know.

He rose suddenly, blew out the lamp and snatched at the quilts he had kept on a cot during the rebuilding of the mill. She lay, resting on one elbow, watching. The music in the room was suddenly loud, and so was Dr. Marvel's voice, promising to cure everything, to heal it all, to make like new.

"Move," said Max Carson.

Esther stood away from the firelight while he threw the coverlets on the floor before the hearth. She stepped from the shadow and helped straighten them on her side and smooth out the wrinkles.

Now he felt awkward. "That skirt . . ."

She stepped back into the dimness. The dress fell over a chair. In another minute she was walking into the light, wearing only the petticoat which hung from her waist to just above the ankles. He saw that her breasts were full and the tiny knobs at their tips had an upward tilt. In the firelight her skin was almost red.

"I love you, Max," said Esther.

He went to her. Now he could be gentle.

Chapter

❧ 19 ❧

THIS TIME Sam drove the buggy alone to the train station to meet Thomas, so they might have a father-son talk on the way home. Mildred did not want to stay behind—she had some idea her sick boy might be lifted down on a stretcher—but Sam insisted.

"There may be something worrying him that he'll only tell another man."

Mildred was shocked. "You don't mean . . ."

"A boy away from home for the first time . . . you never know," said Sam uncomfortably. Mildred went straight upstairs to read the Bible ("A wise son maketh a glad father; but a foolish son is the heaviness of his mother"—Proverbs) and to ask the Lord not only for strength, but that He might reach into time and erase from past events anything bad that Thomas might have done.

When she felt fortified, she went downstairs and asked Esther for the tenth time to be especially nice to Thomas, who had never before this been sick a day in his life. Never given her a minute's worry. She had sometimes feared for Esther, or even for David—but Thomas was fine. He had always been fine.

Rosa interrupted. "Is Silas coming home?" It was not the first time she had asked. Mildred explained again that Silas would not be coming home anymore. This was Thomas—her son, Thomas—arriving from Chapel Hill on the afternoon train.

"Well, I'm not going to have this baby till Silas comes," said Rosa petulantly, "if I swell up as big as a barn!"

Esther went to the front window as though she were watching for the buggy. Actually it was to look across to the mill, where Max Carson was. The last seven days, she thought, she had been at least seventy people, and sometimes as many as a dozen at a time. Sometimes she felt wise like that Esther in the Bible, who got what she wanted by clever planning, leading on Haman and Ahasuerus from banquet to banquet.

Then, just as she began to feel competent and satisfied, it would strike Esther that she had snared Max Carson the way one traps a copperhead, by pinning it to the ground with a forked stick. What next? Who is in whose trap?

Often she felt simply bewildered and believed she had been helpless and overcome. It all reminded her of a game she had once invented to play with her young brothers on rainy days, called "When I Get To Be God." The idea had been to look into the future and plan all the changes one would make when it was—at last—one's turn to be omnipotent. It was daydreaming on a cosmic scale.

Now it seemed to Esther that as she grew older, everything else got to be God except herself; and she was not even in charge of the rhythm of her own heart.

She saw the buggy coming rapidly between the rows of houses. Too rapidly for much serious conversation, she thought. "Mama! David! They're here!"

She ran into the yard to meet them. Her father's face was set. He got out of the buggy like a man escaping and went directly into the house. Esther threw her arms around Thomas as soon as he stepped down. "Welcome home! You look just fine, Thomas! We were afraid from your letter you might have wasted away, but you look wonderful! And you must have grown another inch!" She heard her voice babbling. Thomas was stiff as a board. She drew back and studied his face again. "It's good to have you home."

"You're glad, aren't you?" asked Thomas. He gave her a searching look.

"I'm glad to have you home," she said again, hesitating.

"I thought so." He followed his father into the house.

They could hear Sam Allen's raised voice. "I tell you, it's your kind of problem and not mine. Something to do with religion. All about Calvin and the elect and the damned."

Mildred, flushed and nervous, bustled out of the parlor, held him tight, kissed him on the cheek. "Welcome home, son."

Thomas said defensively, "Anybody can get sick."

"Why, certainly they can! And we'll soon have you fixed up on good home cooking. You've worked yourself half to death, that's all," soothed Mildred. She shot a glance at Sam. Behind her David put up a very casual hand and rotated it in the air. "H'lo, Thomas."

"I want to see Aunt Rosa," said Thomas in a particularly gloomy voice. He pushed out of the family group and went into the parlor and pulled up a footstool near Rosa's chair.

"And how are you?" he began. Rosa said she would be fine if all the birds would stop singing. "It's November," Thomas said, "and there aren't any birds to sing."

Rosa's eyes widened. "That's just awful!" she breathed. "It must be the hens have taken it up, and the horses! Think what the spring will be like, when all of them start in, and the birds besides!"

"I'm going to be right here," said Thomas, "and I'll take care of you."

"That's all right," said Rosa, beginning to feel confused. "Silas will be home by then."

"Some people," Thomas stated, patting her hand, "never had a chance."

Mildred swept in then and pulled him right off to the kitchen for buttermilk and a large piece of chocolate cake. David, frowning, went along in hope of getting in on the cake.

Esther was wearing her own frown, but her attention was caught by someone coming out of the mill office. She moved to the window to see if it might be Max. She wondered if she would be able to slip down the stairs tonight. It looked like Max. She felt suddenly warm and the ends of her fingers tingled.

She did not hear Aunt Rosa lean forward and ask in a loud whisper, "Who was that funny boy?"

"Damned if I know," said Sam.

Time to go, thought Esther. She had been sitting near her bed-room window, knitting by moonlight the red wool scarf she was mak-ing for Max Carson's Christmas present. The holiday was only a week off; and every night she sat knitting in the dark until it was late enough and quiet enough to slip from the house. The scarf—which was a secret from everybody—had a number of lumps where stitches dropped in the dark had been picked up twisted in daylight.

Esther stored the knitting deep in a bureau drawer, fluffed out her hair and picked up her shoes, which she would not wear until she was safely down the back steps.

Quietly she eased down the hall. It had been simpler to slip from the other house, with its porch roof and its convenient chinaberry tree. She remembered now, with a pang, the night she and David had crept away to spy through Ellie Faye's bedroom window. Esther felt old and disillusioned. No, she felt grown up and full of confidence. It was hard to know just how she did feel from one minute to the next.

She was especially careful passing the door of Thomas' bedroom. He had treated her so strangely since he came home from college that she half feared he knew about Max. Certainly Thomas blamed her for something—and what else could it be?

Beside the back porch she buttoned every other loop on her high shoes and ran for the black shadow of the mill, by the new boiler room, around the back so no one might spot her from the windows of the Allen house.

The mill office was dark. She wondered how much longer Max would be able to justify spending his nights there, now that the mill was again operating on a full schedule. And how long it would be before she miscalculated and bumped into the night watchman on his regular rounds.

She circled the mill, eased open the office door and closed it softly behind her. "Max?" She gasped when his arms came out of the dark and pulled her to him.

Much later, when little was left of the fire but a bed of coals, she saw Max holding his pocket watch toward the hearth to catch the faint glimmer of light.

"Must I leave already?"

"No." He put the watch back on the table. "We've got time to talk."

"Too lazy to talk," she sighed.

"I've got to tell you something." He stared at the crusty andirons. "I'll build up the fire."

He sounded serious. Esther sat up to watch him. She knew with certainty that he must be about to settle a wedding date, to talk about the Boston house. Maybe even to suggest they live in Greenway. "Whatever you want, Max," she said with a dreamy smile, meaning to answer all the questions which hung in the air between them.

"I'm transferring to Kentucky. The first of January," he said.

"That's not much time." She reached out to touch his bare back. She would never get over the curve of his spine. She walked her fingers down the bone stair steps.

He shook suddenly loose. "I'm serious now."

"All right. Serious." She hid her smile.

He threw the log onto the fire and sparks sprang out. "I'm going to miss you," he said. She could see the harsh line of his jaw in the flare of light from off the hearth. She held herself very still for a minute, then began to put on her clothes. "Why do you have to miss me?" she asked. Even to her own ears, the voice was calm. She stood and pulled her skirt on with great care, not wanting the fabric to whisper or the hem to brush the floor.

"You always knew I'd be moving on someday."

She waited for him to add he could not move on alone. All he did add was, "I've told you that a dozen times."

"Yes. You have." The blouse now—over her head. Esther wanted to stay there, hidden inside the little tent it made. For one second she allowed the terror to pour across her face while it was safely covered. Then she drew the neck down and finished working her arms into the sleeves and began to concentrate on the buttons.

"There were no promises," he said. "You're so young."

Her voice nearly failed her. "Weren't there?" She tore a buttonhole getting it into place. "No. No, I guess not."

"You always knew," he repeated. "You're not even sixteen! And I told you I'd not be here forever. You always knew."

That was like saying you knew earthquake to be possible, or pestilence, or flood. It did not mean you held yourself in readiness. She sought for a breathing place in this conversation, a clearing from which he would be able to list the clothes she would need in Kentucky and tell her when to catch the train. She said, "You ought to clean out that fireplace. Carry out the ashes."

"It isn't that I want to leave Greenway. You know that, Esther. I don't want to leave you. But I work for the machinery company." His words were orderly, almost dogged. "I stay until a mill is well under way and making money. I protect my company's investment."

"Oh, let's do that by all means," said Esther in a strained voice.

"The fire kept me in Greenway long after I would normally have been moved to some other mill. Your father talked me into staying. And I talked my company into letting me."

Esther could not control her sudden, bitter laugh. "So in a way everything's my father's fault! I think that's neat and tidy, keeping all the guilt in the family."

There was something about that word "family" that stopped him. "Esther, you're not . . . not going to have . . ."

The possibility of that lie made her dizzy with hope. "Would it matter?" she asked. She was tempted to invent a baby if that would work.

She saw that if he had looked miserable before he now looked martyred and resigned. He caught hold of her shoulders. "Just tell me if you are."

Esther raised her right hand as if, once more, she would touch tenderly the dark scar sunk in his face. Instead she hit it with all her strength. "*No!*" she yelled so loudly the watchman and the Allens and all the mill village could hear. "No, and you can go to Kentucky or Hell; it's all the same to me!"

She slammed out of the office, banged the door loudly behind her and headed straight for the woods. For no good reason she threw herself into a pile of brown leaves, grabbed up an armful and slung them out in all directions. She was half growling behind her teeth. She saw Max come to the door and heard the night watchman running. Esther pulled back into the leaves.

Max Carson could not tell which way she had run. "It was the wind," he explained to the puffing watchman. "Everything's fine."

But he stood there, looking out into the night long after the watchman had gone, trying to decide if he should call her name. Had she not been so young . . . If he had held to his usual resolve never to mix love and business . . . If he had just followed his own rule of finishing the work, then taking a few days in some strange town with a strange woman he would never see again . . .

Finally he called into the dark, "Esther? Esther, are you out there?"

Not to you, she thought, watching him go into the office and close the door. She wiped her wet cheeks.

Carson believed that in less than a month he would be gone from Esther's mind, layered over first by guilt, then by some new face, at last by forgetfulness. But out in the dark Esther's first thoughts of pain were already sinking under the new ones of anger and wounded pride. Country Girl Betrayed by City Slicker, her mind was spitting. She saw herself captured forever in some anecdote about one of Stone County's best-known spinsters.

Oh, she could imagine how her house would be pointed out to visitors. "Old Miss Esther lives there, with her dotty aunt. It seems a long time ago, when the mill was first started here . . . She wasn't much more than a child . . . and this Yankee fellow . . ."

Not about me, they won't! And I wouldn't have married him anyway! Not forever would I have married Maxwell Carson! He was somebody new, that's all, and he had that hole in his face and told that story about his mother not being a bottle of milk—and that was all it was! Nothing but that!

Esther half feared all this was true. She might really have arrived in this place by choice, and stupid choice at that. That made her angrier than ever. She searched in the dark until she found a fragment of broken brick, which she hurled through the night at the office building. It fell short.

Esther walked to the river and watched the brown water pulling by. What had Miss Bethesda thought in that moment she stepped out on to her floor and landed on nothing but air, and plunged right through into the Katsewa? Or maybe Miss Bethseda had looked into her own future and seen something black and horrible and—holding her nose—had jumped gratefully into the dark.

Well, I couldn't, Esther thought. I could get on a raft and float off someplace new, but I couldn't jump.

This made her feel her heart must not be broken, after all, and she was a little disappointed. She pressed her hand against the bark of a tree until the ridges were marked in a pattern on her palm. Silly. She walked as quietly as she could to her own home, checking her buttons and ribbons and smoothing her hair. In the kitchen she waited at the table till her mother, yawning, came down to make breakfast.

"What are you doing up?" said Mildred when she saw her in the early-morning light.

"I've been up a long time," said Esther. She allowed her face to look sleepless and gloomy. If she asks me what's wrong, I'll tell her. I'll tell her I love Max Carson and he's going away.

"Well, don't be getting in my way. Your Aunt Rosa hollered with bad dreams half the night. I could bite a nail in two."

Esther wandered outdoors, saw Jube going into the store the back way. She followed him, and when she found herself alone in the storeroom, moved the keg of pickles to one side and took up the loose board in the floor. Light winked on the rows of whiskey jars beneath. I could get drunk. When a man was jilted, he sometimes got drunk. Very silly. Esther slammed the board back in place and stood on it spraddle-legged. I keep waiting to have the right reaction. Silly.

Big Jube had come quietly through the curtains. "You put them pickles back where they belong."

"Put them back yourself," she said. "I got things on my mind."

She waited for Jube to ask what they were. He lifted the keg and placed it in the exact center of the board. "You not even suppose to know about that," he said. "Your daddy don't want you to know about that."

Now Esther whirled, laughing, on one foot. The things she was not supposed to know and the things they were not supposed to know —if all the secrets in the world were spread out in a big field in the sun, who would be really surprised?

She pushed through the curtains and started down the aisle. Sam Allen was coming in the front door. "Your mama says come eat some breakfast."

She stopped and looked mournful. "I'm not hungry."

"Everybody ought to eat breakfast," he said, distracted.

"I feel funny."

"Get something in your stomach and you'll improve." He was already braced for the payday crowds and the arguments he would have about debts and payments and store accounts.

Esther ran to the narrow porch across the store front. It was still early. Houses along the street were just waking up; the smoke was barely beginning to thicken at all the chimneys. A brisk December wind made her eyes sting. Her nose was running. She wiped it with her gloved hand; then, irritably, jerked the glove off and threw it toward the road as hard as she could. Let somebody find it and carry it home to his wife. She took off the other glove and slung it out, and the wind carried it off to one side.

When she went back inside the house, Thomas was hanging his coat on the rack in the hall.

"Been carrying in wood for Mama?" she said. Thomas had been so hostile since he came home from college that she found herself making nervous conversation with him.

"I do my share around here," he snapped, "which is more than the favored ones do."

Esther had never felt less favored. It seemed to her important, at just that minute, to settle whatever quarrel was between them. She might even talk to him about Max. She might ask his advice. "Thomas," she began.

He said through tight lips, "I know about you."

Esther swallowed. "Who told you?"

"Nobody had to tell me. You can't have your way forever, don't you know that?"

"I know it," she whispered, and closed her eyes.

"I'm not going to put up with it any longer. I'm going to change things!"

Her eyes flew open. What could he mean? He was going to tell everybody about Max and what a fool she had been? "Nobody can change it now," she said uneasily. "Besides, it's all over." Her throat began to hurt and she knew she was about to cry.

"You're right about that; it's over. Because I'm fighting back. I've gotten strong. There's power that's given and power that's taken."

"I don't want anybody to know," she managed to say. He was confusing her with all this talk of power.

"You're just like her," he said. "You think you've got some kind of gift."

"Just like who?"

"Well, I wasn't on the end of her string. I'm not on the end of your string. Nobody spits a curse on me."

Esther was shaking her head. "Thomas, I don't know what you're talking about right now, but I am asking you—don't tell anybody. I can stand being stupid. I can stand having you know I've been stupid. But I can't stand everybody knowing it. I'm not going to be somebody for people to talk about all over Stone County. I'm not going to be Pearlie Winters, who fell in the river; remember how Grandfather used to talk about her?"

Now Thomas blinked. "The sleepwalker?"

Esther gave a harsh laugh. "Oh, yes! The sleepwalker." For with Max she had surely been walking in her sleep, and had waked up from a pleasant dream. "She fell into the cold water," said Esther, remembering how they called out to Pearlie and she toppled in the river and died.

Her brother's eye bulged. "How did you know that?" he hissed. "How could you know that?"

She drew back. Something in his face frightened her.

"You must be really evil," he said, "to know things you couldn't know by any normal way. You must be really evil. It's not just being favored, or having the luck. It's something worse than that." He clapped both hands to the sides of his head. "Now you've made my head hurt!" he cried.

"Evil?" she whispered. She ran up the stairs. Gracefully, thought Thomas, watching her from the corner of his eye. He rubbed the heel of his hand against his eyebrow, for there—right there—where Miss Bethesda had cursed him last, was the sharpest edge of the pain.

Esther stopped and looked back at him. She looked honestly bewildered. "You really hate me," she whispered, "and I don't even know why."

Now that it was in words he saw that he did hate her. He hated her white neck. He could have thrown her down on the stairs and hated her entire body with his. He saw suddenly that Esther was the cause of everything—it was her fault about Zelda Dowdy, and Christine, and Miss Bethesda Lee Michael, and the University of North Carolina. Between tight jaws he said, "People ought to pay for looking like you look."

She easily vaulted the last steps and ran down the hallway to her room. Easily, he thought. No matter what she does she's always dancing. He pressed the coat onto its hook too hard and the fabric tore. She made me tear my coat.

At suppertime, Thomas was sent to call her to the table. He started softly up the stairs, thinking he might find her lying with her clothes off across her bed, and he might strike her someplace soft. Stealthily he put his foot on each tread. The front door began to bang. Max Carson burst in as he turned.

"Where's Esther? I've got to see her!" he blurted.

"I guess she's upstairs."

"If she won't come down at first, you tell her I've changed my mind. Tell her I don't care how young she is. Tell her I want her to marry me. I want her to go with me to Kentucky."

Thomas, astounded, folded up on the stairs. Esther and Max Carson? He had not thought them so much as friends!

"I'll tell her myself," said Max, and passed him, running up the steps.

Thomas had begun to smile. He saw how it would be with Esther married and out of the house! How he would be at his mother's side. How he would build a business with his father. How he would see that David settled down, and never mistook himself for someone favored, with a gift of power. His headache disappeared and he started up the stairs behind Carson.

But Esther was gone. It must have happened when Sam closed down the store for supper. Two dresses, Sam's chestnut horse with the streak of white down its forehead, some money from the shattered cash drawer in the mill store were gone with her. A keg of pickles had been overturned in the back room of the store, and the juice poured under a loose board, over a lot of broken glass. They found a pair of her gloves dropped in the street outside.

PART III

David

❧❦❧

Chapter

❧ 20 ❧

HE LEANED AGAINST the brick wall of the small building. Beyond it, on the broad green lawn, the crowd was still milling and laughing. The women who smelled of custard were putting their lace handkerchiefs away. Sounds of their laughter seemed to fall over the low roof the way balls had flown across when the three of them played here with Nellie, on long ago summer evenings.

"David?"

His name was like one of the tossed balls of memory appearing at the wrong spot above the peak of the roof. "Back here," he called.

"What you doing here off by yourself?" Sam Allen, wiping his face on a handkerchief, came around the corner. "Thomas will be wondering where you are."

"The hell he will," said David.

"If it's this hot in June, I hate to think about August. What's that?"

"I came out here for a drink. I can't taste anything in that punch but lemonade."

"By God, that's a fine idea. Pass it over." Sam lowered himself, with care, to the ground and rested his back against the wall. "Nathan used to practice law in here," he said, thumping the bricks. "And his father and grandfather before him."

David passed him the whiskey and Sam took a long and grateful swig. "You're bad as Henry Grady," David muttered. "You think when you mix Grimes blood and Allen blood, you get the New South, just like that!"

Sam made an awful face. "Jubilee Jackson never made this stuff."

"I get it out of the next county. It's cheaper than yours." David walked the length of the small building and back again. "I was back here remembering how we once played in this yard. At Nellie's birthday parties there was a game about throwing the ball over the roof. I never was any good knowing where it would come, but Esther—"

Sam began to shake his head rapidly and push the whiskey away. "No talk about Esther today. We promised your mama."

"And Mama promised Thomas."

"You know how he is." Sam looked suddenly depressed. "It's bad enough Nathan didn't live to see this wedding. Makes me feel old." He reached out a hand and jerked his head until David understood he was to heave him to his feet. "I'm getting to sound just like old Angus Mackey. The more years go by, the more I miss the old hellion. You better come on. It's almost time for them to leave."

"They don't need me for that."

But he followed his father through the crowd, saying polite things into an assortment of upturned faces. Inside the house the two of them joined Thomas at the foot of the stairs and waited for the bride.

"Mother's upstairs. Probably making Nellie nervous," Thomas said.

David said, "Well, you're not nervous." That was not quite true. Thomas had measured out to himself just the required amount of nervousness. David studied his brother's face. The smile, fleeting and self-conscious, seemed as carefully chosen as the flower in the lapel. Bridegroom's flower; bridegroom's smile. Tall and handsome, Thomas looked older than his twenty-three years, looked sober and settled.

If I had made that face with a knife, its neatness would have nagged me, David thought, and I would have forced on it dents and dimples until it was mutilated forever.

He said aloud, "I wonder if Esther's married. I hope she married a man with a crooked nose."

Thomas pulled his eyebrows into a frown which was perfectly symmetrical. "Do you have to talk about her now, of all times?"

"No."

"Boys. We promised your mother."

Thomas said, "You were only nine years old."

"I remember her well enough."

He knew, of course, what Thomas thought—that Esther was now a group of loose bones somewhere in the river's bottom between Greenway and South Carolina. More than eight years had passed without a word; detectives sent out on a hundred leads came back without one sign of her. But the horse which left with her had wandered home in a couple of days, and other horses had vanished for two-day periods on a line northward through Virginia all the next week after she disappeared. Coincidence, Thomas said. She had drowned herself over Max Carson, whose child she was probably expecting.

Thomas had been watching David's angry face. He smiled. "Matter of fact, I wish Esther could see me today. She might have been surprised."

As if on cue, the bride appeared and began to descend the stairs. Nellie Grimes Allen lifted one lace-gloved hand in a private greeting to Thomas, then she smiled at all the guests waiting in the downstairs hall. Her hair, the color of the cherry stair rail, was turned in a series of smooth rounds atop her head. She was tall but very thin, with cheeks caved in slightly on bones which must be no thicker than eggshells. Her entire face looked translucent, like a bowl of fine china.

Nellie had almost been an old maid, nursing her father through his long illness. Perhaps it was those years which had made her white and small, like something to be kept inside a cage.

David's taste ran more to buxom farm girls. Watching her come cautiously down the curving stairs, he thought that even her breasts must grow long and narrow, with sharp tips. The hipbones would rise like scythes below the stacked blades of her ribs. He began to smile. And I would have carved Nellie out of bone, little bone, sparrow's bone; and for the hair one strand of copper wire and under that one small wood shaving of brain curled in a snowy skull.

"You must be very happy," he said to Thomas, surprising him with his gleeful face.

"I am."

"Here it is!" cried Nellie, and the bouquet sailed past them over a circle of girls who batted wildly so that it shattered and rained in bits among them all. Nellie ran down the stairs and Thomas took her arm.

"Run for it!" He laughed. Rice grains rattled on the shining floor as they went down the hall toward the open door.

They sprinted for the new car Thomas had bought only the week before, one of the few in Greenway, with its spoked wheels and knobby running board. Sim Etheridge had started it well in advance and now waited behind the high steering wheel until Nellie was settled in her vibrating seat. He leaped aside for Thomas. The car lurched once before it began the noisy trip out the oval drive. Its top had been put down in accordian folds and Nellie's white parasol jiggled like a flower on a long stem.

David had turned aside before they drove into the dusty road and turned left to Greenway and wherever beyond that they were taking their wedding trip. He ambled off to the scuppernong arbor and had another drink. Once, he knew, Esther had been punished in this very arbor for slipping away from Nellie's birthday party, stuffing herself on grapes and spitting their seeds at the bees, and staining the only white dress she owned.

Now the arbor, the house, the thousand acres—maybe even the bees—would all belong to Thomas. Just as the store and most of the mill would someday soon belong to Thomas. I don't know who inherits the earth, thought David, but it sure ain't the meek.

He lay in the spotted shade. Last week he had flatly refused to help out in the mill while Thomas was on his wedding trip. Thomas had gone storming to their father, vowing that David would come to a bad end; he was lazy; he had no ambition. "If you'd give me a freer hand with him . . ."

"Son," Sam Allen said, "if you had a much freer hand I think it would get chopped off at the wrist."

"Well, I never got to loaf around the way he does! I never got to whittle my life away!"

David looked up at the fuzzy undersides of the grape leaves. There might be time for a nap before the last guest had gone and the last goblet lined up for counting on the kitchen shelf. He let his eyelids drift downward. I hope when he takes her tonight her very edges are sharp—he grinned to himself—and she peels him like a stick.

When the Allens moved away from the mill village in 1906, after Sam's controlling interest in the mill was secure and undisputed, they built a grand house on the outskirts of Greenway, heavy with towers and turrets and illogical gables, rimmed with knobby woodwork and banisters which looked as if they had been crocheted.

David took over the gazebo in its front yard and he and Little Jube carried it way down to the back edge of the property. They were both sixteen that year. They made the transfer late one night on the strength of a fruit jar full of peach brandy; and David wanted to move somebody else's privy onto the front lawn as a joke, but Little Jube wouldn't.

In the two years since then, the airy latticework structure had been so changed by David's whims that it looked like everything from a corn crib to a cathedral, depending on the angle of view. Tarpaper had been tacked against the inside walls so he could use it in winter. A crooked pipe with a sooty iron rooster screwed to its top let smoke rise from a squat black stove. He had added a long, low room—more like a hallway than a room—along one side and fronted this with a row of columns which were not even joined to the roof but simply imbedded in the earth like naked posts. Some of these had been shaped into totem poles and others into false grandfather clocks or mammoth oblong tears, and one into an elongated old woman with a melting chin. He was always changing them; cutting one shape away and superimposing something new, and a few had been hacked away to such thinness there was nothing left for them to be but spears or Aaron's rod in bloom.

Scattered around the building lay a clutter of broken barrels, half-rotted logs, saw horses, a grindstone and a lumpy carpet of wood chips. Here and there a visitor might stoop to pick out of the thick debris a small, polished walnut colt, or a smiling doll with outstretched arms—later discovered to be in the process of crucifixion— or a perfectly egg-shaped round of wood with a hole driven all the way through, the way among river rocks a child can still discover arrowheads.

Inside the little house, the regular wooden benches ran around the octagon-shaped walls of the main room, but now these were littered with pieces of wood which were ripening, pots of polishes and waxes, discarded knives and blunted screwdrivers and rusted straight razors, different-sized bags of sand, chisels and mallets and hammers, small hatchets and files and rasps.

The added hallway room contained finished carvings or those being polished or waxed or discolored, for sometimes David colored his largest wooden figures with melted wax and turned them into garish saints with orange hair and veins which dripped purple blood. It pleased him to know the clean wood with its curving grain lay underneath this horror.

The entire structure, known in the family as David's Playhouse, was an abomination to Sam Allen, who had never set foot inside it, and who had himself carved out over the years elaborate insults to his son—David the blockhead, the woodbrain, to whom life seemed as easy as falling off logs, whose bark was not only worse than his bite but took its place entirely. A boy whose only talent was to turn good stovewood into shavings. A whittler!

Sam spat this last word out with real disgust. His son, David Allen, a whittler!

"Look at your brother Thomas," the conversations usually ran, for Thomas was a vice president in the mill and everyone admired him. Thomas was ambitious. Thomas had never given the family a minute's trouble.

"I don't like to look at Thomas."

"Nothing on God's green earth you can do to support yourself! If you'd make something to sell, if you'd fix furniture or doorstops! But no. It's all deliberate! And if I should stop—if I just stopped buying your rosewood and walnut, what would you do?"

"What Esther did," said David coldly.

"You, who know nothing? Who can't add a column of figures, or gin cotton, or even sweep out a mill floor? If you ran away to any city in the world, you'd be dead in two weeks! You'd be dead of hunger and laziness!"

"But you'd never know for sure. Whether I was dead in some other city or in the closest river—you'd never know."

It was the same stalemate. And from it Sam would head into the splendid new house to hear Mildred offer the same excuse: "David is still so young!"

Young! Sam was tempted to tell her how much it had cost him to move the whole Mayberry family to South Carolina, with their Betsy carrying one of David's bastards. It was one of the many times he was tempted to speak honestly to Mildred, and never did.

But every time Sam got ready to come down on David with all four feet, Thomas, sensing his father's mood, would begin to nag and criticize and accuse and urge his father on. He prodded to have David disinherited or at least thrashed. For the first few days his words were effective. "You're right," Sam would mutter, banging one fist into his palm. "That boy will never be any account unless I make him."

But just as Sam was ready to stride down and enter that heathen playhouse with blood in his eye, Thomas would press too hard, say too much, go too far. Sam would turn to him, suddenly suspicious. "You got no natural feelings for your brother? You don't see any one single thing in that boy that's any-count?"

Thomas backed off—but never fast enough.

After these periodic flurries, Sam would ask Mildred to read him again that piece in her Bible about the Prodigal Son, for he thought somehow that parable must be full of clues. She was always delighted at this awakening interest on his part, and tried to give him the whole Book of St. Luke at one sitting, but he only wanted that fifteenth chapter. When he heard it read, the story was never quite as he remembered. He kept wanting to put things in and take things out. Besides, it never did say in the end how the family fared when the Prodigal had fitted back into it and the Elder had stopped his sulking.

He finally told her, "Never mind that one. Read me that other mystery, one more time."

Mildred said softly, "What good does it do to go over and over?"

He yelled, "Just read it. And read slow!"

So Mildred leafed back to the part she had pondered so often the past eight years, the words she and Sam had talked about, and read, and spelled out silently in the dark.

Sam listened as carefully the hundredth time as he had the first. She pronounced the words slowly, always waiting to have them revealed by the Holy Spirit. They went over it line by line, the second chapter of Joshua, about Rahab and the spies; and how she let down a scarlet thread to warn the spies to flee straight back to the Israelites if they wanted to live.

"No," said Sam, for the hundredth time, "it can't mean anything."

"I never said it did," stated Mildred, the hundred-and-first time. "I just said, that day when I first saw it, that I was reminded of this story in the Bible."

What they both meant was that, on the day Esther disappeared, somebody spotted a long and wavy red thread strung out her upstairs window. It was tied onto a table leg in her bedroom and led nowhere. Indeed it looked like nothing so much as some strand that had been unraveled from a knitted red garment; but everyone knew how clumsy Esther was with knitting needles and how she hated to try. Rosa had wound the yarn into a ball for Mildred, who kept it now in her washstand to look at sometimes.

"I guess we'll never understand it," Sam said. "Put that Bible away. It only confuses me! The red thread meant nothing!"

"Everything means something." Mildred said stubbornly. If she could only settle in her own thoughts whether Esther—like Mama, like Rosa—had been strange in her mind. Or whether she was as healthy as Thomas and had simply run away, leaving that scarlet thread like a message.

But what message? What message?

"Come on," said Little Jube, who was no longer little. He had to stoop to come through the small doorway where David was working. "You going fishing or not?"

"I'm right in the middle. Wait a minute." David rested the block of apple wood on a sandbag and looked at it from a new angle. The wood was a pale yellow and would take a high polish; he was planning to carve a head of Moses because the color made him think of bullrushes. Hell, for all he knew, bullrushes were as brown as cattails.

Jube fingered a length of cedar on the bench beside him, a cypress knee, a hickory mallet. "What you going to do when you get this place stacked full?"

"Burn it out and start over." David drove a chisel into the wood, cutting with a swooping stroke along the grain. He let out a breath he had been holding. "If you ever go in wrong, against the grain of the wood," he said, "the whole thing yells at you. I mean it. Cries out. Tells you about it."

"Go on," said Jube scornfully.

"It makes a hollow noise and splits way down to the heart. That's what I like about wood. It gets ripe, but never quite dead the way rock is, or clay."

"I thought we was going fishing."

"I'm coming, I'm coming." He turned the wood and studied it again. "Maybe I ought to do Miriam in the bullrushes and not fool with Moses." But all David's women looked alike, with tall skulls and faces pulled out long and unreal and beautiful. He threw the mallet down. "Let's go."

"Is the bridegroom back?"

"He's coming today so let's get out of sight."

Jube rolled up his eyes minstrel fashion and splayed out his palms, a trick he often pulled because it irritated David. "Lawdy me," he said in broad blackface. "De boss man is coming back!"

"Shut that up," said David.

Jube threw his six-foot length around in a few ungainly dance steps. "They will be singing and dancing in the quarters tonight," he crowed, "to hear that the massa is come!"

David slugged him lightly in the chest with his balled fist. "I told you to shut that up." Jube blocked the next one. They began to shuffle warily around and to jab at the air between them.

David was surprised when a woman's voice from the doorway called his name. His mother, Aunt Rosa, Ellie Faye—no woman ever came out to the playhouse. There was a knock at the makeshift door, which hung open on one clumsy hinge to the midsummer sun, and Nellie put her head around the edge. "Your father says come out front and have some lemonade with us."

"When did you get back?" David took his hands out of the air.

"An hour ago."

Little Jube stuffed his fists into his pockets and managed by so simple an act to shrink six inches. "I see you around," he said, ducking his head.

David whacked him one between the shoulder blades. "I told you to cut that out."

"Yassuh," said Jube politely, his eyes twinkling.

David took his anger out on his new sister-in-law. "How was it?" he asked her in a contemptuous tone. "You finding married life . . . rewarding?"

She colored and looked at Jube, who had begun to collect his bait bucket and ease to the door. "Hello, Jube," she said. He gave her a deferential nod.

"You come back here. We're going fishing." David began to rummage on one of the cluttered lower shelves for his pole.

"You got family business." Jube's tone was extra soft. "I see you some other time." He collected his own pole and glided quickly outdoors and between the pine trees.

David ran to the door and hollered at him. "Damn it, Uncle Remus!"

Nellie had begun to wander around and he had to turn back to see what she might be messing with. "I've never been in your workshop." She took up a woman's head, done in dark rosewood darkened even more by the polish he used. Its long, sad features were the color of a bruise. "Is this Esther?"

He almost struck it from her hand. "No. Of course not. What makes you think that?" With great control he took it from her and carried it to a high shelf in the other room. "It's an Indian," he lied.

Nellie thought David Allen looked something like an Indian himself. There was the same enclosing of the face, as if his eyes had drawn back slightly behind his cheekbones, his smile out of sight under a straight lip. He was dark like an Indian and his body seemed less to move than to drift. "You look a little like Esther," said Nellie thoughtfully, "except her skin was lighter."

"No, I don't," he said.

"You might at least say, 'Welcome to the family.' "

"I'm sure Thomas has covered all the expected remarks." He maneuvered her out of the building and closed the door. "How was Wilmington?" he asked, grudgingly.

"Very pretty. I like the moss on the trees."

Thomas was coming across the wide lawn to meet them. David examined him for hollow eyes or worry wrinkles. As far as he knew, the bridegroom had just had his first sex of any kind. He never heard gossip about Thomas and the local girls. David grinned, remembering his own first time and the girl laughing at him that she could have got more from a bean pod.

But Thomas seemed confident, high-spirited, pleased with himself. Must have gone well, thought David in some surprise. Unless he's pretending. He's good at pretending.

"Don't tell me you got to enter the sanctuary!" Thomas was saying. He held out his hand and David shook it gravely, as if they had been separated a long time. "You should feel honored, Nellie. None of us have ever been inside."

"I am," she murmured. She moved her hands in a sudden nervous flutter and would not meet her husband's eyes.

Now David looked more closely at her face. Two hollow eyes, he counted. Well, honey, that's what you get from inexperience.

Sam and Mildred were seated in wicker chairs under the huge twin pines whose limbs interlaced and shaded a carpet of needles. Heads of the family and founders of the line. David poured himself a glass of lemonade at the white wicker table. Mildred spread her fingers on his arm.

"Have a good morning?" She kept up the fiction that he worked in his little house at some sort of profession.

"How's Aunt Rosa?" was all he said.

"Asleep." Rosa was now almost entirely an invalid. The veins in her enormous legs broke so often they looked like trunks of dark rosewood. She lay alone most of the day in one of the upstairs bedrooms. Sometimes, late at night, she said, Silas came home for a little while.

Thomas was asking if Rutledge could load up a wagon of his clothes. "You won't stay with us tonight, children?" Mildred asked.

"I think we'd like to be in our own home tonight." Thomas sent Nellie a warm smile. Perhaps from the cold lemonade, she shivered.

Thomas and Sam moved off to one side, talking about orders and shipments, whether business had slacked in Thomas' absence. This must have been how it looked to Cain, thought David, when Adam and Abel discussed their flocks and when the lambs were due.

He felt Nellie's eyes upon him. Irritably he said, "It's business as usual for the bridegroom, Nellie." He put his empty glass on the table.

"I hope you'll come visit us often," she said. There was something pleading in her voice.

David started to tell her he and Thomas seldom walked across the upstairs hall to see each other. He saw how white her fingers were against the wet glass. "I might," he said, finally.

She looked up uneasily and saw none of the others were listening. "I feel," she began, "that even though I've known the Allens all my life, there's so much I don't . . . don't understand."

"You better ask Thomas."

"Yes, of course." She took an enormous swallow of the lemonade. It nearly choked her.

Something very wrong here, David thought. "It takes time," he said. He let the words hang there more like a question than anything else.

Nellie had lowered eyelids as thin as rice paper and looked down at her long, pale fingers. "I guess," she said softly.

The barest glimmer of an idea came to David. He looked across the yard to where Thomas and his father had their heads together, then said abruptly, "I never did kiss the bride!" He saw his mother's happy smile.

Stooping there over the white chair which held Nellie like a cage, he pursed a decorous mouth and kissed her where the corner of her smile pushed into her cheek. But no one saw the quick flash of his warm tongue where it flicked into that corner and parted the startled lips and, for an instant, made a sharp thrust into her mouth.

He straightened up. "I'll come see you often," he said, holding her eyes with his. "I owe my brother that."

Nellie turned aside. Lifting the cold glass, she laid it on her face over the very spot. "Please do," she said, keeping her head down.

Chapter

⋖§ 21 §⋗

I WILL NEVER, thought Nellie, lie more stiffly in my coffin than I now lie in my own bed.

The words had a poetic sound to her. She whispered them aloud. The bed in which she lay alone was the same she had used since she was twelve, and attended Miss Tilley's Academy and memorized sayings which were supposed to cover the whole of truth.

At one time this four-poster bed with its white ruffled top had seemed protective, like something in which an ailing queen might be carried onto a balcony to wave a white hand to her people. Now Nellie crouched under it, afraid, and remembered that the far side of the ruffling was torn.

Thomas was still downstairs, pacing through the huge, high-ceilinged rooms and saying something aloud to the whiskered gentlemen and flabby-chinned ladies in the picture frames.

Nellie jerked her nightgown up and began to explore her body with damp hands. She was thin, yes. Her flat stomach lay between the sharp hipbones like some shallow bowl—that might be it. Her breasts were not large and, when she lay on her back, they spread out and flattened.

I don't know, she thought. I don't know whether it is one failing or all of them that makes him like that.

Not until we were married . . . not until he saw me uncovered . . .
Nellie swallowed. He was not this way before.

All the years Nellie and Thomas had been growing up, he had been
so respectful it was almost wearying. He had taken her elbow as if
it might splinter against his hand. She tried to rediscover now, with
disbelief, that boy whose shoes were always polished, who wrote
the delicate Spencerian hand in the copybooks, who bowed from the
waist at dancing class.

Night after night, while Nathan Grimes lay upstairs giving up his
life one degree at a time, Thomas had come to sit with her in the
parlor. He had read Tennyson aloud, and been especially moving with
such lines as "better to have loved and lost/Than never to have loved
at all." Often he brought her lily of the valley which had a new,
damp odor.

Somehow, from all this, Nellie had thought the future predictable.
She had lived their wedding night a dozen times in her mind, and
always in her mind Thomas was grateful and almost reverent. Always he kissed her knuckles, lightly, and said she was precious to him.

On their wedding day, it was planned they would drive straight
ahead until nightfall. Nellie did not understand why they stopped
in Greensboro. The tiring trip, Thomas said. The heat. The dust.
She had gone down the hotel corridor ahead of him smiling, already
having the daydreams delivered to her. The twilight supper at which
he would sometimes touch her wrist. The slow, almost lazy, ascent
of the stairs afterward. Inside the room in the dim light, gentleness.

They made pleasant but uneasy conversation walking to their
room. The late sunlight still lay in a patch on the floor and she
wondered nervously how they would spend the time till supper.
Thomas paid the boy and locked the door. "Take off your clothes,"
he said. He put the two suitcases, which held all her lace and embroidery and tiny hand stitches, roughly into the closet.

At first Nellie thought she had not heard him right. Change
clothes for supper? Before it was even dark?

The slamming closet door was like a blow. "I said take off your
clothes!"

She fumbled into the closet, stooped down and opened the bag,
took out her gown. He stood in the center of the room, watching.
She felt awkward and did not know whether she ought to look at
him or not, or what she was expected to say.

"I don't care about that," he finally said.

She held the gown to her waist. "I do."

In the other room, she undressed. It was hot and muggy; her underarm curves were damp and looked to her darker than they had ever been in all her life. Against her body, her own fingertips were surprisingly cold. She slipped into the soft gown with its lacy top.

Then she did not know what to do next. She stood there clearing her throat until it felt raw, waiting for him to hear and call her. It was so still she thought the other room might be empty; he had gone downstairs, after all, to order supper. Perhaps it would be carried up to them in silver dishes on a silver tray.

She tiptoed back into the empty bedroom, but he was there, waiting in a chair with his legs stretched out and crossed. He looked so unfamiliar to Nellie that she almost spoke his name. He put his right hand into the air toward her and opened and closed the fist in a gesture she mistook for entreaty. "Take down your hair."

Nellie had begun to smile while she unpinned the long coils before the mirror. Surely he was as tongue-tied with the newness of marriage as she was herself. The fact that it was yet afternoon was a miscalculation, a measure of his own state of nerves. She was turning to say so when he caught the ends of her hair from behind and gave a cruel jerk, scattering the last bone pins. She gasped with the unexpected pain.

The apology did not come. "Lie on the bed."

Nellie saw that he was still fully clothed; should she mention that? No, it was husbands who instructed. This must be part of the ritual. While her eyes were discreetly on the ceiling, he would attend to that.

As an added precaution she closed her eyes and lay down. She felt cold and faint. The bed sagged when he sat by her. She felt him sliding the cool gown up her legs, touching her curiously—almost scientifically—around the knee joints. I must be blushing, she thought, all the way down. I must lie still.

He pushed the skirt further, pinched up flesh from inside her thighs. Then the gown went suddenly to her waist and she contracted her face and closed her eyes as tightly as she could. He slipped a hand under one leg and she flexed it obediently. Then the other. She lay in a tremble with her knees up and waited. And waited. There was nothing else.

Finally her eyes flew open—was he undressing *now?*—and she would never forget his face and the way his mouth was turned as if some word lay inside it too hateful to speak.

"I like to see what I get," he said, his lip curling. He bent forward suddenly between her paralyzed knees and bit her savagely on the stomach. Nellie cried out and backed away, flailing the bedclothes.

It was then he took her, himself barely uncovered in an awkward tangle of clothes, and she with her neck twisted painfully against the head of the bed, turning her face back and forth. She remembered how tears had run down into her open mouth. She had pushed at him with both hands and he, catching hold of them in one grip, had banged them back into the bedpost and held them there and kissed her in such a way that she could not breathe. She writhed against him, seeking to draw in air, and the harder she struggled the more she heard him grunting with satisfaction.

Later, when he was asleep, she tried to get out of the room and could not find the key. No supper arrived and she huddled on the floor in the growing dark, still hiccuping with tears. In the middle of the night he found her there, stood over her and put his hands at the sides of her head and pulled it in to him. "There," he ordered. Nellie, weeping, jerked her face aside. He caught it again and let his two thumbs rest lightly where the pulse was jumping in her neck. His hipbone was sharp against her cheek. "There," he ordered, and she put her mouth there while he moved. At some point he curved his body down far enough to catch the tips of her breasts between his fingers and pinch them and pull upward.

The days they had spent together since that time had been full of polite attentions, devoted gallantry, sweet compliments, and pleasant conversation. She knew the hotel clerks between Greensboro and Wilmington smiled at such a devoted and respectful husband. The other nights had been as cruel as the first, varying only in detail, and the details had never been in any of Nellie's dreams.

She heard Thomas now coming up the stairs which, only a week before, she had run down laughing in her bridal veil. He was humming under his breath. Now, in her father's house—in the bed where as a child she had felt like royalty . . .

By the time he put his hands upon her, Nellie was already whimpering.

Winona Rickert sat up and plucked pine needles from her hair. She said, "You been in the Grimes house since they fixed it up?"

"Allen house. My brother wants it called the Allen house."

She was agreeable. "I sure would like to see inside."

"I should have taken you to the wedding," David said. "I thought about it." He'd have given a lot to see how Thomas would look if he ever brought a mill girl to that house.

"You're sweet," said Winona. She looked as if she were thinking of something else. Winona was a very practical girl who made love for hair ribbons and diversion. There was very little real passion between them. Sometimes, of course, Winona did daydream about being his wife and living in a large house with blue-velvet chairs; but David seldom appeared in these dreams at all. Only the chairs, and the carpet and the napkins and the silver spoons and the china gravy boats.

From where they lay, the roof of Sam Allen's house and the comb of the iron rooster who guarded David's workshop could be seen against the hot sky.

"We ought not be so near," said Winona. "The way your crazy aunt looks out the windows."

"She can't tell anything." He lay back, rested his head on his folded arms and looked at Winona critically. She had the pale, indoor look of girls who worked in the mill: tan hair and lashes, light-blue eyes, some haphazard freckles and plump flesh which looked as if it would retain the imprint of a finger. If I were carving Winona, I might use mushroom; David grinned. She dipped snuff with a willow-twig brush, but not when she was with him; and she always rinsed her mouth ahead of time. Still the odor seemed to cling to the roots of her teeth. He had only kissed her once.

He closed his eyes. It's all downstream with Winona. Summertime and bumblebees.

"How do you like your new sister-in-law?"

"Prissy old maid," he said drowsily.

"But she's married."

"Prissy old maid anyway."

"Hold still." She wet a finger and took up a red ant from his arm. "I hear he fixed the house up pretty for her."

David swung suddenly to his feet, opening his eyes on the way up, and extended his hand to pull her. "Come on then. We'll go."

She began to giggle and hold back. "I couldn't! My hair! Look at these wrinkles!" Nervously she patted and smoothed herself. "What would she think if I showed up at her house like this?"

"She'd think you were a friend of mine." Winona missed his smile. "I'll even give you a ride over in the famous Allen automobile; it's home today." He saw she had made herself too neat. Carefully, when she was not looking, he slipped two wisps of pine straw back into her hair.

Winona shrieked half the distance between Greenway and the Grimes—now Allen house. She kept spreading her hands over the road beside the car where the wind was flowing.

When Amy Lee opened the big door of the house to them, air that had cooled in the dim rooms flowed out upon them with a similar rush. The sweat at Winona's hairline dried to a dingy stain. Perfect, thought David. But instantly he was ashamed, and while Amy Lee went up the stairs to tell Miz Allen they were here, he pinched Winona lightly on the rump. She frowned, suddenly proper. She pointed to the faraway ceiling, bulging with plaster grapes and tendrils and vines.

"How high it is!" she breathed. "Ooh, you could dance in a hall like this!" She lifted both arms above her head and made a slow turn, flatfooted and without rhythm.

David saw Nellie on the landing, watching the girl with some surprise. "Good afternoon!" he called. Winona's hands came slapping down by her sides.

"It's about time you came to see me," Nellie said with a quick smile.

David made a mocking flourish as she came down the stairs to them. "Mrs. Thomas Allen, Miss Winona Rickert."

"How do you do?" said Nellie pleasantly.

"Yes, ma'am," Winona stammered, and suddenly she turned on David a look of such pure hatred that he took a step backward.

"Let's go into the parlor where it's cool." Nellie's eyes had become fixed on the pine straw hanging from the girl's hair. Her voice faltered briefly. "Hasn't this heat been awful, Miss Rickert?"

"Awful," the girl said miserably.

The rug on the parlor floor, while faded, had once been a rich crimson and still showed a complex design of blue and black and gold. There were new chairs, new window hangings of a pale silk, and marble-topped tables on grotesquely twisted legs.

David stopped suddenly behind the two women. "When in the world did you get that?"

It was a new pump organ, built on the lines of a Gothic cathedral, and it rose in tiers and towers and balconies to form platforms for small vases and china ladies and round doilies. The stool was covered in white velvet with a row of tassels and tiny snowballs.

Nellie said it was a present from Thomas. "He had it waiting when we got back from our wedding trip."

He thought her tone a little sour. "Do you play?"

"Not much."

Winona, awed, had gone to the organ to finger the little balustrades, the curving rims and fluted edges. Into the music stand were cut two treble lines of music with the notes made into winged birds. She ran her fingertip along those lines and spaces as if she were blind and deaf and yet could somehow hear a melody by touch. "It's bigger than the one at church," she sighed. "Play something, Mrs. Allen."

Nellie raised an eyebrow at David. "What would you like? 'Love's Old Sweet Song'?"

"Something more spiritual."

With a bored face she sat at the organ, played badly a few bars of Chopin's "Funeral March," trickled into the beginning of the "Moonlight" Sonata and ruined it with wrong notes. She then put two fingers on E flat and D flat and pressed the black keys and pedaled furiously until the organ sounded as if it were in pain. "I said I couldn't play much." She lifted those two fingers and looked at them curiously.

"It was grand!" Winona giggled, then choked on it. "I do relish music," she added.

Nellie said politely, "Do you play?" She made a gesture as if she would move aside.

"No! Oh, no!"

"Guitar," David put in. "Winona plays guitar at the lyceum on Saturday nights."

"That's not music," said Winona, giving him another ugly look.

Nellie closed up the organ. "I'd like it better than this."

"Thomas hates the guitar," said David. "He doesn't think guitar is quality."

Nellie said with sudden anger, "I'm not Thomas." She twirled around on the stool. "Do you make up songs with your guitar? I hear Amy Lee making up songs in the kitchen. It seems to do her a lot of good."

Winona didn't like being compared with Amy Lee. "Darkies are all like that," she said crossly.

David was not happy with the way things were going, nor with the high note which had leaped into Nellie's voice and the two deep lines which sprang up between her eyebrows and would not fade. "You could make up songs at the organ," he suggested.

"I don't want to do that. Miss Rickert, do you think you could teach me to play the guitar?"

"Could what?" The girl looked terrified.

"I could come to the village. Or meet you where David works."

Winona shot a look at David, begging him to get her out of this. "I'm not really good on it—just a little strumming I picked up from my brothers. And you wouldn't like it, Mrs. Allen. It's really not your kind of music. . . ."

Thomas wouldn't like it; David was sure of that. As if she read his mind, Nellie said, "It would do me good to get out of the house. This house has . . . memories."

"I don't even own a good guitar!" cried Winona. "And the strings will cut your fingers!"

Nellie gave her sudden, high laugh. "Believe me," she said, "cuts on on my fingers would be the least of my worries! The very least!"

Again Winona looked to David for help. Then she crossed to Nellie and said forlornly, "You have to get hard skin on the ends of your fingers. Like—like this." She held out her own hands with their horny fingertips. Nellie rubbed the calluses.

"I can see that would be an advantage," she said softly.

"And later on," said David, not knowing exactly why he felt ashamed, "later on, Nellie, I'll make you your own guitar. I always wondered if I could."

"Winona was right about the fingers." It was the end of the first lesson and Nellie looked ruefully at the deep red lines cut in the fingertips on her left hand. "That hurts."

Winona had just left the workshop, worried she would be late for work and have her pay docked. She was also very angry with David and had rushed out without answering his question about tonight.

"You didn't sound too bad for the first time." David went on tapping the chisel and taking away the slivers of wood which lay between him and the face of Moses. The head was going badly and he had misjudged the grain. The chatter of the two women had irritated him. It no longer seemed worthwhile to annoy Thomas by involving his precious Nellie with how the other half lived. His earlier, fleeting thought that he might even make love to her now seemed to him insane. He could not remember a woman he had ever found less attractive.

Nor were things good with Winona, who only the night before had picked up his hand before it could slip inside her dress and bashed it furiously against a tree trunk. He could not remember being so surprised in his life. "What's wrong with you?" he'd asked her.

"Why don't you tell *me*?" she had spluttered. "You think you know so much!"

He said now to Nellie without much interest, "What did you learn today?"

"Not but three chords in an hour's time. I think it must be the key of C; Winona didn't know. I can tell when I get back to the organ."

He went on working in the hope that she would leave.

"The funny thing," said Nellie, "is that three chords turn out to be all you really need to sing most of the songs in the world. The bare necessity." She sucked her fingers like a little girl. "The way these feel, I may settle for knowing three chords."

There was no help for it; she wanted to stay and talk. David put the chisel down and found her a bottle of turpentine and a clean rag. "Try this."

She made a face at the smell but rubbed the oil into the long dents in her skin.

"You really like Winona?"

"She's all right."

She handed him the turpentine. Watching his face closely, she said, "I think men don't have to like women at all. There can be a thousand other reasons."

"One's enough," said David shortly.

"Somebody ought to tell the women," said Nellie. "Well ahead of time." He didn't like the tone of self-pity nor the slump which came over her the minute she sat on the bench.

"You ought to hold your head up," he growled. "You'll get a wrinkled neck."

She straightened somewhat. He didn't know how it was possible for anyone to sit erect and still look wilted, but Nellie did. "Why don't you and Thomas get along?" she said, elaborately casual.

He tapped the chisel several times and discarded a series of answers. "Look, he's your husband," he finally began.

"I made my bed and I can lie in it?" Nellie began to laugh, but not with amusement.

"I don't want to talk about Thomas," he said. He concentrated on his work. "You going to stop by and see Mama?" he said hopefully. "And Aunt Rosa?"

Nellie began to wander around, which made him nervous. "You're not going to marry a girl like Winona Rickert?" David said he wasn't going to marry anybody. Out of the corner of his eye he saw she had picked up one of his chain carvings: the snake that was eating the weasel that was eating the rabbit. Hastily she put it down. "Do you . . . well . . . do you kiss Winona?"

She won't even ask what she means, he thought grumpily. He said, "Not if I can help it. She uses snuff." He enjoyed Nellie's shudder.

Nellie had lifted her bruised fingers to her own lips and explored them. She could not think what else to ask him. Her mouth was as full of questions as her nostrils were filled with pine oil. There was the steady thump of his tools against the wood, regular and easy. Easy, she thought. He seldom struck hard, and yet the cut was clean.

"Thomas is going to Boston next week," she said.

David shrugged.

She said, "Your father has another report that Esther's been seen there."

He had learned not to hope. "There've been a hundred such reports. Men all over the North have got rich off Father's guilty conscience."

"Why don't you go with Thomas?"

"No point to it."

"You never know. This might be the time it was true. Anyway, you and Thomas might enjoy the trip. You could talk to each other."

David said that would be a novelty.

The whining note was back in her voice. "David, you could talk to him."

He frowned at her and said flatly, "What about?" She would not look at him. He barked, "Don't slump like that!"

Nellie jerked up quickly and in the sudden shift of her dress he saw below the collar a bruise low on her throat, like a dog bite. Her hand leaped to adjust the neckline when she felt his stare. Then she looked quickly away and, almost involuntarily, the hand fell to a spot near her waist and pressed. Quickly she took it back and said nervously. "These fingers still hurt, even with that turpentine."

David put the chisel and mallet down. "Nellie?"

She said rapidly, "I guess they'll toughen up. I couldn't stand to work all the time in that smell. Don't let me bother you, David. Just keep on working."

With an effort, he turned back to the emerging wooden form. Maybe the jaw was turning out too sharp, more harsh than firm. "I don't mind the smell," he said.

She concentrated on her fingertips. "I hope I can learn enough to make up some songs. Isn't that stupid? I don't know the first thing about making up songs."

David said carefully, "I guess that would be bringing something together, the tune and the words. In the end you'd have something bigger, something new from that combination. Carving, now—that's more a process of taking things away. It suits me better." He rubbed at the wooden jaw; yes, it was too sharp. It had a mean cast to it. It was the face Moses turned on Pharaoh after the gentle arguments had passed and the demonstrations of magic, and there was nothing to say but *"Let my people go."* It was the face he wore when he threw the Commandments down. It was not the awed countenance turned to the burning bush.

"But you make something new," said Nellie. "You find the face that's inside it."

He shook his head. "I don't start out thinking there's some face inside. I start out tearing up the wood. Maybe in the end I can destroy enough wood to drive the rest of it into the shape of a head."

"Destroy?" Nellie sounded dismayed. He waited for her to say something else. She said, "You don't strike hard."

David could not see what that had to do with anything. He tried again. "I can't make things in clay first, though it might help. You'd see better what you wanted to do. But the clay—that would be like putting material together, joining things. I need to cut it out."

Her back had straightened. "I don't think you're that way at all. I think you're more gentle than that!"

He lifted the head and began to point out places where his chisel had been gouging. "You learn—the hard way—just to cut shapes. Not the holes or hollows or indents you'll need at the end. The shape you can always make smaller when you must, but you can never fill in the hollow where you bit too deep." His eyes met hers. "Bit too deep," he repeated, and waited for some reaction.

Nellie reached out blindly, encountered Winona's guitar and grabbed it to her like an infant. Biting her lips, she played the three weak chords, fretting hard with her sore fingers. "How does that sound?"

"Not very good."

"When my fingers get hard, I can play louder." She began to hum one of the songs Winona had been singing. Her voice was reedy and thin, like the rest of her.

David took a deep breath, "Nellie, is something wrong?"

"Some compliment to my singing," she said with a nervous laugh.

"You and Thomas," he persisted, "Is something wrong?"

She worked very hard with the three chords. "It takes time, like you said."

Finally he saw he would have to ask her straight out. "Nellie, does he hurt you?"

She put the guitar down and walked away from him, down the long room between the garish statues under their colored wax. "There's lots I don't know," she told the wooden figures.

David spoke louder. "You know whether he hurts you or not."

"I don't have anything to compare with. I don't know whether it's supposed to be like that or not."

He had begun to feel awkward. He decided to come at it another way. "The bruise on your face. Did you really get it falling on your own banister?"

"That's not so bad," she said, and touched it quickly.

She was at the far end of the room. Now she began to wander back along the aisle between the benches and the carvings. Now and again she ran her fingers into an eye socket or around a shoulder. "These are really very good," she said, "but I don't understand the wax."

"Those are teeth marks, Nellie. On your neck. I saw the marks."

She threw herself onto a bench. "Yes. He hurts me."

David stood by her and looked down at her bent head. "Why? Do you fight him?"

"He hurt me before I even thought of fighting him. Now I don't think of it."

He could not see why she would tolerate it. He caught her shoulders and made her stand directly in front of him. She was nearly as tall as he. "Maybe you like it that way, being hurt. Is that it? Is it a good hurt?"

He saw the tears gathering. "No, oh, no," she said huskily. "I'd rather be dead."

He looked past her shoulder. "Then why?"

She jerked loose and began to cry with a shrill sound. "You tell me why! Is it that crazy streak in your family? Is it the same thing that makes your Aunt Rosa climb out on the roof in her nightgown? And made your sister drown herself in the river?"

"Esther's not dead," he said absently.

"You tell me then. You tell me why!"

He thought she meant about Rosa. "She's always smelling smoke. She can't even walk except when she thinks the house is on fire, which is every week or two."

"Do you hit Winona? Is it always this way? Was Esther full of bruises? Explain it to me!" Her white face was pinched and ugly.

David pulled her against him and held her, but gently, as if she had been a younger sister. "It's not always like that," he said. "Hush. I promise you it's not." He thought: They'll hear her crying all the way to the house. He muffled her face against his shoulder, pressing her head there with one hand. "Don't cry, Nellie."

Now it was easy to see the teeth marks, low where her neck curved into the shoulder. They were evenly spaced and dark in color; one was deeeper and had bled. I'll always remember he has one upper tooth longer than the others. I'll knock the damn thing out.

He rested his cheek against her hair. It tickled his nose. The bruises were so near his eye they seemed to swell and throb, like a set of purple footprints. God, he thought, I'll kill him with a hammer.

"I don't know what to do," she moaned. "I don't know what to do."

David was hypnotized by the marks in her skin. They seemed to pull at him until he bent slowly and put his own mouth on the wound and kissed it, lightly. She trembled. "It's all right," he whispered. He kissed it again. "It's not always like that, Nellie."

Her crying was softer. "It's not," he repeated. "It's not."

His arms tightened around her. The bones felt fragile and near the surface. Well, he thought, she said it herself. Men don't have to like women. There can be a thousand other reasons.

Now he smoothed her forehead with one hand, where the creases of worry had been, kissed her wet eyelids and alongside the line of her nose. He was very careful to kiss her mouth lightly, a child's quick press of lips. He let his face rub hers before he kissed her again, a little longer.

He could feel her softening against him, beginning to sag a little in his arms. He could not stand to look at those teeth marks. He covered the bruise with one hand.

Ever so slightly Nellie rolled her head back against his palm. Her eyes were closed. He let the other hand touch her, tentatively, slide, pause, touch again. Then he laid his mouth precisely over the width of her first, dreamy smile.

Chapter

❦ 22 ❧

It was sam, not Thomas, who made the trip to Boston.
They took him to a theater where a dark-haired woman was appearing in a sad play about the beaten South. She was no actress and she was no Esther.

He stayed in Boston two days, recuperating from the illness of hope and convalescing again to the point where he could believe his daughter dead in the river and not a year older than the fifteen she was when she put her foot into the current.

Then, wearily, he started the trip home, He stopped in Norfolk long enough to buy presents for the family: silk fabric for Mildred, some fine steel knives for David, carpet runners for the stairs in Thomas and Nellie's house. Rosa was a problem. Finally he bought her a spyglass which pulled out to a grotesque length and magnified everything in sight.

Mildred made him deliver that gift himself because, she said, "I never would be able to explain why you bought such a thing."

Sam thought he made it perfectly clear to Rosa when he stood by her bed and pushed the brass tube into her hands. "It's time you got over those notions about the birds," he said firmly. "I want you to look out your window with this thing. I want you to watch them sing. If you could begin by getting over that, it would be a step forward."

"I'm in bed," said Rosa, meaning it was unlikely she would be stepping anywhere.

"Just train it out the window. Look in that red maple and the thicket down the hill."

"It stinks," said Rosa, taking her damp hands off the brass and wiping them on the sheets.

As soon as he had stamped out of the room to tell Mildred it was hopeless to try to help that woman, *hopeless*, Rosa pulled the spyglass out to its full length and began to examine the world. It took her no time at all to confirm her terrible opinion of birds. Filthy things, their nests foul, their nestlings forever strangling on wiggling bugs or caterpillars oozing some thick liquid. And the squirrels, rat-faced and cruel, were worse, with their jerky tails and greedy paws and fleas.

Propped against mounds of feather pillows, Rosa turned the spyglass in her hands. When she had been holding it for a while, her sweaty hands took on the smell of brass. Sometimes she would lie with empty fingers spread over her nose until the sharp odor itself seemed to pierce the darkness and open up vistas of bruised hills, church spires, clumps of daisies. She tried watching the stars at night, but they seemed to be always dancing out of the glass circle. She would have the evening star fixed firmly in the round view and it would take a sudden fiery leap and be gone. The realization that the sky was in such agitated motion all the time made Rosa uneasy.

So soon she watched only horses or men, or the Allen car when Thomas drove it by the house and turned off the mill road. Or she would seek fragments of David moving behind the lattice walls of his workshop. In some places the tarpaper had tattered and fallen down; in others he had torn off great strips to let in whatever summer breeze might wander by, so she only saw a piece of him now and then—a scrap of shirt, a flicker of what might be his head or a moving hand.

She had the glass up, trying to piece him together one such afternoon. There he was—pink the face and blue the shirt. Now the pink lowered . . . He had what? He had laid his ear on the earth? A long green color swam into her lens. It had a reddish topping; who did Rosa know with reddish hair? The blue and the green were against each other. What in the world were they . . . ?

Rosa closed the spyglass and wiped its lens on her pillowcase. The bedroom was warm, perhaps already burning. She heaved herself up to look fearfully into its corners, hung panting from the edge to search under the bed, then dragged her red face back.

She put the glass out of sight among the pillows and drank some water. Two swallows spilled out of her mouth and dropped in a cool splash between her ample breasts and stayed there, dammed into an oval pool. When she probed with a finger, the edges broke and the cool ran down the crease and was blotted up by her gown.

She rubbed at that spot. Surely, with all her other children, she had never grown so large as she was now, too swollen to walk. This child had been so slow to form that it seemed to her the baby created each unborn feature by defacing something of the surrounding shell. In its lazy greed for perfection, the child had slowly devoured her while it pressed against her swelling body; and now she could only lie helpless until it should be satisfied, and leave off sucking her nature into its nature.

By now, she thought, the child was laid down in her like a second skeleton. Its legs were thrust out of her womb and spread inside her own legs. Its broad head had risen high into her throat. The two infant arms were thrust inside her own and the stringy fingers reached down beyond her dimpled elbows.

Rosa began to turn over in the groaning bed; but oh! how the baby punished her for sudden movement! It roared in her belly like a lion. Or it would kick down harder and bloat her legs, and take one scrawny hand and squeeze her heart.

Never a child like this! Sometimes Rosa almost felt she had been waiting its birth for years and still it curled there in the dark, unwilling.

Yet she knew this was only a fancy. The baby would be coming soon now. Already it was in her dreams at night, a large baby with an angry face.

She took the spyglass out again and rolled it down her breasts like a rolling pin on a layer of dough. How proud Silas would be, when he came home at last from his long sea voyage to see his son, when he came home from the cool, wet sea. He had given her this glass so she would see him coming from a long way off. She put it to her eye, smiling.

Then she cried out and drew back, for again she had put the wrong end to her eye so that all she could see was made shrunken and indistinct. She had done this many times, and it always shriveled her eye to the size of a pea. She would have to wait while it pulsated and ached and finally blossomed out again into its socket.

Rosa kept both her eyes closed but turned the glass carefully around and laid it against the other lid, knowing it was somehow tied to Silas in such a way that if she took thought, it would make a tunnel across the earth, through which she could see to where he was. She did not even have to open her eye. First there was dark, and then whorls of light and a set of scarlet cogwheels turning and meshing and fading; but then at last she could see the swelling ocean, and farther off a silver fish, going in gentle leaps away, away.

David knocked lightly on the door. He hoped Rosa was sleeping so he could tiptoe away. In a day or so, he knew, she would forget having sent for him. Today she had jangled her bell at the entire household, insisting she needed to see David now, right now.

"Come in!" called Rosa.

He took a deep breath, postponing as long as possible the stale sweetness that hung in her room, where talcum floated on the sunbeams instead of dust. Then he went in.

"Who's that?" called Rosa, peering out from the hollow she had made in the bed and pillows.

Between visits David always forgot how grotesquely fat she was. The feather mattress puffed out around her like an overflow from her body. Her mouth seemed more and more lost in the spreading face and ascending chin levels; and he would not have been surprised if someday it closed up entirely like a puckered navel.

"It's David. They say you want to see me."

Rosa told him to sit down. Then, very deliberately, she drew the brass telescope from under her pillow and trained it on him in reverse, making him smaller and more manageable; although she gasped in pain when her eye contracted and fell down loose in her head.

"What is it, Rosa?" he said, and moving toward her he seemed to be tumbling through the lens and into her eye. Rosa squeaked. The glass flew over her head into a nest of pillows.

"Don't do that!" she whined. "Don't come inside."

Shrugging, David turned to go.

"Well, sit down," she bellowed to his back. He hesitated, then carried a chair beside the bed. They sat there for five minutes in silence.

A time or two he asked how she was feeling and once he mentioned the hot and humid weather. Rosa would say nothing. He took out a pocket knife and began to clean his fingernails.

Her sudden question made him jump. "What do you do in your little house out there?"

"Make things."

"I see smoke."

"In the winter. I have a stove."

"I watch you," Rosa said.

He nodded. Then he gave her a thoughtful look. "With your spyglass?"

"Get me some water."

He poured a tumbler of water out of the china pitcher but she barely wet her tongue. Carefully she poured a small amount down the neck of her nightgown. "That feels good," she explained.

"I'm sure it does. You say you watch me?"

"I hate birds," she said firmly.

David rescued her spyglass from among the pillows and trained it absently on the window, then on his lattice house down the hill.

"Aren't they just awful?" said Rosa.

"Um," he said, frowning.

"I like your friends."

His eyebrows sprang up. "What friends?"

"The ones standing out there in a row. I like the woman that got her face caught in a door."

"I see," he said, examining the line of statues through the glass. Yes, they were very clear. You could pick up every feature. And where the tarpaper was torn off the inside walls—

"Give it back now, before it gets to smell of your sweat instead of mine."

He tucked it under her pillow. "Is this what you wanted to see me about?" he began cautiously. "Watching me with your spyglass?"

"The woman out there with the long face, yes," she said.

Now he was thoroughly confused. "Why don't you tell me about it?"

Rosa spread her pudgy hands on the counterpane and gave him

a sunny smile. "I want you to make my tombstone in your little house."

He blinked before he returned the smile. "All right, Aunt Rosa. When the time comes, I'll make it."

"Now," she said. "Make it now. Terrible water you poured me." She took up a corner of the coverlet on a forefinger and swabbed out her mouth.

"You won't be needing a tombstone for a long time."

Her eyes flashed with sudden anger. "You think I'm a fool? You think you can throw anything together and stick it up over my grave when I'm not there to argue? I want it now."

He tried to make his voice soothing. "You won't be needing that for years. We can talk about it. I promise to make it exactly as you say."

"You're just like Silas. 'I promise, I promise' " She sulked. "Last night I told him, 'Promise me no more promises.' It hurt his feelings."

"Yes, I imagine it did. But I'm sure he's over that by now."

"I want it now," she said loudly, "because I'm not going to live through this baby."

"Don't say such things. You'll be coming to my funeral."

"Well, if you can't do one little thing for me, I swear I won't even go. They can bury you without me, David Allen; and I won't let Silas come either!"

David looked around uneasily but he had closed the door behind him and he knew his mother could not hear Rosa's voice growing sharper. "If it will make you feel any better, go ahead and tell me now what you want for a tombstone. Then you can forget about it," he said.

"No, I'll never live through this baby." She rolled her head from side to side. "I dreamed it. Mildred is there when it happens. I die the day after the birth. I tell you, I dreamed it." Rosa had closed her eyes to see the dream better; now she raised the lids and said in a loud, and slightly irritated, voice, "The baby lives. It's a very strong baby, you know."

"It takes after you and Silas," said David. "Drink some more water, Rosa."

He handed her a second glass and, without looking, she tossed its contents over the side of the bed and into the rug. "I'll show you exactly what I want," she said. She took the spyglass out and waved it in the air. "I've drawn exactly what I want and every day I'll watch you work. I'll look at you hammering away."

Perhaps if he gave in she would soon forget it. "It does take a long time to make a really good stone, I suppose. All right, I'll start on it, if that will make you feel better. But I promise you it won't be needed for years and years."

"Promises!" she grunted. She laughed aloud and whispered something under the covers to Silas.

"In the drawer of that table," she said to David then, through the sheet. It was so muffled he had to make her say it again before he understood. Then she pulled the sheet over her face and tucked the edges carefully around her skull and practiced at being dead.

He found the folded paper in the drawer. It was covered with drawings, some scratched over, some blacked out, one of them encircled and repeated on a larger scale on the reverse side. At sight of it, David whistled and shot a look toward Rosa, but she seemed to be sleeping in her temporary shroud.

"I've got it," he said. The corpse convulsed with giggles.

The drawing was so involved that it would require something the size of the Egyptian Sphinx to execute it properly. Grapevines curled around the two columns flanking the main headstone, and at least a dozen bunches of grapes were visible, some of them square in shape. These grew toward an arch with a cherub and a lamb and over these a sullen-looking dove which was carrying something in its mouth. Peace, perhaps, or a worm. Between the front columns the central stone had a border of leaves and flowers like Solomon's trumpets, and scattered among the lettered text tiny daisies had been drawn to dot the *i*'s or close the lines. The inscription read: ROSA MACKEY BENNETT. *Beloved Consort of Captain Silas Damascus Bennet, 1864-19——. Her Price Was Above Rubies, Pearls, and Other Gems and Jewels. Gone to Her Heavenly Home but Not Forgotten, After a Short Illness While Her Husband Was in Foreign Seas, and Her Child an Infant. Cut Down like a Flower*—at this point a little flower, something like a violet, was inserted intact for clarity—*To Bloom More Sweetly in a Sweeter Place. Rest in Peace Forever. In Jesus' Name, Amen.*

Beneath this message were an open Bible, a cross, and something David took at first to be a fried egg. No, a sunrise, surely. Or maybe a sunset?

"Rosa!" he breathed through his widening smile. "Rosa, I wouldn't have guessed you had it in you!"

She popped out from under the covers. "I started to say a helpless infant, but this one won't be helpless. You think that's all right?"

"I think that's fine," he chuckled. "I never knew Uncle Silas had Damascus for a middle name."

"He doesn't. I put that in for Mildred's sake. You know how she likes the Epistles."

Now David laughed aloud. "Rosa, I never was asked to do anything this important in all my life! I just hope I can be worthy."

She beamed. "I thought you'd like it."

"It's beautiful," David folded the paper carefully and put it inside the sweatband of his hat. First problem would be stone itself, and then tools. He would need special tools. He would need knowledge and practice. He had never worked with stone. He gave a laugh of pure delight. "Aunt Rosa, I am going to dedicate myself to this thing. I want you to know it."

"Sweet boy," she said coyly.

"They're always wanting me to be dedicated to something. And all this time, I've been waiting for you to finish drawing on this piece of paper and call me in."

David marched downstairs, still chuckling, and told his astonished mother he was taking a horse; he would be in Stoneville for the next three weeks; he had business there.

Mildred ran after him toward the barn. "What are you going to do in Stoneville?" she called when she had got her breath.

"Learn to make letters!" he yelled merrily. He waved toward the the second-story windows in case Rosa had her spyglass to her eye to watch him ride down the road with her tombstone in his hat.

He rode along the Stoneville route, seeing the monument rise in his mind. It would be half the height of the church. By now Mildred must be upstairs asking Rosa questions and Rosa was likely saying, "David who?" And as for this afternoon, let Nellie and Winona amuse each other and sing their songs alone about somebody being gone ten thousand miles!

The horse raced and he opened his mouth to let the wind fly into him. Maybe Esther had felt this laughing way the night she rode out of Greeenway, at least for a little while.

He reined in suddenly. He had forgotten to ask Rosa about the third symbol at the bottom of the inscription. Was it a sunrise or a sunset?

Never mind, he thought, hurrying the horse along. From this minute on, I say it's a sunrise, and a sunrise it will be. Poetic license, I think it's called.

It was nothing but a tarpaper shack set low in a clutter of gravestones, boulders, rocks, stones, pebbles.

As David crossed the yard, stopping sometimes to test his palm against the surface of a stone, he could hear thuds and talk coming from behind it. He called out, then walked through a tangled patch of vetch and blackberry briers until he came upon the man working.

He was half lying in the weeds, pounding at a base slab and talking with the empty air. The back of his blue shirt was wet and so was the glistening bald head. A pair of bulbous ears were almost as red as small handfuls of bristly hair which grew just above them.

Without turning or slowing his work, the man called out, "Who is it?"

David rounded the low stone and stood looking at the prone workman. "I'm David Allen."

"What's that make me?"

David said coolly, "Somebody else, I guess."

The man blew out a whole wad of tobacco with an explosive noise and raised up on one elbow. "What kind of marker you want?" He waved his arm. "See anything in the yard you like?"

"No." He took Rosa's paper out of his hatband and, squatting, passed it to the stonecutter. "I want one like this and I want to make it myself."

The man stared at the drawing, then fell back laughing into the nettles and took his hammer and pounded the red clay beside him. "Oh, the kidneys of Jesus!" he howled several times. He rolled onto his stomach and beat the ground until it gave up small puffs of rusty powder, and finally fell flat on his back and looked up into the clouds for a few last spasms and wheezes. Still squatting, David watched the laughter ebb.

The man said to the sky, "Where you from?"

"Greenway."

"You ain't one of them rich Allens? Cotton-mill rich?"

"No," he lied. He had nothing to do with the cotton mill. Thomas was welcome to it all.

The stonecutter spread out Rosa's paper on his chest and raised it between his eyes and the summer glare and chuckled. "Damnedest thing I ever saw."

"She drew it herself."

He handed the paper back. "By the time that thing could be finished, the lady's corpse wouldn't be any bigger than a thimbleful of dust."

"She's not dead yet," David said. "She'll live a good ten years."

"Wouldn't be long enough if you worked on it everyday," grunted the stonecutter. He laughed one more time and wiped his mouth with a dusty hand. "You come twenty miles to show me this thing?"

"All I want is for you to teach me how to make tombstones. Then I'll make this one."

He spat. "I ought to laugh some more, but—come to think of it— that's right insultin'. You want to learn my life's trade in a day or so. Already I get all the business out of Greenway. You take that from me and it won't be with my help."

David decided to sit down on the hard clay. It was hard to talk to a man who wouldn't do any more than lie there on his back. "Listen, I don't want to make tombstones for a living. I just want to make this thing for my aunt. I've got the ten years to spare."

"At your age, everybody thinks so," growled the stonecutter.

David went doggedly on. "And I'm already a woodcarver, so I thought I might learn fast. As an apprentice. You could hire me as a helper."

"Don't need no helper."

"Then let me watch. Just let me watch you working."

The redheaded man made a face. "I *thought* you was one of them rich Allens. Who else can spare time for watching? You just roll that platform over here to me."

He pointed to a flat slab of wood, maybe a yard square, mounted on large metal wheels. David rolled it into reach; the stonecutter lined it up carefully behind him, lifted himself to a sitting position with his arms, and dragged his body upon it. Last of all he picked up each leg with his hands and laid it on the platform and pulled himself farther back.

When David finally understood, he tried to help with the second crippled leg. Barely interrupting his smooth movements, the man flipped a hard fist into the side of David's neck.

"Don't you ever help me," he said, gritting his teeth.

"No, sir."

Sitting now, the stonecutter turned the back wheels with his hands and rolled himself down a well-rutted path to the back door of the tarpaper shack. The wheels set up a terrible screaming.

"You want some whiskey?" He rolled into the shack and out of sight. David followed.

There were two rooms inside, one for cooking and one for sleeping. The cart had worn deep tracks in the earthen floor to record every act of his daily living—two lines to the fireplace and its iron grate on which stew was bubbling, from there a small road to a table with legs sawed off so it only sat a foot high. Then the grooves marked the route through the open doorway to a low bed.

Both rooms were hot and dim. Food in tins and covered jars was stored on low shelves and atop circular tables made of barrels sawed in half and upended. In double folds, clothes were hung from a row of nails not three feet from the dirt floor. Here and there a sleeve trailed from the careful folding and lay emptied out on the earth.

David was embarrassed. He did not know what to say about the neat arrangement of the stonecutter's possessions. Fumbling, he said, "I didn't see any well outside."

"There's a creek back of the house. I drink it and wash in it." He got two cups off a shelf and filled them from a jug which was swinging from a rope. The whiskey tasted so bad David wondered if he might have been washing in it too.

"How old are you?"

"Eighteen."

"How come you're not in the Greenway mill?"

"Don't like it."

"You don't do *nothing?*"

David thought about it. "I guess not."

"Must be nice. Who's Rosa Bennett?"

"My mother's sister."

The stonecutter reached out into the air and clicked his fingers. Awkwardly David found the paper and handed it to him. The man laid it on one of the shelves, weighted a rock at one corner and began to run his finger down the lettering. "She lives ten years, that infant surviving her won't be much of an infant."

"She has no children."

He raised a ragged red eyebrow. "And what does her husband say? This is a costly monument."

"He was killed when the mill burned eight years ago."

The stonecutter said he remembered that, remembered the name now, and he'd done the stones for the old woman and her granddaughter too. With much squeaking of the wheels, he rolled back to the jug for another drink and left it swinging, bump-bump, against the wall. He took a big swallow, sloshed it around and forced it between the cracks in his teeth, and spit it into the dirt floor. "Do that once a day," he announced, "and your teeth won't rot."

"Why don't you just swallow the whiskey down?"

The stonecutter looked at David as if he were crazy. "What? And move all that rot into your belly? Boy, you sure don't know nothing."

"I'm willing to learn."

"Drink your whiskey. My name's Bungo. Bungo Mayfield."

David debated whether he should try rinsing his mouth out once, just to prove he was a willing student. He decided against it.

Bungo consulted the paper again. "This husband—was he ever a sailor?"

"Never."

"Not even for three days have I ever had a helper. Not even for one job. First thing I knew, people would say I had got helpless. There'd be ladies out here with cakes and chicken pies." He curled his lip, drank deeply.

"I could keep them away," said David breathlessly.

"Even if you learned everything I knew in three days—hah!—I wouldn't like it. I don't like people talking and hanging round."

"I could try not to ask much."

"Hah!" said Bungo again.

"I'd do other things. Fetch water. I could cut some wood for the winter. Go to the store for you." He braced himself in case Bungo should swing his hard fist again. "I could lift things."

David was ready to block the fist but not to dodge the cup half full of whiskey which flew through the air and whacked the bridge of his nose. Only a little went into his eyes. He wiped his chin on a sleeve.

"You learn slow. Already I can tell that," grunted Bungo.

David picked the cup off the floor and set it halfway between them while he thought over what to say. "A waste of whiskey," he finally ventured. He considered adding, "Good whiskey," but the lie was too much for him.

Grinning, Bungo took the cup and poured himself some more. "The boy does hold hisself in," he remarked to the swinging jug. "Don't know what to think of that." He lay propped on an elbow on his cart, his back still turned to David, while he tapped a woodpecker noise on the jug with one fingernail. "You got money?"

"No," said David. "I never thought of that."

"Never thought of it," sighed Bungo Mayfield. He turned to stare at him. "How was you going to live?"

"I thought"—here David could not help the laughter that bubbled out of him—"I thought you might pay me a wage while I was helping you out and learning."

Bungo did not laugh. "Does a farmer pay the cutworms? Could you get any money?"

David ran them through his mind: Mama, Father, Thomas? Nellie? He said, "I doubt it."

Now Bungo lay back, closed his eyes and put his forearm across them, thinking. "Here it is, then, David Allen," he muttered under the dirty arm. "You stay here three days. Right here. Live here. See how much you learn. You live my life a little bit, three days' worth, in this house. Put your fingers on the handle where my fingers go. We'll soon see how you like it." He took the arm down and gave David a fierce look.

David was already flicking his glance around the two small rooms built for a prone man, which seemed to him artificially crushed. Even the top of his head felt thick with pressure. It's like a coffin in here, he thought. He said, "Fine. Thank you, Mr. Mayfield."

"Fine, is it?" Bungo put his cup into a tin bucket in the corner. "Sleep with me in my bed. Next to the wall. I got to get in last. You can see I got to work in from the edge."

David said he could see that.

"Eat my stew. Wash in my creek." The man had begun to enjoy himself. "Meet the mourners. I sure want to see you meet some mourners."

"When do I start?"

"It's still daylight, ain't it?" Bungo took hold of the rear wheels and moved himself suddenly, running across the toe of David's shoe. "Move!" he ordered as he rolled by. David drew back, bent his head at the low door and followed him into the sunlight. The back of his neck was cramped.

Bungo rolled around on the hard-packed earth, examining slabs of stone, some with rounded corners, some with cracks and unfinished designs, one completely ready for BERTHA KANE, 1872–1906, *Home in Jesus.*

"The Kanes," Bungo grunted, "decided not to pay for it. Waste of money, with Mama off in Heaven getting her every wish. Oh, you're going to like meeting the mourners. Here. This one." He leaned sideways off the platform and slapped a hand on something David could not see for the tall weeds. Before he could get there, Bungo bent at the waist and heaved a gray rock, cut in a long rectangle, onto his chest. "Limestone. From up in the mountains." He glowered at David. "Well, here! Take it! I can't roll this thing with both hands busy!"

David broke his spine loose from everything else in his body lifting the stone off Bungo's chest. He staggered along behind the rolling cart, half dragging it at ankle height. When Bungo stopped, he let it go with a gasp of relief and remained folded over, hands flapping, afraid to try straightening his back again.

Bungo was unrolling a long burlap in which mallets and chisels rested in ragged pockets. "Take your choice," said Bungo, and began, without another word, to drive his own chisel along the same stone he had been cutting when David arrived.

David eased himself carefully to the ground beside him. He looked over the tools. "Just start right in?"

"Cut some shape. A head. A bird. Rabbit. Anything."

David took up the mallet and examined the different edges on the roll of chisels. "You're not going to show me anything?"

"I'm going to show you what you did wrong."

Now David rolled his chunk of limestone to look at it on all sides, swallowing down the grunts of effort. He shot a look once at Bungo's powerful shoulders, which bloomed forth above his wasted hips and legs like a deformity. Finally he stood the stone upright, thinking suddenly of Rosa's dove—not flying, as she had drawn it, but tall and still with the wings laid against the body and the head up and turned slightly to one side. He reached at last for a flat chisel and put it to one of the upper corners, intending to cut it out of his way. He came down with the heavy hammer in the usual swooping motion he used for wood.

Nothing at all happened.

He banged harder. Again he struck, this time moving the chisel closer to the edge of the stone. Then he leaned his face into it closely and pounded with all his strength; and in front of the chisel a sand grain's worth of material was crushed into powder, and a fragment flew up into his eye.

He sat, fuming, pulling on the eyelid with his finger until he had washed it away. The damn thing hurt. All Bungo said, without turning, was, "Don't need me to tell you what was wrong with that, do you?"

"No," he snapped. Bungo made little hee-hee whispers of amusement under his breath.

Again David began to work on the corner, surprised to find that the stone did not fly off into chips as he had supposed, but barely crushed in front of his tool. He felt like a sparrow eroding a mountain with one wing. Once Bungo reached over and took the flat chisel out of his hand and gave him a similar tool which came to a point. Although it gave quicker results, David complained at the furrows it left.

"Smooth later. With the flat ones and the toothed ones," Bungo said.

Now it seemed easier and the corner began to round off and move in. At first he tried holding the pointed chisel straight; it made a little dent. Then he turned it at an angle so it would travel along the stone with his repeated blows, leaving a curved track like one of Bungo's wheels. Watching the line form, he suddenly missed the end of the tool and brought the heavy mallet down on the base of his forefinger. "*Damn!*" he yelled with all his power. "Oh, damn! God! Damn!" He threw the tools to the ground and put his knuckle into his mouth.

He saw that Bungo was calmly shaking his head. "Ain't got much variety," Bungo said. "You'll need a lot wider cussing than that, even for just three days." He had rolled himself off the cart onto the hard ground and shoved it beyond him, out of the way. Now he turned halfway and rested one hand on the ground. "You break it?"

"To splinters," said David grimly.

"Short lesson." Unconcerned, Bungo turned back and began his even tapping. David thought what a juicy noise it would make if he drove the mallet into the bald top of that head, between the bristly growths of red hair. He sat back on his heels and took a lot of deep breaths.

Then he began again to bang the point at the edge of the limestone block and watch its slow and ragged rounding. Bungo started to whistle. There was no tune to it, merely a random rising and descending of the scale. It flowed out of his mouth in a series of peaks and valleys.

The noise was so piercing David half expected his hand to be carried off on it and chop a row of uneven mountains across the block. He set his jaw and fixed his eye on two inches of the surface under his tool. After a while he stopped hearing the whistle and discovered that at a certain angle the stone seemed more inclined to give under his blows, as if long ago it had been laid down in a pattern too small to see or understand. Several light and even blows seemed to work as well as one mighty pounding.

He saw, too, that the stone was not entirely gray but had within it lighter flecks, some of them shiny. After a while he stopped and wandered off in the yard and came back with several small stones, which he scraped against the surface of his block. He knew Bungo was watching. He discarded the handful of stones in favor of a hard clod of orange clay, and with it he drew a rude outline of his dove and tried to mark on the top where the head would emerge. The result so depressed him that he scrubbed it out with his sleeve and elbow and redrew the whole bird much larger, so there would be less stone to carve away in order to reach its surface.

Now Bungo spoke. "A buzzard, huh?"

David said stiffly it was no buzzard.

Bungo returned to his work and David began to drive the point into another spot on the stone, not because he had finished with the first but in order to keep his spirits up. Dust from the rock made long streaks in the sweat on his arms. Several times the mallet glanced off and struck his left hand at almost exactly the same place. The skin from the base of his thumb to the first joint in the bruised forefinger turned dark red. In time the whole area went numb. Rosa, he thought, turn your telescope on me.

The afternoon wore on and the shadow made by the upturned stone grew longer and more rapidly than any progress he was making.

At last Bungo said, "Supper, I reckon."

David put his hands atop the stone and dropped his forehead on them. He would have put his entire sore left hand into his mouth if he could have got it crammed between his teeth.

"Put your tools away." Bungo pulled his platform to him, dragged his body upon it. When David had wiped the tools and slipped them into their pockets, he rolled up the burlap and tied it with a string. Bungo then stored it in an oilskin packet which he laid between his legs before rolling himself rapidly to the little house.

Now David set his teeth and began carefully to pull up to his feet. His legs were cramped from half straddling the stone as he sat. One hip felt as if it had been pulled loose from its twin. His back was aching. He thought gloomily of Bungo's narrow bed, and of having to lie carefully alongside the cripple lest in his sleep he might kick the wasted limbs. It would be hot in that airless room tonight. He walked slowly into the house. Bungo was already dipping stew into a pair of bowls.

David took his and, flinching, sat on the floor. Experimentally he spread the surface of his back against the wall. He examined his twinges one by one. He saw Bungo getting two clean cups and said hastily, "No more whiskey for me."

Bungo said, "You never needed it more," and fixed him a cup anyway.

This time it tasted a little better. Between its warmth and the heat of the stew, David's taut body began to ease and feel more familiar. The food, mostly beef, potatoes and onions, was good. David emptied his bowl and turned it up to drink the last drop of liquid. Bungo ate noisily and between spoonfuls he sucked on his teeth.

"I been thinking," David began. "It's so hot tonight, I could just sleep out in the yard. And not crowd you."

"Suit yourself," said Bungo. He washed his dish in a pail of water, dried it on a rag and put it back on the shelf. David did the same.

"All right if I wash in the creek?"

"Straight out back. You can follow my tracks," said Bungo.

He was glad to get out of the room and its heavy smells of whiskey, food and sweat, and into one of summertime's long twilights. The grooves from Bungo's iron wheels were not hard to find. They led across the yard and downhill into what would have been a pleasant tunnel for a curious small boy. It was kept cut back by Bungo's pocket knife to a height of less than three feet. David finally got down on his hands and knees to match its size, after running head on into festoons of briers. Cursing his sore back, he inched through the tunnel and came out at last on a sandy edge where a creek, brown with its load of mud, flowed slowly toward the Katsewa River. He thought of putting a message into a bottle for the creek to carry: JUBE. COME AND SAVE ME.

David took off shirt and pants and stuck them in the water under a smooth rock to soak. His underwear and shoes he left on the bank. He waded in to the deepest point, which was halfway up his thighs. First he scrabbled his feet around to drive off fish or moccasins or crawdads or even sharp pebbles; then he sat slowly and gratefully in the cool water. "Oohhh," he groaned in pure pleasure. Some of the nails driven into his muscles began to dissolve. He let himself lie back so his feet could rise toward the surface. He felt them relax and float. He indulged himself in one more happy groan.

Then he reached for his clothes and began lazily to squeeze them out in the water. With the shirt he wiped off his face and hair. Above the water a dragonfly passed and lightning bugs began to appear against the far bank of honeysuckle. He put the clothes under the rock again, closed his eyes and gave himself up to the touch of the sliding water and the cooling, early-evening sky.

At last he stood, splashed water into his groin and buttocks to take out the last gritty sand, and splashed to the bank, where he put on his underwear and rolled up the wet clothes around his shoes.

Then he stopped and stared at the thick underbrush. The path back to Bungo's house was a problem. If he crawled, his damp skin would pick up more dirt than he had just washed off. He put the bundle of wet clothes over his face and plowed through, upright, collecting a new set of scratches.

There were no lights in Bungo Mayfield's house. A blanket had been thrown out over the tombstone Bertha Kane's family had never bought. David folded the blanket and spread it on the ground, and hung his wet clothes over Bertha's monument. He lay down, smothering his groans. Under the cool surface of his skin, the body seemed to be boiling. His left hand had begun to throb. He moved it here and there but his heart poured down the arm and into the hand and hung there, beating. He propped the hand up on the base of Bertha Kane's stone.

Before he had even fallen asleep, there was a loud thunderclap, a second, and a sheet of rain fell upon him in drops the size of fists. David grabbed up the blanket and bolted for the house and stood in the kitchen, surprised at the coolness of that floor under his bare feet. His head was ringing where he had struck it running through the open door. He waited in the dark for Bungo to speak to him. Nothing happened. David cleared his throat. "Bungo?" he called softly. "Bungo Mayfield?"

"Bad day all around," came a dry voice from the other room. "Come on in here."

"I could sleep in the kitchen," said David doubtfully.

"That floor wets up. Come on. Only crawl over me easy."

The man lay shapeless under a covering. There were no windows in the room and no moonlight, no reflection off a rain puddle, to help David see. He felt around uneasily with one hand until he had located Bungo's feet and legs, jerked quickly away. Then he crawled in from the bottom of the low bed and arranged himself like a rod facing the wall away from Bungo. His straight back began to hurt again.

In the dark Bungo's voice sounded lazy. "I bet you wonder a lot of things about me, David Allen."

David lay, barely breathing, and tried not to move. His nose was itching. He blew upward at it awkwardly, hoping he would not have to shift an arm to scratch it.

"I bet you wonder what crippled me."

Cautiously David said, "I did wonder that."

"And maybe how I go to the toilet?" Bungo's voice was very soft. "Maybe you even wonder about me and women. You wondering them things?"

He swallowed. "Yes." He heard the click of Bungo's teeth.

"Well, it ain't none of your damn business," Bungo snapped, and jerked at the bedclothes once and went to sleep.

Chapter
◄§ 23 §►

THE SECOND DAY WAS AGONY. It seemed to David every other tap of the mallet glanced aside and crashed into his sore hand. No matter how lightly he brought the hammer down, by the time it struck his bruises it carried the force of a dozen men.

When he first came into the stonecutter's yard, stiff but somewhat rested, he was shocked to see how little his stone had changed for all of yesterday's work. Had it rolled down some hillside and struck another rock it might have accidentally broken off—in one split second—that single corner he had so painstakingly eaten away the previous afternoon.

He separated his stiff legs to get the stone where he could reach it with—with comfort? David sneered. There was no such thing as comfort in this work. He looked at Bungo, who, without a word, unwrapped the long roll of tools and spread them within their mutual reach.

"You have enough to eat?"

Three hard-boiled eggs. "Yes," said David.

They set to work. It was still very early in the day. The patch of clover where David sat held onto the last remnants of dew. After ten minutes he was grateful for that one cool spot on his entire body. Sweat gathered under his arms and began to course down his sides

and soak into the seams of his shirt. Relentlessly the sun climbed
into the hard, blue sky. Soon he was wet all over. Where he absently
kept wiping one arm across the beaded forehead, sweat dried in a
salty skim that made the hairs prickle.

The second day, he groaned inwardly. And on the third, he
wondered, who's going to resurrect me?

Bungo, again, had dragged himself off his cart and was working
prone on the ground. Sometimes he lay on his stomach propped on
the left elbow, and managed to locate the chisel just so with the left
hand. Not one of his strokes seemed wasted. Sometimes Bungo
would lie on his back and stroke at the base from the bottom up, se-
lecting his spot carefully, placing the chisel, closing his eyes for the
blow in case dust should fly. Other times he would use those strong
arms to push his torso upward and sit on one side or the other and
drive downward against the stone.

Even with his eyes shut, Bungo never hit himself once. The base
of David's thumb had begun to bleed. He let it drip and clot, hit
it till it dripped again. Blood began to spatter on his working surface.
Then David let fly a whispered curse, reached for his shirt and tore
off a strip with his teeth to tie up the cut. It was hard to maneuver
the cloth over the thumb and anchor it finally around his wrist.
Using one hand and his teeth, he felt his nose would be tangled
in the bandage. Bungo watched him from the corners of his eyes,
but said nothing.

The hand was awkward now and the wrapped cloth made the tips
of his thumb and forefinger thump like an echo of his tools. David
set his teeth and went back to work.

After a while it had the quality of a bad dream. The pounding was
so monotonous. Bungo's tuneless whistle had no beginning and no
end. The climbing sun grew so hot there was no longer any question
of degree; it was an endless heat, without measure or alteration.
When he gave thought, David could smell himself. He stopped giving
thought.

Bungo's voice shocked him. He had not noticed the whistling had
stopped. "Time to eat," said Bungo.

David looked up and saw a small colored boy standing by with
a covered plate. "I buy from the boardinghouse three times a week.
It's the only way I can get bread," said Bungo. He pulled a knotted
rag out of his overall pocket and untied some coins. The boy accepted

two and carried the plate of warm biscuits inside the house, where the potatoes Bungo had set boiling in their skins were now soft and mushy. They ate bread and potatoes with their fingers, David using his wounded left hand for a plate.

"How's the buzzard coming?"

He was too tired to say again it was no buzzard. "I don't know," he said truthfully. "I forgot to look." In the course of the morning he had entirely forgotten the bird or even what he was doing pounding forever on this unyielding stone.

Bungo had himself another cup of whiskey, but this time he did not offer a drink to David. He had little to say. When his cup was nearly empty he leaned over, suddenly, and emptied the balance into the clumsy bandage on David's thumb. The whole hand caught fire.

"Don't want it to fester," Bungo said calmly, just as David had drawn back his good hand to beat him to death. David fell back into the kitchen wall and tried to blink away the tears of pain.

When the two went out again into the summer glare, Bungo tied a red kerchief over his bald head. The sight of that flapping cloth caused David to examine his own skin. It was red and tingling every place he could see. He was not willing to ask Bungo for anything to tie around his neck but as soon as the other man had set to work he poured the tools onto the ground and wound the dirty burlap over his collar. He thought he heard Bungo chuckle, but with the whistling it was hard to tell.

David stared at his piece of limestone. A lump, still very shallow, was coming up out of its top and he realized with surprise it was the emergence of the dove's head. He saw instantly that it was much too wide; there wasn't a dove that fat anywhere in the world. A fat dove for a fat Rosa, he thought. He turned the stone to a different angle. He could not decide whether to continue working down or to start in from the dove's front or back. It seemed to him the beak and the rounded belly would come forth far enough to cut down slightly on the amount of stone he must remove. He thought with loathing of the slender neck and decided there would be no skinny legs and feet on this stupid bird, not unless he could dynamite away the excess to get in to where they ought to be.

He looked up and saw that Bungo was laughing at him. "You

could make a very large frog," said Bungo, reading his mind. David shook his head and began doggedly to pound on the front surface of the stone.

During that second afternoon he tried sitting with both legs stretched out on one side of the stone; he tried squatting; he tried resting on his knees. If it had not been for Bungo, he would have laid himself flat to the ground, and maybe gone to sleep with the hammer in his hand. In no time at all, the heat and the steady effort carried him over again into the numb state of bad dreams.

Bungo spoke to him once. He rolled across the ground and took a critical look at what David was doing. "Have you thought," he said softly, "that if you make the dove this big, it's going to take a right big stone to be that sunset?"

"Sunrise," said David weakly. He had not thought of that at all.

"Seems to me there's a baby on top of that thing too," said Bungo gravely. "Babies is bigger than doves."

"It's a cherub," he said, choking.

Bungo nodded his kerchiefed head. His face was very serious but both corners of his mouth were jerking. "Course," he said, widening his eyes, "if you start too little, you'll never be able to see all them daisies and violets."

David echoed him. "Daisies and violets."

"You can work all that out," said Bungo Mayfield. His chest shook.

David took a deep breath. With tense control he said, "Thank you."

"Welcome," said Bungo easily, and rolled over and resumed his work.

At the end of that second day David did not believe he could get on his feet at all. Bungo rolled up the tools and squinted at him. He fixed his hands on the squeaky back wheels of his cart. "Need a ride?"

"I'll be inside in a minute," David said.

"Don't hurry yourself. I'm washing up before supper." Bungo rolled his platform to the door of the house, threw the tools inside and turned into the ruts which led downhill to the creek. "When you finish with it, throw that piece of burlap in the kitchen!" he yelled.

David had forgotten the burlap. He took it carefully off his neck. The threads seemed to be glued to his skin and he thought there might be a layer of blisters underneath. Heat was radiating from his sunburned arms. Around both eyes the skin was tight and swollen. He started to touch his nose and thought better of it.

As soon as Bungo had disappeared into the green tunnel which led to the creek, David got up on all fours and crawled painfully to the house and inside the dim kitchen. He now appreciated anew the arrangement of every item at such a low point that he would not have to lift his aching shoulder. He pulled the whiskey jug by its rope, jerked out the plug and poured a large quantity down his throat. If he'd had the energy, he might have gagged. Steam, he felt certain, was rising now out of all the pores of his skin. He drank one more time. Then he fell forward on the cool earth floor and spread out his arms.

He heard the wheels of Bungo Mayfield's cart squeaking up the hill. "Oh, God," groaned David aloud, and would have said more but lacked the strength. He pulled himself to his feet and went outside, trying to hold his back straight. It did not seem to hurt any worse that way than sagging. He waved a casual hand at Bungo, who rolled noisily up to the door.

"Think I'll go down if you've finished."

"You forgot the burlap," Bungo said.

David found he was still clutching it in one hand. He had intended to examine it for patches of his own skin. With dignity he passed it over.

This time he was glad to crawl through Bungo's tunnel, although he feared if one brier touched his sunburned skin he would rise straight up through the entangled branches. At the end of the leafy tube he did not even straighten but crawled straight ahead, fully clothed, into the cool waters of the creek. He scrabbled right along under water until the top of his head had entirely disappeared beneath the muddy surface; then squatted, monkey fashion, with his eyes tightly closed and his arms hung loosely at his sides. At last he needed air and rose as briefly as necessary to the top, took in a breath and sank again.

For all he knew, the waters of the creek had started to boil from his heat and to churn turbulently into the Katsewa River. He thought of crocodiles, which spend their lives covered with wet mud; and no life ever seemed to him more sensible. He had to stretch upward and breathe a second time. Then he went to the edge and lay with his head on the sandy bank and the rest of him submerged.

"I'll take my clothes off in a minute," he said aloud to the honey-suckle. The cool water washed across his flaming skin. He fell asleep.

When Bungo shook his shoulder some time later in the evening dusk, David sprang awake and found himself threshing and—he thought at the time—drowning in the sea. He slapped the water, went down and swallowed most of the creek. At last he spluttered onto the bank, dripping, his chest heaving up and down.

Bungo was sitting quietly on his cart, arms folded and a little smile on his face. "I brung your supper," he said. David reached out a wet hand and took the three biscuits with fatback between them.

"Didn't need to do that," he said. He was starved. Quickly he wolfed them down and scooped up a drink of water in the palm of his hand. He was embarrassed to look at Bungo Mayfield.

"You look right tuckered out," said Bungo calmly. "Maybe we ought to turn in early."

"Whatever you say."

"I got rabbit traps up and down this creek. Remind me to look at 'em in the morning," Bungo said. He turned and began to roll uphill toward the green tunnel. David followed, down on his hands and knees again. His clothes dripped and clung to his skin.

Halfway through, Bungo suddenly stopped turning his wheels, so that David crashed into him with the top of his skull.

"I swear, I'm right tired," said Bungo. He looked across one of the huge shoulders with eyes which seemed to David merry and malicious. "Think you could give me a push to the house?"

David stared, shut his eyes briefly. "Hell, yes," he finally managed to say. He pushed the heavy cripple all the way up the hill, through the yard and into the kitchen, where, without a word of thanks, Bungo suddenly scooted away under his own power into the other room.

David stayed where he was, bent over. His right arm was quaking with fatigue.

"I wish you'd get in first tonight," grunted Bungo. "I can't stand being crawled over."

David hunched into the room, threw his body onto the bed and plastered it to the far wall.

Laughing silently, Bungo took off his shirt, pulled himself off the cart to his own half of the bed. He sat there and looked at the boy's dark hair. "You asleep, David Allen?" he asked, holding his laughter in.

But David didn't answer. He was.

When he woke the third morning in his half of the bed, David found his entire right arm had solidified. At first he thought he must somehow be lying with all his weight upon it. No, the flesh was simply hard and knotted. Between the elbow and the wrist ran one long metal rod of pain. When he held the hand in front of his eye, the fingers trembled.

He could hear Bungo moving in the kitchen. David eased out of bed, grunting when cloth rubbed against his raw skin.

Silently Bungo pointed to the second plate. More boiled eggs, a lump of hard hominy. This time there was a cup of milk. Bungo said a woman down the road brought milk sometimes, and left the jars tied by saplings and cooling at the bottom of the creek.

"You sure do eat hearty," Bungo complained. "You're costing me to feed."

David had more hunger than pride. He went on eating.

"How you feel this morning?"

"I'm all right."

"Picked up a rabbit while you was still asleep. I've put it on to stew."

"I could have skinned it for you," said David. Silently he thanked God he was not forced to begin this day disemboweling a rabbit.

"I was afraid you might cut off a finger," said Bungo with a sour face. "I hear old lady Clark died Tuesday. They'll send in Jasper to trade for the gravestone, because he's the sharpest with money."

"How much do you charge?"

"Depends. Size. Kind of stone. How much stuff they want on it. I know them Clarks. They'll want the littlest, cheapest stone on the lot, with words running off the edge to swear how sweet she was. That was the meanest old lady for fifteen counties." Bungo gulped down his morning cup of whiskey. Then, very offhand, he said, "There was somebody come for you early this morning."

"For me?" David stopped, with the cold egg growing thick in his mouth.

Bungo raised his bristly red eyebrows. "Come in a car!" he said. "What'd you tell him?"

"Never told him nothing. Tried to sell him a tombstone. He got right provoked."

David began spooning up his grits. "He's tight with money."

"He said some fellow brung your horse home. Told him where you was."

"Likely he did," said David without much interest.

Bungo turned up the cup and finished the last drop of whiskey. "I had a lot of trouble understanding him. Couldn't seem to remember from one word to the next who David Allen was supposed to be." He rinsed out the cup in the bucket and put it neatly on the shelf. "Fellow said finally it must suit you just right, to be living with some crazy cripple."

"That was Thomas, all right," said David bitterly. He was uneasy about what else he needed to say. "You want me to say I'm sorry for what he told you?"

"You got more sense than that," said Bungo, and rolled out into the blistering sun.

This third day was no easier than the other two, but perhaps David had passed some limit of discomfort. He took for granted, now, that the arm and right shoulder would always hurt. The smarting of his skin was more troublesome. He took off his shirt and tied it over his head and neck to give his back a chance to burn. He was resigned, too, to hammering his own finger, although he did not hit it so often as before. The thought of Thomas somewhat distracted him from his aches. Any minute now, Thomas might come rattling up in that automobile, bringing their mother and father. Better the car than the buggy. Thomas had always held a cruel whip on the horses.

When someone did come into the yard, David threw up one hand to defend himself. It was a tall, lean man in his mid-forties who introduced himself as Jasper Clark. Bungo turned him loose to look over the monuments which were already smoothed into crosses and tablets and open books and folded hands. Clark chose a long, thin stone with an arched top like a church window. He pulled out a long piece of paper and held it out, but Bungo would not stop working. "Just read it out loud," he said. "I want my helper to hear this."

David's heart bounced once in his chest at hearing himself called Bungo's helper. He listened carefully to the man's hesitant voice:

"Mattie Ruth Clark. Born eighteen eighteen. Died nineteen eight.

She trusted in God all the years of her life and he rewarded her with a sweet nature and a house of loving children. Who in her memory erect this stone. Heaven is richer by her presence."

"That's about it," said Jasper Clark. "And I want you to hold it to ten dollars."

Bungo spat a thin stream of tobacco juice. "You just carry some rock out to a field one night and trust in God and maybe He'll send down the lightning and write all that out for ten dollars."

"Well, it's a little stone!" Jasper protested. He thumped it as if it were some watermelon he were testing for ripeness. "Look how thin it's cut. Ten hard winters will wear it out."

"Take a thicker one then," said Bungo.

"Mama was never very much for earthly show," said Jasper stiffly.

" 'Vanity of vanities . . . all is vanity,' " quoted Bungo. "You ought to stick that in."

Jasper pulled back his paper and frowned over it. "You really think so? It doesn't seem to have the right tone to me."

"Let's save that Clark tone for sure," said Bungo. "Thirty dollars. That stone and that writing—thirty dollars."

"You have gone out of your mind in the hot sun!" Jasper exclaimed. He straightened his shoulders. "My mama would turn in her grave to think we deprived the little children of bread to stick up thirty dollars in the cemetery!"

Bungo was bored. "Tell you what I'm gonna do, Jasper. I'll knock that stone in two and just put her name and dates on half of it. Ten dollars' worth."

"No, sir!" cried Jasper. "You know our plot's right next to the Hendersons' that put that angel last year. My mama would be humiliated!"

Bungo grinned over at David. "It do look as if Mama Clark is in for a hard time, either way it goes."

"Damn right!" crowed David, suddenly pleased to be who he was and where he was. He sat up and put his mallet down and looked at Jasper Clark. "For a woman that lived ninety years, thirty dollars is not so much to charge her loving children. That figures out just over thirty cents a year."

The man said in some awe, "Is that so now!"

"Just take me for an example," David expanded. "At thirty cents a year, my memory wouldn't be worth six dollars altogether."

"Is that a fact!" said the man. He looked at David Allen with a certain amount of pity.

David was surprised to hear Bungo say suddenly, in a pleasant tone, "This here's my new assistant. David Allen. David, this is Mr. Jasper Clark. One of the bereaved mourners I been telling you about."

"How de do," said Jasper Clark, ducking his head.

"My sympathy," said David somberly.

Clark now thrust the paper a second time toward Bungo. "Thirty dollars then, but you deliver it to the graveyard yourself. I got too much work in the fields to spare a wagon."

Bungo would not yet accept the paper. "Ten now?" he asked slyly. "Twenty when I got it in place and your mama's quit turning in her grave?"

"For the mercy's sake!" grumbled Jasper Clark. "Five now ought to more than cover it."

"Ten now," Bungo repeated firmly. "David, how many years does that add to?"

"Thirty years," said David. "Three decades. One third of her whole life."

"That long, huh?" said Clark, frowning.

Bungo looked thoughtful. "I figger that would carry Mama Clark right up to about the day you was born, Jasper."

"I ain't that old. For the Lord's sake," he said in mingled wonder and irritation, "take the damn ten dollars. I swear, when it comes to a family's grief, all you can think about is money!" He rummaged in his pocket and counted out some bills. Bungo counted these a second time, put them in his own pocket, rolled up the slip of paper with Mrs. Clark's inscription on it and stuck it behind his ear, under the bristly red hair.

"You got my sympathy too, Jasper," said Bungo. He was smiling. "You can just tote mine right home along with David Allen's."

The man started out of the yard. "How long's this going to take?"

"Not long," called Bungo. "I don't want you to forget the twenty that's owing." He went back to his work.

David, expectant, waited for Bungo Mayfield to comment on the sale. Not a word was said. In a few minutes, the same tuneless whistling rose from the other side of the stone, no merrier than before. Shrugging, David turned back to his clumsy dove, which now looked as if it were falling forward out of some broken mountainside. He began to cut around its breast and allow for feathered wings right and left.

When the sun was straight in the sky, they had more milk, cold grits and part of the rabbit stew. At the end of the meal Bungo said, "You're right good at figgering."

"I've always liked numbers. Like to measure things."

"Never was much with numbers myself, except the ones on money. We better get some work done before that storm comes up."

"What storm?" said David.

But when they went back into the yard he was grateful for the gathering clouds which thinned the hot sunlight. After an hour's work, Bungo told him to put the gravestone Clark had chosen on the cart and roll it into the kitchen. "Might as well get started," he said. "Wait too long and he'll swear he's already paid me in full."

David would not admit how hard it was for his stiff muscles to lift the stone. The two men had described it as thin; and Bungo could probably have tucked it easily under one arm and still managed to roll himself inside the house. David eased it, puffing, onto the kitchen floor just as the thunder broke open some cloud and rain began to drum lightly on the roof of the tarpaper house. Quickly he pushed the cart to Bungo again. The tools were already wrapped and he was waiting. "Sprinkle feels good," he said.

"Want me to push?"

"Hell, no," said Bungo, to David's great relief.

Sure enough, a driving rain did pour into the small kitchen and stand in pools on the hard-packed floor. It didn't bother Bungo, who was up on his wheeled platform, but it did explain why those wheels were rusted and made such a squawking noise.

"You need a door on this thing," said David, moving back. It wouldn't be hard to fix.

"Just be in my way."

David frowned. "You could saw it in half. Hinge it so you could open the bottom part just by rolling that thing against it."

"Someday," said Bungo. He took the paper from behind his ear and spread it on a shelf and began to work. After a while he looked up irritably at David, who was watching. "You ain't got nothing to do, why don't you pour out that bucket of water and let it sit in the rain awhile? Won't have to carry up from the creek."

David threw a sheet of dishwater into the yard. The rain had ended his third day ahead of time; he did not know how long Bungo would allow him to stay. Till the rain ended, at least. He stood in the door-frame and let the cool drops blow into his taut face.

Without looking up at him, Bungo said, "Seems like you're gonna peel all over."

"I guess so," David said.

"I wish you'd just quit standing around. Especially in that door. You're in my light," said Bungo.

"Sorry." David picked up things off the shelves and put them down. At last he took a chunk of pine from the stack by the kitchen fire, pulled out his pocket knife and began to chip at it. For an hour, the two did not talk. Then David said, "Got any nails?"

"Under the bed."

He found a sack of nails, most of them rusted, and tacked up the long rack with its series of notches which he had made. He sighted carefully so he would nail it no higher than the whiskey jug was hung. Into each notch he fitted one of Bungo's enamel spoons. "Is that too high?" he asked.

Bungo looked at it a long time. "Naw," he said finally.

The rain began to slack. David went into the other room and found his extra shirt, twisted it into a thick belt and tied it around his middle. He stood in the doorway between the two rooms and looked down at Bungo, who was carefully cutting MATTIE RUTH CLARK in the face of the stone, between two straight lines he had scratched in with a stubby pencil.

"The rain's stopped," said David.

"Always does."

He stepped outside and saw there was not more than two inches of water in Bungo's kitchen bucket. He carried it downhill to the creek and filled it nearly to the brim. All the way back it sloshed over into his shoes. He set it in the usual place in the corner.

"Well," David began. "I want you to know . . ."

Bungo laid down his tools but he wouldn't look any farther than the water bucket. In a suddenly loud voice he said, "You notice I use script letters for the women and block for the men."

"I noticed that," said David, swallowing.

"Dumb as you are, it's a wonder." Bungo wiped sweat off his face. "Tomorrow you better just sit in one place and watch me work on this one."

David began clumsily to untie the shirt from around his waist. "All right," he managed to say.

"I swear, I don't know how you've lived so long," Bungo grumbled. "Anybody dumb enough to walk all the way to the creek for water and forget about the milk. You know we need milk for supper."

"I'll fetch it now," said David, beginning to smile.

"You oughta been able to figger that out yourself," snapped Bungo, taking up his tools again.

Chapter

❧ 24 ❧

NOBODY REALLY BOTHERED David until September.

Mildred sent Preacher Holt all the way over from Greenway to see him once, but the preacher had grown so deaf it was hard to guess what he understood from David's answers. Several times during the summer Thomas drove by the stonecutter's yard and blew his raucous horn. David would not look up. We both left you, Thomas. Esther first. Now me.

Bungo would say, without straightening, "That's him again."

"I hear it," David said.

Early in September Rutledge drove the Allen buggy into the yard and Sam climbed out alone, wearing his Sunday suit. David heard the horse and the wheels. He kept his back turned and looked across at Bungo.

"It's some Allen," said Bungo, "but I don't know which."

Behind him his father said sharply, "At least it's better than whittling."

Slowly David turned to look at him. He stood and put out his right hand. "How you feeling?" he stammered.

Sam stared angrily at the hand. "How you think I'm feeling? Not one word to your mama or me all these weeks? Wouldn't even come out to speak to your brother Thomas? I'm feeling like hell about it, that's how."

Before David could answer, Bungo spoke off his cart. "My name's

Bungo Mayfield. How do, Mr. Allen. I think it was you I talked to about them Bennett stones. Silas Bennett and that little still-born baby."

"Yes, yes," said Sam to one side, not taking his eyes off David. "I'd like to know what you think you're doing."

David took his hand back and wiped it on his pants. "I'm making a tombstone."

Sam stepped to one side to see it better. It was a lamb stone for a child kicked in the head by a horse. Bungo had done the lamb. David was adding the letters and the dates.

"That ain't bad!" said Sam in some surprise. He wheeled around to Bungo Mayfield. "How much you pay my boy for doing fine work like that?"

"Pay him!" yelled Bungo. "How much do I pay him!" He jerked so suddenly the iron wheels beneath him began to squeak.

"We got an arrangement," said David soothingly. "How's Mama? How's Aunt Rosa?"

"They're fine. What kind of arrangement?"

"He's just learning. Room and board," said Bungo with an effort.

Sam looked as if he might fall over on the ground. "You're living in that thing?" He waved a hand at the tarpaper building.

"I'm fine," said David. "I'm just fine."

"Thomas sure got all the money sense in this family." Sam began to shake his head. "Now look here, Mr. Mayfield. This boy has got a skill with his hands. You know it, I know it. A skill is worth something. You got to pay this boy decent wages."

Bungo's face began to redden and he rolled himself a little nearer. "You standing on my property talking to my helper about paying out my money. If you got nothing to buy here, you tell that buggy to drive on. If my helper don't like the way he's treated, he can ride off on the seat beside you."

Sam stared at him and blinked. To David he said out of the corner of his mouth. "Walk over this way with me. I want to talk to you." Of all three children, only Thomas had really turned out right, he thought.

At the edge of the yard, Sam sat on a lump of stone and gave David a hard look. "You sure are a sight. You look like a tar baby."

"I work outside all day."

Sam wrinkled his nose. "Smell like you been burning the new

ground. I am sure glad your mama didn't come with me. She'd break right down and cry. You nothing but skin and bones."

"I never felt better in my life," said David.

Sam went on morosely shaking his head. Finally he said, "How much money you need?"

"I don't need any money."

"You ain't eating right. Anybody can tell that. How much?"

"Nothing, I said. Tell Mama I'm just fine. I'll come see her after a while."

"Don't kill yourself," Sam snorted. He got off the stone and walked briskly back to where Bungo had begun to work again. "I figure any business you get is a help to my son David. Ain't that so?"

"What you got in mind?" said Bungo evenly.

Sam took some bills out of his pocket and began to straighten them out. "I've put this off a long time. Too long. It didn't seem right with nothing to bury under it. But today I made up my mind."

Bungo said very quietly he didn't take money from people. "I work for my living."

"That's all I'm talking about. Now I want you to make the finest gravestone ever was put up in Stone County. Marble, maybe. Bring it in from Italy or someplace, and I want it to curve. None of them sharp edges. All of it curving. I'll pay whatever it takes to make it just right."

David had gone to the buggy to speak to Rutledge. Walking back, he began to frown at what he could overhear of his father's words.

"You ask David what he thinks ought to go on it. All I know is the name, Esther Allen, and the dates, eighteen eighty-four to eighteen ninety-nine. Something nice after that. Some poetry or—"

David broke into a run and struck the money from his father's hand. "Get out of here!" he ordered.

With care, Sam stopped and began to gather the bills and straighten them out in a neat stack in one hand. Not looking at David, he said, "It would ease your mama's heart."

"She'll have to ease it some other way."

Now Sam got to his feet with all dignity. "I was talking business with Mr. Mayfield when you interrupted. Any price you name, sir. And I'll pay the whole thing today."

Bungo looked at David and shook his head. "No."

Now Sam shook the money into the air. "Don't be a fool! I can go straight to Greensboro or Salisbury or any other town and get somebody else to make it."

"You do that, and it won't stay in the graveyard overnight," said David grimly, "if it's twenty feet high and I have to carry it to the river on my back."

"Mr. Mayfield?"

"You heard me. No."

Sam turned and walked rapidly to the carriage. Rutledge started to drive away but as they were turning into the Stoneville street Sam stopped him and called back. "David? Come here."

David shook his head, "Go on," said Bungo.

Again David shook his head. "You getting to be as stingy as Jasper Clark. Go see what your daddy wants," barked Bungo.

When David did not come as close to the carriage as he wanted, Sam leaned way over and said in a soft voice, "When all's said and done, you got more sense than I give you credit. Greenway's the growing town. It'll pass Stoneville any day; there won't be nothing here but court on Fridays. Everything's going to move to my end of the county." He winked. "I'll start looking around now for some property when you're ready to open up your business."

"I won't be opening up any business," said David steadily. "I'm staying here with Bungo."

Sam's mouth dropped open. "I tell you, all the business is moving out of Stoneville. In another ten years, all the money's going to pour that way. If you don't open up in Greenway, somebody else will."

"That's his worry and not mine," said David.

Sam hardened his face. "Looks like I was wrong," he said angrily. "No matter what you set out to do, it winds up to be whittling! Rutledge, drive on!"

David went back to the lamb stone. There was no sound beyond a few passing bees and the steady clang of metal and thump of hammers. Finally Bungo said, "I see you're still here."

"Till you throw me out," said David. It sounded threatening.

Bungo began to laugh. "How could a poor old crippled man like me throw out a big strong boy like you?"

"Yeah." David grinned. "Looks like you're stuck."

It was early morning. Thomas, alone at the long table, finished his breakfast and rang the tiny crystal bell.

"Excellent, Amy Lee," he said when the cook came to clear his dishes. She nodded without a smile. He added that Mrs. Allen seemed a little tired this morning. "You might carry her tea and toast a little later."

"I might," said Amy Lee, sounding insolent.

Thomas was too well satisfied to care. Amy Lee had worked for Nellie's family twenty years. All right, so in her eyes he would never be Nathan Grimes. He thought: The worms are crawling where Nathan lies this morning and I am sitting in his chair.

Smiling, he lit a thin cigar and began to wander through the downstairs rooms of the Gri—no!—Allen house. He owned everything his eye fell upon—every polished chair arm, all the portraits, each of the silver rosebud vases. Thomas gorged his eye. It made a second hearty meal atop the first. He felt sleepy and replete as he moved from room to room, sometimes thinking, sometimes muttering his thoughts aloud.

". . . And the last surviving member of that fine old Grimes family blends into me. Here I stand in this fine historical house, my house, and by my existence a whole channel is diverted. . . ."

He sneered when he came to the row of family portraits.

"My face and Nellie's, and the faces of all our children, will soon be crowding you off the walls. I will pull Allens out of her belly one by one and drive this—this *maternal* line into the attic. . . ."

He threw back his head and laughed.

Amy Lee appeared at the dining-room door and looked at him. "You call me?"

"No," said Thomas, sobering. Her sudden appearance had startled him. For one instant her face had melted and altered and he had seen behind it the features of Miss Bethesda Lee Michael. What had she told him that night, sifting his cornbread crumbs? "Never want to marry but one girl and that's the one you'll marry. Die of old age right here in this county." Well, what was wrong with that? Thomas swung angrily toward one of the painted gentlemen, who had wobbled slightly in his frame.

Irritably he told Amy Lee he was leaving now for the mill.

Nellie, fully dressed, waited upstairs at the crack of her bedroom door until she heard his car coughing and sneezing on the road. Then she hurried down the curving stairs. Amy Lee was slumped on the bottom step, her forehead in her hands.

Nellie called to her softly. "You feeling sick?"

"Just feeling old," sighed Amy Lee. "What you want to eat this morning?"

Nellie shook her head. "You know I'm going to Stoneville. I don't have time."

"Yessum. I got Halliburton to hitch up. He was to come around when the car left."

"Go have your own breakfast." Halliburton called through the front door that everything was ready and Nellie threw on her cloak and hurried to the carriage.

The October air was crisp and the horse set a brisk pace. There had been frost this week for the first time. Soon it would be winter. For weeks at first, and now for months, Nellie had waited for David to send her some message. Once she had made Halliburton ride all the way to the mill village to see if Winona Rickert had heard anything.

It was not hard to find Mayfield Monument Works. The contrast between the name Nellie had been given and the sight she actually saw made her jerk on the reins and stop the carriage right in the middle of the road. There was one squat black building and a series of sheds and lean-tos being built. Scattered around were sample tombstones in assorted shapes. She thought of giant teeth dropped at random in a patch of weeds.

Nellie could bring herself to go no closer. She rose as high on the leather seat as she could and called for him. "David? Is David Allen in there, please? David!"

A thin man who was building a rough shed at one corner of the lot turned, shaded his eyes and looked at her. For a long time he stood without moving. Since he was the only living soul she saw, Nellie raised her voice to him. "Can you find David Allen for me?"

Almost reluctantly the man began to walk toward her. He was sunburned, very tall, almost bony. His dark hair grew very long on his neck and the shirt was torn raggedly down his chest. He was less than five feet away when she cried out, "David? Is that you?"

He nodded. "How are you, Nellie?"

She was shocked—that's how she was. He looked like more of a stranger than Thomas had seemed that first afternoon, waiting in the hotel room. "You've changed," she said weakly. She could not believe those hands had ever touched her.

"Everybody says that. It isn't so."

Nellie took off her hat and began to pat her coil of hair. "I thought I'd hear something from you. Weeks and weeks I thought so."

"I been right busy. I'm coming home for a few days as soon as I get these work sheds finished."

She looked, disbelieving, at the rickety wall he had been hammering.

"Your father says you're going to stay on though. And work with that . . . that crippled man."

"That's right. Are things . . . any better with you?"

"They're not as frequent," she said with a high laugh. "I guess that's better."

"Maybe in time he won't need to be that way. Especially if you . . . if you help him."

"He'll always need to be that way, and I didn't come here to talk about that," she said. "I came to tell you I miss you. I want to know if I'm the reason you're over here working. In this . . . this place of death," she said with a frown.

"It had nothing to do with you."

He sounded very definite. Nellie drew back as if he had struck her. She stared down the light-brown road and the darker-brown fields. Her lips grew white. "I'm beginning to realize that nothing much has anything to do with me. Thomas marrying me—that was for something else. To get a Grimes and a Grimes house and maybe some Grimes children. And you, David Allen! You were just putting something in the beggar's cup, isn't that so?"

Her phrasing would have made him smile if he had not been so miserable with guilt and embarrassment. "Not exactly," he said.

She swung her face toward his and he saw the tears standing in her eyes. "Does it matter to you," she whispered, "how much harder you have made my life?"

"I'm sorry," he said. He was almost angry. "I don't know what else to say besides I'm sorry."

"And I'm sorry too. Sorry I came." She turned the horse's head, then stopped, as if she was trying to decide whether or not to say something else. She decided to say it, but not to look at him. "One night," she began hesitantly, "that is, one time . . . . Thomas called me a name. A woman's name that was not mine. While he was . . . well, anyway, he called me this name."

"Who did he say?"

She looked at him now, with contempt. "You know what name it was," she said, and lashed the horse down the Greenway road, holding herself very carefully so he would notice her shoulders did not slump.

David worked doggedly on the side wall of the shed where he and Bungo could move things in rainy weather. One end was still open. Here they would build a crude fireplace for winter heat. Here, too, David might do some carvings; he had in mind to make Bungo a new cart, with ornate edges and hand grips and a padded seat and back rest.

He heard the screech of Bungo coming on his rusted wheels. Once he had oiled them but Bungo complained that after so many years the unexpected silence hurt his ears and made him feel he was not moving at all. For the new cart, he would attach the same noisy wheels.

Bungo rolled himself into the shed and held out a new slip of paper. "Come in while you was seeing your visitor," he said, grinning. "They asked to have David Allen himself do this one. What you think of that? It's the first time somebody's asked for your work by name."

"Imagine that!" said David to himself. He felt warm with pride. "Let me see that thing. Is it block or script?"

"It's a woman," Bungo said, passing the note to him.

David stared at the careful inscription. It was for "Miss Eliza Tilley. Teacher of Youth."

"They said she was right fond of wise sayings," Bungo went on, "so we picked one to go at the bottom that seemed to fit her work."

David's eye slid past the dates—was she *that* young?—to the short quotation. "As the twig is bent," it read, "the tree inclines."

Chapter

⋙ 25 ⋘

By 1910, Stoneville began to slide in bits and pieces across the county to Greenway, where the cotton mill was.

The county newspaper moved first, because it needed more subscribers and more advertising. A court reporter telegraphed any important trials to Greenway and mailed in the routine deaths and marriages and land transfers and wills probated. The train now stopped in Stoneville only once a day, because it was busy taking coal to the factory and cloth away. On Saturdays, farmers would drive their wagons right through the main street of Stoneville and pass on down the road to Greenway, where there were more things to buy and more people to watch.

Sam had been right about that shift in business. But since no rival stonecutter appeared, David and Bungo found most of their business still came out of Stoneville, where people were aging and slipping out of sight. Greenway was the source for violent death among the young, for children's accidents and new babies; but the reliable marching of old age (what Bungo called the "steady trade") was still from Stoneville.

The two talked about moving, or setting up someplace halfway between the two towns. By 1909 they settled for buying a wagon to transport the heavy stones that might have to be delivered to Greenway cemeteries or county churchyards beyond.

David built a ramp by which Bungo could be rolled onto the wagon, and a special seat Bungo could reach by using his husky arms. Seeing the two of them riding side by side, you wouldn't have thought Bungo crippled at all—not till you drew very near and saw his legs—no broader than a little child's.

Right after the September rains in 1909, an unexpected flood drowned ten people at various spots along the Katsewa. It took the whole winter to finish all the tombstones. The flood almost got Bungo too. He was washing himself in the creek when floodwaters backed into it without warning, found him lying by the water's edge and sucked him in. Bungo roared for help as he was dragged away. After that he could not work fast enough with those powerful arms and shoulders to pull his head above that churning surface. The current tossed his useless legs about as if they had been rotten logs.

Hearing him yell, David plummeted through the thickets downstream, threw himself into the water and managed to catch hold of Bungo by the ankles. He had a sense of horror when his fingers wrapped themselves so completely around the stringy leg. Pulling with all his strength, he dragged Bungo loose from the swift water and jerked him high on the bank. Then he began frantically to pound him between the shoulder blades.

"Goddamnit, breathe!" he yelled.

Bungo coughed, vomited downhill to the water's edge. "If I ain't dead yet," he gasped, "don't kill me now."

David left off pounding. It was the first time—the only time—David ever saw Bungo's legs uncovered. They hung from his muscular torso like strips of dough, white and limp. Bones like spear points or arrowheads were pushing up that pale skin.

"I thought you were dead," David panted.

Bungo laid his face to the sand on the other side, away from the vomit. "Yeah," he said. "Me too."

Before the cold weather set in, David finished the work sheds and added shelves at two levels—his and Bungo's—so they would be more comfortable when they worked. The shelves he built would not support the weight of stone and the endless vibrations of their hammers. David's high shelf collapsed suddenly at one end one November afternoon and the stone which rolled downhill upon it fell with a thump at the foot of Bungo's cart and bounced alongside. They stared at it. Bungo reached out and gave it a tentative pat.

"Some carpenter," he said tightly.

So that week David went straight to Sam Allen's house in Greenway and asked for a favor. It nearly killed him, but he couldn't think of anything else to do.

"You want *what?*" yelled Sam.

"I want three bales of cotton. I want 'em put on the train and unloaded in Stoneville, and I want help from the mill to get them all into the yard and inside the work shed. I'll have to knock out part of a wall to get them in, so I need to know when they're coming."

Sam fell back on one of Mildred's most delicate parlor chairs. "You got any idea what cotton is a pound?"

"It turns out Bungo Mayfield's neck has been hurting for twenty years because there's no real way to work lying down that doesn't cramp it. All I want is three measly bales of cotton."

His mother came in at the sound of their shouting. David turned to her in anger and said, "Read him about Jacob and Esau. I'm asking for three bales of cotton for my whole birthright. You think you and the Bible might be able to explain it to him?"

Sam sent the cotton.

He sent Big Jube and Little Jube and Rutledge and Halliburton and three other workmen from the mill to help them get it off the train and delivered and set up at Mayfield Monument Works just the way David wanted. David wanted one bale upright and two turned on their sides. He had already worked out a system of ramps and platforms so Bungo could use the two horizontal bales like giant work tables and, by rising to a higher ramp, change the height he would be using to work on a stone. David's own platform was fixed so he could work standing up, which he and his spine had found most comfortable.

When all three bales were well in place, and Bungo had ridden up and down the inclines with hooting laughs, he rolled into the house and came out with a jug of whiskey for every man there. They built an open fire in the yard and sat on the tombstones and sang songs. Bungo told tales about violent deaths and who the local ghosts were supposed to be. Big Jube said Miss Bethesda Lee Michael came back in dreams to his wife, Vinnie, and swore she had been murdered by a tall white man now living in Chicago. Rutledge asked Bungo if he would make him one little tombstone, not more than six inches high, and put a certain name on it so he could hex a man; and Bungo vowed he would. In fact, they worked out a whole new witchcraft system that night which might have made them all rich, if anybody had been able to remember enough of it by morning. Everybody got very drunk. David wanted to walk all the way to Greenway and knock out one certain tooth in his brother's head, and he had just the mallet and chisel to pick the spot. Little Jube had to throw him in the creek to get him quiet.

The next morning Sam sent over a wagonload of burlap, because he figured they would wear out the covering on the bale pretty quickly. First thing they knew, his irritable note said, some iron band was going to whip out and kill them both if they didn't cover and pad. He understood all about Esau, he added, except the part about the hairy animal skin.

David accepted the burlap.

"One other thing," he warned Bungo. "This cotton will burn. Let's watch out with that fireplace and the lamp."

"You'd be surprised how long I lived safe before you come," Bungo grumbled. His head was hurting and his tongue was slimy. "I hope you don't feel obliged this morning to pound nothing too hard."

"No," said David wanly. "Not a bit."

Now they were able to work at a steady pace through the winter in the heated sheds. The cotton muffled some of the noise, although bits of it were always puffing out and—said Bungo—getting stuck inside his nose.

Sometime that winter Bungo told him about the sickness which had crippled him as a boy. Fever and vomiting, he said, with pain in the arms and legs and some soreness inside his throat. Just as the sickness ebbed the pain grew worse, especially behind the neck and down the center of his back.

"When I didn't die, the pain moved down in my legs. It stayed there a long time, and when it finally let go it took all the future pain with it, because I couldn't feel nothing. They wouldn't move. They never did move."

"How old were you then?" asked David, not breaking the rhythm of his hammer.

"Eight. I'm forty now."

"Forty?" said David doubtfully.

"Forty; you heard me. I used to stick myself with a hatpin and try to believe I could feel it more in one place than another, but it wasn't so."

Bungo had learned the tombstone trade from an uncle in Davie County, who helped him start business in Stoneville as a young man of twenty, "some forty years ago."

"How many years?"

"I forget," snarled Bungo, "and didn't them snotty-rich Allens teach you no manners? That uncle was my last kin. Died when you couldn't have been much more than a baby. Left his own marker all finished except for his death day. I put that in for him."

"If you ever got rich," said David hesitantly, "is there someplace you could go, some Northern doctor?"

"Not a thing," said Bungo.

By that time he was giving David 40 per cent of all the money the yard earned. David, in turn, paid some on the food and fuel, and with part of his profit built a small office and scaled the furniture down to size so Bungo could roll directly into the kneehole space of his own desk and talk to the mourners.

David set up a file on the families with whom they did business. That meant when Tom Willett came to bury his father, he could be told right away what kind of marker was already on his plot, its height and style, and how much room was left. David also invested in some books: a Bible, a Shakespeare, and a 1910 edition of Bartlett's *Quotations*. On long winter evenings if work was slow, he worked on a ledger of suitable sentiments for infants, young children, spinsters, mothers, fathers, the aged.

Part of his pay David took out in stone itself. He was slowly working on Rosa's complex monument. The dove had been the first portion completed. It looked rough and amateurish now; but he kept it in a corner of the special lean-to he had added back of the work shed for what Bungo called "Aunt Rosa's Folly." David had already made and joined one of the front columns with its twining rope of grapevine. From time to time now he worked on the second column. Each came up to his shoulder.

I wish Esther could see it, he sometimes thought. *She always liked the things I carved. She'd approve of this.*

Some Sundays David went to Greenway to see his parents. By the fall of 1909, Thomas and Nellie had their first daughter and by Christmas in 1910 they were expecting a second child. There was a strain between David and Nellie. The family talk was all of babies: how Thomas had been, when David had walked and cut his teeth, whether young Melinda looked like Grandpa Sam or not. Nobody ever mentioned Esther. David was glad to escape upstairs to Aunt Rosa, who, at forty-five, looked as if she might well live forever.

"I keep working on your stone," he told her. "A little here, a little there."

"What stone?" she said.

"Just tell me how you're feeling today."

She shook her wide head. The chins wobbled in unison. "I'll be better," she vowed, "if this baby will ever come. My other six never took this long."

As time passed, David went home less and less. Almost imperceptibly, the change took place in his mind which made a trip to his parents' house a "visit," and the Mayfield-Allen Monument Works a "home." He built a second bedroom, full-sized, onto Bungo's little house and put in a regular bed. The construction was the same and he covered it with the same tarpaper.

"Hell," said Bungo. "Way things are going, we could have afforded brick."

"I've gotten used to tarpaper." David shrugged.

Bungo had shifted to his ornately carved new cart, which had the quality of a throne. There were now polished wooden hooks all over the kitchen for his pots, and a divided door had been hung on oiled hinges. David put in a kitchen floor, on which Bungo's wheels passed with a curious rumbling sound, like thunder.

For weeks David worked in secret on a low wardrobe-closet which would be used for storing Bungo's clothes. He made it from a wooden packing box, with a rod and a series of wooden hangers (some ending in coiled snake heads) which slid from left to right. He chose walnut for the double doors and carved on the left a mallet, a chisel and a large and muscular hand. On the second door he cut the letters of Bungo Mayfield's name. He gave it to Bungo in 1911, for Christmas.

"Oh, you damn fool," breathed Bungo when he saw it.

"Your clothes keep hanging in my way," said David.

Bungo tested the smooth wood with his calloused fingertips. "You'd fall over stuff if I nailed it to the ceiling, you damn fool," he said with some effort. "You go outside. Go look at Aunt Rosa's Folly."

David carried a lantern to the back lean-to. In front of the dove and the columns rested the marble cherub. It was scaled to the proper size; the eyes were wide and nearly merry, and the small mouth was pursed. Beside it, David's first dove looked more raggedy than ever.

At the top of his lungs David yelled, "You old bastard, when did you have time to make this thing?"

Bungo bellowed back at him from the door to the tarpaper house. "I ain't got to tell you every way I spend my time!"

Sometime that spring, when David was driving the wagon into the yard from a trip to Greenway cemetery, he saw a strange man leaving Bungo's office, still frowning at a piece of paper he carried before him in one hand. Bungo rolled out behind the man on his cart.

"I don't care what you got to put in front of that or behind that or around it that makes it legal, but someplace in the middle I want them exact words."

"Yes, sir," said the young man.

David nodded as they passed each other on the path. "He looked like you scared him half to death," he said. "You sending out to have your own tombstone made? You don't trust me to get the letters right?"

"You was just lucky with that little wardrobe," said Bungo. "I'm afraid you'll forget to step inside when the time comes and double check that spelling. I sure don't want to go into eternity as Bingo."

The summer was hot and dry. Bungo kept coughing in the dust and complaining that David stirred up more than his share.

"Go see Doctor Newton," said David, "instead of making so much racket. You got so you cough all night. Maybe you ought to be taking some kind of medicine."

"I been to see him," said Bungo.

David wheeled around. "When did you go?"

He waved a dismissing arm. "Last time you was in Greenway. He said I'm fine for my age."

"And what did he allow your age to be?" said David, grinning, for he could never get Bungo to admit to a year past forty. It was hard to guess it. The skin was wrinkled, but wrinkled the same way clay will crack from too much sunlight. His head was bald except for the two red woolly clusters above his ears. Between the waist and the jut of his jawline, Bungo was built like a bull.

"Forty. My coughing bothers you, I reckon I can sleep outside." David said he would live through it.

The dry summer passed into a dry fall. Leaves dried on the trees without color and the scarlet berries in the woods were hard and wrinkled for the birds. Bungo's cough did not improve.

One night David heard the wheels squawking out of the bedroom. The cart thumped the lower half of the kitchen doors as it rolled outside.

"There's water in the bucket," David called out sleepily. Nobody answered. He yelled it: "I brought a whole bucket of water up."

"Go back to sleep," called Bungo. "Can't a man piss in peace?"

David did go back to sleep. When next he woke it was with a feeling of something gone, missing, lost. He could not imagine what it was. He rolled back and forth in the bed. Then he began to hear the silence, without a single cough to mar it. He realized Bungo had somehow creaked his way back to bed without waking him.

"I don't believe that," said David to the dark. He walked softly into the next room and called out to the low bed. When there was no answer, he ran his flat palm across it.

There was no way of telling whether he had slept a minute, twenty minutes, an hour. David ran into the kitchen and forgot to open the top half of the door. Swearing and rubbing his bruised head, he finally shoved his way into the night and called for Bungo. He did not expect an answer, but he did expect to hear the wheels squeak somewhere.

All he could see was tombstones like feather pillows lying here and there in the moonlight. "Bungo?"

Cautiously he began to inch his way toward the creek. What had once been a tunnel was now a wide swath he cut back weekly with a scythe, and he had laid a board runway so Bungo would not wear himself out shoving his weight through the mud. One winter, he remembered, grinning, Bungo had struck an unexpected ice slick on one of these boards and gone straight downhill into the frigid water, bawling like a calf.

"Bungo?" he called. He stopped, waited for the cough or the sound of wheels. "It ain't funny, Bungo! You answer me now!"

He found the cart standing parallel to the creek. Bungo had fallen half off it into the sand, a tin cup hanging onto one thumb. His mouth was partly open and the flesh was cool.

The name broke in his mouth. "Bungo?"

David ran his hand over the face, felt the rough eyebrow with a fingertip. Then he cradled the head on his other arm and tried clumsily to close the eyes. They were swimming in moonlight. One would not stay down and seemed to be winking at him. He laid two smooth river pebbles on the lids.

It was hard to move him, but David pulled on the torso until it was lying on the cart and the flaccid legs were dragging loose behind it on the ground. He pulled the cart uphill and did not look back. It felt as if something bristly, like a pine cone, were hung inside his throat.

David made the coffin himself. He took both doors off Bungo's Christmas present and trimmed them until they fit longways, and nailed the lid down. Twice the hammer crashed into his finger. It was the first time he had hit himself for nearly three years.

David dug a grave at the back of the yard and, grunting with effort, rolled all the completed tombstones he could find until they stood around its border like a wall, ringing Bungo's head, foot and sides. By that time it was nearly noon of the next day and people were coming into the yard to stare at him and whisper. David tugged the last stone into place and went into the tarpaper house and got very drunk out of Bungo's swinging jug.

The next day the young man who had talked to Bungo in the spring appeared and beat on the door and would not go away. At last David opened it and asked him what the hell he wanted.

The man looked away from David's red-rimmed eyes. "I'm Matthew Jordan," he said uncomfortably, "and I'm a lawyer and I've brought you something. It's all taken care of. Filed and everything."

He stuck out a long paper rolled into a little tube. David's eyes smarted so he could barely read. He did see right away that—just as Bungo must have insisted—there was legal talk in front and around and on all sides. But the lawyer had done what Bungo wanted about the middle. He had not only put in Bungo's exact words, but he had glued the ragged bit of paper right into the center of the document. It was dirty, much-creased, much thought about. The lettering was block, neatly and precisely inscribed, and fit to be carved into the finest marble. It said: "I leave my business and anything else I may own to David Allen, because I love him."

That night David began work on the headstone which he would put on Bungo Mayfield's grave. He did not have the dates; Bungo had fixed it so nobody would ever have the dates. He planned to cut into the surface no more than: BUNGO MAYFIELD. MASTER STONECUTTER. 40 YEARS OLD.

Above that David would make an angel. The robe would billow forth over a swelling chest, and he planned that the angel should blossom outward in a pair of sudden and enormous wings, such as would be needed to lift so thick a chest and such heavy shoulders, and carry them upward lightly.

PART IV

Mrs. Andrew Warner

JUNE, 1920

Chapter

❦ 26 ❧

THERE WERE ONLY a few loafers on the benches at Greenway depot, but all of them sprang to attention when the woman stepped off the early-morning train. One of them, Kyle McLees, shook loose from the group and half ran downhill to the nearest barbershop to tell the news. She was the first woman most of them had ever seen with bobbed straight hair, not even covered by a hat or veil.

The three men left on the wooden bench leaned forward to see her better. There was a tall man behind the woman but he did not get off the train, merely leaned from the bottom step and said something to her. The watchers glanced at Marvin, who had the best hearing.

He repeated softly what he could catch of it.

". . . sure you'll be all right?"

"Of course," she said. They could all hear that. Not really a Yankee voice, they decided. Halfway. Maybe from Maryland.

"I'll meet you then," said the well-dressed man, "right here tonight. At seven-ten." He looked around, eyed the men watching from the bench. "I don't like the idea of you here by yourself at that hour."

"This time of year it won't be dark till eight." The woman sounded impatient. She shook a few wrinkles out of her pale-green suit. The conductor leaned forward and said something to the man on the steps.

Louder, he said to her, "Why not just go on with me? We can both come back here tomorrow. Spend a few days. A week if you wanted to."

"I don't want to spend a week," she said. She turned and laid a gloved hand against his coat. "You finish your business. I'll be right here and ready to go at seven-ten."

He bent and kissed her. His hair was gray, slightly wavy. "Forty-five, fifty," said one of the watchers in a whisper. "Hard to tell," said another. "People with money don't show their age."

"Be careful," said the gray-haired man. He disappeared inside the train.

The woman turned her face aside and asked something of the conductor, who nodded before he swung onto the bottom step. He pointed into Greenway with one hand. The watching men on the bench turned their heads all at one time and followed his gesture. Governor House. Anybody could stay in a hotel just for the daylight *had* to be rich, they said to one another.

Now she was passing in front of them, taking small, neat steps in a skirt which narrowed at a hem some inches above her ankles. She had a slender waist. Her eyes were as dark as her short hair, which turned in a shallow curl around her cheeks. They saw then that she wore some kind of pink coloring on her mouth.

"You see that?" sighed one, in awe.

"Nice ankles. I like it when they dip in just before that bone," said another with a grin.

"The paint, I mean. You see the paint?"

"I wasn't looking for paint. Fine figure of a woman. How old you think she is?"

"Thirty?" said one.

"Thirty-five?"

"Rich women, above all, don't show their age."

"Think that fellow was her husband?"

One of the men said surely not. "Who'd let his own wife paint her mouth and go off alone in a strange town?"

When the woman walked through the lobby of Governor House, she was smiling and shaking her head from side to side. Her short hair swung.

"This building certainly has changed," she said pleasantly to the clerk. She registered as Mrs. Andrew Warner. The clerk strained the tendons in his neck trying to read it upside down.

"Ain't you got a bag?"

Mrs. Warner laughed aloud. "I'll pay in advance," she said. "And I'll be leaving this evening. Before seven."

The clerk watched her climb the carpeted stairs, automatically moving his head to the rhythm of her hips. Good-looking woman, he thought, if she *has* got her hair chopped off. Didn't look cheap, somehow, the way you'd expect.

When Kyle McLees came in to ask who she was, the clerk wouldn't even say.

In half an hour the woman came downstairs again and stopped at the desk. "I'm looking for some old friends who used to live in Greenway. An Allen family. Sam Allen."

"I know the Allens," said the clerk, surprised. "Live out on the Stoneville road."

She frowned. "I thought they had something to do with a cotton mill."

"Tom owns the thing. Hey, Kyle? Kyle! Come here a minute." Kyle McLees shuffled from behind a potted palm. "How long's Thomas Allen been living on the Stoneville road?"

"Since he got married," said Kyle. "It was his wife's place."

"Married," said Mrs. Warner to herself. "Thank you, gentlemen." She gave them a friendly smile which so charmed Kyle McLees that he snatched at the hat he was not even wearing on his head that morning. He blocked her path. "You could hire a car if you need to get out there," he volunteered. "I could do the driving."

"No," she said. She gave him a second smile. "Thank you."

Outside the hotel, Mrs. Andrew Warner walked aimlessly along the brick sidewalk. Trumble's General Store, she read to herself, studying signs. Stone County Beacon, Mondays and Thursdays. The dusty street was still unpaved, but the stepping-stones which had once bridged the mud from corner to corner, built for buggies to pass above, were gone. High, open cars—Maxwells, Lexingtons, Hudsons, Model T's—stirred up the summer dust.

The Presbyterian church, considerably enlarged, was still located right uptown, but the Academy next door had given way to a row of shops for dentist, dressmaker, barber. There was one glass-fronted office marked with gold-paper words: MATTHEW JORDAN—WYNDHAM

MORRISON. Attorneys At Law. Next to that Harriet Steele, Milliner, displayed a row of lacy hats, a tray of jeweled hatpins, and one daring cloche, which looked a little sun-faded.

Mrs. Warner crossed the street and went inside the newspaper office. She took a folded paper and a small gold pen from her embroidered purse. She asked to see the editor.

Mr. Hopkins called her behind the railing, moved a stack of papers off a chair and wiped it with his handkerchief.

"Perhaps you can tell me," began Mrs. Warner, "where to locate some people. Do you know a Sam Allen?"

"You don't mean the boy?"

She bit her lower lip. "No."

"Tom Allen's youngest boy—he's the last of ten children—is named that for his grandfather. The old man died in . . . oh, nineteen fourteen, I guess. Fell down the steps at his house, the big one he built on the edge of town."

"I see." She put the cap back on the pen. "And his wife?"

"Mildred lives with Tom and Nellie on the old Grimes place. She's got a rose garden out there you wouldn't believe. Two acres long."

"Nellie Grimes," said Mrs. Warner to herself.

"That's right. Mrs. Tom Allen's in bed a lot. Big family and all, they seem to tire her out."

Mrs. Warner began very carefully to remove her gloves. "There was another son. David."

"Oh! David, sure. Ran the old monument works in Stoneville. You used to know David?"

Her face, which he had just been thinking was very handsome, wrenched out of shape. "Used to?"

"That was right sad," he said, lowering his voice. "Boy was making money out there. Did fine work. Caught influenza two years ago— not a soul knew about it. You know, he lived right much to himself after Bungo went."

"Bungo," she repeated, a little numbly.

"Somebody wanting a tombstone found him dead in his own bed after three, maybe four days. Some said working in all that stone dust and them ragged cotton bales had weakened his lungs."

In disbelief Mrs. Warner cried, "Cotton bales?"

"Anyway, they buried him on the property, since he and Bungo always stuck together. Right alongside. If you ride out that way, you can see this big angel at the back of the lot, but don't let that fool you—it wasn't David's best work. It's all out of proportion. That boy could make anything he set his mind to. And when he died in nineteen eighteen, he couldn't have been more than . . ."

"Twenty-eight," she said softly. "He would have been twenty-eight." She got up to go.

"He left that place to his sister, not that anything will ever come of that. Since you know the family, I guess you know all about that story."

Mrs. Warner sat, almost slumped, back into the chair. Pretty woman, thought Mr. Hopkins. Big-city stuff. "No," she said with an effort. "Tell me about that." She worked one of the gloves back onto her fingers with great care.

"Of course, I wasn't living here then," said Hopkins, expanding. "But one Christmas—eighteen ninety-nine, I think it was—the oldest Allen disappeared. She wasn't even sixteen then, supposed to have been a beautiful girl. Her name was Esther. She absolutely disappeared."

"I didn't know that," the woman said. She started on the second glove.

"All these years, David wouldn't put up any tombstone for her, though it was common knowledge what happened."

The woman jumped in her chair. "What was common knowledge?"

"Some fellow here with the cotton mill got her . . . got her in trouble. She went out on the Old River Bridge and threw herself in. Never did find the body and David refused to believe she was dead. Went so far as to write out a will and leave his business to his sister Esther Allen whenever she came home."

The woman said nothing. She opened her purse and began to look absently inside.

"Her daddy put up one tombstone, the year before he died. In the family plot and everything. David went over there in the night and cut out all the letters and the numbers and beat off the corners and tore up this cross that was up on top. Hauled it with a mule and left it in his daddy's front yard. It was still sitting there, last I heard."

"Thank you, Mr. Hopkins." Mrs. Warner jammed the paper and pen inside her purse. "I appreciate your time and trouble."

"You going out to see them? Friend of the family?" he asked, his newspaperman's curiosity getting the better of him.

"No," she said shortly. She gave him a cool look, as if he certainly had a nerve, taking so much for granted. "I hardly know them at all," she said. "One last thing though. Mrs. Allen—Mrs. Sam Allen. Is she in good health?"

"Never misses church," said editor Hopkins. Since the lady was going to be so stuck-up, he wasn't about to tell her of the time they'd carried Mildred Allen into the vestibule with heart failure. Anyway, she was still living. "She spends a lot of time working with them roses," he added, which was perfectly true.

"I appreciate your time and trouble," said Mrs. Warner softly. She opened the swinging door in the railing which divided his office.

"Should I tell Tom somebody's been asking for him?" the editor called when she had got to the door.

Mrs. Warner gave him a stare. "I don't think that would be wise," she said flatly.

Outside the newspaper office (Hopkins watched) she turned back to the hotel, holding herself very straight. The clerk in Governor House was surprised to see her back so soon. "Find what you wanted?" he called out as she marched past him and up the stairs. He thought he heard her laugh.

All that day she did not come downstairs again. He watched carefully for her, and Kyle McLees sat on the sidewalk with a straight chair propped back against the hotel wall to see where she might want to travel next. He was hoping to hire out his brother's Ford and drive her to the Allen place.

At precisely seven o'clock, Mrs. Warner walked rapidly down the stairs and handed the clerk the small brass key. She gave him another smile, but it was more from habit and politeness than anything else. Not like the one which had shattered Kyle that morning. The clerk decided she was older than he had first thought. At least thirty-five, even if she did hold herself like a girl.

At the depot, she waited alone. All the men were back on the bench to make certain she really got on the train. She did not seem to notice. Sometimes she paced, staring straight ahead. As soon as the train had puffed to a stop, the gray-haired man swung into view. The sight of her seemed to worry him; he jumped off and took three quick steps across the wooden platform. "What's the matter?" he said. Kyle McLees heard him.

"I want to go home," said Mrs. Warner. Her voice sounded a

little pitiful. Kyle always swore later she had been crying. The man put his arm around her and they climbed quickly aboard the train. It gave a sudden scream before it began to chug out of the station.

People talked about the woman with bobbed hair, curiously, for weeks; and Kyle McLees and the hotel clerk had a serious argument about whether she had been in a laughing or a crying mood when she went away. There was a lot of talk, but none of it reached Thomas Allen. The woman might have been some out-of-town girl friend he wouldn't want to know anybody had seen, with her red mouth and shingled hair. Besides, Tom Allen had such a temper it was hard to tell in advance how he'd react to anything.

Nobody, not even editor Hopkins, thought to tell Mrs. Warner about that lean-to at the monument works, where for years David Allen had been building some kind of strange and complex statuary, now deserted and overrun with honeysuckle blooms. Nobody mentioned that Mrs. Sam Allen had, in 1915, donated a fine stained-glass window to the Presbyterian church in memory of Esther, and how baffled the new preacher, the Reverend Worth, had been by its subject matter, which was Rahab and the spies. It was a bright-colored scene, dominated by the open window and the scarlet thread.

Nor did anyone take Mrs. Warner to the Greenway town cemetery, where she might have seen samples of David's careful work —including a recent stone replacing Angus Mackey's old one, edged in a granite vine on which grew flowers and seed capsules which looked suspiciously like dried beans.

Mrs. Warner didn't ask about Rosa Mackey Bennett, so nobody told her that Rosa was long since dead. Thomas Allen had paid $29.88 for her chalky square tombstone, and ordered it out of Sears Roebuck.

ABOUT THE AUTHOR

Doris Betts was born and grew up in the red-clay piedmont country of Statesville, North Carolina, and attended the University of North Carolina at Greensboro (Woman's College), and later at Chapel Hill. She was married after her sophomore year, and won the *Mademoiselle* prize for fiction the following year. Her first collection of short stories, most of them written while she was still in her teens, was published under the title of *The Gentle Insurrection* in 1954, and her first novel, *Tall Houses in Winter*, three years later. Her writing has appeared in *Mademoiselle*, *Red Book*, and many literary quarterlies, and several short story anthologies.

Mrs. Betts lives in Sanford, North Carolina, with her husband and three children.

PS
3552
.E84
S2
1964

90-1683

DATE DUE

DEC 0 4 1989

MAR 1 9 1990

APR 3 0 1990

MAY 1 5 1990

MAR 9   1992

MAR 3 0 1992

MAY 0 4 1993

Please Do Not Remove This Card From Pocket

OCT 1 6 1989

Gramley Library
Salem College
Winston-Salem, NC 27108

Gramley Library
Salem College
Winston-Salem, NC 27108